WinterChild

# WinterChild

Wil Skarra

TreeSide Press

WinterChild by Wil Skarra
Copyright © 2004 Wil Skarra

All rights reserved. No part of this book may be used or reproduced in any manner without prior written permission except in the case of brief quotations embodied in reviews.

*Publisher's note: This book is a work of fiction. Names, characters, places and incidents are the product of the author's imagination or are used fictiously, and any resemblance to actual persons living or dead, events or locales is entirely coincidental.*

Manufactured in Canada.


National Library of Canada Cataloguing in Publication

Skarra, Wil, 1944-
   WinterChild / Wil Skarra.
ISBN 1-897098-21-9

   I. Title.

PS8587.K36W45 2004            C813'.6           C2003-907115-4


TreeSide Press
4511 Fernwood Avenue
Powell River, B.C., Canada V8A 3L4
http://www.electricebookpublishing.com

# One

Howling, shrieking, the Arctic wind blew down along the North Saskatchewan river, driving snow particles that cut like a knife. Deer and wolves huddled among trees, miserably hoping in their slow dull manner that the weather would break. And in crude mud and wood hovels, the last of a once proud and free Plains Indians also huddled around smoky stoves or open fires, praying to the White Man's God to favor them with a warming wind.

The wind howled down along the river valley making the snow obliterate all tracks and limiting vision to ten feet. But when it slowed, a large grey building could be seen overlooking a valley. Behind it were snow-covered hills and stunted poplar trees, frozen grotesquely; bare, and pitiful before the wind. Around the building was a high wall, meant not to keep intruders out but people in. And on the window there were bars, while uniformed guards patrolled the hallways, armed with heavy leather straps attached to their belts.

In the hallways, night and day, there was screaming; the screams of people trapped, forever in the torment of their minds. They were strapped into beds when their behavior became too violent. But not all the patients screamed, for in a room, six by eight feet, a woman sat near a window, staring out at the swirling snow and howling wind.

Helga brushed her greying hair, checking the strands she had laboriously and hopelessly brushed into place that morning. Then, as she tried to ignore the screams echoing down the hallway, she stared, again out at the blinding blizzard. Her face was aged with lines of anguish and her eyes held a peculiar brittle light. A stranger would have found it hard to believe she was not yet forty years old.

"Mein Gott!" she muttered, wringing her hands while tears began to glisten on her cheeks.

"Mein children, Gott! How are they surviving?"

She thought then of Hans, her husband, and muttered, "Dear Gott! Make every thing good for him too."

With the desperate prayer her mind, as always, returned to the homestead and her four children, especially little Gertie. Then a vision of Breslau and the beautiful Prussian countryside came and she heard the strains of a waltz, distant and melancholy.

She had not been born to a hard life but after her parents had died when she was fourteen she had been left without a heritage. She had married Hans, who had promised to rescue her from a life of toil. Instead, she was thrust into a harder life still on the Canadian Prairies where the winters were seven months long.

Helga shivered and pulled the tattered wrap about her thin shoulders for heat rarely came from the rusted steam vent and she was always cold. Then she wondered about the cold and what had caused her to be locked up in a large grey building where guards patrolled at all hours.

Hans had not been a good choice for a young girl desperately trying to escape the hell of menial, demeaning labor. He had been jilted by another and fearing he would be an aging bachelor, had proposed to Helga who was not beautiful, if one did not look deeper than the skin.

They had married and set out for the new world after Hans had seen a poster advertising one hundred and sixty acres for the taking in a Land of Milk and Honey.

But the Land of Milk and Honey had soured for Helga for Hans did not love or respect her. And in winter the howling wind caused her to fear for her sanity with its incessant screeching and moaning. When she was big with their fifth child, her foot had slipped on the crude ladder leading to the cellar. She had fallen headlong, landing heavily on a pole which caught her in the stomach. She had lain in agony until Hans had come home and then had suffered in bed, the child dying within her body. She had carried the dead baby for a week while begging Hans to take her to a doctor. And when she had begun to babble incoherently, Hans had hurriedly hitched the horses to the sleigh and driven her to a hospital. But the hospital had bars on the windows and the nurses were really sadistic guards who carried heavy leather straps. It was an insane asylum for the living damned that nobody wanted. But the admission was free and Hans had thought it a bargain.

He had promised to return when she was well but the years had slipped by and her hair had begun to turn grey.

Helga bit her nails and wrung her hands in anguish, worrying about her children, as she prayed to a God that didn't hear. And while she stared with unseeing eyes out at the swirling, frozen hell, part of her heard a screaming from one of the rooms. Then she heard the quick slap, slap of shoes on the polished floor and the screaming rose in a quick crescendo and then suddenly stopped. But it continued, off and on, night and day until the poor lost soul succumbed to an exhausted sleep for a brief time, only to resume the grating, maddening screams.

It was at times like that, when she had to eat next to others who slobbered like pigs, Helga thought that she too must be insane. To her the grey building was a place for sub-humans; humans who screamed horribly or walked about, carrying on conversations with the dead. For Helga it was the dung heap of humanity: A place where the sad, demented souls were locked away from normal people and guarded by cruel, semi-insane nurses who swung their heavy leather straps with evil pleasure.

The straps and screams were a constant reminder that it was a place of madness.

In the short, sudden stillness, Helga thought of what had been the new world, of Canada. The Promised Land where fat cattle grazed in belly-high grass and calves frolicked in the sun. She also thought of the winter winds and minus forty degree temperatures that had destroyed that dream.

For Helga, the Promised Land had become the land God gave to Cain.


The wind swooped down, across the open plain, all the way from Hudsons Bay and the frozen arctic. It danced and whirled the snow, playing with it while driving particles that stung like driven nails. It slowed now and then, impeded by poplar bluffs but only slightly and then, once it was free, gathered strength and force. It roared past lonely cabins and mud shacks whose occupants huddled around blazing hot stoves in an attempt to forget for a few brief hours the wind's force and fury. The snow, blown by the ruthless wind, drifted up around the shacks and over hay and straw stacks. And the settlers soon found themselves slaves to their stock for when the wind abated in the morning they had to dig the fodder free and carry it to their cold and hungry animals.

The wind cared nothing for the white man's puny attempt to tame a vast and free hinterland, for if he had subdued the Indian and slaughtered the buffalo, the wind was untamable. It moaned on, unmindful of the tiny sod huts or mud and poplar log cabins where the first settlers brave, or foolish enough to venture out onto the vast plain, huddled and prayed fervently in many languages for spring. And after months of the wind's fury the first signs of madness began, with husband and wife quarreling over nothing or sitting listlessly in front of the airtight heater, moving only when the flames flickered to dying embers and they were forced to go out into the gale for firewood.

But not all the settlers huddled around their stoves. There were some who braved the wind and cold to earn desperately needed cash. They earned also, the frostbite and near madness engendered by the desperate, sad feeling of being all alone in the vast expanse of frozen white wilderness.

As the wind rose and slackened, grey blurry shapes suddenly appeared, disappeared and reappeared, plodding slowly onward into the teeth of the gale. A team of heavy horses doggedly placed one foot in front of the other, their nostrils white from frost and their eyes glazed from the gargantuan effort, it took to keep pressing on, one step at a time.

Behind the sleigh, a short bear-like creature walked as heavily as the horses, placing one foot then the other in the sleigh's track, praying for the miles to pass beneath his swollen and aching feet. For protection against the savage cold, the man wore a bulky fur coat and he rocked slightly from side to side as he walked, alien but still pitifully vulnerable. He was short and muscular with a frozen, frost-covered moustache that hung well below his lower lip. Along with the bulky fur coat he wore heavy leather boots under which there were heavy thick felt socks that were supposed to guarantee warmth in minus forty degree temperature. The man walked to keep his feet from freezing and once in awhile he clapped his hands together to keep the circulation going. Occasionally, he reached upwards and pushed back against his fur-lined cap with the heavy ear-flaps that were tied around his chin with a leather thong. He also rubbed against the woollen scarf he had wrapped around his neck and throat. He kept his eyes barely open, just enough to keep the sleigh in view as he wearily placed one heavy felt and leather clad foot in front of the other. It was difficult walking in the narrow track and at times he nearly lost his balance. Still, he kept on.

And finally, maybe from the madness that comes from the wind and driven snow or simply to assure himself that he was still human and not some stumbling primordial beast, he spoke. The words came heavily and slow for the frost numbed his lips and made, talking awkward. Still, the words came in defiance of the wind and cold.

"A sheissing weather. Nothing but sheissing ice and snow." The heavy German accent rolled from his lips as he lifted his head. In the white, grey and surreal world of the blizzard the horses rumps could be faintly seen as they plodded on, in their dumb and trusting manner.

"A nice house in Breslau, for this, a sheissing weather."

He shook his head slowly in disbelief as an image of the gentle Prussian countryside came and he remembered the green of an eight month summer.

"And I am a Craftsman. A maker of fine furniture. All that I leave, for this, a sheissing weather."

As he glanced up again, he could see the snow-covered mail sack on the sleigh and he wondered about the rich people who sat in warm parlors and complained about the slowness of the mail. But for each fifty mile trip he received five dollars, enough to buy flour and supplies for all winter. To buy it he had to once again hitch his horses for a fifteen mile trip through the snow to the tiny hamlet of Berlin. He only went two or three times a year.

The man stumbled on, his feet growing heavier and where moisture from his eyes formed, ice also formed until it was difficult to keep them open. The horses plodded on, their slow dull minds taken with the splendor of a manger full of hay and a warm barn, while the man thought of the airtight heater that glowed with the fire within. And he thought of his four children, huddled around the stove, waiting for their sole parent to return with the wonders of civilization; a bag full of apples and a smaller bag of hard candy that took nearly forever to melt in a mouth and would fill a child's eyes with wonder and happiness. Then the man wondered how he could look forward to the dingy log hut after his youth and young manhood in Breslau.

It took only a slight raising of his head to know why.

So he stumbled on; a stubborn pioneer helping to build a great nation and having no choice but to be stubborn or perish. He glanced up, blinking rapidly to keep the stinging moisture from his eyes and then looked down at his feet.

Suddenly he tripped over the sleigh and fell headlong, cursing the horses for stopping without a command. But when he straightened and gazed about he opened his mouth in wonder. The horses had stopped in front of a poplar log barn, his barn. Fifty feet away was his home, the poplar log hut he and his wife, "Poor Helga", had labored to build during one hot summer. He could barely see a flickering spot of light through the drifting snow. It shone through a tiny, frost covered, window, and he felt the warmth that comes from the soul; from the knowledge that only a short distance away was hearth and family.

He unhitched the numb, stumbling horses and led them into the barn, throwing a fork-full of hay into the manger. With numb fingers he lit the coal oil lantern for it was pitch black inside the tiny barn. Five cows rose slowly, stretched and gazed in wonder with large eyes, manure clinging to their hindquarters. They shook their heads in puzzlement for it was not yet evening and time for milking but the man was still there.

Hans, ignored the cows' dumb wonder and hung the harness on pegs just inside the door, where the frost built up from the cold outside. Then he hunched his shoulders and stepped outside, careful to close the door tight. He walked rapidly, bent forward with his chin tucked into his coat, until he stood at the door. Tomorrow he would complete the mail route but tonight, he thought wonderingly, he would sleep in a warm bed only a few feet from a blazing airtight heater. He banged on the door and the eldest of his children, Anna, stood looking up at him. Her twelve year-old face was older than many in their twenties. It was her duty to feed and take care of three younger than her.

Hans staggered slightly as he entered and slung two sacks on the plank floor. The frozen apples bounced and the candy landed with a hard thump. Three children stood apart from Anna and stared up at him, Marie, Augustine and Gertie, their ages: eleven, nine and seven. From their eyes shone wonder and then joy as they pounced and tore at the bag of candy. They took one each and placed it in their mouths, taking care not to stray too far from the stove. They stood smiling, savoring the alien sweetness that lasted nearly forever if they let the candy lie in their mouths and didn't chew.

"Ah, children," Hans thought as he shrugged his shoulders and smiled awkwardly for the frost had not yet left his face.

"What do they know of the cold?"

He sat heavily on a wooden bench and slowly removed each outer boot. He flexed his toes and massaged them with his hand, feeling the warmth from the stove and again he smiled. Then he stretched them forward until the socks sizzled from the heat and the cold was finally driven away. He removed his heavy fur coat and woollen sweater until he sat in the bright yellow light in his shirt sleeves. He brushed his face and moustache with his hand for the frost had melted and the moisture glistened on his skin. Then he glanced at his oldest daughter.

"Anna! Bring supper," was all he said."

# Two

The blood red sun descended slowly over a landscape as bleak and barren as the moon. The wind had driven the snow into hard banks, covering the brittle brown grass and giving the land a surreal, alien air. The size and redness of the sun meant little for it was the year's shortest day and not yet three p.m. If Hans had a thermometer, it would have registered minus thirty-five degrees Fahrenheit.

He stood by his barn and looked westwards at the sinking sun, over the huge meadow where he cut hay when the summer was in full heat. And he gazed at the poplar bluff where he cut firewood every winter. Closer to the hut stood another stand of poplar, stark, and frozen. The branches were still and lifeless. Snow birds flitted from tree to snow and back again, searching desperately for food.

Hans closed the barn door and walked slowly to the hut, his shoulders hunched against the wind and something more, the irreversibility of one mistake. He thought of the poster in Prussia, proclaiming the New Land of Milk and Honey with fat cattle grazing in belly-high grass and forty bushels per acre wheat. And he thought of how in Prussia there were always two crops in summer and here only one. And how in Prussia, cattle only needed hay from January to March. He gazed at the dwindling hay stack and fervently prayed it would last until spring. As he longed for a bright sun and the sweat it caused, he sardonically wondered how long it would take milk and honey to freeze in the frozen wilderness.

He trudged to the tiny house, his shoulders still hunched and his mind taken with images of another time. When he got to the door, he swung it open, stamped his feet to rid the boots of snow and then entered. The setting sun still cast enough light for the tiny kitchen to be bathed in shadows, and it was not yet time to light the lamp. Hans sat on the wooden bench and removed his clothes and boots, nodding at Anna who was busy at the small cook stove. Marie helped but stayed out of reach for the times were not easy on Anna. She was big for her age, rawboned and tough. An immigrant child used to a hard life of toil. The other two, Augustine and little Gertie played quietly by the airtight heater, but their gaze turned occasionally to the tiny poplar tree with the homemade ornaments hanging from its sparse and grey branches. The ornaments were bits of cloth, a few bright but most grey with age, all that there was to remind the children of the holiest of all Eves. Beneath the tree, wrapped crudely in old brown store paper were the presents, one hard candy for each child.

Hans looked at the cook stove for in its belly roasted a large jack rabbit. That would be their Christmas meal, that and the attempted gaiety. There would be no Christmas Mass for that would mean a ten mile trip to a tiny church in a glade and Hans had had enough of trips.

When Hans finished undressing and once again sat in his woollen pants and checkered shirt with the dark, blue suspenders he had bought before leaving Breslau, he turned to his oldest child.

"Anna! When's supper?"

"In a little while, Father," she replied. She didn't use the normal endearment of Dad or Daddy.

Hans thought of when he and Helga had immigrated, the confusion when disembarking in Montreal. He remembered the never ending train ride west through smaller and smaller towns and finally the last stop, a tiny hamlet named Berlin by the German immigrants who prayed a name bringing up fond memories would also bring luck.

Hans could smell the rabbit and his stomach growled. He remembered how Helga used to roast pork with dumplings and rich brown gravy. Anna had only learned to cook and her meals were rudimentary: meat, when they had it, and too many times, porridge or bread with lard and salt.

"Poor Helga!" Hans sighed. But he would have been more accurate to have sighed, poor me, for life without her was as bleak and barren as the landscape. He thought of her slow, gradual change. How at first she would sing and then how finally she had been silent. Then she had sat by the window, staring out at the brown grass in summer or the grey, white of winter.

"Twelve years," he mused. "Twelve years since we come to this land and two since she leave." He remembered her sad, lonely lament of 'I wish someone would come for a visit,' as she had sat by the window and gazed forlornly at the track leading to civilization. He didn't think of their child dying in her body for that would have brought guilt. Hans had enough guilt to bear when he looked into his children's eyes on a Christmas Eve.

And always when his mood was pensive and he felt the pangs of loneliness he thought of the insane asylum where he had taken her.

"Ah, and what was I to do? When a mind snaps, it snaps." He snapped his fingers and then became aware of Anna's look.

He wondered how long it would take for thoughts to become words and a conversation with himself to begin. He quickly shook the thought from his mind and then succumbed to self-pity. There had been no money and an insane asylum was a free hospital, but a hospital no patient ever left and after all, she had been acting strange. She had even taken to talking to herself and to people from across the ocean.

"She was not made for this life," he mused. Helga had loved fine things while he was a working man, even if he was a Craftsman.

Then he remembered how he had teased her and a small pang of guilt came and went quickly.

Ah! But women are funny, he thought. Besides, he had only teased her to break her out of her dark moods. But it had only aggravated her and now Hans was sorry for he was a man alone with four children.

And now he was stuck here, in this sheising weather and land of snow and ice.

The only way he could have made enough money for passage home would have been to turn to his craft. But a Craftsman who made fine furniture wasn't needed.

Berberi! He thought angrily of the other settlers. They only want rough, crude furniture that can be used for tables and work benches.

There was nothing to do but continue in the eternal cycle of seeding, summer-fallowing and harvesting and then enduring the everlasting winter when everything was buried under the Great White.

"Supper!" Anna interrupted his musings, announcing their Christmas meal from the other side of the room.

At the call, Marie turned her round pretty face from where she had been washing a pot and the two youngest scrambled up from their play. They crowded around the table as Anna set the roaster in the middle. She removed the lid and the rabbit lay glistening and hot, waiting to be eaten. The children moved in closer; their eyes intent and Hans noticed the torn dresses made from flour sacks.

"Wait!" He announced suddenly. "First we say Grace. It is little enough we say Grace around here." He bowed his head and folded his hands.

"Our Father, who Art in Himmel..."

When he finished, the children lunged for the meat. Then they stood around the table, chewing rapidly, using their hands and juggling the baked potatoes until they cooled enough to eat. On the cupboard were frozen apples, one for each child.

"Wait!" The command came again and Hans gave little Gertie a ham from the rabbit for she was the youngest. But already she is helping in the kitchen, he thought.

Hans looked for an instant at his children, wolfing down meat and potatoes with lard glistening on their chins. Gertie wiped grease from her face with a tattered sleeve and chewed noisily, her mouth open.

Two years, Hans thought, since Helga is gone and already they are Little Berberi!

He gazed at tiny Gertie. She was short and squat and her sack dress sizes too big. A persistent thought came into his mind then.

I wonder if someone would take her. Just until she is older.

Hans brushed the thought away along with the worry that his children were growing up illiterate.

When the children had eaten and wiped their faces with dirty, tattered sleeves, Hans gave each a candy wrapped in brown paper. He watched silently as they greedily tore at the wrappings and then, their mouths full, smiled happily from the stove.

Berberi! Even a little candy makes them happy.

Then Anna surprised him with a request.

"Can we sing a Christmas Carol?"

"Huh!" Hans, looked down at her. "A Christmas Carol?" He asked dubiously.

"Tannenbaum?" she said, her eyes misty and bright.

"Yuh! Sure. But, can you sing it?"

Anna shook her head, her black hair bouncing limply.

"I don't know the words."

Hans, cleared his throat then and began slowly, painfully.

"Tannenbaum,Oh Tannenbaum..."

He stopped for he had forgotten the words. Silence settled down upon the little gathering and the wind moaned outside. Anna's eyes remained misty and bright.

Finally Hans, stretched, looked about and walked over to the airtight heater on the other side of the room from the cook stove. He lifted the lid, put a stick of wood in and turned and faced his children. The children looked up at him, as if expecting something.

But what do they want from me? Hans shrugged. Christmas I can not give in Canada. Here in the wilderness.

Finally he cleared his throat.

"It is time for bed. No!"

Gertie's eyes bothered him for they were not demanding or even questioning. She seemed content with just a frozen apple and a rock candy, her eyes round and trusting.

Such a little one, and already she knows not to demand things she can not get.

Hans turned and walked to the other room where he and Augustine slept. The three girls slept in the kitchen, close to the stove on wooden benches with straw for mattresses.

"Don't forget to wash the dishes, Anna," he called over his shoulder and the girl nodded and then turned to the cupboard, her eyes still misty and bright.

A large snow owl stared solemnly from a fence post as the two horses strained into the harness, pulling the heavy sleigh and rack through the two foot drifts. A brisk wind whipped the snow and drifted it across the open field where Hans had sown oats eight months earlier. It piled higher and higher in drifts, until it was hard enough for a horse to walk on.

Hans hunched his shoulders against the wind, his heavy fur coat and hat keeping him from freezing but not comfortable. He snapped the lines and the horses plowed onwards, their heads rising and falling, in the manner of horses, rhythmic and powerful.

Hans gripped the reins with his mitts and stomped his feet on the boards. He hadn't planned to be out in the cold but he was running low on feed and three miles from the barn was a straw pile he had hoped he wouldn't need.

As the horses slogged through the snow, their heavy hooves throwing up frozen chunks, Hans touched his exposed face occasionally, rubbing with the fur on his mitt. By forcing circulation he avoided frost-bite and it had become a habit. As the horses strained onwards, a raven flew overhead croaking hoarsely. Hans swore softly and repeated his memorized phrase.

"A sheising weather. Nothing but snow and ice!"

As he hunched against the wind and the horses faces became white from frost, the straw pile came into view beside a poplar log and mud granary in a little bluff. The wind had blown the snow around the building and there were three foot drifts to get through.

Hans snapped the reins and the horses surged forward, coming to within a foot of the stack, puffing and straining until finally they were past it. Hans kept them going and made a circle past the stack again to break a trail, for a rack load of damp straw weighed nearly a ton. Next he took a large scoop shovel from where he had hooked it onto a two-by-four and plowed his way through the drifts. He bent his back and shoveled until he could climb to the top where he cleared at least a foot of snow from the straw. Then he climbed back to the rack and sat on the rough plank floor for a rest but not for long for his sweat would cool. It had taken nearly an hour to shovel the snow and Hans was beginning to tire.

Then as the horses began stamping their feet impatiently, he stood and painfully straightened his back before climbing the stack. Melting snow had soaked the top of the stack to a foot beneath the surface and was frozen solid. Hans had to dig until he could throw the fodder fork-full by fork-full onto the rack, stopping occasionally to rub his cheeks and blow his nose with thumb and fore finger.


While Hans was away, Gertie and Augustine played quietly in the corner of the kitchen close to the airtight heater. Anna washed dishes and Marie dried in the deep silence. Anna handed Marie a dish and Marie wiped it using a stool to reach the top of the cupboard where she placed it carefully.

Anna's face was grim as she washed, slopping the water angrily. That morning she had forgotten to check the oatmeal as it simmered on top the cook stove for she had been busy doing other chores. When the coffee started to boil, she had run to remove it from the stove and then had noticed the oatmeal. It had burned in the pot and she scorched her hand when she grabbed the handle. Hans had only dry bread and black coffee for breakfast.

He had slapped her for her carelessness; a hard resounding slap in the face and the kitchen had grown deathly still with little Gertie and Augustine watching warily from the corner. Marie had stood meekly by the table but Hans hadn't bothered to punish her. Her turn would come.

Carefully she stepped onto the stool to place the blue and white plate Hans had brought from Prussia. But the stool was old and wobbly.

Suddenly she lost her balance and let go of the slippery plate, just for an instant. It smashed into countless little pieces with a loud shattering clang.

Gertie and Augustine became deathly still again, their play suspended in mid-motion as they crouched in the corner, a rag doll lying inertly in Gertie's hands.

Anna whirled on Marie with a large wooden spoon, hitting her on the head and then the arms. Marie retreated to the corner where Gertie and Augustine cowered. They scrambled desperately to get out of the way as Anna laid into Marie using the spoon like a club.

"Oh such a sowishness!" she cried. "You always get away with it, and I never!"

Tears ran freely down Marie's face as she kept her arms up and large welts appeared quickly on her forearms. Then as Anna began to cry too the beating lost momentum. She dropped the spoon and turned and sat wearily in a chair while Marie stood in the corner, weeping and covering her face with her bruised arms. Gertie and Augustine stood by the heater and then crept quietly to the bedroom where they sat on the large iron bed. Gertie still held the inert rag doll as they sat silently, their eyes downcast.

While the drama unfolded in the tiny mud and log house, Hans finished loading the rack. He threw the fork onto the load, climbed up by way of the horses' rumps and rough planks at the front and then sat on the cold straw. He undid the reins from an upright two-by-four and snapped them impatiently.

The horses threw their combined weight of three thousand pounds into the harness. The chains tightened and after a few seconds of struggle the sleigh began to inch forward, the runners making a grating sound, peculiar to minus thirty temperature and frozen snow.

Once they were on the trail, Hans wrapped the reins around the two-by-four to free his hands, which he clapped together with his mitts on to keep the circulation going. For his feet he could do nothing and the frost slowly penetrated the felt and leather. He rubbed his face and thought of the warm stove and supper. Tomorrow he would unload the straw but first he had to carry some to the mangers for the cows and some wheat straw from the stack by the barn for bedding. And also tomorrow he would clean out the barn, using a smaller fork to throw the manure onto a stone boat, two runners with heavy planks bolted across them to form a crude sleigh. Then he would hitch the horses to the boat and unload it in a field for fertilizer.

When the blood red sun was setting over the frozen and foggy land, Hans stomped to the house and yanked open the door. He quickly removed his clothes and boots and stretched his feet to the heater, massaging the toes and mumbling to himself, "God in Himmel! They are frozen, almost!"

He looked up at Anna and Marie and noticed the whiteness in their faces and that Marie held her arms in the peculiar manner of a child who has been hurt but is too afraid to tell. Little Gertie and Augustine were in their customary corner by the heater but their play was more quiet than usual and they cast fearful glances at Anna whenever she moved about the kitchen.

"Anna! What happened?"

Anna stood by the table and said nothing as Hans glared at her. Then she blurted, "Marie broke a plate!"

"The good one from Breslau?"

"Yuh!"

"My God! What kind off a house keeper are you then? Are you not the oldest? You must know more." This time Hans was too tired to slap her.

"Can I not leave you alone with the children for a few hours with nothing going wrong? Are you a child then? Like Little Gertie and Augustine?"

Anna began to cry quietly as she prepared supper. The sun slipped beneath the frozen, western horizon and Marie lit the coal oil lamp. The yellow light cast shadows on Hans' tired face and he rubbed his two day old beard. Then he glanced at the salt pork and boiled potatoes on the table. He looked at his eldest daughter for an instant and then the thoughts came.

If only I did not have these children, I could go back to Prussia. I could make fine cabinets and get paid well. But no! I am stuck here in this sheising wilderness they call Canada and I cannot leave. My God in Himmel. What is to become of me?

Then he noticed the glistening moisture on Anna's face and the paleness in Marie's. He glanced at the two youngest, crouching in their corner. They had stopped playing, sitting hunched up, Gertie in her tattered sack dress and Augustine in his oversized pants and shirt. Hans noticed the encrusted dirt on their bare feet and the filth on their sad faces.

Ah! Little Berberi. And what am I to do? Hans glanced down at the floor.

A home and family I can not give here in this wilderness. I am only a man with no wife.

Then he thought of "Poor Helga" as the silence settled down upon the kitchen with Anna preparing supper and Marie staying out of her way.

# Three

A cloudless blue, sky encompassed the earth, contrasting with the green of early spring as a gentle breeze fanned the tall brown grass near the slough's edge. A full breasted robin hopped about in the grass close to the tiny poplar log, mud-house, for he had a family of demanding young in a willow tree near the slough. He stopped suddenly and darted forward, grabbing a worm in his beak. He struggled, pulling the desperate worm from the ground and when it wiggled wildly, he flapped his wings and flew to his nest with the prize.

In close to the robin's nest by the slough, ducks nested and crows flapped above on urgent business while just beyond a low hill coyote pups were beginning to wobble forth from the security of their den to inspect the larger and more challenging world beyond.

Above the coyotes in the clear blue morning sky, a marsh hawk circled slowly on a warm air current while gophers kept a wary eye turned skywards. And among the gophers, in the open field, ran little Gertie and Augustine as they followed five cows and their calves who walked briskly in search of green grass.

When they were about a mile from the yard the cows slowed and Gertie and Augustine sat close together in a patch of fresh, yellow dandelions. They placed their tattered hand-me-down jackets on the grass and took out their lunches although it was not yet ten o'clock. The warm oatmeal they had eaten for breakfast had become a forgotten memory and their stomachs growled.

They tore eagerly at the wrinkled brown wrapping paper and then looked at their dinner.

They stared at the hard dry bread for a moment and then Gertie re-wrapped it carefully in the brown paper. Augustine did the same and then they sat for a while longer watching the cows graze. But the cattle needed no herding, content where they were and the children soon became bored. Augustine jumped up suddenly and ran to a tiny slough.

Gertie followed until her bare feet sank into the brown, brackish water. She stopped and stared down at where her toes disappeared in the muddy liquid. Suddenly Augustine stooped and grabbed something.

"What you got?" Gertie asked warily.

"A frog. See!" Augustine grinned triumphantly as the frog wriggled desperately in his clasped hands.

Then he turned and ran back to their torn jackets and lunches and sat down quickly. When Gertie joined him he stretched forth his legs and looked at her, excitement in his eyes.

"Sit! Stretch your legs."

When their toes touched Augustine let the frog loose. It hopped until it came to a leg. Then it turned and hopped in the opposite direction but always, it was brought up short. Finally it sat in the middle of its prison, looking at Gertie with large round eyes.

"See. A fence," Augustine laughed.

Gertie watched the frog and finally reached with a tiny hand and gently stroked it. The frog remained still until she picked it up and held it in her hand, stroking it with the other.

"He's tame," she said wonderingly.

"Yuh!" Augustine answered and then his round little face became serious.

"Marie said that if we keep a frog too long it will get sick, maybe die."

Gertie continued stroking the frog but finally she met his eyes and then placed it gently on the grass. It sat still, not knowing it had been given freedom. Gertie lowered her head.

"Shoo! Go!"

The frog finally came to its senses and hopped away towards the brackish water. The children were silent, watching the place where the frog had disappeared into the tall grass. Then Augustine reached into his oversized pants pocket and produced a frayed bit of twine string. It was about fifteen feet long and had been tied in many places for he had found the pieces in an old straw stack and had painstakingly made a rope.

He quickly made a loop which slid when pulled and then rose and walked with Gertie following towards a mound of fresh earth. A large gopher saw them coming and stood upright for an instant. Suddenly he whistled, diving headlong into a hole.

Augustine ran to the hole and placed the string carefully around its opening. Gertie looked questioningly at him and finally he said, "Pappa said we can get a penny for a gopher tail."

"A penny!" Gertie's eyes were round.

Then they retreated and lay down in the grass facing the mound of fresh earth, occasionally casting an apprehensive glance back towards the cattle.

The cows grazed contentedly while their calves pulled and pushed at their teats. The sun continued its slow, lazy way upwards, nearing the midday point and the heat increased until a low humming came from the insects and frogs. When the full heat bore down the cows lay down with their calves close by and the children rested their heads on their arms. Gradually their eyes grew heavy and they fell asleep peacefully on the warm green grass. Then as the sun began its descent one of the cows stood, stretched and began grazing.

Suddenly Augustine raised his head.

"Hey!" he yelled, wide awake, for the string wrapped around his hand had been given a solid tug.

"We got one!" he cried incredulously, jumping to his feet. He pulled steadily and walked forward slowly. Then a gopher emerged slowly from the hole, pulling back desperately, his tiny forefeet planted in the fresh earth. He struggled with all his might, his eyes bulging and his body rigid. But suddenly, after nearly a minute of terrified effort he gave up, letting Augustine lead him to where they had left their lunches. When Augustine stopped, the gopher sat on the grass appearing to have philosophically accepted his misfortune.

Gertie stared at the little creature and then sat next to Augustine. The gopher looked up at them, not more than three feet away, waiting their next move. When Augustine pulled gently he came nearer but when he was two feet away he stubbornly planted his tiny forefeet again. Then they took turns leading him about and he followed without a fuss until the children again sat on the grass with the gopher between them.

"We have a real pet now," Augustine grinned.

"Yuh!" Gertie grinned too and then became serious. "Let's not kill him for his tail."

Augustine nodded quickly.

"But what shall we call him?" Gertie asked.

Augustine gazed thoughtfully at the gopher who looked steadily back.

"Gerhardt!" he said suddenly.

"Yuh! Gerhardt!" Gertie beamed. "Won't Marie be surprised when we come home?"

Just then Gertie's stomach growled again and she glanced at the brown wrapping paper. They both opened their lunches slowly and chewed on the hard bread, their hunger making it edible.

Augustine stopped suddenly and tore a small chunk free and held it out to the gopher. The gopher sat up instantly and sniffed the bread suspiciously. Then he sat back down, ignoring the gift.

"He's not hungry," Gertie said quietly.

"Maybe it's the old bread," Augustine said just as quietly.

The shadows lengthened and the cows stood and stretched, walking about, grazing and gradually drifting off towards a poplar bluff with their calves following. And as the sun sank slowly towards the nether world, over the sleepy afternoon, Augustine suddenly raised his head.

"My God! The cows!"

He scrambled to his feet and looked about desperately. Then he began running with Gertie close behind.

"What about, Gerhardt?" she yelled.

"Leave him!" Augustine yelled back over his shoulder. "What will Anna do?"

The last was enough to spur Gertie who caught up to her brother as they entered the trees. Sweat ran down their faces and their breaths came in gasps. Suddenly they stopped and stared for the cows had all lain down, their calves close by.

"They was only looking for a place to lay down," Augustine laughed, still puffing.

"Yuh! And we ran so hard." Gertie laughed too, her face red with exertion. But she glanced suddenly back to where they had left their jackets.

"What about Gerhardt?"

Augustine stopped laughing and looked sadly back to the tiny slough. "He'll be gone by now. Besides it's late and Anna will be mad."

"We can catch another gopher, no? Tomorrow maybe?"

Gertie nodded and they kicked the cows and clapped their hands loudly. The cows rose reluctantly and then walked off towards the homestead with the children trudging wearily behind. Their stomachs rumbled and they had lost their pet but they had not let the cows stray.

That was all that mattered.

The withered brown grass stood limp and bowed in an open meadow under a merciless July sun, while above crows cawed from the shade of poplar trees. The crows were the only large birds left, for the ducks had gone in search of water. The sloughs they had nested in were only memories. Dry, withered and cracked ground was all that was left of where the frogs and insects had hummed contentedly a short month before.

In the meadow two horses plodded forward, pulling a heavy mower and a man. The sickle snapped back and forth making sharp, staccato bursts of sound as the right wheel turned a gear which turned a wooden lever. The lever moved the sickle, the business end of the mower and more dry grass fell and became hay.

Hans sat on the hard steel seat, his shoulders hunched forward and his hands gripping the reins tightly for the staccato racket made the horses nervous. His cloth cap was pulled down low but sweat still ran into his eyes and down his cheeks, collecting in the hollow of his throat. It also collected in his armpits, mixing with the sour odor of labor past. After twelve hours of sweat and dust, he was too exhausted to pull water from the well, heat it on the stove and then take a bath.

And the sweat was just beginning for when he was finished with the mower, he would rake the hay into long swaths. Then he would bunch it and pile it with a pitch fork so it would dry. The last part was the hardest, hauling the hay with his wagon and rack and piling it near the barn.

But Hans thought little of that. He let his mind go blank in the manner of a laboring man engaged in thoughtless and mind numbing work. He thought of nothing except to keep part of his consciousness on the horses' rumps and to hold the reins tight. When he came to a corner of the slough, he snapped out of his mental lethargy momentarily to turn the team. Then the doldrums would settle back down and his mind would go nearly numb. It was the only way a normally intelligent brain could stand the countless hours of menial work.

Not far behind Hans ran little Gertie in bare feet as tough as shoe leather. In her right hand she clutched the rag doll Marie had sown during an everlasting winter. The doll had old buttons for eyes and one dangled from a thread, the result of too much fondling and holding, even in sleep.

For little Gertie this was a good time. The cattle were in the pasture and didn't need herding until autumn. She and Augustine were free to play in the brief summer. She had left her brother in the front yard with an old piece of iron that was a plow, making tiny furrows in the hard ground as he pretended he was Pappa and working the land.

Gertie had one more toy besides the doll, Hans' large steel comb. She used it to comb the doll's imaginary hair, but her own she ignored and it hung, tangled and dirty from her head, as she ran barefoot and happy behind the mower. Once in a while a grass stump hurt her foot but she ignored it for out in the open field she was free from Anna's watchful eye.

Hans didn't notice her at first and when he finally did, he saw only the rag doll, not the comb. If he had, he would have ordered her to immediately take it back to the house for it was the only one he owned. Instead he smiled slightly.

"Ah, the little one. So free and careless." He didn't see the smudged face or the filthy hands clutching the pitiful doll.

As the sun sank towards the west and the ache in his shoulders intensified to agony, Gertie still played behind the mower. She didn't notice the comb slip from her fingers and drop to the ground where it reflected the sun's light. Hans made another round and as the pain in his arms and shoulders made him swear softly, he glanced downwards. A sharp glint caught his eye and he pulled hard on the reins.

"Whoa! What is this?"

He got up stiffly from the mower and bent to examine the bright object.

"Bloody Hell!" He swore suddenly and picked up the comb. Then he glared at Gertie, standing warily a few feet away.

"Did you take this?"

Gertie stood deathly still, her eyes dilated and wide.

"Yuh Pappa," she finally said. It would have only made it worse to lie.

Hans lunged and caught her by the arm. He quickly removed his heavy leather belt and knelt, lying her across his knee. He doubled the belt and swung, hitting the tiny rump, hard and viciously. Again and again he swung until his arm grew tired and he rested.

Gertie cried loudly but didn't struggle. Crying helped ease the pain a little and maybe made Hans stop sooner.

Finally he threw the belt on the ground and held the child upright. Tears rolled down her face smudging the dirt as she let her head hang sideways, her eyes on the ground. And slowly guilt penetrated Hans' heat-fogged brain. He released his grip and placed his hand on her head in a caressing manner. Gertie didn't draw away but she endured the caress in the same manner as the beating.

"Poor Little Berberi," Hans said slowly. "You didn't know. But the spanking was not for playing with the comb. It was for knowing better in the future. Yuh! So you know not to do it the next time." He took his hand from her head.

"Now run to the house and put the comb back in the dresser. Moch schnell! Hurry!"

Gertie's bare feet flew over the stubble as she ran the half mile to the house, barely feeling the sharp sting of grass stumps. Hans watched her go for a few seconds and then shook his head sadly.

"Ah, poor Little Berberi." He wiped the sweat from his brow and cast an eye at the afternoon sun and then back to the fleeing child. "But I can not be a father, mother and nurse maid here in the wilderness!"

Gertie carefully put the comb back in the dresser and then ran to where Augustine played in the dirt. He glanced up at his baby sister, staring at the dried tears for a moment. Then he turned his attention back to the furrows in the hard ground.

# Four

Thirty miles east over hill and poplar bluff from where Hans toiled in the hay field, another immigrant family survived. And although their circumstances were similar, they were from a totally different time and place.

Bzigniew Bronski spoke perfect English for he had spent most of his life in the United States, growing up near the Mississippi river, living off fish and wild game and enjoying a life of lazy plenty; if plenty can be measured in things that cannot be bought. When he had reached the manly age of twenty-one, he had wandered to Minnesota where he met his wife Mary who was Metis. Her family came from the Red River district in Canada and was part of a mixed race, born from the merging of European and Cree/Ojibway people. In a brief rebellion against the Canadian government, the Metis fighters had defeated the scarlet clad Northwest Mounted Police at what is now Duck Lake, Saskatchewan. Then after they had been defeated by the Canadian Army at Batoche, her family had fled south to the United States. She, like many others, had forsaken the sad, proud life of a vanquished race, for the promise of a better one with a white man. Mary never talked of the rich culture that had once flourished along the banks of the Saskatchewan river and it became only a fading memory. When asked, Mary would say that she was white.

Bzigniew worked as a laboring man in mills and plants until he became a locomotive engineer. But despite his growing up in America and the fact he drove a locomotive, he was still a "Polluck" and the call to the west became a sweet siren.

One hundred and sixty acres if he could clear it: A Land of Milk and Honey and the freedom of owning his own land had swirled through his dreams. He didn't know that it was the same dream Hans had, only in a different language.

Amid the towering fir and cedar of Oregon, he had staked his claim, bending his back to the promise of good times. He had felled timber, cleared land, planted and reaped but the Milk and Honey didn't come his way. All that did was ache in his back and sweat in his eyes. So Bzigniew had loaded his wife and year old child on a train and set out north east to a still newer land. A province had been carved out of the former North West Territories of Canada after the buffalo had been slaughtered, the Indians herded onto reservations and the Metis defeated. Bzigniew and Mary had stepped from a train at a hamlet of mud huts and three rough frame houses that was called Saskatoon, after the wild berry growing in profusion along the banks of the South Saskatchewan River. Then they had loaded their possessions onto a wagon pulled by two horses and hitched a team of oxen behind. It had taken four days to reach the homestead, forty miles east of Saskatoon and fifteen miles from a one room Post Office and General Store, prestigiously called Peterson, Saskatchewan.

That was how Bzigniew happened to be just thirty miles from Hans although neither was aware of the other. He was alone, for his wife had died of the consumption, the euphemism describing the untimely deaths of so many pioneer women. But none of that concerned Bzigniew as he lay in his iron bed, thinking of the back breaking work to come and the fact that he was a father, mother and nurse-maid; for his wife had left him three children. The eldest two were girls, Helen was ten and Sophie, nine. They did the cooking and housework while Vincent, the youngest at eight, helped by fetching water and doing other chores. That morning he was supposed to rise at six and find the oxen for plowing.

Bzigniew stretched and rolled over. The house was deathly still and sleep fought the sure knowledge that hard, sweating work was the only way to survive the eternal winter. The image of a steam locomotive came and he thought of the days when he had ridden the rail line, gazing arrogantly down at the Chinese laborers. And with the memory came anger for he knew also the image of sweating oxen and his own bent back. His anger always grew in the morning for he could only blame himself for so long.

He thought of how he subscribed to the New York newspapers although they were a month late. And he thought bitterly of how he had no one to discuss important events with. Then he thought of how he could be free if only he didn't have three hungry mouths to feed.

"Son of a bitch!" He swore bitterly and threw the covers back. His muscles were still sore despite a night's sleep and he dressed stiffly and stomped into the kitchen. When he looked at the clock, rage welled up, like a volcano.

"Jesus Christ! Eight o'clock! Helen! Where the hell's breakfast?"

Helen was scurrying about the kitchen within seconds, starting a fire and setting a coffee pot on the stove.

"Where the hell's Vincent?" Bzigniew glared out the kitchen window. "I don't see those Goddamned oxen in the corral."

Then he stomped to the lean-to build onto the house. He yanked open the door and stopped for an instant. Vincent lay in his cot sound asleep, his brown childish face peaceful with a tiny smile on his lips.

"Goddamn lazy brat!" Bzigniew roared. As Vincent scrambled up and dressed in seconds Bzigniew picked up a tug, part of a horse's harness. It was three inches wide and made of four strips of thick cow hide.

When Vincent hurried outside, he stopped, his face white.

"Goddamn lazy brat!" Bzigniew swung and the boy hit the dirt face first. He lay still as Bzigniew swung over and over, the tug making a loud thump when it landed. Then when exhaustion sapped his strength and rage, he disgustedly through it on the ground beside the unconscious boy.

As Bzigniew walked angrily towards the pasture and oxen, he thought of the child lying in the dirt. "But he should have known better. He knows he's supposed to get the oxen," he muttered. Then as the anger subsided it was replaced by a small knot of concern for the boy had lain so still after the first blow. An image of red, coated police officers came quickly but he brushed it aside.

Hell! He'll live. I didn't hit him that Goddamn hard!

While Bzigniew was searching for the oxen, Helen and Sophie carried Vincent into the house. They laid him gently on the couch, brushed the dirt from his clothes and washed his face with a damp cloth. Then they sat and held his hands as they gazed sadly through their tears at the welts and deep gash on Vincent's cheek that oozed blood. But all they could do was hold him, and pray that he would recover.

As they fearfully looked into each other's eyes, Vincent stirred and mumbled. He slowly opened his eyes and gazed through a red haze at his sisters.

"Can I have a drink of water?"

Sophie ran to the pail in the kitchen and brought a dripping dipper. Helen held Vincent's head in her lap, her eyes still wet as she tilted the dipper so he could drink. Vincent's throat convulsed and then he let his head rest in her lap. Both sisters again looked into each other's eyes as Vincent lay still, as if sleeping.

A cool autumn breeze rippled the yellow leaves of the poplar trees lining a field while row upon row of grain stooks stood with wheat heads drooping from the stalks. Along a fence, dry brown grass stood as tall as the barbed wire while above crows cawed in large flocks for harvest was in full swing.

Bzigniew drove his team of blacks down a rough track, the rack bouncing when an iron rimmed wheel hit a hole. The horses trotted briskly with a rare friskiness and as they approached a row of stooks, Bzigniew hauled on the reins, yelling "Whoa!" Then he jumped to the ground and began to throw the sheaves with a pitch fork. He whistled and bent with a youthful vigor for the feel of harvest was in him too. And not only the harvest. It was the company of other men and the banter and joking that made the day pass quickly.

As he threw a bundle onto the rack's floor, the field pitcher joined him. Frank grinned widely and using his tongue, shifted a hand-rolled cigarette from one corner of his mouth to the other, exposing yellow teeth. It didn't take long before they were placing the bundles on the sides to build a good load.

"Nice day!" Frank called as he threw bundle after bundle, rhythmically.

Bzigniew grinned and kept on pitching for no man wanted it said that he tired in the field. When the rack was full he drove his team to the threshing machine and waited to unload. Then as he drove up to the feeder the spike pitcher clambered up the back of his wagon and joined him in throwing bundles into the machine's hungry maw. From the machine a belt stretched fifty feet to the steam engine which shook and trembled as the fly wheel spun and gears meshed. And two other men hauled the freshly threshed straw around to the steam engine's firebox for wood was scarce. Bzigniew and the spike pitcher joked and raced each other but they were careful to throw the bundles head first into the feeder so power wouldn't be wasted.

Close to the machine, inside a wagon box, Vincent struggled to keep up with the golden wheat cascading from the elevator in a nearly continuous flow. The bumper crop waited for no one, man or boy. As Vincent stood, knee-deep in grain, a fleeting image of a schoolroom and teacher flitted by. He shook his head to rid it of sweat and the haunting image as he bent his back and struggled with the heavy scoop shovel that was nearly as big as he. If he didn't shovel the grain to all four corners it would pile up and spill over the sides. His shoulders ached and his arms were leaden for it was late afternoon. And the shovel grew heavier with each push but he gritted his teeth in desperate determination, begging the hours to pass. Once the grain was nearly spilling over the plank sides the teamster hitched his team to the load and left, an empty wagon box. As the man turned his team towards a granary Vincent was in the new box, experiencing a rare break for it took a minute for the grain to pile up.

As he wiped perspiration from his bare forehead, he cast a glance upwards at his father and the spike pitcher. Suddenly the elevator dumped nearly a bushel of wheat onto his feet and he bent his aching back once again. The wheat found the openings in his old shoes and he could feel the blisters forming where the kernels grated against his bare skin. He didn't dare stop to empty the shoes for fear he would fall behind. Besides, he had learned that they would only fill up again in a few minutes. As sweat burned his eyes he cast a sidelong look at his father who drove his team to the open field for yet another load. Bzigniew spread his legs wide for balance and threw his head back, whistling a nameless tune, unaware of his son's eyes.

Half a mile away in the house, Helen and Sophie hurried about the kitchen setting the table and occasionally stopping to check the pies and roast in the oven. Sophie wrapped her apron around a handle to lift the stove lid and then shoved in a large piece of firewood. She breathed deeply and then brushed the sweat from her face, raising her arms to allow air to circulate to her armpits for it was a nearly hundred degrees near the stove. Then she grabbed a broom and began sweeping the floor for the men never bothered to remove their dirty boots. As she swept she glanced out the window. Suddenly she froze, the broom suspended in mid-sweep.

"They're here!"

Through the window she could see the teams driven to the corral where they would be tied up for the night. One man pulled water with a rope and pail, dumping it into a trough while another held his horses.

Helen and Sophie ran as they took the roast from the oven and placed the pies on a windowsill, to cool. The men would be impatient with hunger.

Then they came through the door, tired and dirty. They drank large gulps from the water dipper and then went back outside to wash quickly from a basin of water Sophie brought to them. They returned to the kitchen with Bzigniew in the lead and crowded around the two tables that had been rammed together.

While the men grinned and joked, the two girls ran back and forth carrying trays of potatoes and meat along with loaves of freshly baked bread. When the table was full, Vincent finally entered, his face smudged and his hands and feet blistered. He looked for a place to sit and one of the men got a chair for him. But his father didn't miss his dirty hands.

"Wash yourself! Dammit! We got company," Bzigniew snarled and then turned and grinned at the man next to him.

"Kids..."

When Vincent returned, he sat and gazed numbly at his plate. The same man reached over and threw a chunk of pork on it.

"A man needs food to work hard, eh?"

Vincent only nibbled dumbly.

"He's a hard worker," the man said to Bzigniew who stopped chewing and grinned again.

"Yuh! He's like an extra hired man," he laughed.

Vincent kept his gaze on his plate as he chewed dumbly, his eyes half open.

# Five

An enchanted kingdom of frozen ponds and frost-coated poplar trees, broken by occasional snow covered fields, stretched forth to a grey, clouded horizon. At the edge of a large slough under the leaden sky, brown grass stood frozen, stiff and stark, where once ducks had nested. At home, in the frigid world, a large coyote trotted quickly along a narrow trail, his nose to the snow in the eternal quest for food. The coyote stopped suddenly for he scented and then saw a man and boy approaching clumsily through the drifts. The coyote slunk quickly away under the willows near the slough's edge, to a safer world of dark shadows.

The man and boy approached slowly, lifting their legs high to clear the drifts. Neither noticed the beauty, for hoar frost only meant cold, snow and hard walking. Above, the sun began to penetrate the cloud cover and the day became noticeably brighter but the sun carried little heat. As the man walked he sank into the snow and frost grew on his beard and heavy eyebrows. He carried a rifle and traps on his back while his sheepskin coat kept the cold at bay. He also wore a fur cap with flaps tied tightly under his chin with a leather thong. Cowhide leggings covered his calves, insulating them and keeping the snow from his socks.

Bzigniew walked ponderously, ducking occasionally to avoid a low lying frost-covered branch. Behind him Vincent struggled with little protection against the cold. He wore a tattered toque and occasionally he would reach up with a bare hand and rub his ears for that was the only way to avoid frostbite. His mitts were tattered too for he had only the inner woollen ones which became soaked from the snow. He didn't carry a weapon, only steel traps on his back along with weasel boxes which at first seemed light but began to bear down with an irresistible weight. As he concentrated on each step, desperately pleading silently for a stop, his legs burned like fire. Finally Bzigniew stopped but only because of the business at hand.

"Come here!" He waved a fur clad hand.

The boy approached and Bzigniew took one of the boxes from his shoulder. He also took some bait from inside his coat and placed it on top the pan of a #1 trap inside the box. The box had two openings; one with a screen nailed against it. The weasel would enter through the open end if he saw what looked like an opening through which to escape and he never noticed the screen. The box also protected the carcass from marauding ravens and magpies.

Once he had carefully set the baited box in the snow, near the slough's edge, Bzigniew began walking again with Vincent following, thankful that his load had been made slightly lighter. He still had trouble keeping up though and he continued rubbing his ears. He concentrated solely on surviving, and the thought that he should be in school never entered his mind. Maybe it had been the beatings, but he had lost interest in things that came in books.

What good is he if he can't earn his keep? Bzigniew had shrugged aside the suggestion that education was becoming important. He read and wrote fluently and what good did it do him?

Finally Bzigniew stopped again and brushed the snow from a stump before sitting on it. Vincent approached slowly and when he was near he knelt in the snow and looked up at his father. Bzigniew had told him once that it only made his knees damp but he ignored the boy now. He reached inside his coat and brought out a brown paper bag. From it he pulled a sandwich made from baked bread and salt pork. He chewed thoughtfully; gazing about at the snow-laden world and at the frozen trees and slough. Overhead a raven flapped by looking for food and he eyed it for a while. Then he became aware of the boy's sad gaze.

As an afterthought he reached into his coat and gave the boy a sandwich. Vincent hurriedly tore off his tattered mitts and bit into the bread hungrily.

They remained there, the man sitting on the stump and the boy still kneeling in the snow. Bzigniew didn't talk, for what could you say to a nine year old? He couldn't discuss politics and what did he know about farming or the fact that no matter what he tried, he seemed to fall farther and farther behind each year? It was getting so he had a hard time buying flour. And the price of children's clothes kept going up.

Finally he placed the bag and one sandwich back inside his coat and stood. Vincent watched the sandwich intently as it disappeared but he said nothing. Bzigniew turned and picking up his rifle, continued along the slough's edge. Vincent stood too, taking a handful of snow and licking it for the salt pork made him thirsty. As the man receded, he quickly shouldered the weasel boxes and traps and hurried to catch up for as the day wore on he found it harder and harder to walk. Falling behind only made it worse.

The shadows lengthened and the damp cold penetrated his clothes making him shiver despite the perspiration. Ahead Bzigniew shivered too for the damp penetrated even sheepskin coats.

"Going to be a long winter," he muttered, worrying about the feed for his stock. Then he turned and glared at the boy who had lagged behind again.

"You coming?"

Vincent struggled with the traps and weasel boxes and Bzigniew turned and started on his way home, wondering if the price of weasel skins had improved over last winter.

"Hardly worth the Goddamn trouble," he muttered as behind him the boy slipped and fell. Bzigniew didn't notice for he had his own problems and had no time for a boy's frailty. Vincent scrambled to his feet, his mitts wet and his fingers freezing. But he was careful to shoulder the traps and boxes for Bzigniew had brought too many and he had to carry them the full trip.

At last, when they approached the farm yard, Vincent looked gratefully at the smoke rising straight upwards from the blackened stove pipe on top of the house. Despite it being only early December the temperature had dropped to minus thirty and would be well below forty by early morning, cold enough to burst tree trunks. Bzigniew went to a shed close to the house and deposited the unused traps and then turned and looked at Vincent whose breath turned to clouds of steam as he breathed heavily. Bzigniew waited impatiently and finally growled as he held the door open.

"Hurry up and put those Goddamned boxes inside. We don't want to be out here all Goddamn night."

When Vincent had dropped the frozen steel traps and weasel boxes on the floor, Bzigniew slammed the door and turned the wooden handle. Then without a word he turned and walked to the house with Vincent not far behind. After stomping his feet to rid the boots of snow, Bzigniew hurriedly removed his outer clothing and boots. Vincent did as his father, gratefully kicking off his boots and massaging his toes, feeling the warmth penetrate from the heater. He was lucky. They were not frozen and he would be spared the pain of thawing flesh. And as he drew as close as he could to the heater, he became drowsy. The kitchen was lit by the late afternoon wintry light coming from a setting sun which barely penetrated the frost patterns on the window. Normally they would have been beautiful but all they did was impede the view.

After Helen and Sophie brought out the food; more salt pork, potatoes and bannock made from flour, water, baking soda and lard, the family gathered for the evening meal. There was no butter but there was salt and Bzigniew spread lard on a large piece of bannock. Then he sprinkled salt on the lard and bit off a large chunk. There was no conversation for the girls were tired from walking two miles from school and hurrying to cook supper. Vincent was exhausted and as he chewed slowly, his eyelids grew heavier and he nearly dropped off to sleep at the table.

"What's the matter? You going to sleep?" Bzigniew demanded. "We got chores to do."

Vincent forced his eyes open and reached for a chunk of bannock. But he couldn't chew. He sat very still with the food lying like a piece of straw in his mouth.

Outside, a coyote sat on a snow bank and howled at the full moon rising in the darkened sky. Inside the barn, the cows chewed their cuds and the horses stamped their feet, waiting for the man and boy to feed them.

Bzigniew backed the team of horses and sleigh to the barn door and then jumped off and grabbed a large manure fork. Vincent stood in a stall and started to shovel the partially frozen waste. He grimaced as he lifted the fork and staggered forward. Then he plunked the load down on the sleigh and rested, just for an instant, before going back for another load. Bzigniew glared at the end of the sleigh.

"Throw it farther. It'll pile up," he growled.

Vincent tried but his arms were not yet strong enough.

The frost coming through the door turned to icy vapor as the air warmed. It made the smell worse; an acrid cloying stench that stayed in the nostrils long after they had left the barn. But there was nothing to do, except haul it away, for if they didn't it would pile up and the stock would have nowhere to stand. Outside the cows walked about near the well, exiled from their warm stalls and then stood bawling by the gate for the temperature had barely risen to minus thirty.

Bzigniew stopped for a few seconds and tugged at a flap where an ear lobe protruded.

"Cold!" He muttered and then spit sideways before digging into the manure with his fork.

Vincent rubbed an ear with a mitt but he didn't stop for long. He knew the harder they worked the sooner they would be done.

When the sleigh was loaded, they hauled it to a pile three hundred yards from the barn and the boy began shoveling again. He clapped his hands occasionally to restore the circulation and then dug in until his ears were freezing and he stopped to rub them.

After the barn had been cleaned, fresh straw carried to the stalls and the cows allowed back in, Bzigniew hitched the team to the rack on the bobsled. Then he and the boy were off on a trip for straw.

The horses bobbed their heads and threw chunks of snow backwards with their heavy hooves while snow devils danced in front of them. The wind blew from an open field, making Bzigniew's eyes water. He wrapped the reins around an upright two-by-four and clapped his hands, cursing softly under his breath.

"Jesus! Eight months of winter!"

He clapped his hands again as the horses plowed forward towards the stack in a small bluff where the trees provided shelter. Vincent knew by the numbness that warns of frost bite that an ear was tinged. He rubbed it with a mitt and then removed the mitt to massage it with an open hand. But the circulation didn't return and he nearly froze his fingers.

Bzigniew shovelled the snow from the stack and then threw fork-fulls of straw onto the rack. Vincent piled it evenly and tramped it down, still rubbing his ear whenever he had the chance. Soon, he lost all feeling.

When the rack was loaded Bzigniew drove the team to the barn where they unloaded. Vincent still rubbed his ear and finally his father noticed.

"What's the matter?" Bzigniew looked closely at Vincent. "Jesus Christ! You should be more careful. Rub it when you lose feeling."

"I did!" Vincent couldn't control the tears which froze on his cheeks.

"Well, go in the house. You're no Goddamned good out here like that."

Vincent clambered down from the rack and ran to the house, banging on the door. When he was inside, he pulled off his mitts and toque and Helen came over from the cupboard where she was kneading dough. She examined the white flesh and shook her head.

Vincent's frozen tears melted and mixed with new ones as the flesh began to thaw.

"Quick!" Helen turned to Sophie, "Go outside and get some snow."

Sophie didn't bother to put on a coat as she opened the door and scooped up a handful. Helen rubbed the frozen flesh with snow trying to slow the thawing as needles of pain shot to Vincent's brain. His eyes watered but he didn't cry out. He sat by the stove and let his sister gently massage the flesh while tears coursed down his cheeks.

Bzigniew opened the door suddenly and a gust of freezing air swirled into the kitchen. He took off his coat and boots and looked at the flesh that was turning red.

"Goddamn it! I told him to be more careful. He should have rubbed it more."

Helen looked up from her baby brother and found a rare courage.

"He shouldn't be outside with just that old toque," she said and then took a deep breath, adding "you should buy him a decent cap."

Bzigniew glared at his daughter but said nothing. He glanced about the kitchen and then back at his daughter.

"Why don't you let him use your shawl? He can cover his ears with that."

"But he'll get it dirty with cow manure. It's the only one I got." Helen gazed at the red flesh for a moment and then added quietly, "All right."

She went to a bedroom and returned with a gaily colored scarf, placing it in Vincent's lap.

"Here. Try not to get it dirty."

Vincent nodded but said nothing as the tears dried on his cheeks and Helen looked sadly at the frozen ear and her shawl. She knew it wouldn't be long before it smelled from cow manure. But it was better to lose a shawl than for Vincent to lose an ear.

---

The air in the crowded caboose was cloying as the fire in the tiny heater made everyone sweat under their heavy clothing. It was pitch dark except for the red hot glow shining through cracks around the door on the stove, while the constant rocking motion made everyone slightly nauseous. But it was better than facing the wind in the open. Bzigniew hunched his shoulders in his bulky fur coat as he drove the horses with the reins through two holes. He sat, his face right next to the smudged window, trying to see out into the night. Around him and his children, the canvas walls and roof were held in place by strips of wood set on a sleigh and the blazing red-hot stove made the tiny caboose warmer than the house.

Vincent sat next to the door on the hard wooden bench, next to Sophie and in the dark his eyes were excited for it was Christmas Eve. He sat stiffly for he had been beaten for failing in school but if he didn't move on the hard plank the pain wasn't bad. He pulled his new cloth cap down over his ears despite the heat for it was a new and sensuous comfort. His right ear had turned brown and the skin had peeled off making him lie on his side in bed for a month but it had healed. The soft, cloth cap had been a Christmas present and Vincent smiled in the dark. Beside him, Sophie wore a new pair of wool mitts and Helen had a new red scarf, replacing the one Vincent had dirtied in the barn.

The caboose was silent except for the peculiar grating sound from runners on frozen snow. Bzigniew's mind was in the past when he and his wife had gone to Midnight Mass in a tiny church under the towering fir in Oregon. But what was the use of dreaming? He still had three children to feed.

The horses began prancing, their heavy hooves trampling the snow as they approached the church and Bzigniew slid the tiny window open so he could see better. Then he turned the team and stopped them next to other cabooses and sleighs. He let the reins hang loose and then walked hunched over to the door. When he was outside, he turned to his children.

"Let's go!"

He unhitched the team and tied them facing the front of the caboose with a fork full of hay at their feet. He glanced up at the starlit sky, clear and cold and breathed the pure air deeply. Then he turned and wordlessly led his family to the church where he found a pew in the rear, amongst the fur clad homesteaders out for the first time in months.

Vincent wrinkled his nose from the new and alien scent. Incense had an oriental and exotic flavor; tantalizing and compelling and as he closed his eyes and breathed deeply the world of sweat and cow manure receded. A Mass Server in a white gown with a red vest appeared silently by the altar with a long taper and lit the rows of candles, making the church come alive with shadows and mystery. Vincent breathed deeply again and stared at the crucified Christ hanging forlornly from the Cross. On the other side of the altar was the Madonna: The Virgin Mary, who held the Christ Child in her arms and wept for all mankind. In the shadowy light, she was alive and Vincent felt a slight discomfort for the sight of motherly tenderness was alien to him.

A priest entered from a side door and approached the altar, turning his back to the congregation. Vincent sat very still while inside he felt a simmering excitement. It would be a life long fascination for the mysterious Catholic Church and the sensual incense. Then, exhausted from the day's work and excitement, he fell asleep with his head resting on his sister's shoulder.

Bzigniew knelt and prayed for a moment and then sat back in the pew, noticing that Vincent was asleep. He frowned for it wasn't right to sleep in church, but in the serene incense laden air he felt reluctant to chastize him.

Vincent slept peacefully on his sister's shoulder in the alien world of tranquillity, unaware that he had made his father angry.

# Six

The wind blew, snow devils danced and trees popped in the night as the frost became a living enemy, silent and deadly. Deer walked slowly through the deep drifts, conserving strength while settlers hunched their shoulders as they brought in firewood and wondered: Wondered if through some freak of nature winter would never end. But no matter how vicious the winds, how deadly the cold, seasons change in the endless cycle and spring eventually comes, complete with crocuses and wild flowers bursting forth in myriads of color. Then the song bird joyfully sings, celebrating life and his long sojourn north to build nests alongside the budding leaves and aging pussy willows.

In a yard, thirty miles from where Vincent sweated alongside his father, Hans also sweated for he was building a pig pen. He had bought a sow and now it had a litter and Hans didn't want the pigs to wander off. So he was busy building a fence from poplar logs he had cut the previous winter. Poplar was the worst of all wood to build with, for the poles are heavy and crooked. But spruce and tamarack were a hundred miles north in the jack pine country and buying rails was out of the question.

He hefted the heavy poles and dragged them to near the posts he had sharpened and driven into the ground with a heavy axe. At the heavy end of each pole he used the same axe to chip off chunks of the green wood for they were too thick to drive nails through. When he had paired them down, he held the clumsy pole with one hand and drove a spike with the other. Once the nail had sunk through the pole and bitten into the post, he wielded the hammer with both hands. It was grueling work with no break, for Hans worried he wouldn't be finished in time for seeding. And then would come the haying, the summer fallow and the harvest in the endless cycle.

"Ah, what a life, here in the wilderness," he muttered. Then he wiped his brow with a tattered handkerchief that had once been part of a shirt.

"It is the end," he added softly, gazing for an instant off into the distance. "Deutschland! All kaput!"

He had heard in Berlin, the tiny hamlet that was civilization fourteen miles away, that Germany had been defeated in the Great War. But that was thousands of miles away, across a great ocean and in another world. Besides he had more pressing problems. As he swung the hammer, he thought of his children. Anna, the oldest, had become a martinet who was feared and hated by those smaller and weaker than she. But she was a hard worker and some man would marry her. The same went for Marie while Augustine would take over the homestead.

"But what of the Little One? What of her?" Hans thought, for Gertie was a little savage, her dress torn and her hair wild.

As Hans sweated and worried under the hot sun, little Gertie and Augustine lay on the grass two miles away near a small herd of cattle, and with an old twine string, tried to snare another gopher for a pet. For lunch they had the same dry bread and eating was only a matter of filling their stomachs. Even at home they ate where they wanted, sitting on the floor or taking their food outside amongst the cats.

"Little Berberi," Hans mused and wondered if the man he had met in Berlin had been serious. Albert had seemed sympathetic, even saying that children should go to school.

"School! Ah, but what has it brought me?" Hans wondered, feeling a slight guilt for keeping the two youngest home to herd cows. Marie had gone more often but it was rare that she attended three days in a row.

As Hans worked, the shadows lengthened until finally he glanced up quickly and saw a team driven into the yard. Albert Blute stood at the front of the wagon box, holding the reins loosely as the iron shod wheels bounced over the rutted tracks.

"Gooten Tag!" he called in German and then yelled "Geddown!" in English at the mongrel dog that trotted out barking from the shade.

Hans dropped his tools and walked to where Albert had parked the wagon. The horses reached hungrily forward to the tender new grass for they were in poor condition with their ribs showing. Some felt that a man could be judged by the condition of his stock.

Hans ignored the horses as he and Albert exchanged small talk for a few minutes; each inquiring about the nature of each others crops, his stock, the amount of feed or how it had lasted through the winter and wondered, as all farmers do, what the new season would bring.

As they talked Gertie and Augustine brought the cattle to the well and trough and watched them drink their fill. Then the cows wandered off, looking for a soft spot to lie down in, their calves following obediently. Gertie and Augustine turned from the well and approached the house.

They stopped suddenly and stared when they saw Albert; excited but still not approaching, for the long lonely winter had taken its toll.

Finally Hans noticed them.

"Come here, children!" He called.

Albert stopped describing a crop of oats and stared at Gertie. He noticed the tattered, dirty dress, the smudged face and wild uncombed dark, brown hair. He gazed silently at the dirty, bare feet, tough from running through the dry, brittle, brown grass.

"Is this the one you was talking about?"

"Yuh!" Hans reached down and ruffled the unkempt wild hair. Gertie didn't duck or draw back. She just stood still and endured the caress like a half-wild dog.

"Poor Little Berberi," Hans said softly and then added, louder, "She has no chance to learn about nice things. All she knows is to run through the fields and herd the cows. But she is a good worker. She does what she is told. And you don't have to beat her much."

"How old is she?" Albert asked quietly, his eyes narrow and calculating.

"She was eight in February."

"Yuh." Albert petted the child on the head. "She should make a fine worker."

Gertie stood very still, enduring the quick caress and then warily watched as the man withdrew his hand. It was dirty with black filth under the fingernails while his eyes were cold and unsmiling.

"We would give her a fine home, Rosa and me. Rosa loves children and she wishes she could only have more."

"But what about school?"

"Oh Yuh! Theres a school in Berlin. It's only a mile away." Albert smiled quickly, revealing rotting tobacco-stained teeth.

"It even stays open in the spring and fall and all through the winter. It's the new law, at least in town." Albert's eyes narrowed.

"Not like here, in the wilderness. You are lucky. You got kids at home all winter where they should be working!"

Albert paused and then smiled, glancing sideways at Hans.

"But she can go to school. Yuh. We'll make sure off that."

Hans dug a furrow in the ground with his worn boot. He looked at the fence he hadn't finished, the broken down mud-log barn and the cows lying down in a little bluff. Then he turned to Gertie with her smudged and dirty face, filthy hands and torn, ragged dress.

"But what can I do?" He sighed. "I can not give her a home, like a mother, here in the wilderness!"

"But Rosa and me can," Albert added quickly. "She could go to school and all she got to do is help Rosa in the kitchen. You know with chores and stuff."

Hans still hesitated as he gazed again at the wild, unkempt hair and dirty smudged face. Then he sighed deeply.

"As long as she can go to school, yuh?"

"Oh yuh!" Albert said quickly as he studied Gertie's sturdy frame.

"She'll be very happy with Rosa in the kitchen."

Gertie gazed up at her father, her eyes round and uncomprehending. Hans looked back, sadness and resignation in his eyes.

"Go to the house and get your things. You're going on a long trip."

Gertie stood very still. She sensed that this was a momentous occasion but she had no idea what a "long trip" was for, she had never left the farmyard. She glanced at Augustine but he was just as puzzled. Then glistening appeared in her eyes as she looked back up at her father.

"Moch schnell! You don't want to make this good man wait do you?" Hans snapped and then added, "You'll get to go to school and you won't have to herd the cows no more."

Gertie walked slowly to the house, her shoulders slumped. She stopped for a moment by the door, turned and cast a long last glance at her father and then Augustine. Then she pushed the door open and disappeared inside.

Albert gazed down at the ground and smiled. Rosa would be happy, he thought. She would have a maid in the kitchen. Then he looked up at Hans' worried face

"The school goes to grade eight. With grade eight, she could even work in a bank."

Hans nodded and then looked at Gertie who left the house, clutching her possessions in her dirty hands, a torn spare dress and a worn and tattered shawl along with a rag doll. She had no shoes, for in winter she hadn't gone outside. She stood glancing uncertainly up at the man who had come from nowhere and who stunk from sweat and tobacco.

"Well, we better get going," Albert said suddenly, looking at Gertie who clutched the doll to her breast. The button eye Marie had sewn had come loose and hung by a thread. The rest had deteriorated and stuffings, could be seen peeking from a leg. She clung to the doll with a fierce determination, her eyes moist.

"Come!" Albert said gruffly and turned and then climbed into the wagon box. He grabbed the reins from where they had been wrapped around a two-by-four and glanced down at Hans. Hans silently lifted Gertie up to Albert who grabbed her under her arms and then sat her down in the box. She stood clutching the doll, her eyes swimming as she looked at Augustine who gazed upwards from where he stood beside Hans. Anna and Marie had come out of the house and they too looked up at their baby sister.

Albert suddenly clucked to the tired horses and Gertie grabbed a rough plank for balance. As the wagon left the yard she turned her head and looked back at her family, standing in a semicircle. She didn't wave and neither did the other children for they didn't know they meaning of it. Hans too stood still, his hands at his side.

"Where is she going?" Marie finally asked.

"She is going to the Blute's. She'll go to school and they can feed her, better."

Marie looked sadly at the departing wagon and then at her father. He avoided her eyes as he thought, little savages. What do they know about feeding four mouths or the work in the field?"

As the wagon bounced over the ruts, Gertie lost her balance for an instant and dropped her doll. Albert glanced from the horses to the rag doll bouncing on the wagon floor. Then he bent and picked it up, gazing thoughtfully at it. Suddenly he grinned and with a flick of his wrist, tossed the doll over the wagon side.

"No!" Gertie cried out, her eyes wild. Albert grabbed her roughly by the shoulder and shook her.

"You got no time for that foolishness. Work is all you'll get and the sooner the better you know. Dolls are for kids and rich folk!"

Gertie gazed numbly at the bundle of rags lying in the dirt and the tears welled up and overflowed, coursing down her cheeks. She didn't cry out or struggle; she only gazed at the receding bundle of rags and wept silently.

"Now cut that out!" Albert snapped. "I got no time for kids crying or dolls."

Gertie turned her face away to hide the tears but they wouldn't stop and her last look at her home was through blurred, swimming vision.

Hans still stood in the yard and watched the receding wagon.

"She'll be better off. She'll get enough to eat and go to school," he said softly and then turned to other matters.

"Anna! When's supper?"

The yard Albert drove his skinny horses into wasn't much different from the one he and Gertie had left. It had a run down barn, a couple log sheds and pigs in a pen along with a mongrel dog who rose lazily from the shade. The yard however did have a greying, two storey frame house. Water came from a well a hundred feet away and the family stored perishable food in an ice cellar; a hole in the ground, cribbed with boards and filled with water in the winter.

The tired horses stopped by the house on their own, their heads drooping. Albert turned to Gertie and then nodded curtly towards the kitchen window through which a large woman peered.

"Go to the house! Rosa will see to you!"

Gertie got slowly off the wagon and Albert snapped the reins. Then, as the wagon bounced towards the barn she stood alone, clutching her tattered dress until the woman came out. Rosa was a tall, raw-boned woman with tough, hard lines on her face. Her blond hair was just beginning to grey and she wore a faded blue print dress that covered her knees while on her feet were scuffed patent leather shoes. She stood stolidly, arms akimbo; glaring down at the tiny eight year-old child who looked fearfully up at her.

"So this is the Little Berberi that Albert brought. Well, we'll soon see about that!" She turned to the house, adding over her shoulder, "Come!"

Gertie followed slowly until she stood in the kitchen. Rosa went to the wood stove and placed a large kettle on it. Then she took a poker and stirred the fire, adding another stick.

"So now! So this is how you think you should go visiting. Dirty like swine!"

Gertie hadn't known she was dirty but she cringed nonetheless.

"Undress!"

Gertie obeyed meekly, taking off the tattered dress. Then she stood in grey worn panties, naked and vulnerable. She glanced frightfully at the water kettle as steam began to escape from the spout.

"Come here!"

Gertie obeyed meekly, her eyes round and dilated.

"Here!" Rosa took a wash cloth and poured water from the kettle into a wash basin, pushing the cloth down into the water.

"Mein Gott!" she swore suddenly and yanked her hand back for the water was boiling.

"Here! Wash!"

Gertie gingerly sponged herself with the hot cloth until her skin began to turn red.

"Soak it in the water!" Rosa commanded. "Like this!" She took the cloth and pushed down. "And don't be scared to wash. Rub with it!"

Gertie's skin became redder and sore but she obeyed meekly although the tears again coursed down.

"Stop that bawling! What do you think this is? A pigsty? We wash here. We are not savages!" Rosa growled as sweat ran down her neck and mingled with yesterday's, giving off a rank smell.

Finally when Gertie stood dripping and cowering, her skin red and hurting, Rosa had enough. She turned to a chair and grabbed Gertie's tattered dress. She threw it at the child and laughed loudly.

"Is this all that Polluck Pappa of yours can afford?"

Gertie shivered as she hurriedly dropped the dress over her head just as Albert came through the door. He stopped and stared at the child for a moment.

"I see you give her a good wash," he finally said before sitting at the table.

The family sat down to their evening meal, Rosa and Albert along with their fourteen year-old son, Donald. Gertie stood by the table not knowing what to do as the three strange people ate noisily. Donald plopped down a piece of meat on his plate and after half cutting, half tearing off a chunk with his knife and fork, rammed it into his mouth. Albert did the same, swallowing loudly before cramming more food home. Suddenly he stopped and stared at Gertie, his head turned sideways and his fork suspended in mid-motion. He chewed rapidly for a few seconds, swallowing most of the pork.

"Why she not eat?"

"Sit!" Rosa commanded and Gertie sat, her eyes round and wondering.

"Eat!" Rosa snapped. Then she grinned at Albert and Donald as she plopped down a small piece of meat and some potatoes onto the child's plate.

Gertie stared at Rosa for an instant and then looked down at the plate. Then she took the meat in both hands and bit off a chunk with a sideways motion of her head. She chewed quickly for despite the fear, her stomach growled fiercely.

"But what is this?" Rosa suddenly, demanded. Albert and Donald stared at the child, their knives and forks suspended in mid-air.

"Albert! What kind off Polluck, berberi brat have you brung us? Why she eats like an animal!"

"Polluck," Donald laughed, wiping his mouth on his shirt sleeve. Albert grinned at his son, displaying brown, yellow teeth.

"Why, we'll just have to train her," he said to Rosa.

Gertie stopped eating, a lump in her throat stopping her from swallowing as the meat lay like a chunk of straw in her mouth. Her skin was hot with shame and the tears started again. But she kept her eyes down at her plate. Then more hateful words came.

"That Pappa of yours. He thinks he is so good, speaks the High German and says he is a Craftsman, maker of fine furniture. Pshaw!" Rosa laughed.

"He cannot even raise his children so they eat like humans."

Gertie had no way of knowing that her grandfather had immigrated from Poland to Prussia as a tradesman, and had been what was called a "Prussian Pole."

"Here!" Rosa suddenly grabbed her hand and jammed a fork into it. Then she grabbed her other hand and pushed a knife into it.

"Here's how you eat! You cut the meat and use the fork. You don't gobble like the pigs in the pen!"

Gertie held the knife and fork uncertainly in her tiny hands, her hunger gone.

"Cut with the knife! Dumpkoff!"

Gertie slowly began cutting, holding the fork awkwardly until eventually, after tearing off a piece she placed it inside her mouth alongside the un-chewed portion. Then as Rosa glared she forced herself to chew but her throat ached and she nearly retched.

Albert stared at the child for a while and then grinned suddenly, saying, "Hans asked if we would send her to school." He laughed outright, un-chewed food rolling around in his open mouth.

"We would take in an extra brat, just to send her to school, eh!"

"First we must teach her to wash and eat like a human," Rosa guffawed. "Not like some pig or savage Polluck."

# Seven

A blood red sun rose lazily over the eastern horizon, hanging low as it woke the countryside. On top a pole fence in the Blute's yard a large red rooster opened his eyes, shook his feathers and gathered air into his lungs. Then he gave forth a mighty crow waking the mongrel dog who slept by the porch. The dog rose, stretched, sniffed the air and then trotted down to the barn. In the pasture, cattle stirred where they had lain in a bluff and chickens began pecking about the yard for unwary worms. A small flock of ducks flew above the two-storey house, the wind whistling in their wing feathers as they circled to land in a large slough.

Gertie glanced at the chickens by the barn, as she rested for an instant, her hands on a five gallon milk can. She rubbed her eyes and sighed and then looked at the four cans she had to take to the train station, for the Blutes shipped milk to the infant city of Saskatoon, forty miles away.

As Gertie rubbed her eyes, she closed them for an instant for she had been up since five thirty a.m. Rarely did she get to sleep until after midnight and there were permanent bags under her eyes. In the two years since Albert had brought her to the farmyard she had grown but not upwards. Her shoulders had widened and her hands were bigger but she was just as short as she was when she had been eight.

She wiped her hands on the old print dress Rosa had re-made to fit her and then gritted her teeth and hefted the can. It was all she could do but with an extra effort she pushed and shoved the forty-pound can until it was near the front of the cart. She did the same with the rest, resting after each one. Then she walked around to the front, took the reins and clambered onto the board seat. The mare raised her head and Gertie snapped the lines. A mile away, a train whistled and she snapped the lines again. The horse jumped forward and then settled into a quick trot, dust rising where her hooves hit the soft ground.

Along Berlin's main street three stores displayed barrels in the verandas and merchandise in the windows. The owners were not yet up and all that could be seen through the glass was a dark gloom. Across the street was the railway track. She turned the horse into the station, backed the cart to a three-foot high platform and once again lifted the forty-pound cans, resting between each one. When she had all the cans on the platform she hurriedly took a receipt from the station agent and clambered back onto the cart's board seat.

When she was back at the barn, she led the mare into a stall and began unharnessing her. She couldn't reach so she stood on a manger and pulled the harness from the mare's back. It fell with a loud jangle, the steel parts rattling on the stall floor. Gertie half dragged, half carried the heavy harness to a peg, wrestling with it, before she could get all the parts properly hung up.

Then she ran to the house, stopping just long enough to splash water on her face at the porch, ignoring her armpits and neck. She clambered up the stairs to her tiny attic room and grabbed a grade two reader and scribbler along with a worn pencil stub. As she ran through the kitchen Rosa glared from the stove.

"And make sure youre home by four!" She yelled.

Albert had brought home the news that it was now law that a child under fifteen must attend school and that she couldn't miss more than one week at a time.

Gertie ran out the door and down the trail to the road. It was over a mile to where she could faintly see the convent and as she got closer she could see children being shepherded into the building by black robed nuns. Gertie picked up speed but it was too late. The doors closed and she was forced to knock. Finally, as Gertie stood panting by the door, her face red from exertion, an aging face framed by white above a black robe appeared. Then the door opened all the way.

"Late again! Did you bring your lunch this time?"

Gertie glanced down and hid her hands in the folds of her hand-me-down dress. The ancient nun glared at her for a moment.

"Well, go to your classroom. Maybe we can find you something at dinner."

Gertie ran to the room and opened the door quietly as an attractive young nun glanced up from a reader. She stared at the perspiring child who was at least a head taller than the other students. Gertie kept her eyes downcast as she crept silently to her desk that was too small.

"So, you have decided to come back to school," the nun said quietly. "That's nice, but it would be nicer if you could be on time." The nun smiled and then added, "Today, we will be reading page eight.

"Gertie! Did you finish the homework I gave you last week?"

Gertie looked up quickly, her mouth dry and constricted. Then she lowered her eyes to her desk as slowly she shook her head. She had been busy planting potatoes and Rosa wouldn't let her use the coal oil lamp after dark.

"Why not?"

Gertie remained silent, growing smaller in her desk. One of the children laughed and she felt the hot tears start down her cheeks.

"Thats enough!" The nun snapped and then added, "Maybe Gertie has a very good reason not to do her homework." Then she glanced down at the reader continuing, "We will finish reading anyway."

The unexpected kindness made Gertie's tears run unchecked and the other children smirked. She tried desperately to make sense of the figures in the book but her vision was blurred and her world became more constricted, until all she was aware of was the droning sound of the nun's voice and the blurred book. Finally, after an eternity, the class ended and others followed in a daze until it was time for lunch. The children filed outside, carrying their lunch bags and sat in the shade to eat.

But Gertie had no lunch and she feared the other children would mock her. So she sat at her desk, not knowing what to do and praying the lunch hour would soon end. Her stomach growled fiercely for she had eaten only a scrap of bread for breakfast, six hours earlier.

As she sat, her book open and her eyes on the words but not reading, she saw a serene pastoral vision of her and Augustine herding cows on a hot summer day. She saw the frog they had played with and Gerhardt the gopher and she could feel the freedom of the open fields. Through the hot tears, she wondered what Augustine was doing and if he had caught another gopher for a pet.

Suddenly her dream was shattered. The nun came slowly into the room and Gertie looked up quickly and then just as quickly back down at her book, trying to make herself as small as possible.

"What's the matter? Why aren't you out eating with the other children?"

Then, as Gertie stared straight ahead, swallowing painfully, the nun took a brown bag from her pocket and laid it on the desk. She smiled warmly and nodded towards it. Gertie stared at her for an instant and then at the bag. Wonderingly, she reached forth a timid hand and when the nun nodded again, unwrapped the gift slowly, her eyes round. She found a sandwich; canned meat between buttered white store bread, and she glanced back at the nun, her eyes filled with wonder. But what was more surprising was the cake that fell from the bag. Gertie sat very still for a moment, staring at the sandwich and cake.

"Eat! Don't be afraid."

Gertie bit hungrily into the sandwich, swallowing quickly. Her jaw convulsed and the bread and cake disappeared in seconds. Then she sat very still, staring straight ahead.

"Come. Tell me," the nun said quietly, "why don't you do your homework?"

Gertie swallowed and the familiar lump in her throat became painful while hot tears again began rolling down her cheeks.

"Those people you live with, the Blutes. Won't they let you?"

Gertie stared straight ahead through the haze, afraid Rosa would somehow find out if she told the truth. The nun gazed sadly at her glistening face.

"It's okay," she finally said and then added thoughtfully, "I tell you what. Why don't you stay after school? You're bright and you like reading. I can tell. That way you can catch up and pass grade two."

Gertie remained quiet, staring straight ahead and the sister sighed deeply.

"What do you think of that?"

Gertie nodded quickly but it was only to help her swallow for her throat ached horribly. The nun however, thought it meant yes and she rose, smiling.

"I'll see you after school then. We'll go over the reading."

Gertie could only stare straight ahead, afraid to offend the gentle sister, while her tears made the letters blur on the blackboard and the room swim. The nun smiled, confident that she was doing the right thing and walked to the door, closing it quietly. When she was alone, Gertie sat rigidly at her desk, fighting the panic which made her stomach contract until she was nauseous.

Suddenly, a boisterous, happy group of children burst into the room and ran to their desks, glancing at the crying child that was much bigger and older than they were. They smirked and laughed at Gertie, for children are at times are unwittingly cruel.

Gertie burst from the convent, her books clutched to her breast, running hard. An image of Rosa, red faced and enraged, spurred her to even greater effort and her breath came in quick gasps as her legs burned, for the last part was uphill.

She stopped just outside the house, panting and out of breath. Then she breathed deeply and pulled open the door, closing it softly as she tried to sneak upstairs to her attic room. But as she crept through the kitchen, Rosa came from the living room.

"So this is what you do!"

Rosa's face was red and she clenched her fists, taking a menacing step closer with each word. Gertie retreated, still clutching her books to her breast.

"We send you to school, and what do you do? You come home late after playing and fooling!"

"But Sister made me stay."

"Pshaw." Rosa's upper lip curled. She snatched the books and hurled them into a corner.

"Wasting your time! You think that we feed and cloth you just to fool around?"

Rosa didn't bother to get the strap. She used her fists, hitting the child in the face, on top the head and on her shoulders.

"Lazy! Good for nothing! You're just like that Polluck Pappa of yours."

Gertie retreated into a corner, cowering and protecting her face with her arms. Then as Rosa's rage was diminishing and the blows losing force, Albert suddenly slammed the door and stepped between his wife and the child.

"Here now! Stop that!"

Rosa stopped, took a deep breath and then slumped into a chair, her chest heaving.

"Nobody cares about me." Tears ran down her face. "All I get is work. Work all day and nobody cares. And you bring me this Polluck brat that is good for nothing just fooling."

"Well, don't beat her like that." Albert's voice was harsh. "What if someone sees you. They would call the police. Then what would you do? And what help would you get then?"

Gertie still cowered in the corner, her face glistening as she wept silently. Albert turned to her suddenly, his face angry.

"Take these darn books to your room. And start in with the work. Moch schnell!"

Gertie bent quickly, snatched her books up from the corner and ran upstairs. Albert pulled up a chair and sat down next to his wife.

"What's the matter? Why did you get so mad?"

"She was an hour late, the little brat!"

"Well, she can just stay up longer til she's finished with the work," Albert said soothingly, wondering about women and their ways.

"But we must be more careful. If some one found out..."

When Gertie returned, she began washing dishes piled up since breakfast. She washed hurriedly, casting occasional apprehensive glances at Rosa. When she was done she set the table and brought food from the oven and pantry. When the family sat down for supper, Rosa turned and glared at her, her cheeks their normal color but her eyes flashing fire.

"Since all you are good for is fooling, you can wait on the table. You eat when we're through."

So Gertie stood by the table and fetched water, butter, or anything else Albert and his family wanted. And it remained so for she was too frightened to protest.

# Eight

Months passed and summer changed to autumn in the endless cycle. Gertie still wore the tattered dress that had become too small. But she had shoes, an oversized pair Rosa didn't want and she stuffed paper into the toes so they would fit better. She still hauled milk in the heavy cans to the station but she was getting used to the weight and didn't strain as much. She rarely was free until midnight when she dragged herself upstairs to the attic and flopped down on the old cot. It took only a second to fall asleep and it seemed like a second before it was five thirty again and she rose dazedly to start breakfast. She still served the family and ate what was left while her hunger grew with each passing day until she began secreting scraps of bread into her pockets. Late at night, in the dark, she chewed on the dry bread, keeping the hunger at bay.

School reopened and her face set in hard lines for she had failed and had to run the gamut of ridicule along with the sister's kind but insistent questioning about homework. As hunger and fatigue fought for prominence, school receded farther and farther.

One evening, when she was milking, she clutched the cow's flank for an instant as blackness closed in. But only for an instant, for she was growing sturdy and tough, even though she experienced more and more migraine headaches. They would come and go, starting with blurred vision, a deep feeling of nausea and eventually a splitting headache that lasted for hours. She had mentioned the migraines once.

"That's a sign of craziness. That's what that is. You're gonna end up like your mother. Crazy!" Rosa had laughed raucously.

No matter how hard she tried or what she did, she couldn't please Rosa. Rosa lived a hard life too, seldom leaving the farm and spending hours by the window, wishing for company. Whenever she saw the child, trying mightily to do her work or simply to please her, a spout of rage would erupt and the original dislike hardened to hate.

As Gertie was milking the familiar migraine started. One eye became blurred while the other remained normal. She closed the affected eye but the blurriness only switched and she sighed deeply.

Her throat was dry and sore for Rosa had begun denying her water after she had wet her bed.

"That's just a sign of laziness!" Rosa had snapped and then had laughed. "Water makes fat." So Gertie drank from the well or in the middle of the night when she sneaked down to the kitchen.

As she rested her head against the cow's warm flank and closed her eyes, she thought of the warm, rich milk being squeezed into the pail. It landed with a loud sizzle, a peculiar sound heard only in a galvanized tin pail. As she milked, she could smell the rich warmth and then on an impulse she bent downwards and sideways, putting the cow's teat close to her mouth. When she squeezed, she was rewarded with rich milk, straight from the cow. She closed her eyes again and breathed deeply.

Her mistake was in not keeping a constant vigilance.

"So this is what you do! You, lazy brat!" Rosa screamed from just outside the pole corral. "You even suck the cows dry. You lazy good for nothing Polluck brat!"

Gertie straightened quickly and directed the milk back into the pail while Rosa kept up a steady tirade. Gertie closed her eyes and rested her head against the cow. She was becoming accustomed to even scorn and spite.

At supper Rosa added more scorn, looking at her husband and son, grinning broadly. "She was sucking the cow so even the snot ran."

Donald grinned, casting occasional glances at Gertie but Albert only grunted as he ate noisily.

"Aw is it not enough that she works so hard. Why you not leave her alone?" He finally demanded.

Rosa bit her lip and anger welled up but she said nothing, only casting Gertie a baleful look.

Gertie stood behind the table, waiting for an order to bring more food or water and her body swayed slightly. She fought to keep the tears dammed up for if she had become used to the beatings and scorn, Albert's unexpected kindness had caught her off guard. She closed her eyes for an instant, the searing headache was a steel band around her temples. She opened them and the room swam slightly in front of her but nothing else had changed. The family still ate noisily with Rosa muttering to herself and Albert hungrily ramming food into his mouth.

"Gertie! Bring water!" Donald suddenly demanded and Gertie went to the pail by the stove and dipped down into the cool depths.

She turned and carried the dipper to the adolescent boy, waiting until he was finished drinking. Donald pushed the dipper away then and grinned at Gertie, his eyes lingering on her worn blouse where her budding breasts pushed against the cloth.

"Looks like a good crop this year," Albert finally said, ignoring Gertie. Rosa stopped muttering just long enough to answer.

"Yuh! And as long as there's no frost."

While the scattered conversation ebbed and flowed, Gertie thought of the kind nun and the cool convent while she suppressed the painful memories of class. The black robed nuns became angels instead of flesh and blood, and gradually the Catholic religion became the Heaven they were always talking about. For Gertie it was peace and the image would stay with her the rest of her life.

"Bring bread!" Donald suddenly commanded, scattering the dream.

Gertie walked with Rosa and Albert to the high spired church at the end of Berlin's main street. It was the center of town in more ways than one; being a place of worship and of social gatherings, even the odd play that Rosa called "A live show." Gertie kicked the inch of snow that had fallen during the night and felt the dampness through the thin leather of her cast-off shoes. Her feet had grown and she no longer had to shove paper into them but they provided little warmth. She clutched a worn green coat to her breast, which she had been given by one of Rosa's relatives. The buttons didn't match and one elbow had a tear through which stuffing could be seen.

They stopped at the door and exchanged greetings with neighbors. One man stopped and grinned, baring brown, tobacco-stained teeth. He wore a shiny black suit coat and faded brown pants from a different, older suit.

"Morgen!" He said for nearly all the settlers near Berlin were from Germany.

"Gooten morgen!" Albert nodded, folding his hands behind his back and leaning slightly backwards. Rosa and Gertie stopped beside him and waited. Donald was sick so he had stayed home. The three had driven in the Model T Ford Albert had recently bought and he was a proud man, the owner of an automobile. But the neighbor wasn't interested in cars.

"Gertie's growing so." He looked at the twelve year old girl.

"Yuh! She'll make a fine woman. Make a fine Frau." Rosa fondled Gertie's hair and displayed her large teeth. Gertie stood solidly under the rare and transparent caress. Then the people moved inside the shadowy church and found pews. Gertie sat next to the wall, just beneath a picture from the Way of The Cross; a series of paintings, depicting a bleeding and battered Savior, scourged and tormented on his way to a lingering and agonizing death on the cross. In front, she could see the statue of the Blessed Virgin, her arms spread wide and a red, pierced heart on her chest. On the other side of the altar, Joseph, the surrogate father of Christ stood, gazing stolidly over the congregation, his black beard hanging down over his chest.

Above the altar, Christ hung on the cross, his left side ripped open and bleeding bright blood, while his bearded sad, white face bore an agony that touched Gertie deeply. She gazed at the sculptured Christ and as the seconds ticked by he appeared to weep. Gertie wept too, the agony of the Christian Lord weaving a sad, melancholy spell deep within her soul.

"Our Father who art in Heaven," she prayed and then switched to the "Hail Mary." After that she let her mind go blank and prayed without words, a deep trusting feeling that comes from suffering, and hopelessness.

Gertie believed like her ancestors, in their ancient Gods and eventually the newest one, Christ. She laid her soul bare at his feet and the feeling changed from an infinite sadness to a primitive belief and longing that he, and only he, could make the world better.

As Gertie prayed, the mass servers and priest entered and began the mass. The nuns took their places in the front pew and she could see the backs of their heads, again caught by a mystical, melancholy feeling that their world was without pain.

The priest intoned the sacred Latin while the servers swung the incense bottles and the church was filled with the heavily scented smoke. Gertie breathed deeply but it had to end and it did.

As they were filing from the church, Gertie suddenly caught her breath. There was her father, her brother and two sisters. Augustine saw her too and hurried over.

"Good morning," he said, once they were outside, standing on the steps.

"Good morning," Gertie replied and then they shook hands, in the manner of adults. After that they both stood and looked at each other for a brief time.

"How are the cows? Do you still herd them?" Gertie finally asked.

"They are good. But I don't herd them no more. We have a fence now, and I do more important work," Augustine said and then hesitated.

"How is your job?" He asked shyly.

"Job?" Gertie was puzzled until she realized he meant her position with the Blutes.

"Oh. It is good."

Augustine looked steadily into his sister's eyes. Then his attention was taken by Rosa.

"She is a fine worker," she said, again fondling Gertie's hair. "She does the work of a full grown maid."

Augustine and Gertie looked at each other for a while longer. He was puzzled by the moisture in her eyes for he had been told she was doing well. Then Hans appeared from out of the crowd.

"How is my Fraulein?"

"Oh, she is fine," Rosa said, placing a hand on Gertie's shoulder. "She is a fine worker."

"Good!" Hans said and then added, "Does, she go to school?"

"Oh yuh! She goes all the time."

Hans looked from Rosa to Gertie and smiled. Gertie wanted to cry out but it was too late for he and Albert turned and left, talking of the harvest and other important things. Marie and Anna came up to her and Marie looked sadly at her little sister.

"How are you?"

Again Rosa answered, "Oh, She is fine" and the hand stayed on Gertie's shoulder. Gertie swallowed but the words again wouldn't come. Then when Anna looked down at her, her eyes hard, Gertie finally found her tongue.

"Maybe I could come for a visit?"

Anna stopped from turning. She gazed down at Gertie, her mouth thin and cruel.

"And we can do without you too!" The words cut sharper than the sharpest knife.

Moisture appeared in Gertie's eyes, but she was tough too and fought back the tears. As she stood, her body numb, a migraine started.

"Yuh and there are two of you. We need her with us. She is such a fine worker," Rosa laughed.

Anna left and joined her father, the words forgotten. Marie cast Gertie a glance, her eyes sad and worried and then she left too. Augustine had joined Hans and Albert in men's talk of the harvest. That left Gertie and Rosa standing on the church steps, the hand still resting on her shoulder.

"Come!" The command was harsh and the familiar knot in Gertie's stomach tightened.

# Nine

A coyote trotted down a familiar path under a full moon that filled the magical world with silvery beams and dark mysterious shadows. The coyote was alert, for in the shadows were tiny animals to eat, but also in the shadows lurked danger. He stopped suddenly, sniffing the air and then made a wide detour for he had come to the Blute's farm. In the distance he could hear a dog bark suddenly and he slipped away into the shadows.

Above the coyote and then the farm, a large owl glided silently, looking for mice or other unwary creatures. The farmyard was lit by the silvery beams that played with the shadows and a ghostly stillness lay on the land.

The beams shone through a dirty window into the stifling tiny attic room where Gertie lay on her cot, drenched in sweat. The sheets were hot and cloying and despite her great fatigue, sleep wouldn't come. She had turned thirteen and her body was maturing, for she was experiencing her first menstrual cycle. She had fearfully asked Rosa about the strange feelings that filled her with longing and fear but Rosa had only glared and then had laughed raucously.

"That's a sign that you will be wild and run around with crazy men."

Hot tears glistened on Gertie's face as she stared upwards into the shadows. Bits of tar paper hung from the rough planks and two-by-fours that served as a ceiling. Gertie didn't notice as the tears flowed and she clutched her hands together in a silent prayer.

"Please God! Forgive me. I'll not be wild," she prayed desperately, fear and guilt intermingling. She had never mentioned the subject again to Rosa and the anxiety simmered as she prayed for forgiveness for a sin she didn't even understand.

A faint odor came to her and she knew she was unclean, as she clenched and unclenched her hands until the knuckles were white. And the guilt settled deeper and deeper into her soul, until all she knew was a deep shame: A sense of worthlessness and an abhorrence for anything remotely sensual.

Gertie gazed in wonder, for there were all manner of wondrous things. Under the glass counter pocket watches, jack-knives and various utensils lay while in a glass jar, hard candy waited with an alien sweetness. Deeper into the store's dark interior and piled neatly on another counter were men's coveralls, work pants and gloves along with heavy leather boots. There were even harnesses hung up on a wall, for Gertie was in Berlin's largest General Store; a place where all things could be bought, even flour and sugar.

But the most enthralling of all were the women's dresses, hanging in a row on a rack, so many, they were kaleidoscopes of color. They hung, dark and lustrous or brightly colored, *Off the Rack*: Dresses made for the poor, for a couple nights out a year and to be worn in dusty dance halls, filled with sweaty farmers and their women.

To Gertie they were beauty. She stood in the cool store, Rosa's discarded, tattered dress hanging loosely from her shoulders, as she clutched a five, dollar bill in her work-hardened hand. It was the first time in her life that she was allowed to make a decision on her own for Rosa had let her enter the store by herself.

"Have you decided?" The store owner's wife asked softly. Gertie turned like a frightened animal.

Confusion followed the sudden fear and on a whim, she pointed mutely to a long sleeved green dress. Where the folds were deepest, the soft dark color shone with a, rich velvety sheen. The woman silently removed the dress and beckoned Gertie to follow. Then in a tiny change room she tried it on and it fit. Gertie couldn't keep her eyes from the mirror as she kept turning back and forth, wonderingly touching the material. The woman smiled for she had grown accustomed to shy young girls whose eyes were round with wonder.

Then, as the woman rang up the price of two dollars and ninety cents on the cash register, Rosa entered. She stopped and squinted, eyeing the dress box uncertainly. Then she glanced at Gertie whose eyes had become guarded.

"I hope you bought something that you can wear for work," Rosa said, displaying large teeth in a smile for the store owner's wife.

"We just paid her wages and she mustn't blow it on some frilly thing."

The woman smiled back but didn't say anything. The dress was made for parties.

"She is only fifteen and already we pay her good. I hope she bought something worth while," Rosa continued, still displaying her large yellow teeth in the unaccustomed smile.

Gertie kept her eyes downcast as she felt Rosa's hand on her shoulder.

Albert had been the one to suggest pay for he feared that sooner or later she would leave. He had reasoned that if they paid her, it would make leaving all the more difficult and Rosa had reluctantly agreed. What Gertie didn't know was that maids normally made fifteen dollars a month. Albert had been ready to point out that she was only fifteen and deserved only five. At least he had been prepared, but Gertie had offered no argument.

She placed the change carefully in an old, soiled leather purse Albert had discarded and together they left. The store owner stared after the woman and child while his wife aired her thoughts.

"I don't like that Mrs Blute. I don't know why but I just can't like her."

On the way home Gertie sat in the rear of the Model T with Albert and Rosa in front. She clutched the box to her, trying to shield it from the dust as she thought wonderingly about the shiny, deep green material that was soft and silky to touch. But her wonder was chased away by a hard knot of anxiety in her stomach. Rosa hadn't said anything but the hard thin line that was her mouth, betrayed her feelings. Gertie had come to fear that hard thin line as much as the violent rage.

Once they were home it didn't take long.

"So this is what we get, eh! We pay her good money and she wastes it on some stupid dress." Rosa gnashed her teeth, spitting out the words. Gertie cowered in a corner near the stove.

"Well, she can just wear it for work," Rosa snapped. "I am not giving her more dresses to wear." She snatched the box from Gertie and tore the dress from it, holding it up to the light that came through the kitchen window.

"Look at that! It's too darned thin. It'll only last a little while and wait until she spills milk on it or gets it dirty in the barn."

"I won't wear it in the barn," Gertie said meekly.

"You'll have to, you Polluck brat." Rosa glared from the dress to Gertie. "I don't care if you go naked. I will not give you my old dresses." Her eyes held a wild light and Gertie cringed.

"You can go naked for all I care," Rosa repeated and then suddenly laughed uproariously.

"That's all you know anyway."

Donald had come into the kitchen and sat on a chair. He grinned at Gertie and laughed too, and as usual his eyes lingered on where her young breasts pushed against her worn blouse. Unnoticed by Gertie a button had become undone and he thought he could faintly glimpse a grey-white bra. Donald's eyes held an unfathomable light for at nineteen, his body's urges were strong and he tossed and turned at night.

"Ah, leave her be!" Albert suddenly took Rosa and Donald's attention as he scratched his head.

"Aw you, you always take her side. You must care more for her than me," Rosa snapped and Albert glared at her.

"I don't give a damn for her. I am just sick und tired of all the bitching und complaining I hear. Can a man not come into his own house once in awhile and not hear bitching?"

Rosa bit her lip and glared at Gertie. Then she threw the dress at her.

"Here! Take it. It'll teach you a good lesson. Buying a cheap thing like that. That's why I let you go in alone und pick it out. Just so you'll learn a good lesson."

Gertie caught the dress and held it to her breast, slowly climbing the stairs, her eyes glistening. When she was alone in the attic, she tried it on, turning about and looking downwards awkwardly for she had no mirror. Then she removed the dress and carefully hung it on an old wooden hanger. As she sat wearily on her cot, her eyes glistening, she determinedly formed silent words.

I will not wear it in the barn. I don't care if I freeze to death. I will not wear it in the barn.


Dark, grey clouds scudded over the earth, spurred by a relentless wind. Below, the ground lay barren and used; grey-brown stubble, the only reminder of the rich, golden wheat, that had once flowed with the wind. The grain had been separated from the straw, and the straw lay in piles, settling and waiting for the onslaught of winter.

The clouds were a damp, cold harbinger of worse to come, making men hunch their shoulders and put, from their minds the future minus forty temperature. Even children played inside while the mongrel dogs sought shelter by the house or barn.

The Blute's house stood forlornly in the yard, its grey, peeling sides as grey as the weather. Inside its occupants ignored the sudden gusts of wind blowing dry, brittle leaves about the yard and bending the forlorn, leafless branches. In a bedroom, Rosa lay in an iron bed, her eyes shut tight against the never-ending days of sameness. After they had returned from Sunday Mass, she had felt a headache start in her forehead and spread. So she had left Gertie washing dishes and retired to bed even though it was only mid-afternoon.

Albert and Donald were in the barn hunched over a harness damaged when a horse had caught it on a nail. Donald held the leather while his father riveted the torn pieces back together. They worked silently, Albert wielding the hammer to drive in the rivets and then flattening the ends once a washer had been put on. Donald held the leather absentmindedly for his mind was not on the work. He had been noticing how Gertie had grown and how her worn and tattered dress pushed forward whenever she took a deep breath. She wasn't pretty; her face was square and sad while her eyes held a preoccupied look as if she existed in some Never Never Land. Her body had grown more sideways than upwards but still, he couldn't help looking at her. As he bent over the harness, his body's urges wouldn't go away and all he could think of was the girl in the house, drying dishes and muttering to herself.

Muttering had become a habit, or rather a way of thinking out loud. And since Gertie was alone, it didn't matter.

"Sure, and Rosa says, I am no good for nothing," she whispered, the words barely audible.

"But I can wash the dishes and mend the clothes. I can milk the cows and sweep the floor. I can even sew. So how can I be no good for nothing?"

She finished the dishes and gave the floor a quick, cursory sweep.

"If I am no good for nothing, how come I can bring the milk to the station?"

When she finished, she went upstairs to her room in the attic and sat down on her cot, her lips still moving.

"Sure, and Rosa says, I am not capable of handling money. But the new green dress," she still referred to the dress as new, although it had been months since she had bought it, "is only for silly things. Sure, and she says that from now on I won't get paid, just because I waste money."

Gertie spread her arms wide then as if speaking to an audience.

"You have to look good. If you don't no man will want you."

She slowly removed her worn tattered dress and in her petticoat, hung it on a nail. Then she lovingly took the still shiny and lustrous green dress from its hanger, smoothing the material with her hand

and feeling the soft, exciting touch of imitation silk. She had never worn the dress in public, only when alone in the attic with her dreams. She sat again on the cot, rocking gently back and forth, the dress clutched tightly to her chest, all the while muttering, quietly.

"Sure, and I shouldn't spend money on a nice dress. But you have to look good. If you always wear dirty, sweaty clothes what man would want you?"

Then she stood slowly and slipped on the dress. It fell to near her ankles, the dark green, darker where there were shadows. She turned this way and that, looking at the dress as best she could for she still had no mirror.

As she gazed downwards, turning her head to see the dress behind her, she heard a faint rustle on the stairs. She dismissed it for rats often scurried about, even in the daytime.

She turned slowly, back and forth, as she smoothed the material with her hands and a far-off look, came into her eyes. She was dancing in a gay ballroom filled with smiling, happy people and she was slim, and beautiful: Beautiful like the woman she had seen in a picture. She smiled dreamily as she danced in a dashing young man's arms and the room swayed with the soft, melodic music. Then she turned slowly and faced the door a dreamy smile on her lips.

She gasped suddenly for she was face to face with Donald. That was the first time he had been in her tiny room and she felt a sudden needle of fear for his cheeks were red and his breathing rapid. She wondered if he had seen her in her petticoat.

Donald took a step forward, placing his hands on her shoulders, his breath evil.

"What you want?" Gertie asked, unable to meet his eyes. A sharp fear gripped her for she knew instinctively what he wanted.

"It's okay! I won't hurt you." Donald's breath came faster and Gertie squirmed for his grip hurt her shoulders.

"Please no! We just went to church."

"Church! Pshaw!" Donald snorted, his evil breath coming in quick bursts. "I only go so Mama won't bitch. What is that, church?"

Gertie cast her eyes frantically about her tiny room. Rosa's name suddenly gave her an idea.

"Rosa! She will know. What will you do then?"

"Pshaw! Momma is sleeping, like she always is. She'll never know."

Donald let his hands slip down the smooth material. Then he brought them together and cupped the adolescent and tiny breasts.

"Come! I will not let her yell at you so much, maybe."

The promise only frightened Gertie more. Desperately she thought of the bleeding, dying Christ near the Altar. She thought too, of the Virgin Mary with her outstretched hands and her pierced heart. Tears formed and coursed down her cheeks as she squirmed, afraid to antagonize Donald.

"Please! We mustn't! It would be a sin!"

"A sin! Pshaw! That's only for the priests and kids. But you are not a kid. You are a woman!"

"Our Father in Heaven!" Gertie began praying, her face glistening.

"Now cut that out!" Donald snapped, angry and slightly fearful. But he couldn't control his hands and his words. "If you yell, I'll tell Momma you wanted to. Then where will you be? Out on a snow bank!"

"Hail Mary! Full of Grace." Gertie's body shook with gasping sobs.

"Crazy, Fraulein!" Donald snapped, grabbing the dress and tearing viciously. Gertie heard a loud, ripping and when, he pushed roughly and she fell onto her cot.

"Rosa will hear!" She tried one last, desperate time.

"Naw! She wouldn't hear a gun."

Donald ripped the dress down the middle until he came to the under-pants. Those he ripped too, until he stood over the crying and trembling, naked girl, his mouth parting in a grin.

"Hail Mary! Full of Grace, in this hour of need, protect me!" Gertie's voice broke and she became incoherent.

Donald lay down on top the girl and placed a hard, dirty hand over her mouth.

"Shut up with that stupid praying. God won't hear you!" He gritted through his teeth as he loosened his pants while still keeping his hand over her mouth.

But the words still came through the dirty hand and the cot shook with Gertie's sobs. She was too terrified to scream or fight so she only mumbled the "Hail Mary" and then reverted to, "Save me, in this hour of need!"

Donald grinned, his breath coming faster as the cot began to rock with his motion. He glanced down at Gertie who had shut her eyes. Then as the motion became faster his grin widened.

"God, won't hear you," he laughed.

The cold light filtered through the tiny, smudged window telling Gertie it was close to supper. But she was immobilized by confusion and guilt. She lay on the cot in a fetal position, her torn and tattered green dress laying, wrinkled and ripped beside her. And as she lay, her hands together and close to her face, she prayed and trembled violently.

"My God in Heaven, what is to become of me? I have sinned terribly." The tears started again, running unhindered down her cheeks.

She didn't bear any anger against Donald, who had left, walking softly and guiltily down the stairs. She only felt revulsion and a great shame as she lay on the bed sobbing, stopping only when she heard a rustle in the wall.

"Hail Mary! Forgive me." the incoherent prayer continued, the guilt settling down in her mind and soul.

Finally, after an eternity, she rose, for eternity it had been. As she stood, her shoulders drooped and she gazed downwards at her toes. Then she turned slowly and picked up the torn dress.

"If it wasn't for this dress, this would not have happened."

Gertie bunched the material in her hands and hurled it into a corner. It fell slowly and settled in a green tangle, the dark wondrous sheen lost in the gloom. Then Gertie lay back down on the cot in the fetal position, pulling a torn blanket over her as her tears soiled the sheet. But she didn't stay that way for long.

"Gertie!" Rosa yelled from the kitchen below. "Where is supper? Where is that lazy brat?"

Donald and Albert sat by the table and Donald looked out the window when his mother yelled. Albert looked too and they ignored her rage as best they could.

Gertie rose slowly, her shoulders slumping even more as she pulled the tattered old dress over her. Then she numbly walked down the stairs.

"Where have you been? You lazy Polluck!" The angry words hit her in a wave but she kept her eyes, downcast and began making supper. When she came close to Donald, she avoided looking at him, and he kept his eyes on his boots. Then he cast her, a sidelong glance and slowly a grin appeared. It vanished quickly when Rosa came near.

Gertie woodenly set the table and took a roast from the oven before taking her customary place behind a chair, waiting for an order. It didn't take long.

"Gertie! Bring coffee!" Donald commanded, the words loud and harsh. Gertie went to the stove and brought the coffee pot, keeping her eyes from his face as she poured. When she placed the pot back on the stove, she returned to behind the chair.

The only sign of her anguish was the whiteness of her knuckles as she gripped the chair. And then, as always when the pain was at a peak, the blurred vision and nausea came. This time her vision was so blurred, she could barely make out the kitchen and her stomach ached terribly. She closed her eyes and stood, rocking back and forth. She kept her lips tightly closed but still the prayer was there.

"Hail Mary! Full of Grace, help me in this hour of need."

# Ten

A large black raven flew purposely over the blinding white world of frozen poplar and brittle brown grass standing stiffly at the slough's edge. The raven croaked hoarsely as it passed over a teenage boy who trudged ponderously through the three foot drifts. He was alone, shouldering the traps and boxes along with a twenty-two, caliber rifle. He carried the rifle in case he saw a prairie chicken or rabbit for too often bannock and potatoes were the mainstay of his diet.

Vincent lifted his leather clad leg over a drift, only to sink to near the ground before lifting the other one. He wore an old cloth cap that had ear flaps covering his ears and a web belt, fastened tightly around a worn coat. His pants were woollen and warm and the leather leggings kept the snow from his feet.

He had grown since he had frozen his ear and at sixteen he considered himself a man, capable of doing the hardest of work. He was a man in his mind, although he knew nothing of manly things or the things men hunger after. He knew only the harsh wind whistling through the frozen poplar limbs and the squirming weasel caught in a steel trap.

Whenever he woke with natural urges turning his mind from the frozen slough and open fields he felt guilt for it wasn't right for a boy to think of such things. As time passed, he relied more and more on the preaching he heard in church from a man clothed in black and one given to saintly sayings and prayers.

As Vincent walked ponderously through the drifts to where he checked a trap, his swarthy face contorted and his nose twitched. It was a habit he had developed and he constantly felt the urge to twist his face into various contortions as if energy built up and it was the only way of relieving it. As he stopped, he let the bundle of boxes drop to the snow and his thick lips twisted while his tongue emerged from his mouth. His head shook slightly and he hesitated for an instant as the face settled. Then he bent and checked a weasel box. Vincent didn't think of the faces he made and if someone would have told him that they were ugly, he would have been surprised and hurt.

As he bent, he peered into one end of the box and a large buck weasel glared back, his teeth bared and his eyes cruel. Vincent pulled the chain attached to the trap and the weasel squirmed and spit death. When the weasel was free of the box, Vincent held a leather clad hand out as a target. The weasel snapped viciously and Vincent's other hand moved like lightening. The weasel twisted and struggled, sensing the encounter as his last. Vincent moved suddenly and held the weasel in both hands, placing his thumbs on the squirming weasel's chest. He squeezed with all his strength, with the thumbs pressing brutally down. Suddenly, the white killer went into convulsions, his heart torn from the arteries.

It never occurred to Vincent that what he did was cruel. It was simply, the best way to kill a weasel without damaging the fur.

When the weasel stopped struggling, he placed it in a bag and took some bait from his pocket. He set the trap and placed it back in the box and straightened. He reached down for the other boxes, continuing his round near the slough's edge. As he walked, he hesitated occasionally, his face contorting and twitching, while he hummed a tuneless melody and kept his eyes on the trees near the slough's edge. As the sun sank slowly, Vincent turned towards home. He walked slowly, carrying the traps effortlessly for he weighed over one hundred and eighty pounds. And as he walked his face twisted and his head trembled.

When he was in the yard he went to the barn and skinned the weasel, carefully stretching the hide onto a board, tacking the legs and tail so they remained in place. Then he went to the house and removed his boots, cap and coat. Helen and Sophie looked up from where they were preparing supper and then back down. Vincent sat near the stove, the warmth making him drowsy. Just then Bzigniew entered from the living room where he had been lying on the couch.

"Catch anything?"

"Yuh! A big buck weasel!" Vincent jerked his head sideways, his eyes excited.

"Did you skin it?"

"Yuh! I left it in the barn. On the board." When Vincent answered his face contorted and his head trembled. Bzigniew noticed but said nothing.

Then the family set down to a meal of pork, potatoes and bannock. Vincent reached across the table for a bucket of lard, spread it on some bannock and sprinkled salt before shoving half the slice into his mouth. His jaw worked convulsively as he chewed with his mouth open, and the bread and saliva could be seen rolling about. Then he helped himself to the meat and potatoes, jamming more into his mouth. As he ate, his jaw worked quickly until bits of food dropped and landed unnoticed on his pants.

He waved his arm, his mouth open. "There's deer tracks, near the slough." He chewed as he talked with more food falling from his mouth. "Looks like a big buck!"

"Is it fresh?" Bzigniew asked thoughtfully.

"Yuh!" Vincent waved his arm again, still chewing. "Maybe I could take the big rifle tomorrow and we could have some fresh deer meat."

"I better come with you," Bzigniew said, keeping his eyes from his son's face as it contorted. "I'll take the rifle. You can come along with the twenty-two in case we see some rabbits."

Vincent kept on chewing, the food rolling around in his open mouth, and if the insult of not being trusted to bring home a deer registered, he didn't show it. He reached across the table, cut a large slice of bannock with a knife and spread more lard and sprinkled more salt, his jaw convulsing as his father looked away.


A full moon rode high in the black sky, sailing slowly over the white snow and stiff, frozen poplars while coyotes wandered the winter wasteland in search of food. In the snow banks, field mice tunneled out homes and survived the winter, keeping a wary ear tuned for a coyote's footsteps. And into the tunnels the weasel burrowed, looking for the mice.

The coyotes and weasels were not the only ones out in the moonlit night. The men and women who, braved the cold however, were searching for entertainment, a break from the endless days of doing chores and surviving. They gathered in the old one-room school and forgot for a very brief time, the blistering cold and silent loneliness.

Inside, one man with a fiddle, another with a guitar and a third with an accordion played a lively tune to a near empty floor. Against a wall, young girls smiled timidly at young men who passed by and pretended not to notice. When the girls smiled they kept their eyes downcast for it was a man's world and unseemly for a girl to appear too bold.

Around a cast-iron, pot-bellied stove near the door, a group of teenage boys gathered and cast occasional glances at the dance floor. They were the ones who were too old to stay home and too young and shy to boldly ask a girl for a dance. In the group Vincent sat on a wooden chair with his arms folded across his chest. Straight ahead he could see his father against a wall with other men, discussing the weather or farming. When he turned he could see his sisters sitting with their backs against another wall, casting timid sidelong glances at the single men.

Vincent was drowsy for it was ten p.m. and he had been up since six and if it came to a choice he would have preferred the cold, open air or his warm bed: Except for the biting loneliness.

And whenever he was in public, he became nervous which caused the urge for a facial contortion to become irresistible. He fought the urge and his jaw trembled but it was only a minute before his tongue protruded and his head trembled slightly. This time it mattered.

The boy sitting next to him suddenly grinned.

"What's a matter, Vincent?" Metro, asked innocently. "The sight of all them girls making you nervous?"

The rest of the boys turned their attention to Vincent, grinning and nudging each other. Vincent couldn't prevent a foolish grin that caused his mouth to widen. It always happened. Whenever he was the object of mockery, he responded by grinning foolishly.

"Look at that one!" Metro, continued and Vincent felt the eyes of the other teenagers on him. His swarthy face darkened and the silly grin stayed on his face.

"Wouldn't ya wanna roll round in the hay with her, eh?" Metro, pointed to a young woman, dancing a polka. Vincent couldn't help himself. He looked and the red flush deepened.

"I'll bet you'd give up trapping for her, eh! I'll bet you'd even stop making all them faces too once you get a look at her naked," Metro added and the teenagers laughed uproariously.

"What would ya do with a woman like that?" one of them demanded.

Vincent's face remained dark. The grin remained too, plastered on his face.

"I don't know!" He said suddenly, the words coming in a rush.

"Don't ya know what to do?" Metro persisted, chewing on a straw he had picked up from the floor. He rubbed his neck which was red from unaccustomed scrubbing. Then he brushed his long dirty blond hair back from his face and grinned. He was a year younger than Vincent but still, he felt immeasurably superior.

"Oh come on Vincent! Tell us. What're ya gonna do on your wedding night?"

"I don't know!" Again the words came in a rush.

"Oh come on! You've seen cows and bulls do it."

"I don't know! I never think of things like that." The dark blush and foolish grin stayed on Vincent's face.

"If you don't know now, how in hell ya gonna have kids?" Metro demanded.

"He probably thinks an angel will bring 'em," one of the boys said and the laughter came at Vincent in waves. "Come on Vincent! Tell us. Do angels bring the babies or do men and women make them like cows and bulls?"

The band switched to a waltz and older couples took to the floor but still the teasing continued.

"Come on Vincent! You watch the cows and bulls, don't ya?"

Vincent didn't answer. His face was still dark while the irresistible urge to make a face came and he wiped his mouth with a callused hand. As the contortion shook Vincent's head Metro finally tired of the game.

"Aw Shit!" He spat the straw out onto the floor. "He probably thinks a piece of ass is donkey meat."

Vincent's grin slowly vanished. He looked at his tormentors for a moment and then a slow, dull anger formed. His lips twitched and his head trembled. Metro laughed, suddenly nervous.

"If you make faces like that in front of a girl, you'll scare the shit 'outa her and that's the last you'll ever see of her."

The boys' laughter caused adult heads to turn but they were only boys having fun and no one interfered.

"It's a sin to talk like that!" Vincent said emphatically, the trembling stopping for an instant.

"A sin!" Metro, glanced at the other boys and then grinned back at Vincent. But he had a hard time meeting his eyes.

"Now who in hell told you that?" He demanded.

"Father said in church that we mustn't think of dirty things, or it'll be a sin."

"What the hell does he know?" Metro snapped, the humor gone. "He probably thinks a piece of ass is donkey meat too."

Vincent clenched and unclenched his hands, the knuckles white where he gripped the back of the chair.

"People who talk like that will go to hell!"

"Aw, who in hell believes in shit like that?" One of the boys snapped and then turned to Metro. "Come on, let's go and see if we can bum some tobacco off my old man. He went to town today so I know he got some."

The teenagers left, walking across the dance floor, taking care not to bump into any of the dancers or to step on the feet of men and women seated on the long bench against a wall. Vincent remained in the chair, close to the warm stove and his eyelids drooped. He glanced over to his sisters but saw only Helen. Sophie was dancing clumsily with a young man who held her awkwardly. Vincent felt a sudden urge to talk to Helen but as he was about to get up a man approached and she stood and then began dancing.

Vincent settled back in his chair and his lips twisted while his tongue protruded. He held the contortion for a few seconds with his head trembling. Then he looked down at the dusty floor, at his boots and then up again as another contortion began while the dancers swirled and the musicians played mightily.

As he sat alone, Vincent thought of the weasel traps and how he would begin trapping muskrat once the weather broke. He thought of the large slough and wished he was there under the leaden sky, with the traps on his back and his twenty-two in his hand.

There, the facial contortions didn't matter.

# Eleven

The late spring sun shone through the dirty window, casting shadows in the kitchen and illuminating dancing dust particles. The light fell on the table, the old scarred chairs the cook stove and ancient cupboard that housed the family's dishes. While beneath and in the walls rats raised their families.

Near the cupboard, Gertie stood hunched over a washbasin, making quick jerky motions as she lathered her face. When she finished washing, she dried herself on a tattered towel and then opened a container of face powder. She shook the powder from the can into one hand and then liberally spread it on her face. The white powder turned her ruddy cheeks, a whitish grey as she rubbed briskly, her whole body moving with the motion.

A full year had passed since Donald had appeared in her tiny attic room. He had returned a few times, always telling Gertie that if she told, he would tell Rosa that it had been her idea and that Rosa would throw her out. Gertie believed him and bore his brutish attentions, while weeping and praying silently. Oddly, she didn't become pregnant and maybe it was her poor diet. She lay awake at night in sweat-drenched anxiety, never knowing when he would return or whether Rosa would find out. And she feared being thrown out more than anything, for no matter how miserable her life was, Blute's farm was still home.

As Gertie applied the face powder, her body still shaking, her lips moved.

"Sure! And it's a sin!" She stopped for an instant and spread her hands wide in the familiar gesture. "But what was I to do?"

Next came the nun's admonishments about people who sin and the punishment of burning in hell for eternity. Gertie's lips tightened and she began mumbling the Hail Mary. She wiped her hands on the towel but her face was white from powder. She didn't notice and she also didn't notice the dried sweat under her arms and the area of her neck she had missed. She grabbed the container and hurried to the attic where she dressed quickly. The green dress had become a rag Albert and Donald used when they worked on machinery and it too was lost in the fog of memory and dreams. As she dressed, she continued mumbling.

"Sure! And it's easy to say I should leave." Again she spread her arms wide, "But where can I go?" She dropped her old dress over her shoulders and ran downstairs, meeting Rosa in the kitchen.

"Where have you been? We'll be late for church!" Rosa snapped and then led the way to the wagon. As the depression had deepened, Albert had quit buying gasoline and the Model T occupied a place near the barn, a sad emblem of happier times. Rosa and Gertie climbed into the wagon box, sitting on apple boxes behind Albert and Donald. Albert snapped the reins and the skinny horses lifted their drooping heads and shuffled off down the trail to Sunday Mass.

When Albert tied the horses alongside the other wagons, they entered the church under the tall gothic spire that could be seen for miles. The cross on top was the highest point, towering over the poplar trees lining the street and over the people who hurried into the building fearful of being late and angering an angry God. Once inside, Gertie knelt on a tiny bench and bowed her head. On her right were Albert and Rosa while Donald was on her left.

Donald never spoke to her, unless it was an order during mealtime and Gertie avoided him whenever possible. The only time he noticed her was when he appeared unannounced in her tiny room.

As she knelt, she made the sign of the cross quickly, bobbing her head and barely touching her forehead and shoulders with her finger tips. Then she began praying in a loud whisper, the words indistinguishable. Rosa turned and glared at her but she said nothing for talking in church was bad luck.

"Our Father in Heaven," Gertie whispered fiercely and then the words became jumbled and she finished with, "Hail Mary! Full of grace."

After all the other parishioners had sat back in their pews, Gertie remained kneeling and praying for forgiveness. Finally she stood and edged her way past Donald, keeping her eyes averted. She walked with bowed head to the confessional where a priest sat behind a screen, his hands folded as if in prayer. But he was lost in a daydream for he had heard all the minor sins countless times before. When a shadow fell across his face he knew someone was on the other side of the screen. Gertie knelt, making a hurried sign of the cross, her lips moving.

"Forgive me Father, for I have sinned." She stopped, for she couldn't bring herself to mention Donald's furtive visits to her room.

She sat confused, her knuckles white as the priest grew impatient. He was about to raise his hand in a benediction, when Gertie suddenly found her voice.

"Oh yuh! I committed the sin of anger. I was mad at Rosa last week. And I stole some food. I ate a crust of bread and didn't tell, her." The sin of lying with Donald in her tiny cot slipped beneath her consciousness, suppressed into the hazy quagmire of guilt and shame.

The priest raised his hand again.

"Oh Father." A hazy memory suddenly raced through her mind and the priest sighed and lowered his hand.

"I committed the sin of indecency!"

"What?" The priest sat bolt upright.

"Yuh Father! I thought of a man."

"Oh," The priest settled back down and hesitated. When he heard no more, he ordered, "Say the Our Father and Hail Mary twenty times each and light candles at the altar. He raised his hand again.

"Now go in peace, My Child."

Gertie made a hurried sign of the cross and with the last words still ringing in her ear, she walked slowly back to the pew, where Rosa kept a watchful eye on her. She knelt and began praying again, reciting the Hail Mary and the Our Father the prescribed number of times, her lips moving in an audible whisper.

When the priest began the mass, Gertie rose and stood, knelt and prayed and then sat back on the bench with the others. If she would have been asked why she attended Mass, she would have been hard pressed to answer. She knew only that if she didn't, she would be overwhelmed with searing guilt and her days and nights spent in fearful prayer.

When the mass was half way through, Gertie again left the pew and stood in line with the Blutes to receive the Holy Communion. She lifted her head to the priest who towered over her.

"The Body of Christ," he intoned and Gertie allowed him to place the wafer, that was the surrogate flesh of the Savior, onto her tongue. She swallowed slowly and the wafer disappeared. As she walked slowly back to the pew, she concentrated on not chewing for that was all the food she had eaten that day. It was the Catholic law that no food was to be eaten in the morning for it would contaminate the stomach which was to receive the flesh of the Lord. Gertie swayed slightly as she sat on the hard pew.

As she knelt and prayed, her whisper became louder and she gazed longingly at the Madonna with the pierced heart. Then as her vision blurred, the Mother of Christ smiled. The harder Gertie stared, the more she saw a smile on the marble statue.

Suddenly she felt Rosa's bony, hard finger in her ribs.

"Gettup!" Rosa whispered fiercely, forgetting the superstition about talking in church.

"Everybody else is sitting already, and you are still kneeling like a dumpkoft!"

Gertie sat up quickly and then looked at the Virgin Mary. The smile had vanished and all she saw was a marble statue with outstretched hands and a pierced, bleeding heart.

---

The hot, searing sun broke weakly through the dust clouds as the relentless wind whipped the soft, pliable soil into the air. Plants withered and died while men and animals constantly found the fine dust in their nostrils. In some areas of the dust-bowl; rain became a memory.

Desperate men sold their land or lost it to the banks and it was said a man traded a quarter section of land for a pair of shoes. Still, the weather didn't let up and the wind whipped the soil that became sand and the land dried up under the blistering sun until it became a desert. Men hitched their horses to a wagon and piled their possessions on top. They used old canvas for a tent and tied a cow behind setting out from the devastated homestead in search of a better place, anywhere. Some simply gave up and drifted to the cities, hoping to be put on relief while others set out for the jack pine country, north of the Saskatchewan river. Others stayed and *toughed it out*, living on eggs, and bannock.

Single men, some young, some old and withered like the dry, parched soil beneath their worn and tattered boots, walked hopelessly from farm to farm, begging for food, willing to chop wood or do anything for a meal, just to keep them going for another sad, desperate day.

And the years passed. The seasons changed gradually from the withered dry grass of summer to the cold, howling wind of winter. The drought and depression could be seen in the dirty, sad faces of children, dressed in old flour sacks or holding a torn burlap sack to their bodies, for decent clothes were also a memory. The children suffered the most, their small minds not able to fathom the silence in the farm houses when there was only bannock to eat, or the sudden quarrels between parents who had never quarreled before. They were the true sufferers in a time that would be written about in history books. They should have been the next step in the immigrant's dream of a good life in the new world, given opportunities, their parents could only pray for. Instead, they had less chance as they played in the hard, baked ground that cracked and splintered in the blistering heat. It was the children who bore the brunt of the weather and the settler's mistake of plowing too deep and leaving summer fallow unprotected from the howling wind.

And it was the children who had the least say in things.

On the farm, not far from the hamlet of Berlin, people passed by occasionally, some begging for food or looking for work, any work, and the message was not lost on Gertie or the Blutes. Her wages of five dollars a month were still agreed upon but she was never paid for there were thousands who would gladly work for mere board and room.

So Gertie sweated in the hot sun, waiting on the table while Rosa and Albert ate or she helped in the barn, for Donald had wandered off in search of a better life in a city. Gertie was spared his brutish attentions in the middle of the silent night. But that was a mixed blessing for the loneliness made life an eternal hell, a sentence to be borne stoically. As she worked, her thoughts swirled, lost in a lonely world of imaginary events and people, a world she couldn't escape. As she stood over the wash basin, vigorously scrubbing the dishes, she muttered and dunked them viciously, her whole body shaking with the motion.

"Sure! And Rosa says I'm ugly and no man would want me." She spread her dripping hands wide, again talking to an imaginary audience.

"But what can I do? I have no nice clothes. All I know is hard work. Sure! And it would be easy to be like other girls, always chasing after men. But that would be a sin!"

Then a memory came, of a neighbor who had listened to her complain. The young woman had grown impatient.

"Why don't you leave then?" She had snapped.

"Sure! And it's easy to say leave. But where would I go? Every day there is people who go by looking for food." Gertie spread her arms wide again as she thought of the withered old man who had walked alone, carrying his belongings in a bag slung over his shoulder. She remembered how thirsty he had been and how the dirt and sweat had creased his face. She had given him water and then watched as he split wood, the requirement of the Blutes before he could eat a cold meal of hard bread and lard.

The years passed until she was in her early twenties, an unwed, unloved young woman, stolid and suffering, torn with guilt for an event she couldn't remember. Then came fear; fear that she would remain a servant of the Blutes with no man or children to call her own and no real home. And as always, she expressed her fear and guilt when she was alone.

"Sure! And it would be easy to get a husband." The hands spread from habit, "And all I got to be is rich. If I was living in a nice home and with nothing to do but look pretty. And I could find a man real easy. But, here with all this work!"

Then, when she felt especially desperate, the prayers would come.

"Our Father in Heaven," or "Hail Mary, Full of Grace,"

And always the prayers went unheeded, for it seems the only answer to a truly desperate person's prayer is, more prayer.

At night, the dreams would come, winding their way unhindered through her subconscious, giving expression to hidden fears and desires. If she dreamed of a man and remembered the dream, she would pray for forgiveness. As time passed and the wind howled, the lines settled on her sad, square face until she looked much older than twenty-four. And in her dreams she returned to the happy, hazy existence of herding cows with her brother. In others she ran from an enraged father who swung a belt. But as time passed the image of her father became less fearful and she wished fervently that she could be with him.

As she slopped the dirty dishwater, the screen door was suddenly opened and slammed shut. Albert and Rosa entered the kitchen, their faces hot from riding in the wagon from town. Gertie turned her head sideways and gazed at them over her right shoulder, so as not to have to turn and slop water on the floor. Rosa gazed back, some of the hardness gone from her face but the words were still cruel.

"You better get ready."

"For what?" A sudden spasm of fear shot through Gertie's body.

"For the funeral in Berlin."

"Funeral! Why?"

"Your Pappa has died."

"My Pappa." Gertie's face slowly lost its color as she dried her hands on a towel. "But he is not that old."

"Maybe, but he is dead anyway." Rosa sat heavily on a chair. "Albert will take you to town. The Mass is at nine tomorrow."

As Gertie turned and began drying dishes, the thoughts swirled. Memories of her father bringing home an apple or rock candy fought with memories of the belt and in the end the apples and candy won out. Slowly, in a dream, tears slid down through the sweat on her face. She turned and gazed numbly at Rosa and Albert.

"I have to wash my dress. I can not go to the funeral like this."


The rows of headstones stood bleakly in the tiny graveyard, an emblem of what the ground was for. There were names inscribed on the stone; some Ukrainian, others Polish or German and even a few English. They all said the same: the date of birth, when there were records, and the time of death. And always, there was the *Rest in Peace* in many languages. The headstones were final, cold hard marble over the cold, hard and final resting place.

Gertie gazed at the priest whose black smock was whipped by the wind and who intoned the words, "Ashes to Ashes and Dust to Dust." Then her brother sprinkled dirt onto the plain wood coffin and the crowd prayed.

When the praying was done, Augustine came to Gertie and placed his hand on her arm. Marie and Anna were there too, having come from their husbands' farms. Augustine's eyes held a vacant worried light, for not only had he lost a father but now he must live alone in the tiny house and scratch a living from the hard soil. He stood beside Gertie for a while, neither saying anything. Finally he found words.

"I have to get back. I milk cows and I have to get back."

Marie's eyes were moist as she gazed at Gertie but Anna had grown still harder from the toil and broken dreams and her eyes were dry and cold. For a while longer they stood together, no one saying anything for Gertie was a stranger. But the silence was unbearable.

"If you ever want to come for a visit, you're always welcome," Augustine said softly.

"Sure maybe," Gertie answered and then they followed the small crowd out through the iron gate with the two tiny winged angels on top of the posts, guarding the hallowed ground. When they were on the street, Albert approached. He had been on the other side of the crowd and his sudden appearance was a reminder that all things of the past must take second place.

"You ready?" He demanded and then nodded to Augustine.

Augustine nodded back and then awkwardly stuck out his right hand to Gertie. And he repeated what he had said earlier.

"Come for a visit some time."

"Sure maybe," Gertie repeated, with Albert at her side. Then she followed him to the wagon. Albert snapped the reins and the thin, tired horses began a shuffling walk back to the farm.

---

Heat waves rose from the hard, baked soil along the edge of the field while crows cawed lazily from the wilted leaves of the poplars. Overhead a hawk circled, rising on the hot air as he searched for prey in the dusty grass in the pasture next to the field. In the shade of the poplars the cattle lay, lazily chewing their cud, their ribs showing through the tough hide for there was little to eat in the August heat.

In the field, four horses plodded forward, their heads rising and falling in a bobbing motion while sweat ran in streams down their backs and became white foam. Behind the horses a three-section harrow bit into the soil, turning it into thick dark dust as it rose from the steel teeth. And behind the harrow walked Vincent, only his eyes and teeth showing from his blackened face. He walked in a clumsy rocking manner, not unlike a bear, and the inevitable facial contortion came and went as he occasionally snapped the lines on the horses' rumps. Whenever he made a face, his lips twisting and tongue protruding, his step would slow and then he would take a larger one, keeping pace with the horses and harrow.

Under the dirt his skin was tanned a deep brown, a reminder of his Metis mother. But he had only a hazy image of a warm, gentle woman, lost deep in the recesses of his mind for Bzigniew never talked of her. If Vincent would have been told that he was one quarter Indian, he would have denied it vehemently.

When he came to the end of the field, he turned the team and then cried "Whoa!" The horses stopped, their heads drooping while sweat glistened on their backs. Vincent took a soiled handkerchief made from an old shirt from his bib trousers and shook it vigorously. The dust came loose and ran in little rivulets down the cloth. He wiped his neck where the sweat and dust had mixed, turning his skin to nearly black. He then wiped his forehead vigorously before blowing his nose loudly. The horses ignored the sound, their heads still drooping. When Vincent blew his nose and looked at the cloth, he noticed that part of it had become darker than the rest. His nose had been clogged with dust and together with the mucus, it formed a dark sticky mixture. He eyed it for a moment and then put the handkerchief back into his breast pocket. He straightened his back, placing one hand behind the vertebrae and pushing. Then he scratched his shoulder under the short-sleeved shirt. His back was bare, except for the shirt and the shirt, which had once been blue, was totally black from dust and sweat.

Slowly Vincent removed his cloth cap and wiped the sweat from the band. Then he replaced it and snapped the reins. One of the horses lifted a hind leg, hesitated and then stood still. Vincent snapped the lines again and yelled "Gettup!" The horses eased their weight into the collars and the harrow began to move with clouds of dust rising in Vincent's face. Slowly, the team walked the half mile to the other end of the field, their sore aching muscles pulling the man-made contraption they were chained to. It wasn't any easier for Vincent for his worn boots sunk deeply into the soft ground and his calf muscles burned.

Over in the next field Bzigniew drove a second team, pulling a gang plow, with its two furrows. When he was, finished Vincent would move over and harrow the turned earth. They rarely spoke, only when it involved an order from Bzigniew. As the years passed, father and son became strangers in the same house, talking occasionally but rarely knowing what the other was thinking. Sophie and Helen had married and moved to the city, so there was just the two of them, taking turns cooking the meals and washing the dishes when the pile grew too high on the cupboard. As for housework, occasionally either would sweep the floor in an attempt to keep the dust at bay. But it was a losing battle for the wind blew the fine particles through the door and window sills.

Occasionally, Vincent would go to town with his father and together they would sit, for a while on a hard wooden bench in the Barbershop/Poolroom. And the thought of being a slave to the land, a single lonely man with no wife or children to call his own caused Vincent to fear the future. He was normally happy in the field or trapping but occasionally, in town, the sight of a girl would break through the barrier of denial and he would feel more alone than ever.

He tried once. One Sunday afternoon he hitched a team to the wagon and drove three miles to a neighbor, where a young girl named Julie lived with her parents. He accepted coffee and sat in the kitchen with the puzzled parents, talking of the weather, the price of grain and cattle for more than two hours. Julie sat at the other end of the kitchen table, her legs primly crossed at the ankles and her arms folded but she didn't join in. When Vincent noticed that she glanced at him, amusement in her eyes, he looked down quickly. Then the irresistible urge for a facial contortion came. He fought it for a moment, his jaw trembling, but the urge was too great. His lips twisted and his tongue protruded while his head trembled. He hoped she wasn't looking. But she noticed and saw a shy, young man who had a dark swarthy face and who talked of the weather and grain when his mind was on something, much more urgent. She also saw a young man whose face twisted into grotesque, tortured contortions. She felt a slight pity, nothing more.

When the sun hovered near the horizon Vincent finally stood, his cap in hand, ready to leave. And then, desperately summing up his courage, he turned to Julie, while her parents looked on, their eyes meeting for an instant.

"Uh," Vincent scratched his head and looked down at his worn boots. Then he glanced back up, "There's a dance in Berlin this Saturday."

Julie looked at him uncertainly, her hands folded in her lap. Then she looked at her mother who said nothing.

"Maybe I could come and and take you." Vincent stammered.

"A dance!" Julie finally answered. She had expected the question but was slow to answer.

"I can't dance. I don't know how," she lied. A sudden silence settled down on the kitchen with both parents again exchanging glances. Vincent looked down at his old boots again.

"Uh, I didn't know." He remembered seeing her dancing but lacked the courage to mention it.

Then with shame and relief fighting in his soul he put his cap back on his head and turned to the door.

"Well, I better be going," he said quickly and left the farmyard, driving the wagon back to his father's farm while the humiliation settled. He thought of the cold wind in the winter when he set traps and wondered why; if he felt happy then why couldn't he forget a girl's face? A month later he went to a different dance and saw Julie dancing with another man. He didn't talk to her and when she noticed his eyes on her, she quickly looked away.

So Vincent walked clumsily behind the sweating horses, under the broiling sun, with sweat mingling with the dust and wondered if that was all he had to look forward to, walking behind sweating horses and setting traps in the winter.

His face contorted and his head, trembled but it didn't matter, for there was no one to see and no one to care. As he walked, in that rocking manner of his, one of the horses lifted a tail and a pungent odor hit his nostrils as droppings fell to the soft earth. He merely walked on, snapping the lines and casting an eye at the sun to check the time.

# Twelve

Vincent tied the team to the wagon, gave them some hay and then straightened his cap. The horses reached forward hungrily, the ropy muscles in their necks showing. Vincent left the horses and hitched his trousers up and walked toward the one room building. Teams were tied around the school/dance hall and other farmers were approaching.

Years had passed and he was a man, in his late twenties, strong and hard working, but ignorant still of the ways of men. Vincent looked down at his worn shoes and slacks that were shiny from too much ironing. Suddenly he felt a great shyness and as he approached the door, he saw Metro.

"Hello Vincent!" Metro cried loudly. Vincent stopped, his hand on the door knob and again the silly grin came.

"Come to give the girls a whirl?" Metro grinned, chewing on a straw he had picked up in the yard. He brushed his dirty blond hair back from his forehead and continued, "I'll bet ya just can't wait 'til the band starts, eh?"

Vincent grinned and stepped back from the door. Then he rocked backwards with his right leg behind his left and his hands in his pockets. Metro opened the door and beckoned.

"Well, what'a ya waiting for? I bet ya been practicing all week, eh!"

"I don't know!" Vincent's words came suddenly, in a rush.

Inside, the married couples and young girls sat while the single men gathered in a circle by the door. Vincent joined them and he swayed backwards in that peculiar placating, manner of his. And as always, the conversation was about farming, hunting and the weather while occasionally one of the men would look at the single girls, pretending he was looking at something else. Then when a silence settled down upon them, Metro turned to Vincent.

"Vincent here, says he's gonna dance with every girl in the house. Ain't that so, Vincent?"

"I don't know!" The same quick rush of words came as Vincent swayed backwards and the men laughed. Then one of them pulled a small brown bottle from his hip pocket, nudged another and winked. The men all turned quickly and made for the door. The first man stopped suddenly and nodded towards Metro

"What about him?" He asked.

"You kiddin? We can't give a guy like that a drink. He might go Indian," Metro snapped and Vincent glared down at his worn, grey shoes.

On a bench, not far from Vincent but unnoticed, Gertie sat with the Blutes. Her worn dress was neatly folded over her knees and her square, sad face set permanently in a forced half smile. She glanced down at her work-worn hands, the skin toughened from milking cows and washing clothes with lye soap, as she felt the same, awkward and painful, self-consciousness that Vincent knew.

Just then the whirling thoughts were scattered by the scrape of a fiddle. The married couples were the first to dance while the shy single girls cast sidelong glances at the single men, never looking directly at them.

After a few tunes some of the braver ones walked self-consciously across the wooden floor and asked laconically, "Dance?"

Vincent remained standing by the door, fighting the urge to make a face and his jaw trembled. He folded his hands behind his back and rocked backwards. Then finally he looked about for a place to sit, away from the countless eyes he was sure were upon him. He turned to his right and saw a place beside Gertie. She still sat, gazing down at her work-worn hands, wishing some man would ask her to dance, but fearing it.

Vincent walked toward her, his eyes on the floor and his body rocking in his clumsy manner. Then he sat, too shy to ask permission. He placed one leg over the other and looked down at his worn, grey shoe while he folded his hands and his head trembled. Gertie kept her eyes downcast too, wondering if his sitting next to her was purely accidental. She cast a quick sidelong glance at Vincent and saw a dark young male face that ordinarily would have been considered handsome, except for the redness from unaccustomed scrubbing and the nicks from a razor.

The band continued, the fiddler drawing the bow vigorously across the strings. Vincent gazed at the dancers, again stifling a wish that he could be among the cattle and horses. Gertie thought too, of her tiny attic room where she was free to dream of a world far less threatening than the dance hall. Finally the music stopped. As the couples were breaking up Vincent kept his eyes straight ahead. But then Gertie took out a handkerchief and blew her nose. When she was about to place it back in her purse, it slipped from her fingers and fell to the floor.

Vincent saw it land out of the corner of his eye and impulsively reached down to retrieve it. He shyly gave the "hanky" to Gertie, not knowing what to say.

"Thanks!" Gertie mumbled, placing the cloth back in her purse.

Vincent nodded quickly and shrugged his broad shoulders. Then they sat beside each other in silence until he finally cleared his throat.

"Nice weather."

Gertie glanced uncertainly at Vincent, not sure he was talking to her. Then, after a few seconds, she found her voice.

"Yuh! And just as long as it don't rain during threshing."

Vincent fought the urge to make a face as he added, "Yuh, but if it snows early it'll be easy to track deer and the weasels will have nice long fur."

"Oh. You trap?"

"Yuh! I trap by my father's farm, about three miles from here." He waved his arm in the general direction.

"Oh," Gertie said softly.

Rosa and Albert looked at her and then at Vincent. Neither said anything but Rosa placed her hand on Gertie's shoulder.

"I live only a mile from here." Gertie glanced at Rosa. "I work for these people."

Vincent nodded quickly to Albert. Albert nodded back while at the same time scratching the back of his neck.

"What's your name?"

"Uh, Vincent!" Vincent said and then realized they wanted more. "Bronski. My father's Bzigniew, you know he got a half section three miles from here."

"Oh yuh! Bronski. I think I know that name," Albert said slowly, gazing upwards at a tiny window that let in the dying sunlight.

"That's Polish. Ain't it?"

"Yuh."

Albert was silent for a moment and then asked suddenly, "Your mother was an Indian, eh?"

"No!" Vincent said loudly. He looked down at his boots and then at the door, his dark face turning darker.

"Oh. Well that's what I heard," Albert said.

Vincent stared down at the floor and a heavy silence settled down upon them. Then the band started again; a slow waltz and once the floor was filling with slowly turning couples, Vincent turned to Gertie.

"You know how to dance?" he asked gruffly. Gertie looked at him quickly, focusing on his green eyes.

"Yuh! Sure, I know how."

Rosa looked quickly at Albert and grinned, displaying her large teeth.

"Do you know how?" Gertie asked quietly.

"Oh yuh!" Vincent answered and then looked down at the floor. Then he looked up.

"You want to?" He asked, the words coming slowly, barely audible.

"Well," Gertie said softly and Vincent sighed involuntarily, thinking of Julie and her cheerful lie.

But Gertie stood and smiled awkwardly. Vincent rose and they walked to the edge of the floor and then stopped, looking at each other. Gertie barely came to Vincent's shoulder and she placed a timid hand on his arm. Vincent took her hand and slowly they tried keeping time to the waltz. Vincent didn't really dance. It was more a series of clumsy bear-like steps while he desperately tried to avoid Gertie's feet. He glanced at the door and noticed Metro grin and nudge the man next to him. Vincent turned his head quickly and concentrated on dancing.

When it was over, both Gertie and Vincent gratefully went back to the bench and sat, their shoulders touching.

Vincent moved suddenly so they didn't touch. Then their conversation continued, haltingly.

"You work for them long?" He indicated the Blutes with his chin.

"Yuh. Since I was eight."

"Maybe when I get older Pappa will give me a quarter of land," Vincent said, letting his lower jaw twitch sideways.

"Oh. And that would be nice."

Then, the same question he had asked Julie came haltingly as Vincent looked at the square, sad face that was Gertie's.

"Uh, Maybe I could come to your place. Maybe we could go to a dance, eh?"

"Okay," Gertie said softly and Vincent sighed deeply. Then they sat in silence while the band played and Vincent didn't ask Gertie to dance again. When lunch was brought out, Vincent rose and then stopped self-consciously looking down at Gertie.

"You want coffee? And a sandwich?"

"Yuh. Please," Gertie used the alien word and then glanced down at her hands.

Vincent clumsily carried two cups of scalding hot coffee and two sandwiches. He spilled some on his pants but he ignored it as he passed a cup to Gertie and concentrated on eating. He made loud smacking noises as he chewed rapidly, his mouth open. Gertie noticed but he had been the only man to ever ask her to dance and eating habits can be changed.

Then, when lunch was finished and the band had played some more, couples began leaving. Vincent rose and looked down at Gertie again.

"Saturday maybe, I'll come to your place."

Gertie nodded and he left, his body rocking sideways in his bear-like walk.

"He's a Polluck Half-breed," Rosa laughed once he was out of earshot.

"Ah! And what of it? We're in Canada now!" Albert said. "Besides, his Pappa has two quarters of land. And maybe he'll get it."

"Yuh! But he's still a Polluck Half-breed." Rosa wiped her neck where perspiration had gathered, for the school house was hot and cloying. She lifted her arms, letting the air circulate to her armpits. Then she cast a sidelong look at Gertie who sat with her hands folded and her eyes, downcast.

"And maybe that's all she can get."

# Thirteen

The sun sank slowly into the west as gradually the heat gave way to the coolness of the long shadows. In a pasture along the dirt road, a horse neighed from where he cropped short grass and cattle came out from their afternoon hiding places. Vincent let the reins hang loose from his tough hands and the horses took their time for in the coolness of dusk, a softness had settled upon the land and they sensed their master's patience.

Vincent cast a sidelong glance at Gertie who sat primly on the hard buggy seat next to him. She kept her eyes on the horses' ears as they passed between stands of stunted poplars. In Vincent's pocket there was fifty cents; thirty for admission to a movie and twenty left over for coffee in a Chinese café down the street. Vincent debated whether he should take Gertie for coffee or save the twenty cents for twenty-two shells.

They passed a wheat field which had headed out and was only a couple of weeks away from harvesting.

"Nice crop," Vincent said for the Great Drought had not reached quite as far north as Berlin. The depression had however, and Vincent reached inside his pocket and played with the two quarters.

Gertie nodded but said nothing as the horses continued their shambling walk. In the distance they could see the gothic church spire with its iron cross towering above the town. The spire gave rise to a concern of Gertie's that had been gnawing at her for weeks.

She turned her square, sad face to Vincent, her hair pressed into curls that were coming undone. Vincent noticed she was looking at him but he kept his eyes on the horses. As he looked at the church spire his face contorted and his jaw trembled.

"You go to church?" Gertie suddenly asked.

"Oh yuh!" Vincent kept his eyes on the horses. "Pappa and me go all the time."

"Where? I didn't see you last Sunday."

"The church in Peterson. Why?"

"Oh, I was just wondering. I'm Catholic."

"Yuh! Me too," Vincent said quickly, glancing at Gertie. "Maybe Pappa will let me bring the buggy to Berlin on Sunday. Then we could meet in church."

"That would be nice."

Their conversation died then as the church spire became larger and larger. Eventually they passed the spire's shadow and Vincent turned off the street and behind the dance hall/movie theater. He vaulted from the buggy and unhitched the horses, tying them to a hitching rail. Gertie waited until he was finished and then climbed down.

Vincent turned with Gertie following and walked around the hall to the front door. While he walked, he again played with the two quarters in his pocket. They stopped for a moment, both looking at posters and notices nailed to the door. Then Vincent paid the thirty cents admission and they found a hard bench. He looked about and saw Metro sitting with two other young men near the front, and then the lights dimmed and an image appeared.

"The Talkie," was a new marvelous invention and the hall was packed. It didn't matter that the plot was weak with a Canadian Mountie continuously chasing a wayward Eskimo in a land of forever ice and snow. Gertie was enthralled by the fleeting images. But the fact the story unfolded in her land, Canada, didn't occur to her.

They sat close together but Vincent made no move to place his arm about her or to hold hands for whenever he looked at the bottom of the screen he could see a head silhouetted against it. He knew it was Metro's.

When the final serial ended and the flickering had died on the white canvas, the lights suddenly were turned on. Vincent looked about quickly, surprised at how fast electricity fills a room with light. Then he and Gertie walked to the door, Vincent wishing she would hurry for he saw Metro approaching. Then, once they were outside in the warm, late evening he heard his name called.

"Vincent! Vincent!" Metro, hurried to catch up, a grin spreading on his face.

"Well, will ya look at this?" he said to the two young men with him. They stopped and stood looking from Metro to Vincent and Gertie.

"Well, did ya do it?" Metro suddenly demanded of Vincent, at the same time winking at the two men.

For once Vincent controlled the foolish grin while Gertie looked at Metro and then at him. And then Vincent displayed a rare sense of humor.

"Where's your girl?"

The sudden question caught Metro off guard.

"How come you got no girl?" The second question made Metro's cheeks turn scarlet and the other men laughed. Then Vincent turned and with Gertie beside him, walked to the buggy.

"Jesus Christ! He got you there," one of the men said to Metro.

"Aw shettup!" Metro snapped. "A guy like that don't know what he's saying."

Vincent drove the team to Blute's farm as he played with the twenty cents he had saved by not taking Gertie for coffee. Gertie's mind kept going back to the Mountie who had chased fur clad Eskimos in the imaginary world within the silvery screen. She was so enthralled, she was surprised at how little time it took before they were in Blute's yard.

"You want some coffee?" She asked timidly.

"No. Pappa will be mad if I get home late," Vincent answered and then sat, while Gertie clambered down, from the buggy. He knew vaguely that he should help her, but instead he merely watched and when she was on the ground and looking up at him, he added, "Maybe I can come again, eh?"

"Sure, and I'll be waiting." Gertie answered. She stood by the wagon for a while longer and then added, her words halting, "Well I better be going in. Thanks for the show."

Vincent grinned broadly and then he snapped the reins while a nameless tune came from his lips.

Gertie walked to the circle of yellow light on the ground, cast by the coal oil lamp shining through the kitchen window. When she entered, she stopped for Rosa and Albert sat at the table.

"Well, how was your Polluck half-breed boyfriend?" Rosa grinned broadly, her knuckles pressed against her hips as she sat on a kitchen chair.

"Aw, we're in Canada now," Albert snapped. "So what if he is a Polluck half-breed."

Gertie didn't answer. She just stood in the middle of the kitchen, a conflict of emotions ebbing and flowing.

"Yuh! And the next thing we know, she'll get married," Rosa said.

"Well, that's okay," Albert answered, casting a glance at Gertie who still said nothing. "Then her man and her can both work for us! Wouldn't that be some thing, eh Gertie?"

When Gertie nodded, absentmindedly, Albert added, "We could give you a couple cows and a team of horses. Then maybe you could start on your own somewhere, some day."

Gertie nodded again and a gleam appeared in Rosa's eyes as she caught Albert's meaning. Her voice softened as she looked at Gertie.

"What was the movie about?"

"Oh," Gertie replied slowly. "It was about the north. A Mountie chased an Eskimo in the snow."

"What is Eskimo?"

"I don't know. But they live in the north somewhere in houses made of snow. There's snow all the time and it's dark for over six months."

"But then," Rosa was momentarily lost in thought. "If it's dark for six months, how can they do the chores?"

"I don't know," Gertie replied. Then she lifted her head, the curls undone and hanging limply. "I'm gonna go to bed." She looked quickly about the kitchen, checking if any work remained.

When she was gone, Rosa shook her head.

"That don't make sense," she muttered. "How can they do the chores if it's dark all the time?"

"Never mind the chores," Albert snapped. Then he added softly, "Maybe we can get him to work for us too?"

Rosa stopped muttering and looked at Albert for a second.

"Yuh! Maybe he will. He seems kinda foolish." Then she grinned. "You see him make faces all the time?"

"Yuh! But still, he would make a strong worker," Albert added thoughtfully.


The priest stood before the altar, the red and white robes appearing from a different time and reality as he performed the sacred ceremony. Above the priest the ceiling rose, lost in gloom and above the ceiling the gothic spire reached to the heavens. And in the tower, pigeons gathered and raised their young, unaware of the sacred gathering beneath.

The priest smiled kindly down at the two would-be-newlyweds. He looked at Vincent, at the swarthy rough, work hardened face and hands and the occasional facial contortion that Vincent mightily fought against but lost to. Then he looked at Gertie, the tanned square, sad face, not one of beauty but of hard work and hard times. She stood gazing past the priest, at the Christ that bled in tortured agony, nailed to the cross for eternity.

The priest looked at Vincent. Vincent stared back and the priest whispered, "Do you have a ring?"

Vincent shook his head, a slight blush spreading on his dark face. Rings cost money and were for rich people. The priest nodded quickly.

"I now pronounce you, man and wife." The words penetrated the fog. Gertie re-focused her eyes as a blurriness and wrenching of her stomach told her, yet another migraine was on its way.

"You may now kiss the bride," came next.

Vincent's jaw trembled and the priest looked at him inquiringly. Then Vincent turned to Gertie, fumbled with her veil until she raised her hand and held it away. Vincent lowered his head, the color spreading on his face. He aimed for Gertie's cheek but she moved slightly and the kiss ended up on her nose. Vincent straightened quickly and the veil fell back into place. Then the newlyweds turned and Vincent saw his father gazing at him steadily. Beside him were the Blutes, Albert's face breaking into a grin while Rosa smirked at Gertie.

After the smiling priest and neighbors had shaken Vincent's hand they left, riding the buggy to Bzigniew's farm. The Blute's had left the ceremony, disappointed they had lost a servant.

"So now! Now she is gone," Rosa muttered. "We care for her. Took her in when she was a brat. And now she is gone."

"Who knows? Maybe they won't get along with Bzigniew. I told them they could always work for us." Albert snapped the reins as he talked.

"I don't think Bzigniew would give him a quarter anyway. Not when he makes them faces all the time. Don't worry. I told Gertie that if she comes back to work for us with Vincent we would pay her the wages she thinks she has coming."

"You promised her wages?" Rosa glanced sharply at Albert.

"Well, what you say and what you do are two different things!" Albert laughed.

As Vincent drove the team to Bzigniew's farm, Gertie tried closing her eyes. But the blurriness had finally cleared and a searing headache had taken its place. She was grateful that she could see clearly again but the pain in her temples made her cheeks turn nearly white and she clenched her hands. When Vincent drove into the yard, he yelled "Whoa!" and the team stopped by the house. That was the only word spoken during the one hour ride. He glanced quickly at Gertie and then clambered down from the buggy.

He stood with his hands at his sides as Gertie carefully climbed down, taking extra care not to tear the white dress she had spent hours sewing from a pattern in an old Eaton's catalog. Then she followed Vincent to the two-storey frame house where he entered, not bothering to hold the door. Gertie sat at the kitchen table, while her head throbbed and Vincent sat opposite her, neither saying a word.

There was no wedding celebration for that would have cost money and Vincent was uneasy in a crowd. So he, his father, bride and two sisters and their husbands sat at the kitchen table for a while, talking about the weather, the feed or coming harvest. Vincent let his work roughened hands rest on the table.

Suddenly he grinned and yanked off his tie and threw it onto the floor.

"I don't got to go out no more. I don't have to dress up no more. I'm married now."

Gertie stared at her husband, her head pounding, as the tears fought to break control. But she said nothing as a contortion came to Vincent's face. He didn't try to prevent it and as his tongue protruded, Gertie gazed down at her hands. Then Bzigniew spoke.

"If you stay here and work for me for a year, I'll buy you that land not far from Forest Grove School. There's not much open and there's a lot of rocks, but it'll be a start."

"Yuh! I could break a few acres a year, maybe."

Gertie silently watched Bzigniew and her husband discussing their future and she thought of the offer from the Blutes. They had promised her two cows and back wages plus fifteen dollars a month for Vincent's labor. But as she sat, the familiar guilt suddenly crept into her consciousness and she forgot about Blute's offer. Her mind slowly succumbed to the turmoil and finally, without conscious effort, the words came silently.

"Hail Mary, Full of Grace!"

Then it was time. Bzigniew rose and Helen and Sophie retired upstairs with their husbands.

"Well, I guess it's time for bed," Vincent finally said when they were alone.

"Yuh," Gertie answered, the word coming out as a sigh.

Together they rose, Vincent's mind filled with anticipation and apprehension for he had been mocked mercilessly about what they were about to do. While his jaw twitched and his face contorted, Gertie's mind was filled with familiar words.

"Hail Mary, Full of Grace!"

When they were in the bedroom, next to the kitchen, Gertie hurriedly removed her dress, laying down under the covers with all her underclothes still on. Vincent sat on the bed and removed his shirt and pants but not his long underwear. As he undressed a facial contortion came and went, his jaw and head trembling. Gertie watched as his tongue protruded out of the corner of his mouth and her anxiety built to a crescendo. She had suppressed the memory of Donald appearing in her attic room so instead, she felt only a great shame and guilt. The prayers became an audible whisper.

"My God! Forgive, me! It must be right. Hail Mary, Full of Grace. In this hour of need!"

# Fourteen

Vincent rubbed his forehead with the back of his hand, for the early fall sun still had enough heat to make him sweat. He walked carefully, for the stubble at times penetrated a place where his boot was torn. He bent and lifted a bundle, placing it upright next to another and leaned the two together, building a stook. He placed still more bundles against the first two and when he was finished he continued along the row of golden, loose bundles dropped by the binder which Albert rode behind four horses. Vincent followed the great, clacking noise of the machine as he started all over, bending and holding a bundle upright while placing another against it. He glanced occasionally at the crows flocking in preparation for their long journey south, his eyes passing over the dry brown grass in the pasture and the cows who lay in the shade.

He wiped the sweat from the band of his soft cloth cap, put it back on his head, pulling the visor down tight and then bent his back once more. Albert had refused to give him a pitch fork, saying it cost too much. So he was forced to stoop, an area in the small of his back aching painfully, as the hours crept by.

A facial contortion came and went as he stooped for the thousandth time, wondering how he had come to work for Albert. It had all started innocently enough. He and Gertie had been sitting in his father's kitchen on a Sunday afternoon with the dinner dishes still on the table. Bzigniew had laid down on the couch in the living room and Vincent and Gertie were alone for a brief time. Gertie had suddenly become playful, sprinkling water in Vincent's face.

"Don't be doing that," he had grinned.

Then Gertie had gone too far, smearing butter across his face and Vincent had grinned foolishly, unaccustomed to play. Suddenly, Bzigniew was in the living room doorway.

"Jesus Christ! Wasting food! Don't you know that's a sin?" He had yelled.

"We was only having fun." Gertie had faced Bzigniew.

"If that's the way you act, you might as well get the hell outa here," Bzigniew had snarled. He had not really meant it, but the words couldn't be retrieved. Silence had reigned momentarily in the kitchen then, for the mention of sin had made Gertie's face lose its color.

She had hated Bzigniew after that, whispering late at night in their bed and convincing Vincent to pack their meager belongings to move to the Blutes. Albert and Rosa had been pleased but when Gertie had brought up the promised cows, Albert had become suddenly evasive.

"Uh." He had glanced quickly at Rosa. "Maybe we better wait 'til spring. Then we'll see how things are going."

"Then could you pay us? We need clothes," Gertie had asked.

"Uh, maybe we better wait 'til threshing. Then, we'll see how things are going."

So Vincent labored in the field, stooking without a pitch fork and Gertie resumed her role in the kitchen. When winter came, he cleaned the barn, hauled feed and straw to the stock, even when it was minus thirty degrees in the afternoon. Albert stayed in the house on cold blustery days, boasting that he had a hired man and had no need to go out. As time passed Gertie grew for she was pregnant with their first child, and if she was sick, she ran to the outhouse. Then she was back at the washbasin, scrubbing dishes or the floor while Rosa complained of a headache and retired to bed. When a migraine came, Gertie bore it stoically, biting her lower lip until it was white. As the months slowly crept by she slipped more and more into a quasi-dream world, filled with men and women, past and present. When she was alone, she carried on conversations with those who had hurt her.

"Sure! And Albert and Rosa won't pay us. Oh yay, I says and if you don't pay us we'll leave. Then where will you be?" She would spread her arms wide and pause dramatically for an instant. But as always, she expressed her anger only in her dream world. So the two of them labored in the barn and fields and in the house, living in hope of two cows and promised wages.

As Gertie's body swelled so did the buds on the trees until the geese heralded spring with their lonesome cry from the heavens. As the grass grew and colts and calves frolicked in the pasture the time came closer until one evening Vincent hitched a team and drove hurriedly to Berlin. When he returned with a doctor Rosa and Albert were sitting at the kitchen table. The doctor glanced quickly around.

"Why aren't you with her?" He demanded of Rosa.

"What do I know of babies?"

The doctor shook his head and ordered water to be heated and then left for the attic room where Gertie lay, drenched in sweat and anxiety.

"You're gonna be a Pappa. No?" Albert grinned at Vincent in the kitchen.

Vincent couldn't control a foolish grin and a contortion began.

"What you gonna call it?" Albert asked.

"I don't know!" The words came quickly.

"And what if it is a girl?" Rosa demanded.

"Ah! A man should have a son for his first. No?" Albert laughed.

"Yuh!" Vincent bobbed his head, the word loud in the kitchen.

During this, the doctor administered to Gertie in the attic, marveling at her stoic manner. She had turned scarlet when he had removed the covers but she made no complaint and silently did what she was told.

In a short time, Vincent heard the cry of a baby and glanced up quickly at the ceiling. He stopped in the middle of a face and then he reddened. In a little while the doctor came into the room.

"You have a son," he said laconically.

Vincent stared at the doctor and then down at his boots. The doctor stared back at Vincent and then at the Blutes. After Albert had paid him the three dollar fee, advanced from Vincent's wages, he muttered under his breath, "Strange people."

"You may go and see your child," he added louder.

Vincent stood and walked slowly to the stairs and then climbed to the attic. At his step a rat rustled in the wall but he didn't hear it. He slowly climbed the stairs and then stood in the doorway, his face a ruddy red.

Gertie nearly sat up in bed.

"Look!" She held the tiny infant, wrapped in an old towel. Then she asked shyly, "Ain't he nice?" The baby's red face was framed by the towel, his eyes shut tight as he sucked a tiny thumb.

Vincent stood very still. He had thought of the moment, many times when shoveling manure in the barn but he had never been able to picture the baby. And now, he stood in wonder for there it was, a baby boy who yawned mightily in his mother's arms. Gertie turned and regarded him proudly.

"What shall we call him?"

"I don't know." This time the words came slowly.

"Maybe Gerard," Gertie said softly. "Yuh! I like that name."

Then Gertie and Vincent gazed down at the tiny, red and wrinkled face of their first born.

---

The deep green, summer grass grew tall near the fence where the cows couldn't reach and the grain stood limply in the fields as overhead, young crows prepared for their long flight south in the timeless ritual. Vincent walked behind the harrows, his blackened face contorting as he slowed his step and then took a giant one to catch up. The sweat glistened on the horses' backs and ran down between Vincent's shoulder blades making the worn and dirty shirt stick to his back. At the end of the field he stopped the team and took out his old handkerchief blowing his nose. He glanced at the moisture in the middle where the dust mixed with the mucus before returning the filthy cloth to his breast pocket. Then he snapped the reins and the horses reluctantly resumed the long slow journey as Vincent wondered in his slow, dull way, how things had not improved. He still walked behind the harrow, piled hay or cleaned the barn and his boots sunk just as deeply into the soft dirt of Albert's field as they had in his father's.

When the sun was in its descent to the western horizon, he stopped the team and sighed in thankfulness for it was near the supper hour. He unhitched the horses, throwing the tugs and chains over their backs before driving them to the barn. He walked stiffly, the muscles in his calves and back burning. But complaining didn't occur to him; for sore, aching muscles were part of the natural order of things.

While Vincent unhitched the horses, Gertie hurried to place the supper dishes on the table. She had set her child in an old high chair near the water pail and she cast occasional glances at him as he waved his tiny fists in the air and cried, for he was hungry.

"Hurry up!" Rosa growled from the stove. Then she cast the child, a spiteful glance. "You care more for that brat then you do for your work."

Gertie looked quickly at Gerard who broke out into a lusty bawl. She ignored the baby, telling herself that he would get plenty once she was through. She breast-fed the child and the sight of the naked breast and the baby's hungry mouth had driven Rosa into a fit of rage. So Gertie always took him upstairs to the attic. As she hurried, the thoughts swirled and danced in her consciousness and eventually became an audible whisper.

"Sure! And I do my best. I wait on the table. I wash the floors and what do I get? Complain und complain!"

As Rosa came near Gertie, she stopped suddenly and demanded, "What are you whispering about?"

"Oh! Nothing."

"Every time I come, near you, you are always babbling to yourself."

Gertie looked quickly at Rosa and then bent to place a plate on the table.

"You're gonna go insane, just like that mother of yours. The first sign is them headaches you always complain about and the next is talking to yourself. The next thing we know we'll have to send you to the Battle Fords. They'll lock you up, just like your mother," Rosa grinned, arms akimbo.

Gertie's body shook as she ran about the kitchen and a small well of anger began to bubble in her mind. She let the thoughts simmer as she forced the words down to an inaudible whisper.

"Sure! And I can not even feed my baby when he's hungry."

The door opened suddenly and Albert and Vincent entered, both dusty and tired. Vincent glanced at his wife and the child who still cried from the high chair. Then he pulled a chair out from the table. They had washed by the well but his neck was still streaked with dirt. He glanced at his wife who took up her customary spot with her hands on the back of a chair. He didn't say anything for what was the need? He was hungry and the food was in front of him.

Albert and Rosa joined him and supper began. Vincent scooped up mashed potatoes with his fork and shoved in a piece of meat. He chewed convulsively, his mouth staying open. Just then Albert stopped eating and looked at him.

"Think you'll finish that field tomorrow?"

"Yuh!" Vincent waved his arm and kept on chewing, bits of meat and potatoes dropping unnoticed to his lap. "Then I'll go to the next, where you're cultivating."

Rosa suddenly glared at Vincent.

"Why do you have to always eat like a pig?"

Vincent stopped chewing and looked at her, puzzled.

"Every time you eat, you are like a berberi. A savage!"

Vincent felt a flush grow on his face but he didn't answer.

"Don't you even care what people think of you? You act like a Polluck savage."

Gertie's knuckles went white as she clutched the chair and finally the simmering anger broke free.

"My God! Can you not leave him be? He works hard all day and you haven't even paid us yet. You don't even let me feed my baby."

Rosa stared at Gertie, surprised at the venom in her voice, and surprised that she had the courage to speak up. Vincent stopped chewing, his mouth open and he took courage from his wife.

"Yuh! If you got nothin' good to say don't say nothin' at all."

"Why you, you Polluck half-breed!" Rosa's face turned white while Albert glared at Vincent. Then Rosa turned to Gertie whose face had also gone white.

"Why you, you Polluck brat. We took you in when you was a snotty, nosed kid fed and clothed you and taught you nice manners and this is the thanks we get."

"Yuh! And where's the money you owe us? And the two cows?" Gertie began to tremble violently.

"You got paper?" Albert demanded. "If you don't got paper that says we owe it, we don't owe you nothin."

"But you owe it. You promised." Gertie's voice lost some of its anger and Vincent looked down at his plate.

"Promised! What's that? You don't got paper. And if you don't like it, you can quit." Albert grinned triumphantly.

"Even his old man don't want him, the way he makes faces all the time. Like a savage half-breed swine," Rosa laughed.

Tears started in Gertie's eyes and she bit her lower lip. Her square face turned whiter still as she fought the humiliation. Vincent looked up again and a slow, stubborn, anger began to glow from his eyes.

"Maybe we should quit, unless you pay us."

"Go ahead and quit!" Albert laughed. "The summer fallow's almost done anyway."

"Yuh!" Rosa kept up the attack. "Pack your rags and get out!"

Then she thumped, the table with her fist and screamed, "Pack your bags and get out!.

Gertie stood deathly still while confusion played across Vincent's face. Then Gertie slowly unclenched her hands and left for the attic to pack their belongings. Vincent rose and silently followed, his clumsy bear-like walk out of place in the house. Rosa glared after them.

"So, now! Now they are quitting. After all we did for them."

"Aw, let 'em go. We can do without them. Besides, word would get around. We'd have to pay them sooner or later," Albert muttered. Then he began eating again.

Gertie and Vincent reappeared very quickly for they had little to pack. Gertie picked up their child who'd stopped crying from fatigue. Then they left, neither saying anything or looking at Rosa and Albert. Albert kept on eating and Rosa ignored them. The door slammed and they were outside. Then, together they turned their faces towards the track leading to Berlin and beyond to Bzigniew's farm.

As they trudged off into the early dusk, Vincent's face twitched and Gertie opened her dress and let the hungry baby suckle. Her mind was full of swirling images and a whisper escaped her lips.

"My God! What is to become of us?"

Vincent looked at her and then back to the dusty track. He made another face as together they trudged into the setting sun. Gertie turned to him then.

"Are we going to your Father's farm?"

"Yuh," Vincent sighed.

"Will he take us in?" Gertie asked softly.

"I don't know." Again Vincent's words came slowly as his jaw trembled and he cast an eye at the setting sun.

Gertie closed her dress with one hand and held her baby with the other. On a poplar branch, a bird sang sweetly and a gentle breeze ruffled the grass near the track. But neither Vincent nor Gertie noticed.

# Fifteen

A warm breeze rustled the blooming crocuses in the open field next to the aging pussy willows by the slough's edge while above, an azure sky with fleecy clouds encompassed the earth. A small flock of ducks flew overhead, the wind whistling through their rapidly beating wings. They wheeled and then hit the water, their webbed feet spread wide. They slowed and glided until they stopped, quacking loudly.

Vincent eyed the ducks for an instant and then spit over the wagon side as his jaw trembled. Then he glanced at Gertie beside him on the hard plank seat.

"Nice day," he said and let the reins hang loosely over the horses' backs. He glanced at the rear of the wagon where two more horses were hitched, their harnesses hanging loosely on their backs. In the box, were various utensils and tools along with an old battered chest full of Gertie's belongings.

"Yuh," she answered while Gerard, who was nine months old, squirmed in her arms. He was clothed in a worn suit covering his entire body and he had tiny boots on his feet. A miniature fist waved in Gertie's face but she gently took his hand and placed it back in his lap. She gazed at her first born wonder still in her eyes.

Vincent glanced at his son as he chewed on a straw and his face contorted. Then he asked, "He hungry?"

"No! He shouldn't be. I fed him before we started."

Vincent nodded and clucked to the horses, slapping the reins on their rumps. They turned their ears backwards for an instant as they continued their slow shamble.

Gertie looked ahead at the track that wound around the slough and through stunted poplars trees, disappearing over a hill. To the left an old buffalo trail ran, its deep indentation still visible. They passed an unseen Cree Indian grave, the rocks still in place, marking the last resting place of a young warrior.

"Is it much farther?"

"I think it's over that hill. I remember when I was hunting deer. It should be there."

"I sure hope there isn't too much work in the house," Gertie muttered, lifting the baby and shifting him to her other arm.

"I don't know," Vincent shrugged and again spit over the side. "Pappa said the Smiths moved out a few years ago."

The three hundred and twenty acres of rocky hills and poplar bluffs the Smiths had given up on was Vincent's, as long as he paid his father three thousand dollars.

"Since you wouldn't stay and help, leaving me in the lurch," Bzigniew had said, "You can work for the winter and in spring we'll see." The price had been more free labor and the debt of three thousand for the half section they were approaching.

Gertie worried, in her agitated manner, about the work to put the old shack in order. Vincent wondered how he would bring the old plow and disc along with the harrow from his father's farm. He worried about bringing the two cows that were included in the price. Later, he would buy a pig if he made enough money trapping and in the wagon were the number one and two traps wrapped in old burlap. Beside them an ancient 44/40 Winchester rifle lay, its scarred stock an untold story about the usage it had been through.

Finally the horses crested the hill and Vincent and Gertie could see their new home. The three room tar-paper shack, stood forlornly surrounded by stunted poplars while to the east a hill rose steeply. To the south a long winding track ran down a hill and led to Forest Grove School, three miles away and where Gertie planned to send Gerard. Past the school and eleven miles farther southeast was the hamlet of Peterson with a church, general store, a Barbershop/Poolroom and four wooden houses.

They passed a crumbling mud and log barn and crooked poplar pole corral, and Vincent and Gertie stared at the decay. On top a gradual hill which rose from the barn stood the sad, grey shack they would call home. Vincent pulled on the reins and the horses stopped instantly, reaching hungrily towards the tender green grass growing by the front door. Together they clambered down from the wagon, Gertie clutching Gerard tightly to her. Vincent pushed on the old door made from rough wooden planks and it swung awkwardly, catching on the floor. He pushed again and it swung open, the hinges protesting loudly.

Suddenly a squirrel chattered, its bright eyes open wide in fright. Then it squawked loudly, running the length of a counter under a cupboard before jumping out a broken window. Gertie stopped, frozen for an instant, her heart pounding from fright. Gerard began to cry as she held him tightly, looking quickly about the dust and debris-strewn kitchen.

An old, rusty cook stove was against the wall by the cupboard and a scarred, rickety table stood in the center of the kitchen. In a tiny living room, a stove pipe hole indicated where the air-tight heater would be. Gertie stared from the doorway as the sun shone through a streaked window and dust particles danced in the suddenly moving air. In a wall a rat rustled, frightened by the sudden intrusion of humans and Gertie turned and sat tiredly on an old chair by the table in the kitchen. Vincent stood in the middle of the room, looking at the first real home he could call his own.

"My God!" Gertie muttered and he stared at her.

"So much work to do. The carpet's all worn out and every thing needs washing. So much work." She hefted the baby who had calmed down and shifted him to her right arm.

"Well, what of it?" Vincent demanded. "You didn't like living with Pappa. Here we got our own place."

"But so much work." Gertie shifted the baby again and her voice rose to a whine as she nagged, "You hafta fix that tarned window. So much work."

"Well what of it? Who wants to live in a big house where you can't even sit down without getting something dirty?" Vincent said and then turned and walked outside to the wagon.

Gertie sat in the kitchen, the evening light throwing shadows across her face as she rocked back and forth on the rickety chair. She stopped suddenly when she heard a rustle in a wall. Then she thought of the hard times and how their luck always seemed to get worse.

"Hail Mary, Full Of Grace. So much work and no one to help." She held Gerard with one arm and spread the other in the familiar gesture of helplessness. "And for what? He doesn't even care."

Vincent stood outside by the wagon gazing at the woods to the north, until he walked around the tar-paper shack to relieve himself. When he finished, he glanced at the azure sky and a fluffy cloud, sniffing the air and mumbling, "Gonna rain. Maybe." Then he looked at the track winding down the hill and leading to civilization as a tuneless whistle came softly from his lips.

Time passed. Vincent rose early every morning, put on his old coveralls and labored in the fields or barn. He patched the old barn with discarded pieces of lumber and clay and waited for his small herd to grow. He had two cows, two healthy calves and a young bull along with chickens and a sow; and eventually he began a small flock of sheep. He hunted year round and kept his growing family fed with wild meat: Grouse in the fall, deer in the winter and in summer they made do eating old potatoes or frying dough and lard in an iron pan. Gertie refused to make Bannock, saying it was Indian bread.

They bought flour and at times coffee with money from trapping and when a neighbor shot a skunk, Vincent walked five miles and skinned it. The stench stayed with him for months but he got five dollars for the hide and they had flour and coffee for nearly half a year. Gertie however had to throw away Vincent's ancient bib trousers for there was no way she could rid them of the noxious smell.

It didn't seem long before Vincent drove Gertie to Berlin in their old wagon and she gave birth to another boy. She held him just as proudly as she had Gerard, who was two years old, for the wonder of the newborn had not yet worn off.

After the birth of their second son, whom Gertie named Allen, Vincent grew restless. He would leave for days to go hunting near his father's old house, father and son speaking little but an understanding growing between them. Bzigniew left Vincent alone and ignored his facial contortions for he was a willing worker, staying to cut wood or help with the chores. Vincent was comfortable in his old bed without Gertie's constant nagging and he stayed longer and longer.

A year later, Gertie wandered through their huge pasture in search of four cows and their calves. Gerard, who was a little older than three, puffed to keep up while she carried Allen. Beside her was a mangy dog named Nellie and together they searched for the small herd. Vincent had been gone for two weeks and Gertie worried that something might have happened.

"Sssh!" she suddenly stopped and held up her free hand. The dog stopped too, a paw suspended in midair while she, cocked an ear. Gerard panted besides her, his face red and his breath coming in quick gasps for they had climbed a hill. Gertie looked down at the dog.

"Can you hear them, Nellie?" She asked and the dog wagged her tail furiously.

Vincent had tied a bell to the oldest cow to make it easier to find the herd in the brush. And finally Gertie was rewarded by a faint tinkling coming from the red willows surrounding a small slough about a quarter mile away. She took Gerard by the hand, still holding the baby with the other, and walked as fast as she could for it was getting late. She found the cows lying down and chewing their cud and she quickly herded them together, letting go of Gerard's hand to throw a stick. Nellie barked happily at the cows whose tails swung back and forth. Gerard ran and then slowed and then ran again for Gertie, in her hurry had increased her stride. When his breath again came in quick gasps, they were walking up the hill to the barn and corral. A small herd of sheep followed and they passed a pile of wool and bones, the flies buzzing in the early evening heat. The head had no eyes for magpies and maggots had been busy devouring what was left of the kill. Nellie ran to the rotting remains and sniffed about until Gertie called and she ran to catch up.

"Tarned, stinky dirty coyotes!" Gertie muttered. "Hanging around and waiting just so they can kill the sheep."

Then she thought of Vincent.

"But where is he?" She sighed. Then she herded the cows into the corral, closing the heavy pole gate and setting Allen on the grass before turning to Gerard.

"And watch your brother!"

Gerard sat next to Allen, who drooled on the worn suit he had inherited from him. As Gerard watched, he brushed a tiny hand against his forehead to wipe away the sweat. His face was smudged and his tiny shoes covered in cow manure. His skin was light and his face had an air of complaint, pinched and unhappy; almost on the verge of tears.

Gertie found a shaky milk stool and set it next to a cow. Then she squatted and began to squeeze the rich, white milk into a pail. The cow contentedly chewed her cud and switched her tail while Gertie rested her head against the warm flank. She felt a migraine coming and as she milked her lips moved while her oldest child looked on in wonderment.

"Sure! It's easy. Run off to Grampas." Then came the inevitable spreading of her arms in the gesture of hopelessness. "But someone has to stay home and do the work."

She milked vigorously and then moved over to the next cow. When she finished, her lips still moving, she called to Gerard who was standing by the fence gazing through the poles at a large ewe, who gazed back.

"Oh, why aren't you watching your brother?"

Gerard's face went white and he ran back to Allen who still sat on the grass. Gertie picked up the baby in one arm and carried a full milk pail with her other hand. Gerard struggled with a couple cups of milk in a second pail and together they walked up the gentle hill to the tar-paper shack. Once inside Gertie sat the baby in a crib and put the milk on the cupboard to cool. In the morning she would use a large wooden spoon to skim the cream to make butter. She took extra care in covering the milk, for she had found a dead rat floating on the surface one morning. Gerard went to a chair and wearily clambered up, his tiny legs dangling above the floor. As Gertie worked, her body twitched and she continued muttering.

"Sure! And it's easy to say move." The spreading of arms came next. "We could of stayed at Blutes. And what's the difference anyway? All I get is hard work." She had reached the point in her loneliness and anguish that she blamed Vincent for being fired by the Blutes.

She began sweeping in quick jerky motions, the broom brushing against a hole near the wall where the rats came out at night. She swept dust and rat droppings as the boy watched from the chair, his legs still dangling and his eyes wide in wonder. Then she lit a coal oil lamp to wash the dishes, for the sun had set and darkness was shrouding the earth. When the dishes were done she sat and mended clothes, all the while talking in the stillness.

Gerard looked attentively at his mother and smiled as if he understood. Gertie smiled back and as she mended and talked she looked at Allen sleeping in the crib. His face was round and full while Gerard's was thin and pinched. Allen reminded her of her brother Augustine; when they had been children, herding cows in the hazy, Never Never Land of memory. She continued muttering as she sewed with quick jerky motions.

Suddenly the door banged and Vincent stood in the kitchen, holding his rifle in one hand. Gertie jumped up, dropping her sewing.

"Where was you?" She demanded, running up to him.

Allen woke and Gerard cringed involuntarily.

"At Grampas."

"And I didn't even know if you was dead. Two weeks! Oh why didn't you come home?"

Gertie's voice rose to a whining pitch.

"He wanted me to help with the plowing." Vincent offered an explanation, nothing more.

"But we missed church."

"I went with Grampa," Vincent scowled as he leaned the rifle against a wall. Gertie bit her lower lip.

"What about your plowing?" she asked softly.

"I'll start on it tomorrow." Vincent looked about the kitchen. "Where's supper?"

Gertie placed bread and Saskatoon berry jam on the table. Vincent cut off a large slice and spread jam on it and then jammed it into his mouth. Jam stuck to his cheeks and his jaw convulsed as he chewed rapidly with bits falling to his pants. Gertie made a face.

"And how you eat…"

"What of it?" Vincent demanded, waving his arm. "I gotta eat, don't I?"

"But how," Gertie said softly as she looked down at her work worn, calloused hands. Then she had another thought.

"Those tarned coyotes killed a sheep!"

"Where?"

"By the corral. The dirty suckers are sneaking right up to the yard."

"I'll fix them. I'll take the rifle tomorrow," Vincent said grimly, his mouth open with food rolling around. "Just wait boy. We'll see."

Then they both lapsed into silence, with the coal-oil lamp throwing a yellowish light on their faces. In the silence, Allen stirred in his crib and a rat rustled in a wall.

Outside, a young coyote practiced his howl and Nellie answered with short barks.

"The dirty sucker can howl," Vincent said angrily and Gertie looked at him from across the table.

Days blurred into weeks and months as years slipped by. The hardness deepened in Gertie's eyes and Vincent's face became more and more lined. Time was an element in itself, the greater evil between drudging work and crushing boredom. Gertie rose early, made breakfast, usually bread and black coffee if they had any and then Vincent would do the chores. As Gertie swept and washed dishes or patched old clothes he cleaned the barn for his growing herd, or sawed firewood with a backsaw or hauled hay for the cattle and his six horses.

The time came when one bedroom wasn't enough for a family of four, so Vincent found old lumber and built an extra room. It was next to the living room, next to their sleeping chamber with the door by the airtight heater. Gertie called it "The boys' room" for that's where they slept. But while Vincent and Gertie's family grew so did the colony of rats who became bolder and bolder, eating from the slop pail full of soaking oats and table scraps for the pigs. When it was dark and silence reigned, their rustle and scampering could be heard and Gertie knew they were eating oats or running along the counter under the cupboards.

The monotony was broken every Sunday when Vincent hitched a team to a second hand buggy and they loaded their two sons, driving the fourteen miles to church in the tiny hamlet. With the horses trotting most of the way it still took over an hour so they had to leave just after eight a.m. Even when it rained, Gertie insisted they go and when the temperature dropped to minus forty, Vincent hitched the team to the caboose with the family riding inside, warm and stuffy, from the tiny stove that gave off as much smoke as it did heat.

One day Vincent stepped inside the kitchen, slamming the door shut behind him. His swarthy face was filled with excitement as he stopped dramatically, his jaw, twitching. Gertie stared up at him from the kitchen table where she was peeling potatoes.

"There's a war on!" He announced loudly, jerking his head sideways. His words crashed off the walls and both Gerard and his three-year-old baby brother cringed.

"Huh!" Gertie's face turned white.

"Over in Yurrup." Vincent jerked his thumb in a vague direction. "Hitler's attacked Poland and then France. He's run all over France."

"But why?" Gertie, demanded.

"I don't know," Vincent shrugged. "I read it in Grampa's paper." He had laboriously traced the words and then carried the excitement home.

"They're calling men up," he added; the excitement succumbing to the silence in the kitchen.

"Oh!" Gertie stared at Vincent, a sudden fear clutching at her breast. "They wouldn't come for you, would they?"

"Naw!" Vincent grinned. "I'm too old. Besides, I talked to a man I met, who said they need farmers for food."

"Oh," Gertie repeated and then returned to peeling potatoes. That was all that was said about a war that was tearing nations apart with millions dying or fleeing the terrible new German weapons. It was nineteen-forty and the war had been raging for over a year but Vincent hadn't visited his father for some time. They had no way of knowing for they didn't have a radio. And again the days blurred into months and years as the war raged in a distant, alien world while Vincent and Gertie made the best of their lives.

It wasn't long before Gertie struggled awkwardly onto the buggy for she was heavy with child again. They went to Berlin where she bore a daughter, stoically bearing the pains of childbirth in the tiny hospital. When it was time, Vincent was called into her room.

But the wondrous joy of beholding his firstborn had worn thin. He only looked down at the tiny bundle and the miniature fist sticking out from the wrappings. His face twitched but he said nothing.

Gertie was beside herself.

"Look! A daughter. My very own daughter!"

"Yuh," Vincent answered, wondering how soon they could get back to the farm.

"You already got two sons that can help you outside." Gertie smiled radiantly, her eyes sparkling. "And now I got a daughter that'll help me in the kitchen." She lifted the baby whose eyes remained closed.

"Ain't she nice?"

Vincent shrugged his shoulders.

"Aw you!" Gertie snapped, her mouth thin and mean again. "You got two sons. Now you don't give a damn that I got a daughter."

Vincent gazed down at his dusty boots for an instant and then glared at Gertie. "Sure I give a damn. But I'm thinking of the work. I always got so much to think about."

"I wish I could have another daughter," Gertie said after a brief pause. "Then I'll have two, and when one grows up and leaves, I'll still have another to help with the work."

"Yuh." Vincent's face contorted and he looked out the window while Gertie held her daughter fondly, gazing into the tiny, uncomprehending face.

# Sixteen

The old horse walked slowly past sloughs, over hills and by poplar bluffs. Overhead ducks winged their way south or practiced for the long journey, while crows flapped about and cawed excitedly in large flocks. The leaves had turned a golden red with the semi-prairie country a place of beauty; if only for a brief time. When the arctic winds and blowing snow came, the leaves would shrivel and drop from the trees while tiny sparrows hopped about in a desperate search for food.

Gerard stood at the front of the tiny cart Vincent had built from old lumber and a Model T axle and wheels. He let the reins hang loose as he gazed at the horse's rump. Whenever the gelding stopped to grab a mouthful of grass, he snapped the lines and yelled, "Gettup!" but the horse did as he pleased and Gerard's face pinched in annoyance and his eyes narrowed.

At first Vincent had taken him, leaving him alone to face the strange children and stranger adult, but after a few days he was on his own. And it wasn't easy. The older children teased him, throwing rocks at the horse until he trotted the first few hundred yards from the school. But it wasn't only the older children who bothered Gerard, for he had trouble with his lessons. He didn't start school until he was seven for he possessed mediocre intelligence at best, struggling to master what brighter and younger children skimmed over.

He was also terrorized by the teacher, a retired and bitter army sergeant who had lost an arm in the war. He sat in the front of the class, his one good arm resting on the desk while an empty sleeve proclaimed his misfortune. In the army he had been feared and respected by the lower ranks but now he commanded only a gaggle of reluctant school children. At all times, a heavy webbed strap lay on top of the desk.

One day Gerard came home with welts on his back and Gertie rocked back and forth in her chair. Vincent looked at her sadly and then down at the floor, his face twitching for if beating a child was easy, facing another man was not.

"If you don't go and talk to the teacher he'll fail and then he'll have to work like us," Gertie's whining voice expressed her constant fear.

During this Gerard sat hunched forward on a chair, his face white and pinched and his eyes narrow.

"Okay! I'll go." Vincent finally raised his head. "I'll go tomorrow and talk to him." Then his face twitched again and he added, "Beating up on a boy with a strap," He thought of the one arm the teacher had.

"Just wait 'til tomorrow. We'll see."

In the morning he drove Gerard to school, meeting the teacher in the yard. They stood and talked for a long time, Vincent waving his arms and the teacher looking out at a slough and then down at the ground.

"You can't beat a boy like that!" Vincent's face contorted and twitched. "How would you like it if someone beat you like that?"

The teacher kept his eyes on the ground or on the slough, anywhere but on the agitated face that was terrible to behold. You can't tell what a guy like that might do, he thought and then added, out loud, "Okay! I won't beat him no more with the strap."

They parted, Vincent to the farm and the teacher to sit and brood at the head of the class. But he left Gerard alone, even when he had trouble with simple lessons. He didn't allow his new tolerance to spread however and beatings continued until father after father made the trip to the one room school. Then, only children with callous, uncaring parents were beaten.

All this didn't make Gerard any happier, for he still was teased and struggled to master English, speaking in a muddled accent he learned from Gertie.

When the leaves had all fallen from the trees and the crows had left, the gelding ambled along the trail while Gerard's face grew more pinched and irritated, until finally he passed through the yard and clambered down when the horse stopped at the barn. He unhitched the old horse, led him to a fence and removed the harness by standing on a pole and dragging the leather straps and steel buckles from the horse's back. Then he stood on an old milk stool and hung the harness on a peg on a wall, before walking the hundred yards to the house. The horse wandered off in the corral, finding a soft spot to lie down and roll in.

On a bench, in front of the house, Allen sat bored with being alone. When he saw Gerard, he jumped up and ran to meet him. He wanted to ask about school and how it would be when it was his turn.

Suddenly Gerard's two tiny fists hit him in the face and Allen cried out in pain. Gertie heard the commotion from the kitchen where she was kneading dough. She ran outside and saw Gerard on top his younger brother, his arms flailing. Blood ran from Allen's nose as he fought back as best he could. Gertie stooped and yanked Gerard away.

"Here now!" She held Gerard firmly by an arm. "Why are you doing that?"

"So now," Gerard pulled away from her grip, "now I know how to fight."

Gertie let him go and then helped Allen to his feet, brushing his clothes off with quick jerky motions. She looked into Allen's hurt and bewildered eyes and then turned and glared at Gerard.

"Don't you ever do that again, or else."

Gerard cast his eyes down to the dust. Gertie left then to the kitchen where she continued kneading dough, her body shaking as she muttered. Allen looked at Gerard, his eyes filled with tears. Gerard stared back, his eyes narrow and hard but he didn't hit him again for he feared his mother's insane, wild swings more than the teacher's. And more than his mother he feared his father, for at times when he had been especially bad she had told Vincent to punish him. But she watched carefully for Vincent had a hard time stopping, once he began beating a child.

So Gerard only glared at his younger brother until finally he wandered off. In a while Allen joined him and they played together warily. In the house Arlene, who was six years younger than Gerard, began crying in her crib. Gertie ignored her, having been told that if you pick up a child when she's crying, you'll spoil her.

Outside, Gerard played with Allen but a pattern had begun and he began to realize the power he had over those weaker than he.


The seasons changed, over and over, in their timeless ritual. Vincent's herd grew and so did the colony of rats. He laid out poison and traps but succeeded only in keeping the population at bay. But his herd and the rats were not the only things growing for once again Gertie was heavy with child. And in late June, Vincent again hitched the team to the buggy and drove to Berlin, impatient that he had to take time from plowing. It was also nineteen-forty four and the brutal Nazis were being driven back to their homeland but that was thousands of miles and a world away.

It wasn't long before Vincent again stood in a hospital room, looking down at Gertie and a new-born baby. His swarthy face didn't show surprise or disappointment for, he no longer wondered about the miracle of birth.

Gertie lay listlessly on the bed and stared dully up at Vincent while he crumpled his cloth hat in his hand. Beside her, the new born baby squirmed in his wrappings, his tiny fists waving in the air. Gertie glanced at him for an instant but she made no move to pick him up.

Then as she stared at the child, a horrific memory flitted through her mind. For the briefest of instants she was back in their tar-paper shack, nine months earlier. Vincent had been gone for a week when the visitor had come. Walter was Vincents first cousin and his face was dark with high cheek bones and his hair jet black and straight. He had been everything Vincent was not. Where Vincent was shy Walter was bold and when Vincent had felt a deep reverence for the Catholic Church, he had felt only a deep contempt for the White Man's God who had allowed a race of people to be nearly destroyed.

They had sat in the living room on the old couch, the afternoon sun slanting through the dirty window. Gerard and Allen had both been in school while Arlene slept on the bed. Suddenly Walter had grinned and moved closer to Gertie until his arm was about her shoulders. Gertie had squirmed, a look of panic crossing her square face.

"Please! Don't!" She had said, the sudden knot of anxiety in her stomach immobilizing her.

"Why not?" Walter had grinned. Vincent won't care. He had let his hand slide down until it was cupped one of Gertie's breasts.

"No!" Gertie had yelled, still immobilized by fear. In the bedroom, Arlene woke for an instant and cried out and then was silent.

"Ssh," Walter had laughed, "You'll wake the baby." Then he had pushed Gertie down onto the couch.

"But we mustn't. It would be a sin," she had said, her body trembling but fear again making it impossible for her to fight back.

"A sin! What's that," Walter had snorted. "You pray all the time and what the hell has it got you?"

"But Vincent might come home," Gertie had tried one last desperate time.

"Vincent!" Walter had laughed. "If he cared, would he be gone now?"

So Gertie had submitted once again, as she had to Donald when she had been a teenager. And once again, her only recourse had been prayer.

"Dear God! Help me in this hour of need!"

And Walters response had been the same as Donalds.

"God don't hear you."

This time though, the result was a fourth pregnancy and Gertie had resorted to her only defense, denial. The memory of the rape slid down into her subconscious along with all the other hurt and pain, while only a deep sense of guilt remained.

When she stared at the tiny, uncomprehending face of the infant, a deep dislike began to fester. In the months to come, if Gertie would have been asked why she felt such a deep dislike for her child, which was fast growing into hate, she would have at first denied it. Then she would have explained how he was guilty of a litany of sins such as bed wetting and crying. And every time she looked at the child, the guilt and pain buried deep in her subconscious would fester and threaten to break the surface.

Gertie turned and looked up at Vincent who still stood with his cloth cap crumpled in his heavy hands.

"I wanted a daughter," her high-pitched whine made him crumple his hat some more. "Now you got three sons. And I wanted another daughter." She looked sadly up at her husband.

"I already got two sons," Vincent said quietly, trying to console her. "I never wanted another one anyway."

Gertie's tears started then and he crushed his hat in his strong hands.

"But we still can have another daughter. We can have more children," he said.

Gertie stopped crying suddenly and stared up at Vincent, her eyes glistening but showing a spark of enthusiasm.

"Yuh!" She sat up. "We can still have another daughter. We're young!"

She lay back down then and turned her head, gazing again at the tiny red face that belonged to her third son. But she still didn't bother to hold him. She nestled into the pillow, gazing up at Vincent who still held the crumpled hat in his hands. Her eyes fluttered and then opened for an instant.

"Tell the nurse to come and take the baby."

Within three days Vincent and Gertie stopped at the church to Christen the boy. Vincent stood with the same crumpled hat in his heavy hands while Gertie swayed slightly. The priest started the ceremony and then looked at the parents.

"What is the child's name?" He asked, impatient that they hadn't told him and irritated he had forgotten to ask.

Vincent's jaw trembled until he noticed the priest staring at him. He reddened and turned to Gertie, his voice harsh.

"What's its name?" The words were loud in the hallowed silence of the church. The priest's eyes widened and then narrowed.

"Uh," Gertie looked at Vincent and then at the priest.

"Metro!" The name popped into her head. "Yuh! Metro!"

An image of Metro's mockery flashed through Vincent's mind along with the memory of how he had been gone for nearly a month nine months before. A growing suspicion began to form but he said nothing. His jaw trembled and he looked down at his crumpled cap.

The priest hurried the ceremony, sprinkling water in the child's unsuspecting face and making him cry.

"Ssh!" Gertie hissed loudly, shaking the child in her arms. He broke out into a lusty bawl and she muttered bitterly, "Oh, he's gonna be a miserable child."

When they started on the long trip back to the loneliness of the farm, Gertie worried out loud. "I sure hope Gerard didn't make too big a fire in the stove." A sudden fear clutched at her chest, for guilt and anxiety had married in her soul and she seldom felt one without the other. Vincent only contorted his face, saying nothing.

"Vincent! Hurry up! I'm worried about the fire," Gertie's voice rose and the baby began to cry. "Ssh!" she hissed loudly and shook him roughly. The shaking only made him cry louder and she began muttering.

"Oh what a miserable child. Oh why couldn't I have another daughter?"

# Seventeen

Three years passed as Vincent tried mightily to wrest a living from the dry soil and rocks, with sweat running down his face in summer and the cold, a living enemy in winter. No matter how hard he tried, the crops failed and the price of mutton and wool kept dropping. And his ancient, rusting equipment and the unyielding soil made grain farming a losing proposition. But he had no choice and his contortions turned his face into a picture of torment. Gerard was twelve and when he saw his father make faces or the food dropping from his mouth, he said nothing. But he began hating his father: For his clumsy bear-like walk, his faces and eating habits but most of all, because he was poor.

He and Allen, along with Arlene in her first year, attended the same school with the stunted poplars and willows growing around the fenced playground. But they had a new teacher who didn't use the strap as often. Allen and Arlene mastered their lessons quickly while Gerard bore a grudging resentment, remembering his grueling hours of study by the coal oil lamp.

One Sunday afternoon, when neighbors came for a visit, Gerard watched his father talk, his face twitching and jaw trembling. The neighbor listened, his eyes wide as Vincent waved his arm in a northerly direction. His wife sat near Gertie and talked of washing, cooking and chores about the house. They were of Ukrainian descent and Gertie looked down upon them as "dumb Galicians." Still, they were company.

"Yuh! I chased that buck north." Vincent waved his arm again. "The dirty sucker ran into the hills. I jumped on a horse and went after him. Cold! Why, it was forty below. But I kept on. After awhile I rode close to a bush." Vincent paused for effect, his hand suspended in the mid-air.

"There he was! I jumped off the horse! I shot! Down he went!" He dropped his arm in a chopping motion.

While Vincent was boasting, Gerard and Allen and the neighbor's daughter went outside. The only children left were Arlene who sat by her mother and Metro who slept fitfully on a bed.

"I think I'm gonna trade some deer meat for baloney," Vincent said, crouching slightly forward in his chair, his hands clasped together. "We got so much. We get tired of it."

Vincent made a face and wiped his mouth with his hand. There was dirt under his fingernails but the neighbor didn't notice for his were the same. The room grew quiet then as they listened to Elias' wife explain how to get rid of rats. But the men soon lost interest and both looked down at their worn shoes. Elias brushed his worn, shiny Sunday dress pants with his hand, and then glanced at Vincent's clean bib trousers.

"Nice weather," he finally said.

"Yuh!" Vincent replied and then, "Those darned coyotes are sneaking up again and trying to kill sheep."

The conversation continued in a haphazard and scattered fashion.

"I think I gotta dig a new well," Elias said slowly. "The old one's filling up with dirt."

"Those darned coyotes are getting brave. But we'll, see. Just wait til I get more bullets."

Just then Elias' daughter ran into the room from the kitchen, her face red. She caught her breath and cast a quick glance out the window where Gerard and Allen were playing catch with an old softball.

"Mama! Gerard said fuck!" She blurted suddenly and then glanced out the window again.

The room became deathly still. Arlene looked up from an old box of toys she was picking through, and Metro stirred on the bed and whimpered.

"What!" Gertie's cheeks went white. Then, her voice rose, to a high-pitched whine.

"Vincent! Do something!"

"Aw gosh darn it the heck anyway," Vincent grumbled as he stood. "Always something. I never got time to do nothing." He walked ponderously through the kitchen, slamming the door behind him. Gertie watched through the window as he approached the two boys. Vincent didn't hesitate or even talk. He grabbed Gerard by an arm and half dragged, half carried him to the bench just under the window. Then he grabbed a thick, willow switch.

The switch landed with a sharp crack and the silence deepened in the house. Vincent swung again and again, his rage gaining momentum and his face twitching. Gerard, bent forward, the switch landing on his haunches as he closed his eyes and gritted his teeth, enduring the sharp pain of the willow. Gertie bent to watch through the window and when Gerard's face was glistening and white she ran out the living room and through the kitchen.

"Vincent! That's enough!" She yelled.

Vincent looked up, the willow suspended in mid-air, and his face filled with pent up rage. Then as he stared at Gertie, he slowly lowered his arm. He pushed Gerard roughly away and threw the switch on the ground before going back into the house without a backward glance. Gerard straightened slowly, his pinched white face glistening but filled with a silent rage. Allen watched warily, an old ball glove in his hand.

Vincent returned to his chair in the living room, puffing slightly. Then he folded his arms as his face twitched.

"Those darned dirty suckers better not hang around here. Boy! Or they'll be coyote skins," he said and grinned.

When the neighbors had left, Gerard approached Gertie. This time he allowed the tears to flow freely.

"Momma!" He began, "I never said that dirty word. She was only mad cause we wouldn't let her play catch."

Gertie stared at her son for a moment. Then she ran into the living room where Vincent slept on the couch. She poked him with her finger, her voice rising to a whining pitch.

"Vincent! Wake up!"

Vincent sleepily opened his eyes and stared. Gertie continued, her voice frightening the rats in the walls.

"Gerard says he never said that dirty word."

"Huh!" Vincent was wide awake.

"You should check first. Oh, why didn't you ask him?"

Vincent made a face, his heavy coarse hand brushing his lips.

"I can't be thinking of that all the time. I got so much to think about," he said and then lay his head back down on his arm and let sleep reclaim his consciousness. Gertie looked at him for a moment and then returned to the kitchen where she washed dishes and Gerard dried, his face still wet. It wasn't long before Vincent's face succumbed to peaceful repose and Gertie became involved in a conversation with imaginary and ghostly people.

She spread her arms wide in the gesture that was habit. "Oh yay, I says," she began but was interrupted suddenly by Gerard when he couldn't control his muscles.

The loud fart made Gertie look quickly at him. His face whitened and he took a quick backward step. But Gertie did nothing, for the nuns had never mentioned fart and sin in the same sentence. Then she farted too, her laughter mingling with the sound. Gerard's white pinched face relaxed and he repeated the noise, while he and his mother enjoyed a moment of perverted togetherness. During all this, Vincent snored peacefully and Arlene played on a bed with her baby brother.

Finally the light was extinguished and the house filled with silence except for the odd snore. As the clock ticked, a full moon rose and shone its ghostly light into the living room. Arlene rose from her bed on the couch and sleepily approached the kitchen with its slop pail, filled with crushed oats for the pigs. It also served as a "potty pail" for there was no bathroom, not even an outhouse. Even little Metro at three, had learned to squat without getting his clothes dirty.

But as the moon cast its ghostly beams through the window a large black rat crouched inside the pail, chewing quickly and casting occasional darting glances about the darkness. All was still, as the thin wail of a coyote drifted in from the hills outside. Just then Arlene appeared in the doorway, silent and wraithlike in her long robe as she rubbed her eyes sleepily.

When she was close, she turned to sit on the pail. The rat saw her just in time. He froze and then jumped quickly over the pail's rim and down to the floor, his claw like feet making a thump and then a quick, patter as he ran for cover.

Horrified screams filled the house as Arlene froze, screaming and screaming. Gertie rose in one motion and ran into the kitchen. Vincent lit the coal-oil lamp, as Gertie held her daughter and tried to comfort her. Arlene screamed hysterically, the horrendous feel of the rat's fur still on her skin. Gerard and Allen looked on from behind Vincent, their eyes round, while in a bedroom Metro screamed too and the house was filled with a cacophony of horror.

"There, there. It's all right. That big bad rat is gone now," Gertie consoled her child. Then she turned on Vincent.

"Oh why don't you make a toilet? Every one else has one."

"Aw gosh darn it. I got no time for that," Vincent grumbled and then went back to bed.

Gerard and Allen did the same and then Gertie took Arlene to bed with her. Metro still cried from his crib and finally Gertie rose and picked him up.

"Ssh!" she hissed loudly. She walked back and forth, the coal-oil lamp casting ghoulish figures on the walls and making Arlene afraid to close her eyes.

"Ssh! You got no reason to cry." Gertie shook Metro and then lay him back down in his crib. He whimpered awhile and eventually fell into a dream-infested sleep.

Next morning Gertie rose, her eyes red and her temper short. She railed at Vincent to build an outhouse while the three oldest children left for school. When she finished washing the dishes, she went to the crib where Metro slept fitfully. She yanked back the covers and lifted him quickly, setting him barefoot on the cold linoleum. Then she reached and felt his underclothes.

Suddenly she slapped him viciously and then half dragged, half-carried him to the kitchen as his terror-stricken, cries rose, and fell.

Gertie set him in a large tin washbasin and stripped his clothes in a couple jerky motions.

Metro's face went white for he had been beaten for being naked. As the cold air made him shiver, Gertie dipped a can into a pail of colder well water and dumped it into the basin. Then she grabbed an old wash cloth and began washing vigorously, her lips moving.

"Dirty! Stinky lazy boy!" Her voice rose in a singsong as Metro howled in terror, trying desperately to cover his private parts with his tiny hands.

"Piss and shit in the bed. Filthy! Stinky lazy! Filthy! Sinful, lazy boy." The sing song rose and fell along with Metro's screams.

Gertie's temper suddenly broke free and she began beating the naked child, the loud slap on bare flesh mingling with his cries. The blows rained down until she was out of breath. Then she began washing slowly, and then faster as the words built momentum once more.

"Dirty! Sinful! Filthy boy! Piss and shit in the bed!"

Her temper broke again and her hands failed as Metro crouched in the basin, hunching his shoulders to shield himself from the blows. Then once again, exhaustion made her slow down until she was washing with quick jerky motions; her words a wild singsong as the madness ran its course. It built to a crescendo again and again until finally she roughly dressed the child in hand-me-down clothes and just as roughly sat him on the floor, shoving him away. When he wandered off, his chest heaving, she turned and finished washing the dishes.

"Oh why couldn't I have another daughter?" Her body shook and she wept as she dunked the dishes and washed violently.

The days passed slowly and snow piled up outside the living room window while Vincent wore a heavy parka just to do the chores. Gertie muttered and worked in the kitchen and during weekdays the three oldest children went to school, riding in the stuffy caboose for with the wind blowing from open fields, exposed flesh would freeze in less than a minute. During this time Metro played by himself as best he could, a prisoner in the house for the only warm clothes he had were for church only. He also had one more disadvantage. His left eye crossed inwards and upwards, and in the place he lived it was enough evidence to condemn him as retarded. Still, he spoke at two and displayed positive signs of a high intelligence. All that did was irritate Gertie further.

One early afternoon when Metro was three and a half, a large, grey female cat sunned herself on the window sill, as the sun's rays illuminated dancing dust particles in the tiny living room. Gertie had brought her from the barn to help keep the rat population at bay but she could do little by herself. So she sunned while the heat from the airtight heater made her eyes heavy and she purred loudly with her paws curled up in front of her.

Metro sat next to the heater, warming himself. He could hear his mother working in the kitchen and the incessant mutter coming from her lips. He stayed in the living room close to the heater, wishing his sister would come home from school. When he tired of sitting, he walked to a worn cardboard box, stopping when he heard a rustle in the wall. Then he cautiously reached forward and stuck his tiny hand into the box, rummaging about for a scarred, wooden horse he was fond of. But a large female rat had chosen the toy box to raise her litter in. She lay quietly for it was close to her time.

A sudden stab of pain, shot up Metros arm as the rat sank her needle sharp teeth into his finger. He screamed and jumped backwards as the rat squealed and thumped about in the box. Metro clutched his hand, staring at the blood dripping from his finger. He screamed and screamed, the horror echoing in his mind as he froze, unable to move.

Gertie ran into the room, a broom in her hand. She began beating the box with quick jerky strokes as the cat jumped down from the window.

"Tarned, dirty sucker!" Gertie screeched as she swung the broom. The rat stood at bay on her hind feet for an instant, her needle sharp teeth bared. But she turned and fled suddenly with the cat one jump behind. Metro stood still, screaming and staring at the blood dripping from his finger.

"Dirty sucker!" Gertie yelled and then turned to the child. She bent and took his bleeding hand in hers as a loud squealing suddenly came from the bedroom.

"Here! It's okay. The cat's got the dirty sucker," she said but Metro still screamed, his feet rooted to the spot.

"Here now!" She snapped. "That's enough of that screaming. It won't do no good." She straightened and glared down at the child.

Metro stood in the middle of the room two feet from his mother while he cried until the sobs subsided and only the horror remained. Then Gertie turned and walked to the kitchen.

"Come!" She snapped over her shoulder. "Come here!" The last was an order and Metro followed slowly, his shoulders heaving. Gertie reached to a cupboard and pulled out a bottle of iodine.

Metro immediately stepped backwards and held his hands behind his back, his face white.

"Here now! Hold still!" Gertie growled. Metro shut his eyes tight and slowly held out his bloody finger. In a few seconds the kitchen was again filled with crying as his shoulders shook and sobs bubbled from his chest.

"Here now! Stop that crying!" Gertie snapped. She stooped with a bandage but Metro jerked his hand away and turned, holding his good arm to his face as the sobs continued.

"The heck with you!" Gertie yelled. "You can go without a bandage then." She straightened and returned to the cupboard.

"All I tried to do was help."

Then Gertie began kneading dough and Metro, his chest heaving, walked slowly to the living room to where the cat had been sitting. He pushed a chair to the window and climbed up on the seat, pulling his stockinged feet up with him as far from the cold floor as possible. He remained like that as the clock ticked away the minutes until the cat returned from the bedroom and jumped up to the sill. Metro cast occasional glances at her as she licked her chops and began a loud purring.

In the kitchen Gertie kneaded the dough as if it needed a beating. Her body shook as she pounded and her lips moved, quickly.

"And I only wanted to help," she growled as again came the spreading of her arms, "But he wouldn't even let me." Then she subsided to muttering about the Blute's and the wages she had never been paid.

Metro sat on the chair, his legs pulled up against his body until the older children returned from school. He played listlessly with Arlene, casting occasional apprehensive glances at the toy box by the wall. When the shadows deepened, he moved away from the bedroom where the darkness grew. Arlene brought the worn, wooden horse and laid it on the floor by Metro.

"Here!" She stood over her baby brother waiting for him to pick it up. But Metro burst into tears and turned away. The fear of the rat had generalized and he began to fear the toy too. He cried quietly by himself, holding his sore finger close to his body for if the iodine had killed any infection, the price was a dull throbbing pain.

Then as the night settled down he lay in his crib in Gertie's and Vincent's bedroom. As the night closed in around him, Vincent began snoring and Metro's eyes grew heavy.

Suddenly, he was awake.

"Daddy! I gotta go potty!" Arlene said from the darkness. Vincent opened his eyes and rolled over in bed, glanced at the faint outline of her nightgown before reaching to a small table for a flashlight. He shone the light into the living room and partially into the kitchen, frightening the rats away from the chop pail. It was only then that Arlene was brave enough to approach, knocking on the wall with her tiny knuckles to warn the rats further. After that the silence settled down again and Metro closed his eyes. Images swirled about in his subconscious and in a dream a heavy weight dropped onto his chest and he saw the cat lick her chops. Sleepily he opened his eyes.

Suddenly, the night was rent with screams. A large black rat had jumped onto his chest, its gleaming, evil eyes shining in the dark. Vincent and Gertie woke and scrambled from their bed as the rat scampered for cover, his claw like feet making a thump and patter in the darkness.

"Here now!" Gertie found the flashlight and shone it in Metro's face. "What is all this screaming for?"

"A rat! A big rat!"

"But there's no rat here."

"What's a matter?" Vincent mumbled sleepily as the other children stared from the door.

"Aw, he claims he saw a rat." Gertie switched off the light.

"Aw, he's always crying anyway," Gerard snapped from the doorway, scratching his ribs through his Long John underwear.

"He just imagined it."

"Yuh!" Gertie agreed and then turned to Metro whose face glistened in the darkness. "Go to sleep. You only thought you saw a rat."

Then she climbed back into bed and the other children disappeared into the darkness.

Metro lay most the night, his eyes open until finally he dropped off. He woke crying and heard his mother's voice.

"Now whats the matter?"

"I see bad things when I sleep."

"Just pretend they're not there," Gertie mumbled sleepily.

"But when I close my eyes, I see bad things."

"Well, hold your hand in front of your face so you don't see them," Gertie snapped. "Go to sleep now, or else!"

The night passed with the parents snoring and the child afraid to close his eyes for fear of a weight on his chest, and the horror of wicked eyes and evil, sharp teeth.

As the nights passed into weeks, Metro finally figured out that if he slept with his head where his feet had been, he could look at the window. It stood out stark and white against the blackness, the ghostly patterns of frost etched on the pane. The light was a great improvement for it kept the horror of the darkness at bay. But when he fell asleep, a large yellow eye would appear from out of the night, swirling and swirling with a yellow tail turning outside the eye. Then the worn, wooden horse would take form and Metro would open his eyes instantly, gasping for air and trembling as he stared at the window.

At times he lay, flat on his back, afraid to cover his head even when it was forty below outside and water froze solid in the pail in the kitchen. One morning he woke, exhausted but thankful it was daylight. But when he turned his head he felt a sharp pain in his ears. He lay still, too frightened to move until Gertie stuck her head into the bedroom.

"Gettup! Stinky lazy! Lying in bed all day!"

Metro rose quickly and managed to dress although he got the buttons mixed up. But as he stood by the airtight heater in the living room, the needle-sharp pain worsened. He remembered the iodine so instead of telling his mother, he cried quietly by the stove as the skin on his ears melted, and Gertie muttered in the kitchen.

"Tarned miserable child! Always crying!" The familiar spreading of her arms came. "And I do my best. I make sure he gets enough to eat."

A few weeks later Metro stopped eating. Gertie felt a sudden fear clutch at her chest, so she held him on her lap and tickled him until he opened his mouth for a spoon. And when he still didn't eat, she cajoled him with soft, boiled eggs. That was how he made it through his fourth winter, growing thin and haggard from lack of sleep and nourishment.

One Saturday, Arlene turned to Metro as they played on the floor close to the airtight heater.

"Come. I got something real nice for you."

Metro looked at his sister warily.

"Oh, come on now," Arlene said soothingly. "If you come here, I got something real nice for you."

Finally Metro approached his sister who knelt by the toy box near the wall. He hesitated and then took a step nearer.

"Here!" Arlene suddenly shoved the toy horse into his face. Metro screamed and ran to the bedroom, climbing up into his crib and pulling the covers over his head, crying loudly. Once he was covered, with just enough light to dispel the horror of darkness, his crying subsided and he sat, whimpering softly.

Gertie walked into the living room.

"Why do you do that?"

"Well, he's always crying anyway," Arlene said.

"But you mustn't," Gertie laughed and then went back to the kitchen and resumed patching an old shirt.

Arlene played by herself for a while until she was bored. Then she went to Metro's crib, pulled the blankets back and climbed in. Metro began crying again.

Arlene pulled the blanket over Metro and herself and sat quietly as gradually the whimpering subsided. Then brother and sister sat together in the dark, under the cover while their mother muttered in the kitchen.

# Eighteen

The golden, evening sun cast long shadows from the stunted poplars just north of the tar-paper shack where the clothes-line hung. A bird sang sweetly from a willow tree, and a gentle breeze ruffled the leaves and grass, as Arlene and Little Metro enjoyed for a brief time the sun's warmth in the coolness of the long shadows. As they sat on the rich green grass, they watched a batch of kittens romp under the watchful eye of the Mother Cat, who was the matriarch of the familys cats. And the kittens had names and personalities only the children could see.

When the sun's rays slanted through the leaves and the shadows were creeping onto the grass, the kittens abandoned their play and began nursing while the "Mother Cat" lay purring on her side.

"They're hungry," Arlene said, watching the kittens who pushed at their mother's stomach with tiny paws, their eyes closed in bliss as the loud purring reached a crescendo.

"Yuh! It makes 'em grow." Metro answered seriously, for at four he talked rapidly and fluently, except for the muddled accent he had learned from his mother.

He still had nightmares and on cloudy or moonless nights when little light came through the window, he was haunted with visions and terrifying images. In the sun however, that was forgotten as he watched the kittens.

Then Arlene lost interest in the kittens and turned to Metro for she had learned something new from a neighbor's boy.

"Lookit!" she said suddenly and pulled Metros pants down. His eyes widened but he didn't struggle.

"See! You're different than me."

Little Metro gazed downwards for a moment.

Just then Gerard walked unseen around the stunted poplars. He stopped suddenly and stared, his eyes narrow and face white. He turned and saw Gertie approaching with Vincent and Allen. Allen carried a quarter pail of milk, his round face red with exertion and pride. Gerard waited until they were close.

"So this is what you do!" He yelled suddenly and ran around the trees to Metro and Arlene.

Metro froze in terror, clutching frantically at his pants.

"You dirty, no good brat!" Gerard's voice was cold and contemptuous.

"What happened?" Gertie yelled, walking around the trees, her face red and her mouth hard.

"The dirty brat was exposing himself!"

As the sudden hot tears ran down Metro's cheeks, Gertie stared at Gerard's cold, white face.

"He's not all there!" He spat the words. "Exposing himself like that. Besides, he's cross-eyed anyway." Gerard's eyebrows knitted together and Allen moved away to stand beside Gertie. Arlene crouched on the grass, too frightened to move. Gertie looked from Gerard to Metro whose face was streaked with tears.

"What he needs is a tarned good licking. That'll learn 'em," Gerard continued with implacable, calculating intensity. "He's not all there anyway, cross-eyed like that!"

Metro retreated slowly, still trying to pull up his pants. Gertie took three giant steps, stooped and beat his bare bottom with short savage strokes. When her hand was smarting and his anguished wails reached a crescendo she stopped and yanked up his trousers, roughly fastening the button. A bit of flesh was caught when the button was forced into the hole but Metro didn't cry out anymore. He gasped for air and his shoulders shuddered as hot tears coursed down his cheeks.

Gertie roughly pushed him away and picked up her pail, taking giant steps to the house. With Allen following. Gerard glared at his baby brother.

"Serves you right! If it'd been me, I'd got a stick. You're retarded anyway. You cross-eyed brat!"

Metro turned and walked slowly towards the trees. His face glistened and throat constricted while his breaths came in shuddering gasps. Vincent stood beside Gerard and raised his arm and pointed.

"Why you! You better watch out. Or I'll get the strap."

Metro continued walking slowly, his back to his father's accusing finger, his face red with shame and fear. When he stood beside a gnarled black poplar tree the Mother Cat brushed up against his leg, and it seemed that despite the shame, at least the cat cared. And finally Arlene came and stood beside him too. His chest still heaved with deep congested pain but then in the coolness of the long shadows the sobs slowly subsided

When the coolness began to penetrate the children's thin clothing, Allen and Gerard came from the house with gloves, tossing an old baseball back and forth. Arlene and Metro walked slowly to the edge of the grass, near the trail running past the house to the barn, and watched. Allen squatted in the traditional catcher's posture and Gerard went into a windup before each pitch. And as they threw the ball, a half-grown pup trotted up from the barn where he had been lapping milk from an old dish. When he saw the ball, he gave chase, with loud happy barks. When Allen caught it, he stood and waited and then chased the ball again. After a few throws, he stood in the middle and tried jumping into the air and catching it.

"Get that tarned dog outa here!" Gerard suddenly yelled.

Allen concentrated on the ball and didn't answer.

"Get that dirty sucker outa here. I'm warning ya!" Gerard yelled again. Then he took careful aim and threw the ball with deadly accuracy. It caught the pup on the point of his nose.

The pup yelped loudly, twisting and turning in a paroxysm of agony. He hit the ground, rolling and whining with tears running from his eyes. Gerard grinned and then gave vent to his feelings.

"Serves him right! Next time he'll know better. Tarned dog!" An evil smile lit up his face and he stood still for a few seconds, relishing the enjoyment of inflicting pain on a helpless creature.

The pup eventually settled down, whimpering and blindly groping about, for his eyes were filled with tears. Allen squatted and watched his dog but he said nothing for the difference between eleven and thirteen is great.

As Gerard began another windup and Allen concentrated on the ball, Metro put his arms about the pup and held him, tears again coursing down his cheeks for the pup's agony was his too.


The days shortened until the dark green of the grain turned golden and finally stood in stooks waiting for the hungry maw of the threshing machine. And as the days shortened, the weather cooled until damp cold winds again blew and Metro was forced to spend more time indoors close to Gertie's constant mutter.

One typical grey day when the leaden, heavy clouds hung low he sat next to the airtight heater, swinging his feet from a chair. There was no fire but he had grown accustomed to sitting there when the cold wind caused dry, brittle leaves to skittle across the yard and rattle against the windows.

While Metro swung his legs from the chair, Gertie stood in the kitchen in her familiar position. Her shoulders rose and fell as she angrily shoved downwards on the kneaded dough. She used her shoulders for extra strength and her lips moved, the indistinguishable mutter making Metro cast an occasional, anxious glance towards the kitchen.

"Sure! And he goes running off to Grampas and leaves me alone with the work."

Gertie's mouth had set permanently into a hard bitter line and so it remained.

"And what can I do?" The habitual spreading of arms occurred and for an instant she stood with her hands outstretched, white with flour. Then she resumed kneading, her shoulders rising and falling and her lips moving. Metro cast another glance at the kitchen and then climbed down from the chair. He looked at the alarm clock ticking on a table for he could tell time. It was two pm, hours before Arlene and his two older brothers would return from school and he looked about, wondering what to do. Then he cautiously approached the toy box, its cardboard sides worn and dirty. He stared at it for a couple seconds and then kicked it hard with his stockinged foot. He waited for a few more seconds and when he heard no sudden thumping from inside, he squatted slowly and reached into it. He felt around trying to tell by feel if he touched the wooden horse. Then he grasped a toy and slowly withdrew it, turning his face away as he slowly lifted his hand. He glanced at the toy quickly and just as quickly looked away. He did that a couple of times, making sure he didn't hold the horse by mistake. He had fearfully thrown it away once but it had reappeared in the box.

To Metro his actions were routine, as routine as Gertie's incessant mutter, his father's faces and wild swings with the strap, and Gerard's cold, calculating hatred.

He walked over by the couch and sat on the floor, running the toy truck back and forth. It was old and scarred and had been played with first by Gerard and then Allen. But Metro didn't notice the scarred tin sides or the two missing wheels.

He squatted and played with the truck until his tiny legs were cramped. Then he wandered into the kitchen and apprehensively watched his mother as she vigorously washed the dishes. She glanced at him and then outside through the kitchen window. She hurried about, trying to do three jobs at once but succeeded in only causing sweat to run down her face, for a fire was burning in the cook stove. She stopped for an instant and looked at a package of raisins Vincent had brought home from the store. Suddenly she impulsively took the package from the shelf and removed three. Then a mischievous grin fleeted across her lined face and she turned quickly to Metro.

"Here!" She held out her hand, the raisins hidden.

Metro's eyes widened briefly, and he retreated.

"Come here!"

When Metro still hesitated, Gertie made her voice cold and stern.

"Come here! Or else!"

Metro stared at the extended arm with the clenched fist. Then slowly, he came forward, like a dog that fears a master but knows better than to run. When he was within reach and trembling, Gertie suddenly opened her hand, exposing the raisins.

"Here!" Her eyes were bright and expectant.

Metro stared and then cautiously took the raisins and put them in his mouth, the fear slowly succumbing to the wonder of sweetness.

Gertie's face lit up with a sudden grin and then she laughed outright, her eyes filled with a bright, brittle light. She reached suddenly and roughly petted him on the head. Metro ducked instinctively and took a quick backward step. Gertie withdrew her hand, the grin vanished.

"Aw you!" She snarled and turned back to the dishes, her face turning red from exertion and her shoulders rising and falling. Then the mutter came.

"Sure! And I try to be nice. And what do I get?" She turned and glared at Metro who quickly returned to the living room. He forced himself not to chew so the alien sweetness of the raisins would stay in his mouth. Then, when he had pulled a chair to the window, he heard a sudden jingle and looked outside. The old black gelding walked past the house, pulling the cart with Gerard holding the reins. Soon Metro heard the door open and slam. He jumped from the chair and ran into the kitchen just as Gertie was holding her hand out to Allen. When he reached greedily for the dozen raisins, she smiled and fondled his brown hair. He didn't duck or draw back for Gertie constantly said that he reminded her of her brother, and how she felt weak when it was time to punish him.

"Me too!" Arlene demanded, holding out her hand and Gertie went to the cupboard and gave her a dozen raisins. Arlene, her cheeks bulging, went into the living room with her books and Metro followed.

"Did you bring it?" He asked, his face serious.

"Bring what?"

"You know. The book with all them cows."

"What cows?"

"You know. All them cows in the big pasture."

"Oh! You mean buffalo," Arlene finally answered. "I forgot."

"Well, will ya bring it tomorrow?" Metro asked, misty-eyed and resigned to no book that day.

"If I don't forget," Arlene said but she never did remember, and Metro had to wait until he went to school before he could read about the buffalo.

When Arlene laid her grade two reader on the table, Metro picked it up and ran to a chair. He sat, his legs dangling and looking intently at a picture of children in the marvelous, far away Never Never Land of the city; where roads were hard and grey and where there were houses, thousands of them. And into each house ran a wire that lit the insides, bright as day.

Metro held the book a couple inches from his face for not only was he cross eyed, he had trouble seeing. But his lips followed the words and he appeared to be reading.

As Arlene changed her clothes in the bedroom and Metro sat by the purring Mother Cat, the door banged and Vincent and Gerard entered. They stopped in the kitchen for a moment and then along with Allen and Gertie came into the living room. Vincent fiddled with the heater, starting a fire for it was growing cold.

"Lookit!" Arlene exclaimed suddenly, pointing at Metro.

"He hasn't even gone to school yet and already he can read!"

Metro smiled self consciously from the book. But not everyone was pleased.

"Aw, he can't read. He's just pretending," Gerard snapped, his face suddenly white with a controlled rage.

"I couldn't read until I was seven, so who's he think he is anyway, pretending to read."

"Sure I can!" Metro said suddenly from the chair. "Dick and Jane live in a, a house, in a," He read slowly and then stopped at the strange word spelled city, the book inches from his face.

Gerard stared at his baby brother whose eyes were crossed and whose hair was tangled and dirty.

"Baloney! You can't read!" He suddenly yelled, his lips white and trembling. Gertie looked on and grinned. She believed Gerard for at fourteen he had more education than she and Vincent combined.

Metro laid the book down and slowly climbed down from the chair. Then he stood by the table as Arlene took out her pencil and scribbler. Gertie went back to the kitchen and began preparing supper while Vincent lay down on the couch. As Arlene pulled a chair up to the table next to the window for light, Metro crowded close, his face again serious.

"Can I have some?"

"Huh! What you want?"

"A paper. So I can draw." Metro's eyes were pleading.

Arlene looked at him for a second and then at the kitchen door. Gertie had her back turned and was muttering to herself while Gerard and Allen had gone into their bedroom. She glanced nervously at their father and saw that he was sleeping. Then quickly, she tore a sheet from her scribbler and gave it to Metro, along with a pencil stub. He pushed a chair to the table and climbed up and knelt so he could reach the paper. Then the room became silent as he industriously drew a picture. After awhile Arlene looked over.

"What you drawing?"

"A fence."

"What for?"

"So Shorty can't get out."

Shorty was the mustang Vincent rode when hunting deer. Metro held the paper so Arlene could see the vertical posts and horizontal lines that were the wire. The lines had little dots signifying barbs and Metro drew grass around the posts. Once he finished the fence, he concentrated on Shorty. The horse was drawn clumsily and childlike but still, there were signs in the careful portrayal of the hooves and the overall perspective. It appeared Metro had a talent that could be developed under proper circumstances.

Suddenly, Gerard's white pinched face appeared above and behind Metro.

"What the heck ya think your doing?" he yelled.

Metro froze. Then he turned, staring up at Gerard's white face.

"I made a fence," he explained quickly. "So Shorty can't get out. See." He moved so the failing light fell on the paper for the house was full of shadows. And in Metro's eyes there was a pleading wish.

"Baloney!" Gerard yelled, his lips losing their color again.

"The gate's too low. He'll jump over!"

Metro quickly drew in more wire and made the gate higher than any horse could jump.

"Now he'll jump over the fence!" Gerard yelled and Metro stared at the paper for it was futile to argue. Gerard went into the kitchen grinning.

"He can't draw. Who the heck's he think he is, anyway?"

Metro left the paper and followed his sister into their parents' bedroom where they both sat on the bed. She had brought out some toys and together they played where they weren't bothered.

But they hadn't gone far enough. Gerard and Allen stayed in the kitchen and the house grew quiet, except for Arlene and Metro's childish voices. Vincent woke and lay on the couch, worried about the weather and work which he tried to escape by sleeping again. Their voices kept breaking into his consciousness and finally he yelled.

"Be quiet! I wanna sleep."

The children looked up momentarily from their play and then continued.

"Shuttup! How in heck can I sleep when you're making all that racket?"

They tried lowering their voices to a whisper but soon forgot and again, Vincent's sleep was interrupted. He rose in one motion and went into the kitchen where he grabbed the new razor strap. He strode into the bedroom and a loud smack and sudden crying made Gertie stop muttering. Vincent was about to swing again at a cowering Metro when Gertie appeared in the doorway.

"Vincent! What youre doing?"

"Aw gosh darn it anyway. I can't sleep when he's making all that racket."

"But not the strap!" Gertie said, looking at Arlene whose eyes were filled with tears.

Metro gasped for air as he shuddered and cried for the strap had knocked the wind from his lungs

But Gertie only looked at Arlene, while behind her Allen and Gerard peered into the bedroom. Gerard's face was again white but an excitement danced in his eyes and his mouth parted slightly in an evil smile. Vincent lowered his arm and turned, while Gertie and her two oldest sons went to the kitchen where she gave each a small piece of raisin pie.

In the bedroom, Metro's shoulders heaved and Arlene's eyes were glistening but they made no further noise.

# Nineteen

Vincent sat proudly behind the wheel of the ancient, nineteen twenty-seven, Chevrolet Sedan. It puttered up hills and coasted down others dust flying in the rear as it whizzed by sloughs, poplar bluffs and open fields. He gripped the steering wheel with both hands, keeping his eyes on the road and advancing the spark with a lever on the steering column to time with the speed of the pistons. He turned and grinned at Gertie as they descended a hill, picking up speed.

"We're going forty miles an hour!"

"Yuh! Be careful!" A sudden stab of anxiety pierced Gertie's breast. She sat stiffly beside Vincent, gripping her old purse with work-worn hands as she fearfully kept her eyes on the road. Her face was covered in powder and her hair curled and set. She wore a brown print dress and a hat with a flower. It had taken two hours to get ready for she had to carry water in a pail to the kitchen to wash.

Gertie had dictated and Gerard had laboriously written a letter at the kitchen table while the coal-oil lamp cast shadows on his white face. Then Vincent had driven to town to post the letter which indicated that they would come on a prescribed date for a visit to her sister Marie who had moved to Berlin. She had married well and her husband had opened a hardware store. They lived in a large frame house on the outskirts of town and Gertie still marveled at the idea of electricity and a well right in the sink in the kitchen.

As the car slowed while ascending yet another hill, Vincent took his eyes off the road for an instant to adjust the spark and then pressed down on the accelerator. The car was twenty three years old and needed constant attention but it was the first he had ever owned. He sat with his chin up and his brown Stetson hat pulled down tight over his eyes.

Metro sat between them, his face white for he was nauseated by the car's motion and the perfume Gertie had doused herself with. He sat very still, fighting back the nausea for he had thrown up before when they had gone to church. He had been slapped and called "filthy!" and "sinful!"

Anxiety fought the nausea and he prayed in his childish manner that the sickness would go away. He looked apprehensively up at his mother who sat, staring out the windshield, her lips drawn and thin. He knew he should tell her that the vomit was crawling up his throat but fear immobilized him and he could do nothing but fight the sickness.

Gerard and Allen had been left home to do the chores and Gerard had bitten his lip but as usual said nothing, harboring a slow, abiding hatred for his parents. In the meantime, Arlene sat in the rear, turning occasionally to look at the receding scenery in the rear window.

In the front, Metro fought a losing battle with the vomit. He clenched his teeth but it forced itself out his mouth and onto his mother's dress, the fluid running down the folds and onto the floor.

"Oh, My God!" Gertie yelled. "Vincent! Stop the car!"

She gave Metro a quick backhand slap and spread her legs so the vomit ran down her dress. Vincent shifted to neutral, jamming on the brakes and the car came to a shuddering stop. Gertie got out quickly, took a hanky from her purse and poured water from a jug. She wiped, vigorously, trying to keep the cheap material from soiling.

"Oh! What a sowishness!" She yelled, her hands making quick jerky, wiping motions. "Dirty! Miserable child!" She slapped Metro across the face with her left hand and kept on wiping with her right.

"You ruined my dress! Dirty! Stinky lazy! Too lazy to tell me."

Metro stood sadly by the car, his eyes filled with tears and his heart with shame.

"Now lookit my dress! Oh, what a shame! How can I go to church like this?" Gertie slapped Metro again, this time with her right hand.

"Why you," Vincent snarled from behind the wheel, pointing the familiar accusing finger.

Metro took a quick backward step, his breath caught in his throat and his chest constricted.

Then Gertie shoved him roughly and he climbed back into the car. When they resumed their journey, with dust rising behind the sedan, Metro's face twitched and Gertie muttered. The wonder of the scenery and the speed with which it zipped by was lost on Arlene who stared pensively out the window from the rear seat.

As the miles passed under the Chevrolet's narrow tires, they eventually traversed Berlin's main street. Arlene gazed in wonder at the sidewalks and countless people for it was Saturday. They puttered past the people and eventually stopped at a large two-storey house at the edge of town.

"Come in!" Marie stood in the door, her arms akimbo. Then she looked at the dusty car for a moment. "So this is the automobile you wrote about."

"Yuh!" Vincent grinned, his jaw, trembling. "I traded two good horses for it."

"Oh, that's nice."

Marie saw the ancient fenders and general rundown condition. She looked away from the car quickly and ushered her younger sister into her house. Gertie walked up the steps, her lips moving.

"Tarned Stinky lazy boy," She brushed at her dress. "He threw up all over me."

Metro moved quickly out of reach and she could only glare at him.

"But he must'a been sick," Marie said. "My youngest was like dat. But he got over it. And so will Metro."

"Yuh! But he doesn't even try not to," Gertie muttered through clenched teeth.

Metro and Arlene both stood in wonder in the middle of the kitchen, their eyes round. They stared at the pump in the sink and the deep brown, varnished floor. And when Marie went to a wall and flicked a switch, throwing the room into instant illumination, they were speechless.

Just then a girl, Metro's age came into the room and looked up at Marie. Marie fondled the girl's hair and Metro wondered why she didn't duck. Then Marie let her hand rest on the child's head and turned to Gertie.

"She's Otto's niece. She's staying with us for a couple weeks." She patted the blond head again and Metro watched, his eyes narrow.

"You must be tired. You want some coffee?" Marie shifted her two hundred and fifty pounds, adding "You want some cake? I just baked one."

Metro stared at the brown cupboards and the door leading into the pantry. He looked down at the floor, brushing his worn shoe against the hardwood. It was slippery from wax and he did it again.

"Stop that!" Gertie raised her hand but then thought better of it. Metro ducked instinctively and Marie gazed in wonder at her sister.

"Oh, that's okay," she said softly. "His tiny foot can't hurt the floor." Then she turned to her niece. "Bonny. Show Metro the house."

The child turned and walked wordlessly into the living room. Metro followed but stopped suddenly in the doorway. He stared at a radio on a dresser, intrigued by the knobs and soft material covering the speaker.

"It's a radio!" Bonny laughed. "Haven't you seen a radio before?"

Metro shook his head and then stared at the leather sofa and chair and the wonder of the steps leading upstairs to more rooms.

Suddenly, soft music filled the room and Metro looked about frightened and puzzled.

Bonny grinned broadly.

"It's coming from here." She pointed to the radio as Arlene entered, gazing slowly about before staring out a large picture window through which she could see the street. Bonny laughed suddenly.

"You must be a," she thought for a moment, "a Stumble Jumper."

Metro wondered what she meant.

"Come!" Bonny added. "I have to go upstairs and wash for supper. You can watch if you want." She skipped and then ran up the stairs as Metro and Arlene followed slowly, the wonder of the stairs and washing before dinner, fighting for importance in their puzzled minds.

Bonny awkwardly poured water from a pitcher into a basin. Then she took a large bar of white soap and began generously lathering her hands. The rich, white soap foamed up and soon was up to her elbows.

Metro stared for a few seconds and then the memory of his mother snarling and slapping him came and his eyes narrowed. He could control himself no longer.

"You're using too much soap!" He said seriously.

Bonny ignored him so he raised his voice.

"You're using too much soap!"

The girl turned and stared at Metro, breaking out into a mocking laugh.

"You must really be a Stumble Jumper." She continued lathering soap, adding scornfully "Too much soap."

Metro stared at the strange girl and her stranger actions. Then he looked down and away, his heart once again filled with shame and guilt.


Gertie's square, sad face set in its normal rigid lines as she walked purposely along the sidewalk. She wore a green dress that Marie had given her. It had been too big so she had worked with Marie's sewing machine until late to make it fit. On her head she wore a hat with flowers and in her hand she carried her worn, imitation leather purse. She had worn the clothes to Mass that morning and had sat with her husband and children, not far from the Blute's pew. She had cast an occasional glance in their direction but her attention was again taken by the Virgin Madonna with outstretched hands and pierced heart, while the bloody Christ hung limply from a cross above the altar. She had breathed deeply for the smell of incense and the incomprehensible Latin always affected her that way. To Gertie the church was a haven that was always cool and where she could rest her tired muscles while she prayed to a visible God: A God appearing as the sad, mutilated and bloody Christ as he hung, crucified for eternity.

To Arlene, it was a place of awe as she stared at the Stations of the Cross, twelve paintings, depicting in succession, the final, brutal hours of the Man/God. To Metro, it had been a place of boredom for his inquisitive six year-old mind soon tired of the paintings and the incense and Latin he couldn't comprehend. He had wondered how long the Mass would take and how soon they would eat lunch.

All that was far from Gertie's mind as she walked along the sidewalk with Arlene whose eyes still widened in mystification at the sight of the town and rows upon rows of houses. Metro had been left at Marie's house to play with old toys while Vincent and Marie's husband discussed the weather and ignored the child.

Gertie stopped suddenly and placed her hand on Arlene's shoulder.

"There! That's the convent!"

"Is that where the nuns live?" Arlene asked staring at the large red brick building not far from the church and under the shadow of the gothic spire. Gertie had told her about the nuns who were kind and gentle and who lived a peaceful life, away from the toil and hardship of the farm.

"Yuh! That's the nun's house," Gertie said softly. "Come! We'll go and talk to them."

An ancient nun welcomed them, her rigid face creasing in countless wrinkles as Gertie and Arlene entered the cool, peaceful hallway and then sat on a soft leather sofa in an adjoining room. Arlene stared up at the paintings on the wall as old priests and nuns stared back down, their eyes piercing and critical. On the opposing wall the inevitable crucifix depicted the final, dying hours of their Lord. The room had a pleasant smell of leather and soap, the floor spotless and shiny.

"So," another nun, younger and with a smooth face came into the room. She sat in a leather chair and continued, "this is your daughter." She smiled kindly at Arlene.

"Yuh! This is my girl." Gertie fondled Arlene's brown hair and then let her callused hand fall to her lap. A silence settled on the trio as the smell of leather and soap and the warmth and non-threatening atmosphere wove a magic and powerful spell in Arlene's childish mind. Then the nun re-opened the conversation, asking about the weather, the crops and other things of utmost importance to a farmer's wife.

After a while she brought out milk and cookies and Arlene bit into the rich, tantalizing store-bought sweetness. The nun smiled warmly at the girl. It was lonely living behind convent walls, with only the company of other nuns and the constant praying and penance for sins they had no chance to commit. Her longing could be seen in the brightness of her eyes but she held it in check. It was also the policy of the church to actively recruit future nuns and priests and Arlene was only five or six years from a convent life herself. So they sat, the nun and Gertie passing the time with small talk, while Arlene listened to the warm and friendly nun who loved children and suppressed the knowledge that she would never have any of her own.

Then, Gertie and Arlene left the cool, warm convent, with the nun smiling down at the girl and telling them to come again. The pure white of her head gear contrasted starkly with the jet black of her robe and she held her hands folded together from habit while a large silvery crucifix hung from a rosary around her neck.

Arlene's eyes were filled with the new and enticing experience and then, as she walked beside Gertie, a decision was reached in her developing mind.

"Momma! I wanna be a nun."

Gertie stopped in her tracks. She turned and placed her hands on the girl's shoulders, a warm and loving smile creasing the normally bitter, hard face.

"Do you really want to be a nun?" Gertie said softly, a knot in her throat as she choked back the tears. Then she looked at a large sign proclaiming, *Woos Café*. She took her daughter gently by the hand and led her into the restaurant where she found a booth to sit in. Arlene gazed in wonder at the rows of utensils on the walls and the long counter that ran the length of the café. Two girls, her age, sat on tall round swivel stools while they drank from glass bottles with straws as they swung their legs back and forth. In the booth was a fascinating machine with rows of vertical buttons but Arlene didn't know it was a "Juke Box."

Then an aging and friendly Chinese approached, his smooth face creased with a smile as he asked, "Would you like some ting?"

"Yuh!" Gertie reached into her purse and placed two dimes on the table.

"Give us two soft drinks. Please."

Arlene let her legs dangle from the leather clad bench as she felt the cold, refreshing taste of soda pop.

"Do you really want to be a nun?" Gertie asked again, holding her straw between two fingers. Arlene nodded as she took the straw from her mouth. Gertie's memory flitted back to the kind nun who had given her food when she was a child.

"I always wanted to be a nun," she said softly, wistfully. "A nurse amongst the children." She gazed at Arlene, her eyes moist and bright.

"If you are a nun you won't have to marry some man. Then you won't have to bear no children or work like I do." Gertie's face hardened for an instant as she stared off into the distance.

"You won't have to submit to no man," she added, a bright anger in her eyes.

As Vincent drove the ancient Chevrolet home and Metro fought the nauseating urge to vomit, Gertie thought of Arlene's statement. And as the sedan puttered around curves, past farms and pastures, she vented her thoughts.

"Arlene wants to be a nun!"

"Huh!" Vincent made a face, wiped his mouth with a heavy hand and then gripped the steering wheel tightly while concentrating on the dusty road ahead.

"She says she wants to be a nun," Gertie repeated and then turned to the back seat where Arlene played with an old doll Marie had given her.

"Ain't that so, Arlene?"

"Yuh," Arlene answered, keeping her attention on the doll. "I want to be a nun when I grow up." She lifted the doll and then held it in her lap, like a mother holding a baby.

Vincent stared into the rearview mirror at his daughter. His face contorted and then he smiled. From then on Arlene was "his daughter."

When they were home and Gerard and Allen were each given a present for doing the chores, Vincent lay down on the couch. It was near supper and too late to start in the fields. Arlene pulled out the old toy box and Metro played with her doll along with the ragtag toys. Metro still felt an unreasoning fear of the box so Arlene upset it with the toys spilling onto the floor. This time Vincent didn't yell at them to be quiet. He lay with his face towards the ceiling, made a face and then scratched himself near his groin.

Finally Gertie stuck her head into the room. "Supper's ready," she said and then turned to the children. "Put those toys away before we eat."

Arlene and Metro glanced up from their play and then Arlene stood and looked down at Metro.

"Put them away!" She ordered suddenly.

"But you took them out. You should put them away." Metro cast an anxious glance at the box.

"No!" Arlene ordered, her hands on her hips. "You put them away."

"But," Metro tried again, "I put them away the last time."

Vincent turned on the couch and glared.

"Metro! Put those tarned toys away!" he yelled and Metro cringed. Then slowly he gathered the toys, dropping them into the box and looking away quickly.

When they ate, Metro sat quietly beside Vincent and his open chewing, mouth. He kept his eyes from the nauseating sight until he lifted his head.

"Butter?" He asked.

"What!" Vincent yelled, his mouth open with the food and saliva exposed.

"What the heck ya mean? Asking for food like that? You go some place and they'll give ya butter on the head." He contorted his face and wiped his lips with his hand while Metro cringed on his chair.

"No!" Gertie snapped. "You just waste it anyway." Then she began a singsong. "He doesn't care. He'll just waste and waste until it's gone. Then he's happy. He doesn't even care."

Metro felt the guilt creep into his consciousness and the tears start while the food became straw in his mouth. His throat was so constricted he couldn't swallow so he sat very still, trying to make himself as small as possible. Vincent turned again and glared, his mouth open. Blood from a gum mixed with the food and saliva.

"Now cut that out! There'll be no crying at this table!" He yelled and then looked at Gertie.

"Where's the strap?"

Metro fought back the tears and forced himself to swallow. He sat very still, the image of the strap in his father's hand making it impossible to move.

"Now eat!" Vincent yelled, the blood still in his mouth.

As Metro's vision swam and he choked on the food. He could see Gerard's cold, implacable stare from across the table. His thin lips compressed and his eyes were bright and brittle. Arlene sat next to her mother and ate, basking in the new and surprising warmth. Metro could also see Allen spread large chunks of butter on his bread. He looked down and forced himself to eat the food that was straw, for Vincent still glared.

Later that evening, consumed with an undeniable curiosity about the wonder of butter and why it was such a treasure, Metro crept into the kitchen. The dishes were still on the table and the butter uncovered. He cast an apprehensive glance about, noticing that Gertie was in the living room while Vincent slept on the couch. He quickly grabbed a spoon and scooped up a large quantity of warm, soft butter. He closed his mouth, expecting an exquisite taste but all, he got was a feeling of near sickness.

Allen entered the kitchen and saw Metro just as the butter became a sticky disappointment. He laughed.

"Serves you right for stealing butter!"

The tears started again for the harshness in Allen's voice and his father's face and yelling suddenly combined into a heavy weight in Metro's chest. He quietly left the house and in the late summer evening sat on a bench under a window. The large Mother Cat jumped up and joined him and he let his arm rest over her. She began a loud, purring and Metro sat with the cat until darkness once again shrouded the earth.

After Gertie had been given an extension of her dream by Arlene's announcement that she wanted to be a nun, she became more and more immersed in prayer and the primitive, mystical faith in the Blessed Virgin who stood with arms spread and heart pierced. Every night when the chores were done and the sun's descent into the netherworld was casting long shadows in the yard, Gertie would announce with a sudden intake of breath.

"Vincent! We didn't pray the rosary!"

Vincent would rise from the couch and go to the cupboard in the kitchen where he kept a little brown cardboard box. In it was a rosary that had been blessed by a Bishop. He would rattle the box and turn it upside down, emptying the beads into his large hand. Then the family would gather in the living room, on their knees and begin a repetitive and monotonous reciting of the rosary.

Metro wasn't spared the need for prostrate prayer to a God that no one saw. But to him the praying was a ten minute span when he moved from knee to knee and mumbled meaningless words while he gazed at the toy box, the walls or the picture of the Bless Virgin hanging on the wall. At times he scratched where he had been bitten for rats weren't the only things that came out in the darkness. During all this he felt a great, crushing boredom. All it took for a quick nauseating anxiety was for Vincent to rattle the rosary box.

Every evening the grey tar paper shack was filled with adult and childish voices reciting "Our Father Who Art in Heaven" or "Hail Mary, Full of Grace." One time a neighbor knocked but no one heard. He opened the door and walked into the living room and into the middle of a loud prayer that sounded like someone had died. He stood for an uncertain instant and then quickly knelt and mumbled the meaningless words along with the family.

Metro felt shame when the neighbor looked about in a puzzled manner. But he kept his position, shifting from one sore knee to the other and wishing mightily that the praying would end. It didn't take Gertie long to notice his lack of interest.

One day, Metro wandered in from outside. It was Sunday and Vincent lay on the couch in his familiar position, letting sleep drain the ache from his muscles and worry from his mind.

"Vincent!" Gertie yelled suddenly. "You should take an interest! Make 'em pray!"

Metro stopped dead in his tracks and cast a wild glance at the door leading to freedom. But it was too late.

"Come here!" Vincent ordered as he sat up on the couch.

Metro stood still, the quick nauseating fear immobilizing him.

"Come here! Kneel!"

Metro slowly did as he was told.

"Pray!" Vincent's voice was loud and harsh as he made a face and clasped his hands together, leaning forward on the couch.

Metro's body went rigid and his memory lost the words.

"Pray!" Vincent yelled and Metro started to tremble. Still, the words wouldn't come. The terror made Metro's throat constrict, and the urge to urinate, strong and pulsating. Vincent contorted his face with his tongue protruding out of the corner of his mouth.

"Pray!"

Metro's trembling increased and he fought the growing pressure in his bladder. Then he felt a wetness in his pants and the trembling made his shoulders heave.

Vincent suddenly swung, his one hundred and ninety pounds behind the fury and Metro landed six feet away, writhing and gasping on the floor for the blow had landed in the small of his back.

Gertie stopped muttering in the kitchen for an instant when she heard the loud thump but then resumed darning socks.

Metro lay gasping and shuddering, tears coursing down his face. He didn't cry out for he needed all his strength to get the air flowing back into his lungs.

"Now pray!" Vincent yelled and rose. But he had expended all his suppressed rage with the one blow so he stomped out of the house. When the door slammed Metro started breathing again, gasping for air. Gertie looked in from the kitchen, her face worried but when she saw he was breathing she went back to the socks and her incessant mutter.

Later that day Metro, urinated blood but he told no one.

The order to "pray!" continued, as the weeks passed and the first day of school approached. The more threatening Vincent was, the more impossible it was for Metro to remember the words. So he knelt and hunched his shoulders, waiting for the inevitable blow.

One evening, Metro sat outside on the bench under the window as tears ran down his face. He was losing a tooth, the new one forcing the old out of the gum. Inside, Gertie turned to Vincent who lay on the couch.

"Vincent! Do some thing! Pull his tooth!"

When Metro came into the living room, Vincent rose with the familiar order "Come here!"

Metro froze, the color draining from his face.

Vincent lunged, grabbing Metro by the arm and dragging him to the couch. He sat and then with one arm holding Metro firmly forced his mouth open. When he stuck his thumb into Metro's mouth, searching for the tooth, Metro could taste cow manure for Vincent hadn't bothered to wash.

"Hold up!" He yelled hoarsely. "Gosh darn It! I can't get it!"

Metro suddenly felt a tearing, crushing sensation and hot blood flowed onto Vincent's hand. Vincent grasped with his thumb and forefinger and twisted and pulled while Metro struggled desperately, frantically pushing upwards at Vincent's arms. Vincent held him firmly as the silent struggle continued and he made a face. Then suddenly he grinned.

"Got it!" He said, holding the tiny, offending tooth to the light and gazing at it for a moment. Then he shoved Metro aside and walked ponderously to the kitchen and threw the worthless tooth into the slop pail.

"Did you get it?" Gertie asked from the cupboard where she was wiping dishes.

"Yuh!" Vincent made a face and then left to relieve himself, walking to the stunted poplars for, he still hadn't built an outhouse.

Metro lay on the couch, his chest heaving. Gertie glanced quickly at him through the kitchen door and then went back to her dishes. Gradually, the heaving in his chest slowed but he still could taste cow manure and blood. He spit and stared at the red specks on the linoleum as his sobs became slower and slower until he lay quietly on the couch. In the meantime Vincent relieved himself in the bushes. When he returned, he glanced at the couch and Metro rose and jumped quickly down to the floor. Then he stood by the toy box, his body trembling again and the tears starting all over. In his confused and childish mind, he thought he was punishing his father with his tears.

In less than a minute Vincent's loud snore filled the room.

# Twenty

The black Geldings clumsy, ambling walk pulled the four children in the tiny cart over hills and down trails, winding around dry sloughs and cracked, seamed ground where once ducks swam. Crows flapped and cawed in poplar bluffs and the air carried a fresh tang that could only mean winter was not far away.

The children crowded together as Gerard held the reins loosely and clucked to the horse who ignored the fifteen year-old. Allen stood beside him, his hands on the rough boards as he balanced against the cart's bumping motion. Arlene and Metro stood on either side, their eyes on the slowly moving scenery. Arlene held a reader and scribbler but Metro held onto the board, raising his hands to shoulder height for he was only six. He didn't carry any books for it was his first day of school and his eyes were wide. As the cart bumped over a stone and Gerard clucked to the horse, Arlene pointed suddenly.

"Look!" She called. A dead garter snake lay close to the trail, its long body bloated and grotesque in death. Metro gazed at the dead snake as it receded slowly. Then he turned to the slowly approaching, greying one-room schoolhouse that had the improbable name of Forest Grove.

Gerard drove the cart past the red willows and open prairie, to the sagging mud poplar log barn in a corner of the fenced school yard. With Allen's help he unhitched the horse and tied him in a stall. Then he threw a fork full of hay into a manger and the horse gratefully stretched his ropey neck forward. Gerard closed the rickety barn door and the four children walked to the school, fifty yards away.

Metro kept close to Arlene and Allen for the world was fast becoming a strange and bewildering place. But he stayed away from Gerard and his cold, implacable look.

"Who's this?" A girl suddenly asked and Arlene looked down at her baby brother.

"That's Metro! He's starting today."

Metro looked up at the stranger, his hands by his sides until Arlene poked him.

"Come on! We're gonna go in now."

Once inside, Metro's world held still more surprises. A middle-aged man stood at the front of the room, a pointer held firmly in his hand and in the back, near the coat hangers, there was a shelf full of books. Metro stared for there were more books than he had ever imagined existed. He approached slowly and placed a small hand on the shelf, examining the books carefully.

"Boy," he marveled, "I sure can read a lot here." And for a very brief time he felt happy anticipation.

"Sit down, Class," the teacher ordered suddenly and Metro ran to a seat beside his sister.

But the teacher approached, the pointer still in his hand.

"Not here! That's for older kids."

The teacher led a trembling Metro to the front and set him in a smaller desk. Metro glanced back at his sister but the teacher again took his attention.

"Okay now! My name is Mr Jones. Or you can call me Teacher." He glanced at Metro, his face stern. He was a kind and gentle man but to Metro he appeared hard and capable of great violence.

"I'll get to you right away," he said and after awhile Metro was looking at a brand new grade one reader. He kept part of his attention on the teacher but when the man made no threatening gesture Metro concentrated on the book. The only other child in grade one, Frankie, sat idly and looked dully about the room. Then the teacher stood over Metro.

"Can you read that?"

"Yuh!" Metro glanced up quickly and then turned and looked back at his sister. But he saw only the cold, calculating, stare of Gerard and he turned and faced the front of the room.

"Read some words." The teacher said dubiously.

Metro held the book inches from his face.

"The black cat chased the black rat," He began, his childish voice pronouncing the words correctly and using "the" instead of "de."

"Amazing!" The teacher said, scratching his head. "Most kids can't read when they get to school."

Metro looked up, puzzled. It was the first compliment he had ever received.

Then the teacher turned to Frankie and asked, "Can you read too?"

Frankie only shook his head dully.

"Oh well I guess it was too much to expect," the teacher said and then looked back at Metro.

"I can get you something else to read." He walked to the rear and returned with another book. "Here! Read this while I teach Frankie."

Metro turned the cover and soon became immersed in a story about a baby wolf who had run away from home and who was alone in the wilderness. In a full page picture, a huge, mangy bear lurked behind a tree. Then Metro read how the baby wolf had taken a drop of water and a crumb of bread before running away from his parents and getting lost in the woods.

Snow fell and the little wolf was cold. Soon he ran out of food and huddled miserably under a large spruce tree, the boughs heavy with snow and hanging nearly to the ground. Metro was only vaguely aware of what a spruce tree was but he sounded out the word slowly, reasoning that it was a new kind of tree that grew in the new world he had just entered.

Suddenly, he sucked in his breath for when he turned the page the bear was towering over the little wolf, saliva dripping from his huge, yellow fangs. But when Metro turned another page, the baby wolf's parents were in the picture and together they chased off the hungry bear. Then they took the little wolf home as he declared that he would never run away again.

Metro knew the sadness and terror of the little wolf but when he finished the story he wondered about the statement of never running away again. He also wondered why the baby wolf's parents didn't beat him. Then he turned and gazed at the rear of the room for a moment. He turned quickly back to the front for all he saw was Gerard's cold, calculating stare.


The golden, fall leaves soon changed to wrinkled husks, rattling against the windows. While gusts of rain and cold wind blew, the warm lazy heat of summer became a vague memory and the family settled in to withstand the onslaught of yet another winter.

During this time, Metro rode the cart with his brothers and sister and learned to read better and to add and subtract, growing impatient when he had to listen to Frankie stumbling over the words. But the easy instinctive manner in which he mastered the written symbols only made Gerard's face whiten.

On a day when the snow fell softly and muffled the sound of the sleigh's runners, Gerard hastily unhitched the horses and put them in the barn. Then he ran to the house and banged the door shut. Inside, was a puzzled Gertie along with Allen and Arlene. Metro stood apart by the stove.

"Allen says Metro's got to get glasses," Gertie blurted.

"Yuh Momma!" Gerard answered, standing in the kitchen in his boots and coat. "The nurse says that's why he holds them books so tarned close."

A health nurse had appeared that day and had given all the children an eye test.

Gertie's face was a mirror of anxiety. Metro was suffused with guilt when he saw the concern on his mother's face and the hard look she gave him.

Vincent entered just then, stomping his feet to rid the snow from his boots. He contorted his face and removed his coat. Then he sat at the table, his clothes smelling from cow manure.

"They say he needs glasses!" Gertie blurted, indicating Metro with her chin.

"Aw, gosh darn it, the heck anyway!" Vincent's jaw twitched. "How much does that cost?"

"The nurse said, twenty dollars," Gerard said disgustedly. "And she said if he doesn't get 'em, he'll have trouble seeing in the future." He gave Metro a cold, calculating look. Gertie looked down at her worn shoes for a moment and then back up.

"Oh No!" She yelled suddenly. "He holds the book too close. That's why he can't see. He's always holding them tarned books too close and when he wants to see some thing far away he can't cause he's not used to it."

"You quit holding that tarned book so close or you'll go blind," she said vehemently to Metro, her sad, square face, hard and lined.

"Yuh!" Gerard added. "And it's cause you read so tarned much. That and that tarned drawing. If you didn't read or draw so tarned much, you could see better."

Then he got his twenty-two from the bedroom and announced, "I'm going hunting." He held the rifle proudly for he had bought it with money he had made trapping weasels. He also had a secondhand violin he couldn't play. He practiced for hours and when Allen joined him with an old, scarred guitar, all they ever accomplished was frighten the rats in the walls.

As Gerard walked up a hill in search of rabbits and Allen and Arlene went into the living room with homework, Gertie glared at Metro.

"You and that tarned reading. That's why you can't see. That's what you got for holding that tarned book so close."

After that Metro tried holding the book at arms length but the words were blurred, and it only gave him a headache. So he still read with the book inches from his face but when he heard an approaching step he held it out and pretended to read what he couldn't see.

The winter ground on, the drifts piling high near the willows and the children riding in the caboose, gladly suffering the smoke from the tiny heater. Christmas came and went, the Midnight Mass and large meal after, etching a lasting and wishful memory in Metro's mind.

Vincent brought home an old battery-operated radio one day. From then on, in the long and dark wintry evenings, the family gathered around the airtight heater in the living room and listened to tales of love and death in the far off Fairy Tale land of the city. Then when it was time for bed, Vincent would grab the rosary box and the house would be filled with mumbled prayer. Metro knelt with the rest, dutifully going through the ritual but never understanding the meaning. Arlene however, expressed a profound interest in prayer. Whenever she prayed Gertie's face would soften and Vincent would say, "That's my daughter."

Metro avoided his mother and on rare occasions when she was in a good mood and attempted holding him, he would squirm to get away. Then Gertie would shove him roughly saying, "Aw you. You're such a miserable child." At other times when he got in the way her hand would snake out in a quick slap to the back of his head.

Vincent found that if he mocked Metro, the child would stand forlornly, his hands by his sides with tears in his eyes. When Metro wanted to join his brothers on a small slough where they played hockey with the skates they had been given for Christmas, Vincent contorted his face, grinned and glared at him.

"Can you skate?"

The words were mocking and when Metro felt the hot tears of humiliation, Vincent's grin widened.

"He can't!" Gertie snapped, her voice rising to a whining pitch. "He only walks on the sides of the skates."

Metro had an old pair a neighbor had discarded. They were too big anyway so he only watched his brothers as they skated back and forth, practicing slap shots with a wooden puck.

One afternoon, after Gerard and Allen had been playing hockey, Allen complained bitterly that the skates he had been given for Christmas were no good. Vincent sat on the couch leaning forward and clenching his hands as he listened, his jaw trembling.

"You should be thankful you got that!" He yelled suddenly and beat Allen with the strap until Gertie ran into the room, wringing her hands in agitation.

But it was Metro who was his main target. At six, he couldn't tie his shoes but in school when the teacher asked softly, he would write or read with amazing ease. In the house, when Vincent or Gertie demanded it, emotional paralysis would grip his soul and he would sit dumbly, hunching his shoulders and waiting for the inevitable blow.

One wintry evening, when the snow softened the relentless cold, Gerard and Allen were by the woodpile loading a hand-pulled sleigh. They had played in the house, forgetting about the wood until Vincent had yelled and they had dressed hurriedly and were outside. As they loaded the sleigh, Allen suddenly stopped and looked at the snow banks.

"Hey! Let's see how much we can put on." He grinned and Gerard stared, not knowing what he had in mind. But when they had stacked the wood as high as they could, Allen looked at the house, a hundred yards away. He gazed skyward at the falling snow while Gerard looked on, his shoulders hunched forward and his face white and pinched in that complaining manner of his. Then Allen grinned at Gerard.

"We'll never be able to pull this load. Why, it's way too heavy for us."

Gerard nodded, his face still white and pinched.

"Let's get Dad! I bet he'll pull the wood for us." Allen laughed and finally Gerard's thin mouth lost its complaining look. Then slowly, it widened into a calculating and knowing grin.

Both boys ran into the house, knocking snow from their rubber boots and removing their mitts. Allen looked at his father who sat by the kitchen table.

"Did you get the wood?" He demanded gruffly.

Allen's thirteen year-old face was solemn and he spoke slowly.

"We couldn't! It's way too heavy."

"Huh!" Vincent stared from the table.

"That's right!" Gerard added. "It's too heavy and the snow's too deep."

Gertie looked on and then opened her mouth with a sudden intake of breath.

"Vincent! It's too heavy. Pull it for them."

Vincent stared at Gertie and then rose from the table mumbling, "Aw gosh darn it, the heck anyway." He pulled on his coat and then his boots. He grumbled some more and cast a hard look at his sons but he did as he was told.

Gerard and Allen quickly removed their coats and boots and stood by the stove. As Gertie hustled about the kitchen she didn't notice their grins while outside Vincent pulled the wood to the house.

Metro sank deeper and deeper into an emotional morass of self deprecation and feeling of minimal worth. In school, the teacher called the two first graders to the front and announced that he had invented a new game for them. He wrote words on the blackboard in two vertical rows and gave each child a ruler.

"Okay! When I call out a word you point to it. Whoever points first gets a point."

"Dog!"

Frankie and Metro both stared hard at the blackboard with Frankie sounding out the word, his eyes traveling slowly up and down the rows. Metro squinted desperately but all he could see was two blurred rows of greyish white. Eventually Frankie sounded out "dog" and pointed. When Metro's eyes followed the ruler, he could barely make out the letters. But it was too late.

Frankie gained a point and the game continued. He stared dumbly at the board, sounding out the words in a loud whisper while Metro desperately squinted, trying to penetrate the blur. Whenever Frankie pointed, Metro would be able to barely see the word but always it was too late. Soon the score was nine to nothing.

"Aw, let's give Metro a chance," The teacher said jovially and marked a point next to Metro's name on the board. The students laughed and guilt and shame sank deeper and deeper into Metro's consciousness. He looked desperately to the rear but he was met by Gerard's cold, calculating glare.

Finally the teacher called off the game and Frankie's face was flush with victory and Metro's red with shame.

"You'll just have to study harder, Metro." The teacher said not unkindly. Then he turned away, ignoring the child who held a book inches from his face when he read.

When the horses plodded into the yard, Gerard stopped them so Arlene and Metro could dismount from the caboose. Arlene ran into the house but Metro stayed by the snow-covered bench. It was cold and starting to snow but he felt a deep unfathomable fear. It wasn't long before he saw Gertie walking rapidly from the barn, her face hard.

"Come in the house!" She snapped, opening the door. Metro froze, the tears starting.

"Come in the house!" The command came again and he followed slowly, his throat constricted and chest full of pain. Then he stepped through the door and stood in the middle of the kitchen, his body trembling.

Gertie appeared suddenly from behind the door, hitting him on the head with the strap. She swung wildly, her face white with rage, spittle flying from her mouth.

"Dirty! Stinky! Lazy! Good for nothing!" The words came in gasps as she swung and yelled. Metro bent forward slightly, hunching his shoulders and enduring the wild beating. As long as he kept his head tucked in, his coat took most of the strap's force. And finally Gertie stopped, her arm heavy and sore. She shoved Metro roughly and he fell to the floor. As he rose slowly, his face glistening, Gertie glared at him.

"Next time you mind in school!"

Metro went slowly into the living room, the fear receding once the beating was over. But the shame remained as slowly he climbed onto a chair by the window. The large Mother Cat opened a sleepy eye and then closed it. Metro looked at her through a watery mist and wished he was her kitten.

Meanwhile Arlene played with a doll in the bedroom and Gertie rushed about the kitchen, her mouth moving incessantly in an audible whisper. Just then the door banged open and shut and Gerard entered. He kicked off his boots and then stared at Metro from the kitchen door. When he saw the glistening face, a cruel smile spread on his thin lips and his eyes held a brittle triumphant light.

# Twenty-one

The cold, implacable winter finally lost its grip and a softness settled upon the land. Soon all creatures who hibernated or migrated, were going about building nests and breeding new generations.

As the old Gelding pulled the cart along the well-worn trail, past sloughs and poplar bluffs, gophers stuck their inquisitive heads from their holes and then stood upright, whistling sharply. Above them robins circled and then landed on the fresh green grass, looking for unwary worms while a hawk rose on the hot air, looking for unwary gophers.

The old horse's head bobbed up and down and he occasionally stopped to crop green grass. Allen held the reins loosely for there was no haste. Metro stood beside him at the front of the cart while Arlene stood in the middle, her eyes darting about the green countryside teeming with the rebirth of life.

"Look!" She cried suddenly. Metro and Allen swivelled their heads as a large jack rabbit bounded away, her strides long and effortless.

"She'd have a nest around here. She probably got young ones already," Allen said to Metro. Metro remembered a young rabbit a cat had brought home to her kittens the preceding summer. As he watched the rabbit disappear around a bluff, he thought of the other rabbit's limp body and the anger he had felt when he had seen its dead, glazed eyes.

But the cat had only wanted to feed her kittens and he had been confused for what is death to one is life to another. He pushed the problem of killing to eat from his young mind as he stared at where the rabbit had disappeared.

"Maybe we could find the baby rabbits," he finally said.

"If we took them from their nest they'd die," Allen answered.

"Oh!" Metro's eyes were round. He didn't say anymore, keeping his eyes on the track in front of the horse and hoping to see another rabbit. As he stood, with his small hands on the rough boards, his shoulder touched Allen. He didn't draw away for on this trip Gerard was absent, staying home to help with the seeding. Metro would remember the alien sense of companionship, for events like that were islands in the sea of grey, misty misery.

Then the horse walked through the school yard and Allen let Metro help unharness. There were still a few minutes before nine and the other children played in the yard.

Suddenly, Frankie picked up a small rock and threw it. It struck Metro in the face and the familiar tears began. Arlene grabbed Frankie and threw him to the ground. Metro stood still for an instant and then enraged, he jumped on Frankie, flailing with his fists until he was pulled off by the teacher.

"Here! What's this about?" He held Metro who shook with fury.

"Frankie threw a stone and hit Metro in the face," Arlene blurted. "See! There's a bruise already." Then she took a hanky and wiped the dirt and tears from Metro's face.

Metro stood in angry confusion, surprised at his sister's attention. Then he drew away to stand by himself by a small willow tree near a barbed wire fence. But he was learning that aggression can be its own reward. Later that day, he was given another lesson. During the last recess Allen hit fly balls to the other boys and Metro watched.

"Can I catch the ball for you?" He asked suddenly but Allen didn't hear.

As he held the ball in his hand and prepared to swing the bat, Metro ran closer until he was right behind him. Metro called again but Allen still didn't hear so he took another step closer.

Suddenly the bat filled his vision and he heard a loud crack Blood spurted and he fell limply to the grass. It was a lucky blow for it didn't break any bones.

When he came to, Metro's mouth was full of blood and his face wet. Pain spread and the tears started, while through a red haze, he saw the teacher bend over him, his face etched with concern. Allen threw the bat to the ground and wrung his hands.

"I didn't mean it! I didn't even see him! All of a sudden he was there."

"It wasn't your fault." The teacher said and then Metro felt his body lifted and carried to the two-room house where the teacher lived. He was placed gently on a bed and the teacher fussed about. Metro lay in a daze, trying to understand the concern that was all about him. Behind the teacher, students crowded into the bedroom, their faces white, for Metro was soaked in blood. The teacher held a damp cloth to his nose and applied it gently.

"Hold it but don't blow! The bleeding should stop soon."

Metro nodded as Allen pushed his way through the children to stand beside Arlene who looked solemnly down at her baby brother.

"I'm sorry!" Allen said, his face white and sad.

"That's okay." Metro heard himself say as the tears slowly stopped. Then as he lay on the soft bed, a tiny smile crept onto his face.

"Try to sleep," the teacher said. "Don't move. Later you can go home. Then your mom will look after you."

Metro soon was alone in the wide bed with clean white sheets and a soft pillow. His body stopped trembling but his eyes were wide for he was trying to sort out the events. Then he nestled deeper into the pillow as the comfort of concern and warmth arrested for a very brief time, the normal harshness of his life. He was woken by his brother and sister.

"The horse's hitched up and we're ready to go," Allen said softly. Metro rose, his sister and brother on either side. He allowed Arlene to help him into the cart as the children stood in a semi-circle and watched. As Allen took the reins, the teacher approached.

"Don't trot the horse or the bleeding may start again."

Allen nodded and snapped the lines. The gelding began a shambling walk and the cart moved out of the school yard, past the red willows and along the narrow dirt track.

After they had gone a quarter of a mile, Allen turned to Metro.

"If we let the horse walk we won't be home before supper. Would you mind if we made him trot?"

Metro looked up puzzled. It was the first time he had been consulted concerning his well being. Then he slowly nodded his head and Allen snapped the reins. The gelding broke into a loose jointed trot and the cart bounced over holes and rough ground.

"Hold on tight!" Allen admonished. "Don't let the bumps jar you!"

When they were in the yard, Arlene helped Metro from the cart. Allen drove the horse to the barn while Vincent and Gerard approached, hot and dusty. Arlene solemnly told her mother what had happened and Gertie glared at Metro.

"You should watch!" Her voice rose to a whining pitch.

"It's your own tarned fault. Next time you be more careful."

The alien sense of caring was quickly dispelled by the familiar anxiety and guilt as Metro stood alone by the house.

Spring passed with the grass turning a brittle brown and the hot sun broiling down upon Vincent's back as he labored in the fields. The days grew shorter as autumn approached and he finished the summer fallow and hauled the dry hay, using a pitch fork and his aching muscles to unload it onto a stack. Gerard and Allen worked with their father under the hot sun and their youthful muscles grew hard and strong. When they worked together, there was a companionship for Vincent called them his two hired men and they grinned from the compliment. When the blisters broke on their palms they said nothing for it was all part of doing a man's job and a man never complained.

Arlene helped her mother in the kitchen, learning how to cook and bake but mainly sweeping the floor or washing dishes. Gerties hard face softened when they were together and she didn't carry on conversations with ghostly people of the past.

"I wonder what it'll be like?" Arlene asked dreamily one evening as she wiped a plate with a dish towel made from an old shirt.

"Oh." Gertie stopped for a moment and regarded the soapy dishes, her hands on the counter.

"You can work amongst the children. It'd be like having your own family but you won't have to have no husband."

"But every woman has a husband, doesn't she?"

Gertie's face hardened.

"Not the nuns. They don't have to. They pray all day and they don't have to submit to no man." She pushed a dish down hard into the water and vigorously washed it. "Husbands are always demanding things!"

Then she spread her arms wide, soaping dripping from her hands.

"Sure! And if you give 'em their way all the time. Sure! Then it's fine. But dare, and complain." Her face remained hard and Arlene's eyes widened.

Then Gertie's face softened.

"When you're a nun, you won't have to do what a man wants."

Arlene gazed at the dish in her hands, her mind filled with her mother's admonishment.

Vincent's friendship with his two older sons and Gertie's companionship with Arlene left Metro alone for he was too young to help. He played by himself or read from a few tattered books that had been brought home, wishing he was in school for it was still summer vacation. At times he sat in the living room and drew pictures on old scrap paper with a worn pencil stub. Soon all the scrap paper was gone and he wandered listlessly into the kitchen and looked up at his mother.

"Mom! I got nothing to draw on," he said forlornly.

"Yuh! And I can't help you." Gertie spread her arms wide in the gesture of helplessness. But as she returned to the stove Metro persisted. She snarled suddenly and Metro ducked, taking a quick backward step.

"Aw you! You and that tarned drawing,"

Arlene watched warily from the kitchen table, her hand suspended in mid-air as it held a plate she had been drying.

"That's all you ever think of!" Gertie yelled. "Tarned drawing! Only lazy people draw."

Metro wandered outside, guilty and forlorn for the desire to draw was strong.

One evening Vincent sat in the cool shadows on a bench near the house, his face contorting and his hands dirty, and folded in his lap. Metro approached timidly. He had a torn booklet in his hand; the adventures of Mickey Mouse and Goofy in the far off Never Never land of the city. He had read it many times and it had lost its wonder so he had turned to the last page and an advertisement. For five cents, a new booklet could be ordered.

"Dad! Can you buy me this?" He held the book up with the advertisement. Vincent ignored him, tired from the day's labors.

"Dad! Can you buy me this?" Metro looked up at his father, a serious pleading in his eyes. Vincent still didn't answer although Metro was two feet away and right in front of him.

Metro tried for a third time.

"Dad! Can you—"

"No!" Vincent yelled, enraged.

Metro froze, his face white.

"You and that tarned reading!" Vincent's face was red and ugly.

"What the heck do ya get from that anyway?" He yelled.

Metro stood very still, his breath caught in his lungs.

"I'll buy you an ice cream cone. There! You got something with that. Not that tarned reading." The words tumbled forth in an enraged torrent.

Slowly, the tears began their way down Metro's cheeks as he stared upwards at his father's anger. Then the explosive rage subsided and Vincent gazed down at his hands.

Metro turned and walked slowly to the soft grass by the house but some distance from his father. He sat in the shade and laid the tattered booklet beside him. The Mother Cat joined him, purring and rubbing against him while her kittens romped on the grass. Metro put his arm around her and watched the kittens through blurred, teary vision.


Grey, heavy clouds scudded across the sky as the seasons once again changed and the ground became hard as iron. Early frosts froze the water in the sloughs, a frigid blanket, covering the hibernating swamps. In the yard, gusts of wind blew shriveled leaves and a fine rain against the window. Inside, the airtight heater turned a dark orange as the fire heated the metal and the house. In the kitchen the family gathered around the table with the coal oil lamp casting deep shadows in the corners, for they had company.

Gertie's brother, Augustine, had loaded his wife and children onto his two-ton truck and driven the winding track through the hills to Vincent's farm. As the visitors gathered around the table, the conversation ebbed and flowed.

"I bought it in Berlin," Augustine talked of the truck he had driven with his two oldest children riding in the box. "It sure the hell can haul a load."

"Yuh! Maybe I can get you to haul my sheep," Vincent said for he had examined the new truck parked beside his ancient Chevrolet. If he was embarrassed, he didn't let it show. Gerard's face however, had become more pinched and whiter than usual.

Then, as the lamp threw its flickering shadows in the primitive kitchen, the conversation changed.

"What's that? Halloween?" Vincent asked, his jaw trembling.

"That's when all the ghosts come out and haunt people," Anna, Augustine's sixteen year-old daughter, answered.

"Oh Yuh! Now I remember," Vincent said and turned suddenly to Metro who stood by the table.

"You better watch out! Or the ghosts will get ya!"

Metro took a quick backward step, his eyes wide and face losing its color. Vincent grinned broadly, thinking it was the ghosts, that frightened the child.

"The ghosts will get ya!" He made a face inches from Metro and then laughed.

"I know a new game for Halloween," Anna said suddenly.

"What's that?" Gertie asked.

"You get a tub of water and put apples in it. Then someone tries to pick up an apple with his hands behind his back. It's called dunking and he can only use his mouth."

Arlene quickly got a tub and the table was cleared. Then water was poured into the tub and half a dozen apples floated on the surface. Anna turned to Metro, her eyes mischievous.

"Come! Little Metro. You try and get an apple."

Metro looked dubiously at the tub but his stomach rumbled with hunger. He nodded and then slowly climbed onto a stool, placing his hands behind him. As he lowered his head, he saw Gerard's cold, calculating stare. What he didn't see was that Anna had moved to stand directly behind him. Slowly he lowered his head, trusting in the strangers and his family.

Suddenly a rush of water hit his face and the hard tub bit into his throat. Anna had pushed down hard on the back of his head and as the water splashed he fell off the stool. His throat throbbed and he swallowed desperately. Then he saw his mother rocking back in her chair, spasms of insane laughter bubbling forth while she waved her hands in the air, her whole body shaking. And as Metro's shoulders shook with fright and pain, he heard a voice amongst the laughter.

"Aw, serves 'em right. He's always crying anyway," Arlene yelled while Gerard watched fascinated, a thin happy smile on his thin lips. Vincent's face turned red as laughter choked off his wind. He leaned forward in his chair, his face shaking and his eyes watering. The only one not to laugh was Augustine who knelt by Metro's side.

"It's okay. Don't cry," he said softly and then turned to his daughter. "Oh why do you have to be so mean?"

A silence settled down then with Gertie and Vincent controlling their laughter. Anna bent again to Metro, her face red from mirth and the effort in making her voice appear normal and persuasive.

"Come on Little Metro, I didn't mean it."

"Aw never mind him. He's always crying anyway," Gertie snapped but Anna looked up, a mischievous glint in her eyes.

"Come Little Metro. I promise not to do it again. We'll let you have an apple," She said soothingly. Metro stared up at her through wet eyes as his shoulders heaved and his chest constricted and filled with pain.

"I promise. We'll be real nice to you if you dunk, for an apple."

Augustine didn't notice Anna's wink or that Gertie grew quiet as she watched intently. As hunger rumbled in his stomach, Metro again stood on the stool and slowly lowered his head with his hands behind his back. As he reached hungrily for a floating apple, he glanced sideways at his mother. A bright light shone from her eyes as she watched, fascinated. Then she winked and nodded her head quickly.

A sudden spasm of fear shot, through Metro's body as desperately he tried lifting his head.

It was too late. The same sudden rush of water came and the same hot pain hit his throat as Anna put all her weight behind her hands, forcing his head beneath the water. This time Metro didn't fall off the stool. As soon as Anna released him, he jumped down, gasping for air, water and tears streaming from his face. He ran into the living room while, amid the raucous laughter, he heard Augustine yelling at his daughter.

"That's enough! Oh why do you have to be so mean to someone smaller?" He took a threatening step forward. "Do you want me to get the strap?"

Anna's laughter died quickly, caught in her throat as Augustine turned and followed Metro into the living room. Metro heard his mother's voice again.

"Aw, leave him. Serves him right for crying all the time."

Augustine ignored his sister and knelt beside Metro who stood by the heater, his body trembling.

"Don't cry, Little Metro," he said soothingly. "Come! We'll go back to the kitchen. I'll make sure they don't hurt you no more."

But Metro refused to believe his uncle a second time.


Metro squinted at the chart on the blackboard. It was twenty feet away and all he could see were the first two rows of letters. The rest dissolved into a sea of blurry grey and white. Beside him the traveling nurse stood, her hand on his shoulder.

"Try the top again."

"R-A-K," He read quickly but when it came to the second row the reading was slower. When his eyes were on the third he only got one letter and then was silent, hunching his shoulders, waiting for the blow. But as the tears came, the nurse only patted his head, wondering why he ducked instinctively. Then she wrote in a note book, her anger growing.

When the day was finished, she approached Gerard who stood at the rear of the room, his face pinched and his eyes narrow. The teacher followed and stood beside the nurse.

"I thought I told you to tell your parents that he needs glasses a year ago."

Gerard looked down at his boots. Then he cast Metro, a spiteful, sideways look. The nurse didn't notice the look but Metro stood by a desk, his eyes widening and his breath becoming shallow and rapid.

"Well, you better tell your parents that if he doesn't have glasses next time I'm here, I'll report you to the authorities." The nurse's voice was harsh in the silent school house.

"That must be why he couldn't see those words on the black board," the teacher suddenly said. "It wasn't because he was stubborn."

"Remember! He better have glasses by the time I come back, or else!" The nurse said to Gerard. He nodded quickly, the pinched complaining look more pronounced than ever.

Then he left with his brothers and sister as the nurse watched from a window.

"Boy! That sure makes my blood boil. I can't understand why they wouldn't get him glasses. Surely they can't be that poor."

"I don't know," the teacher said slowly. "Gerard, the oldest, brings along a twenty-two to shoot rabbits with. And at the Christmas Concert he had a violin. You'd think if they could afford a violin for him and a guitar for Allen they could afford glasses for Metro."

Then he gazed out through the window as the sleigh left the yard with Metro sitting in the rear.

"It's strange," he added softly. "He seems talented. He could read when he first came to school and he's way ahead of the other boy. But if I speak loudly, he ducks and starts to cry. If I speak softly, he's only too eager too read or write.

The nurse gazed thoughtfully at the teacher for an instant.

"It's hard to understand these people sometimes. It seems the only reason they have kids is for free labor on the farm."

"I met his parents," the teacher said. "They're a strange pair. His father makes faces all the time and his mother seems half crazy. And Metro never runs to her like a normal child. He always keeps his distance."

The teacher looked down at the floor and sighed deeply.

"There nothing we can do. They're his natural parents and it's their right to do what they want," he added.

As the two adults talked in the school, Gerard clucked to the horses and glared at Metro.

"Tarn you! You can read when you want to. You just pretend not to see, so you can get attention."

Metro sat at the rear of the sleigh, his eyes downcast.

When the horses were in the barn and the family gathered in the kitchen, Gerard stood before his mother and recounted the day's events. Vincent sat by the table, his face contorting and his eyes hard. Metro stood by the stove and said nothing, his body trembling.

"She says that if we don't get those tarned glasses, she'll report us to the authorities," Gerard said vehemently. "But as far as I'm concerned he can see. He just pretends not to just so he can get attention."

"Vincent!" Gertie yelled. Metro winced, his breath caught in his lungs.

"What are we gonna do? If we don't get them tarned glasses, the police might come."

"Gosh darn it, the heck anyway," Vincent grumbled. "I guess I'll have to sell a steer. How much do those tarned things cost?"

"The nurse said twenty dollars," Gerard snapped.

"Twenty dollars! Gosh darn it! I could buy a gun for that."

"But we have to," Gertie whined. "The police might come."

At supper, with Vincent's face contorting and the food dropping from his mouth, anger crackled in the room. Metro felt the hot tears start again for Vincent kept glaring at him and if he turned away, he saw his mother chewing rapidly and the cold, calculating stare of Gerard. In Allen or Arlene's eyes there was no sympathy for what they saw was normal. So they ate, Allen spreading chunks of butter on his bread and Vincent chewing with his mouth open. Finally Metro reached for the butter.

"Take it easy on that tarned butter!" Vincent yelled. "I just bought it and it better last."

"He doesn't care. He just wastes and wastes until it's gone. Then he's happy," Gertie whined in her grating singsong.

"You're supposed to spread it so you can't even see it," Vincent yelled again and then glared at Metro's plate. It was still full for the food was straw. The familiar order followed.

"Now eat!"

Metro forced the food into his mouth and down his throat, fighting the rising nausea.

That evening he crept away to bed early and the thoughts and images swirled in his confused and frightened mind.

"God! Why can't I see better? Maybe if I could they wouldn't get so mad," Metro prayed with hot tears on his face. He stared at the white, frozen window and a deep congested pain settled in his chest. But the God the family prayed to didn't seem to hear.

As he lay on his cot, his face turned to the ghostly patterns of frost on the window, sleep wouldn't come. When his parents entered the bedroom, he lay quietly while his mother nagged his father.

"Oh why did you want more children?"

"I never wanted no more children," Vincent snorted.

Metro lay, afraid to close his eyes for the image of the horse would come and he would stare at the frost-covered window with his heart pounding. In desperation he turned on his stomach and pressed his eyes into the pillow. This time he saw snakes, a pit of writhing snakes, that made his breathing rapid and his body rigid. But instinctively he forced himself to breathe slowly in and out and the image began to clear. The snakes writhed to the outside and eventually all he could see was their wriggling tails as they left the image. Then wonderingly, he saw a gentle scene with cattle grazing in a green pasture and in the distance, snow capped mountains. He lay still, trying to preserve the image and understand what it meant. His breathing slowed and he didn't feel the stab of fear anymore, only a gentle, peaceful serenity.

He could never recapture the image, but he never forgot it.

Next morning he was late in rising and missed breakfast. As the other children were in the kitchen, he sat by the heater in the living room and slowly pulled on his clothes. His body was gripped by a great, lethargy and his life was in slow motion. He saw his hand reach slowly for a sock and then rest on his thigh as he stared off into the distance.

Suddenly, he heard Gertie's whining voice.

"Just go and leave him! Serves him right if he's too lazy to get up in time."

A sudden spasm shot through Metro's body and he grabbed a sock. But it was too late.

"Vincent! Go in there and give 'em one!"

Metro desperately pulled on the other sock just as Vincent stomped into the room, his face contorting and terrible to behold. He grabbed Metro by the arm and began beating him with an open palm. Metro's shoulder went numb as the hollow, muffled sound of a heavy hand hitting bare flesh filled the house. Gertie muttered to herself in the kitchen but with the sound of the blows a small warning bell went off and she dropped a dish cloth and ran into the room.

"Vincent! That's enough!"

The urgency in her voice penetrated the enraged madness and Vincent straightened. He shoved Metro away and Metro collapsed on the floor. Vincent turned and went into the kitchen, pulling on his coat and boots. Once outside he walked rapidly to the barn, the anger still in him. But when he reached it the rage had dissipated and he began whistling a nameless tune.

In the living room Metro climbed back onto the chair, the feeling slowly coming back to his shoulders and neck. His chest rose and fell in the familiar pattern as he fought for breath. After a while the heaving stopped and only the tears remained until even they were gone. Metro slowly got off the chair and hunching his shoulders, walked into the kitchen. He eyed the bread and butter that was still on the table but he came too close to Gertie.

"Serves you right!" Her quick backhand caught him on the back of the head.

"Serves you right for being so tarned stinky lazy. You'll just have to wait 'til dinner," Gertie snarled as she removed the bread and butter from the table.

"Next time you know better than to be so tarned, stinky, lazy!"


It wasn't long before Metro sat in a strange office with an eye chart, while a strange man in a white gown fussed about, fitting a pair of wire rimmed glasses. The traveling nurse's threat had borne fruit and Vincent had sold a steer and driven the forty miles east to Saskatoon, while his face contorted and he glared at Metro. Gertie had sat in the ancient sedan, her face white from powder and her mouth hard and thin. Metro had made himself as small as possible between his parents and the anxiety and guilt had made his stomach knot and his vision blurry.

In all, the glasses along with fuel and meals cost forty dollars. On the way home Gertie turned to Metro.

"And don't you dare and break them. Or else! And don't wear them outside!"

Metro stared at just above the dashboard for Gertie had discovered that if he sat on a pillow and could see where he was going, he didn't throw up

A couple of days later when Gerard told her Metro had been stubborn and didn't want to read in school, she found an old grade one reader and made him sit by the living room table. Metro's shoulders began shaking and the tears glistened as he waited for the beating.

"Read!" Gertie snarled, her face white at the sight of the child that appeared to defy her. Metro hunched his shoulders as his tears blurred his vision.

"Read! Or I'll get the strap!"

Metro began to shake violently and Gertie gnashed her teeth. Then she ran to the kitchen where Vincent had hung the razor strap. Metro made himself as small as possible, his face wet and his shoulders hunched, waiting for the blows.

"Read!" Gertie laid the strap across her knees. A heavy silence deepened and then the door slammed as Vincent entered the kitchen, his face hot and dusty.

When Metro didn't respond Gertie swung wildly, reining blows down on his head and shoulders as he cowered in the chair. When his head and shoulders were numb, Gertie's arm grew tired and she stopped. Metro still felt the sharp sting of the leather and pain spread to his whole body. The tears came faster and he felt a heavy, constricted pain in his chest as he fought for breath but he didn't cry out.

"Now read!" The command came again as Gertie rested with the strap on her lap. As the minutes ticked by and Metro sat very still and silent, her rage welled up again. Again blows reined down upon his neck, head and shoulders until he was numb with pain and the tears found new streams on his face. Then he lost feeling in his upper body. Still, he wouldn't read.

Finally, Gertie tired and rose from the chair, the strap still in her hand.

"Oh what a tarned miserable child!" She turned to Vincent and her whining voice made him wince.

"Oh! Why did you want more children?"

"I never wanted no more children," He said disgustedly.

The beatings continued and when Gerard and Allen played catch or Arlene played with her doll, Gertie would sit with the strap on her knees and a book in front of Metro. At times he would look at the warm sunshine through the window but Gertie wouldn't let him go until she was too tired or frustrated. Then he would sit outside with his shoulders hunched and his face wet while the Mother Cat rubbed against his leg and he wished he was her kitten.

The struggle continued through spring until the grass was high and the wind warm.

There was one exception. One beautiful sunny day when the countryside was filled with serenity Gertie sat beside Metro and pushed the book to him. She was in a rare good mood and maybe it was the weather but the harshness was gone from her voice and she had neglected to bring the strap.

"Metro. Come! Will you read for me?" She asked quietly.

Metro read quickly about a little calf that ran away from his mother and how happy he was to get home. Gertie was surprised at the quickness and ease with which he read.

"If you read like that I won't hit you with the strap no more," she smiled and Metro felt an alien and inexplicable sensation of both embarrassment and wonder.

That was the only time Gertie was in a good mood. After that she didn't force the child to sit until she felt her world closing in and the ghostly people in her mind came alive.

Then the command "read!" was harsh and Metro hunched his shoulders and waited for the blows. Gertie swung the strap with a practiced arm until her breath was rapid and a silence would follow until the next command and the inevitable beating.

One day Vincent came into the living room and contorted his face, wiping his mouth with a heavy hand.

"He can't read! His glasses are all smeared from all that crying and he can't see," he announced.

That only infuriated Gertie who blamed Vincent for giving the child an excuse. But Metro never gave in, if it could be said he consciously defied his mother. At times when he couldn't sleep, late at night, he heard his parents whispering in the darkness. Then he lay with his body rigid and his eyes on the window. At other times he would hear his parents arguing and the harsh words caused more anxiety, for at seven he didn't understand anger, only the result.

On a late afternoon when the shadows began to slant and song birds sang in the willows, Metro sat with Frankie on the school steps, waiting for Gerard to bring the cart and horse from the barn. Both boys were quiet until Frankie sighed deeply and looked at Metro. His left eye was discolored and his cheek swollen.

"I wish I had a different father," Frankie spoke softly, his eyes glistening.

Metro gazed at Frankie and then sighed deeply. He looked down at the ground by the steps and then back up.

"Yuh I wish I had a different mother too."

Frankie met Metro's eyes and through the misty tears they understood each other.

"My mother ain't so bad," Frankie continued sadly. "But my father He beats me up all the time."

"Yuh," Metro answered with another sigh. "My mother beats me all the time too. I don't know why."

The two boys sat in thoughtful, anguished silence for a moment. Metro turned and looked at Frankie again.

"Maybe if I had your mother and you had my father, maybe it wouldn't be so bad all the time. At least my father doesn't hit me too much, as long as I stay outa his way."

Metro put his hand on Frankie's shoulder and the boys sat silently together until the jingle of harness told Metro it was time to go.


Eventually the struggle between Gertie and Metro generalized to more things than reading. Gertie cooked carrots in boiling water and they were tasteless but it was the only way she knew. When Metro refused to eat them, the battle over reading became the battle of the carrots and he sat, his shoulders hunched while the rest ate dessert, pie or cake and at times Saskatoon berries. Metro would stare at the carrots while Gertie gave his helping to Arlene or Allen.

"You eat them carrots and you can have some pie," she would say. Pie was the epitome of wealth to a family that measured richness in food so the withholding of dessert was nearly as great a punishment as a beating.

Still, he wouldn't eat the carrots. One time when the family had finished eating and he was left alone with the carrots on his plate in the kitchen, Metro noticed that the slop pail was only two feet from where he sat. Slowly he turned to see if Gertie was watching from the living room. Then he picked up the boiled carrots and quickly threw them into the pail. They sank into the nauseating mixture and were gone. Then he sat quietly, waiting until Gertie returned to the kitchen.

"Now that's more like it. If you eat them carrots like that from now on you can leave the table right away."

At other times when he sat by the living room table and Gertie placed a scribbler in front of him, he relied on the same subterfuge.

"You better write some thing before I come back, or else!" Would be the order and when Gertie went outside, he would write one letter.

When she was back she would notice that he had written on the paper.

"That's better," she would say and Metro avoided a beating.

Finally the struggle that neither could win came to an end. One day, when the kitchen was quiet, Vincent entered, his face twitching.

"We're moving!" His head jerked sideways in excitement and his face twitched. He stood in the middle of the room, rocking back on his heels with his thumbs hooked into his bib trousers.

"What! Oh no!" Gertie jumped up from her chair, her face white. "We can't!"

"Sure we can!" Vincent's snapped. "I talked to a man who said there's a quarter of land for sale north of Prince Albert. He said, if I hurry I can still have it."

"Oh no!"

"Well, what the heck! This land's no good no more. Almost everyone's moved off and I can't get no good, crops."

"But there's bears and wolves up there." Gertie remembered the tales of the north. "There can't be no crops there. It's all bush."

"Like heck there can't. The man said there was good crops."

"But how do you know?"

"Because I know!" Vincent held his hand in mid-air for an instant and then dropped it in a chopping motion.

As Gertie bit her lip in frenzied anxiety the family gathered in a semi-circle and stared at Vincent.

"Oh no! What about the garden?" Gertie sat down holding her head in her hands, tears flowing down her face.

"The heck with the garden," Vincent exclaimed and the argument lasted long into the night with Metro listening in frightened silence.

Vincent had built a stubborn shell about himself. No amount of nagging could sway him and the family began planning the move. Metro silently gathered a scarred and broken toy truck and his toy plow made from an old chunk of iron along with an old discarded teddy bear.

He waited amidst the excited speculation of his father and brothers and the whining, frenzied anxiety of his mother and her fear of the land of "bears and wolves."

# Twenty-two

The red two-ton truck stood by the greying, tar-paper shack, ready for the long trek north. Its tires bore the family's worldly goods, beds, cupboards and household utensils, representing the years of toil, sweat and disappointment. And deep within Vincent's breast a boyish excitement simmered. He had gone north by train, and further into debt in order to buy one hundred and sixty acres of land. Then he had sold most of his cattle and all his sheep and a second trip had been made with four horses. A third would be necessary before all the machinery and an ancient iron-wheeled Case Tractor would be at the new farm.

Gertie stood beside the truck, looking about the yard, her hands clasped together in agitation.

"Where's that Mother Cat?" she demanded. "Metro! Find the cat."

The cat, fearful of the strange truck and adults had melted into the underbrush with her kittens. Metro searched for her near the willows by a small slough but after awhile gave up. Then he thought of another urgent matter. He ran to behind the house and gathered his toys, bringing them to the truck and gazing uncertainly up at the top. He looked at his mother, the toys held in his hands.

"Aw, go away with that! I got no time for toys!" Gertie snapped.

"Gerard! Did you nail that door tight on the dog house?"

She was rewarded by a loud whine from the dog, lost and frightened in the new confinement on the truck.

"But Mom!" Metro persisted.

"Aw, go away with that squach." Gertie dismissed him with a quick wave of her hand. She had begun describing things of no value with a word she had made up.

Metro stood uncertainly, his eyes filling. Then slowly, he placed his toy plow and scarred truck on the grass near the house. He clutched the worn Teddy Bear with one eye hanging from a thread and waited by the truck until it was time to go.

Augustine turned to the boy and Gertie.

"We might as well take the little one with us. No?"

Gertie nodded in agitation as Arlene got into the ancient Chevrolet with her father and brothers. Once Metro had climbed into the truck cab Augustine turned to him.

"We are going on a long, trip. No?"

Augustine hadn't forgotten the dunking at Halloween and he puzzled over his sister's cruelty to her youngest child. Metro looked up at his uncle, his eyes wide while he clutched the Teddy Bear.

"And you even brung along your teddy bear. No?" Augustine laughed. "Now we got every thing, except the cats. But you can get more cats once you're there. Not so?"

"Yuh! He got all his toys." Gertie smiled at her brother, the hard brittle lines of her face softening for the briefest of instants. Metro sat between the adults and said nothing as he gazed at just above the dashboard, his pillow giving him enough height to see.

The trip was a kaleidoscope of moving scenery. At times Metro dozed but mostly he watched, wide-eyed as the houses and fields sped quickly by. Once they were through a small city Augustine called Prince Albert, they entered a land of tall trees and dark, shadowy glades and Gertie's mouth hardened into a thin line. But just as soon as the forest started, it ended. Farmhouses and barns stood by the road and Augustine chuckled.

"See! We are not going into the wilderness. There are lots of farms here."

The thin hard line remained on Gertie's face as Metro gazed in wonder for he could see more trees through the window at one glance than he had known all his life. Once they had left the gravel highway they were bouncing down a narrow, tree-lined dirt road with clouds of dust billowing out behind.

"This is it!" Augustine said suddenly.

He nodded at a barbed wire fence and a line of trees separating two quarter sections of land. Then the truck bounced over a bridge, and a dry creek bed stretched away into a rocky, wooded pasture. He turned the truck onto a dirt track, leading to a yard and a three-room tar-paper shack. South of the house and just beyond some poplars, an open field lay black, and fallow.

After the truck had bounced into the yard Metro clambered down after his mother and stood, looking at the small poplars and willows that were to the west and south. To the northwest was a large stand of poplar trees and beyond, on the other side of the road they had traveled, was a large forest of evergreens. Augustine pulled the boards loose from the dog house and the dog jumped quickly onto the grass and relieved himself. Then he began running and sniffing about. Gertie walked into the house and then stood in the kitchen. A bare board floor, dirty and dusty was, beneath her worn shoes and she gazed at the filthy walls and cracked molding along the floor. She went into the living room and her face hardened. Both rooms were twelve by twelve feet and the wall paper was cracked and peeling. Metro followed and poked about in the dust and filth. Suddenly he stooped and picked up a broken toy car. It was plastic and the sides were cracked but he held it in his hand while with the other, he clutched his Teddy Bear. Gertie walked into the third room. It was twelve by seven feet and just wide enough for a bed to be placed wall-to-wall. Metro couldn't find anything more of interest for the house had been picked clean except for discarded and broken things.

Gertie walked tiredly back into the kitchen as Augustine stood outside and mentally calculated how long it would take to unload. He wiped his forehead and walked toward the house as Gertie sat on one of the two broken and discarded chairs.

"So much work." She looked at the filth on the walls and thought of the sweat it had taken to make her former house liveable. Finally, came the familiar spreading of her arms.

"And for what?" she muttered just as Augustine entered.

He looked into the second room where the children would have to sleep until they built extra rooms. He thought too, of the work but he didn't mention it as he rejoined his sister in the kitchen, sitting on the second chair that protested with a loud squeak. He settled down carefully, fearful it might collapse.

"Don't worry. Once you get every thing settled in it'll be okay. No?"

"Yuh! And it'll take so much work," Gertie muttered again as Metro wandered into the room, holding the discarded, broken toy and his worn Teddy Bear.

"But it's gonna be a nice home once every thing's cleaned up," Augustine persisted. "Wait 'til you got more rooms. Then you'll have a nice house."

"Yuh." The word was a sigh as Metro wandered outside and watched the dog run about, sniffing for rabbits. He still clutched his worn Teddy Bear and the broken toy as he wondered how the Mother Cat and her kittens were.

The heat rose in waves from the freshly tilled earth as the four horses walked slowly from one end of the field to the other. Vincent rode the ancient seed drill and wiped perspiration from his forehead although it was not yet nine a.m. As he held the reins in his dirt encrusted hands he could see his four children walking through the pasture on their way to school, three and a half miles east. Gerard was in the lead while Arlene and Allen took up the middle. A hundred feet back and losing ground was Metro.

Vincent turned his attention back to the field for it needed just as much backbreaking work as the ones he had left behind. And a bushel of wheat sold for the same price as before but still he was filled with a boyish happiness. He cast an eye at the ascending sun and whistled a nameless tune.

In the kitchen, Gertie washed the floors on her hands and knees, her lips moving constantly. She stopped suddenly and rose to a kneeling position her arms spread wide.

"Sure! And it's easy to say Move. But who gets stuck with all the work?" She bent back to the floor then, her lips compressed as she continued to mutter.

"And dare and complain."

Perspiration dripped from her forehead and she reached a soapy hand upwards to wipe it away and then bent again, putting her weight behind the cloth while the mutter never ceased.

Gertie and Vincent weren't the only ones to know fatigue. In a neighbor's pasture, Metro ran for a while, the shambling jog helping him catch his brothers and sister. But when he caught up he slowed to a walk with his legs cramped and heavy. He tried stretching them and taking giant steps but still he fell behind until he had to jog again.

Gerard turned and glared, his eyebrows knitted close together.

"Hurry up! Serves you right if you're tired. You're better off not going to school anyway."

He continued his youthful stride that made the miles pass easily, for he was sixteen and almost a man.

Metro glanced tiredly at the tall spruce to his left and the large white poplars interspersed amongst them. At any other time, he would have stopped and admired the trees for the spruce towered ninety feet. But as he glanced upwards to the crowns he noticed a herd of cattle and a bull walking out from beneath them. Gertie's constant anxiety and admonishments about not playing in the pasture near the bull came and he ran to keep up. When he was out of breath, they finally came to a fence, which Gerard stepped over effortlessly after lowering the top wire with his hand. Allen was next and then Arlene. When Metro reached the fence they were already fifty feet away and he scrambled under the bottom wire. When he entered a large yard, a big black dog barked fiercely while a farmer waved from a pole corral. Metro ran when he saw the dog for again he felt an unreasoning fear. But the dog only barked and soon he was past, still trying to catch his brothers and sister.

When they reached the road, which would take them to a railway track leading to the tiny hamlet and school, Gerard turned and glared once more. Then he halted, holding his books in one hand. When he saw the sweat glistening on the child's face, his lips compressed and his face whitened.

"Hurry up! You're just lazy, that's all. You could walk faster if you wanted too. You're just too tarned lazy to try."

Metro avoided the icy glare but he had no defense against the cascade of contempt and condemnation. He looked at the railway tracks shimmering in the distance and the tall Byzantine Church spire which could be seen just beyond a poplar bluff. There was still at least two miles to go but Gerard didn't give him a chance to rest, walking rapidly as soon as he caught up.

"Hurry up!" he snarled over his shoulder. "Or we'll be late for school."

Ordinarily he would have driven the cart but Vincent had kept only four horses to work the fields. At the time seeding took precedence over children riding to school and it actually helped toughen them. But Metro's calves ached fiercely and he gasped for air. The books he carried in a leather bag grew heavier and heavier and the strap bit into his shoulder like a hot iron.

As the miles slowly passed, Gerard occasionally called a halt and waited for him to catch up. And always when he was close, the cold, calculating glare and harsh words would greet Metro. Finally, his face began to glisten from the shame and humiliation of being too lazy to walk fast.

It was less than an hour before they were walking down the hamlet's narrow street. Despite his great fatigue Metro looked about at the store and the Café with the large yellow sign hanging from two chains. Gerard slowed, realizing they still had time, for other children were walking or riding bicycles to the white, four-roomed school at the other end of the hamlet. They came abreast of a boy Gerard's age who stopped and glanced at the four tired, dusty children. Gerard wore a denim bib trousers when most teenagers would have refused to do so.

The boy didn't say anything about Gerard's clothes or the outdated cloth caps he and Allen wore. Instead he matched strides with them as they approached the school.

"You new around here?"

Gerard took his eyes off the dusty road in front of him, glancing at the boy.

"Yuh!" He shifted his books to his other arm. "We just moved here." He didn't mention the fact it was late May and difficult to adjust when it was nearly exam time.

"Oh," the boy said and then glanced at Metros glistening face. "Your little brother looks all pooped out. How far ya walk?"

"Only three and a half miles. But it's his own tarned fault."

Gerard turned and glared at the seven year-old. He saw nothing wrong with venting his anger and contempt in front of a stranger.

"Serves him right, anyway. He only pretends he's tired."

The boy noticed the tears in Metro's eyes. Then he looked back at Gerard who walked steadily, his lips compressed. The boy kept his thoughts to himself while Metro stared up at the foreboding edifice that would be school for less than two months.


As the early leaves deepened into the dark green of late spring, Metro's view of the world became more and more confused. When the teacher, an overweight, middle-aged woman who spoke loudly, demanded he read, he hunched his shoulders and sat cringing, waiting for a blow. The teacher reported that the child "cries and cries" and came to the conclusion that there was something mentally wrong with him.

Metro would cry at the sound of a loud voice and instead of roughhousing with the other boys he preferred to be alone with a book. But reading on his own meant nothing, Gerard told Vincent and Gertie. Only lazy people read for pleasure and it was a waste of time. Besides, if he wasn't retarded, he would do better in school.

Gertie began to treat Metro like he was truly retarded and although he was nearly eight, he allowed her to tie his shoes and to dress and undress him. When Arlene tied his shoes in school, he stoically bore the mockery of the other children. He existed in two worlds; one in which he constantly heard, "You're just as stupid as Metro," the other where he read any book he could find. He still drew pictures on scraps of paper with a worn pencil stub, living in a hazy reality of dreams and stifled creativity.

When neighbors came to visit, he didn't resist as Gertie carried him about like a two year-old, feeding him while he sat listlessly on her knee. When he refused to eat, she tickled him in the ribs until he opened his mouth for the spoon and the food that was straw.

One day in late summer, when school was out, he wandered about the pasture until he came upon a bush of ripe choke cherries. He sat in the warm sun with another "Mother Cat" called Tabby, rubbing against his side. He stuffed himself with cherries, happy in the warm sun, away from the cold, implacable glare of Gerard and Gertie's incessant mutter.

When he could eat no more, he returned to the house. He stopped and looked at his parents who sat at the kitchen table. Two dishes were before them, with the remnants of strawberries and cream still clinging to the sides.

"Here!" Gertie suddenly said, in a rare good mood. "This is for you." She gave Metro a bowl, filled with strawberries and covered with cream.

Metro quickly pushed a chair to the table and spooned up the rich cream and berries. Vincent was in a rare good mood too, and he noticed the brown stains on Metro's teeth.

"You got choke cherries all over your mouth." He said in a condescending manner for it wasn't often, he had a chance.

"Yeach!" He opened his mouth and let his face contort at the same time. He leaned forward, his face only inches from Metro's.

"Yeach! Them choke cherries must make the cream taste sour. How can you eat 'em?"

Metro couldn't ignore the open mouth and facial contortions only inches from his face. And slowly a small, determined anger grew. He stopped eating, filled with revulsion.

"Yuh!" Gertie suddenly joined in the fun.

"Metro must know better then to eat choke cherries before cream."

As Vincent's tongue protruded and he emitted the repulsive word, "Yeach!" one more time, Metro looked straight at him.

"You're just mad because you ate yours already and I still got mine."

"What!" Vincent jerked his face back and glared.

"Why you!" His face lost its ruddy color and turned white, the whiteness of rage.

"You shut up!" he, yelled and then turned to Gertie whose mouth had set in the hard thin line.

"Where's the strap?"

Metro jumped from the chair, tears starting in his eyes. He left the bowl on the table and ran to behind the log chicken coop, his face to the grey walls. The Mother Cat rubbed against his leg but he ignored her as a battle raged in his mind.

He was angry at his father but greater than the anger was guilt and shame.

Guilt and confusion were a major part of Metro's life for no matter how hard he tried, he was always in the way or guilty of some crime. Whenever he came too close to Gertie, her hand would snake out in a wicked back hand, catching him on the head or shoulder. Metro was eight years old but he still wet his bed and when he woke in the morning and felt the cold, damp sheets, he would lie until the last possible moment when he heard Gertie yell. Then he would cover the cot with a blanket praying she wouldn't notice and go off to school in wet, soiled underwear.

In reading and art, Metro was years ahead of the others but in other subjects he lagged far behind until he lay in his cot and prayed feverishly to the unseen God. When he had brought home his report card, it had indicated that he had been passed on credit. He had failed three subjects and would have to pick them up the following year or repeat grade two. It was enough to keep Gertie from bringing out the strap but still Metro lay awake at night, in fearful confusion.

That fall the children attended a different school, three and a half miles west. Vincent bought three old, rusty bicycles and made a seat from an old plank on the back of Gerard's. Metro rode to school, clutching the back of his brother's jacket while Gerard vented his frustrated shame at being poor.

"Gosh tarn it anyway!" he spat the words loudly as he peddled along a tree-lined road. Golden, red leaves fluttered to the ground and the fine scent of autumn was in the air but he didn't notice.

"I'm not gonna peddle you next year. You can walk for all I care!" he yelled.

"I don't care if you never go to school. I'm not gonna peddle you no more. You shouldn't be going anyway. You just haven't got it. You can't even pass your grades."

While Gerard peddled and carried on his tirade, Metro hung onto his jacket and wondered grimly what the first day of school would bring. And if he expected a continuation of his hazy, anxiety-ridden existence, he wasn't wrong.

Gerard parked his bike, turned to Metro and snapped, "Come on! I'll explain to the teacher."

Metro gazed up at Pete, the grade one and two teacher.

"He's passed on credit," Gerard said contemptuously. "But if I were you, I'd just fail him now and get it over with. He just hasn't got it."

The teacher grinned and nodded and that was how Metro failed grade two. But Gerard's disgusted manner, of speaking, told Pete more than just about grades. He was a teacher who not only believed in corporal punishment, he relished it. But at first he made sure the child didn't have parents who would object to the heavy stick he kept constantly on top of his desk. And Metro wasn't the only child Pete knew he had in total control for later that day Johnny was brought to school by his grandmother.

"He's retarded! So whip 'em real good." The old woman stood before the grinning teacher.

"That's the only way he'll mind. If he gets stubborn, use the strap!"

Metro was seated next to the child who was truly mentally handicapped and both were treated the same. It wasn't long before a hand would suddenly go up and a child would tell Pete that Johnny had been swearing at himself again. Pete's eyes would light up, joyously as, he dragged the child to the front of the room and beat him with the stick as he cried piteously.

One afternoon, a child sitting behind Metro took a small pair of scissors and clipped some of his hair. Metro did the same to the child in front.

"Teacher! Metro cut my hair!" The words caused a sudden, electric stillness in the classroom. Metro's face went white.

"Where? I can't see it!" Pete demanded, as he stood over the child. Then after running his fingers through her hair he turned triumphantly to Metro.

"Oh! Now I see it." A sudden grin spread across his face and he grabbed Metro by an arm and dragged him to the front of the class. He made him hold out his hands and then he swung the stick, the loud smack of wood on flesh shattering the stillness.

Metro's eyes were full of hot salty tears but he didn't cry out. He dumbly obeyed the teacher who gleefully cried, "The other one!" before each blow. Metro's hands and wrists went numb but still he stuck out his hand, waiting for the blow.

As the hot pain shot up Metro's arms, the room swam in front of him. But the most painful part was seeing the other children watching in happy fascination and finally disappointment as Pete tired and shoved him away.

On other occasions, Pete would call him to the front of the class and demand who had spilled water. Or it would be any other reason and Metro would stand dumbly before the teacher, fighting the tears and the sudden knot of terror that twisted his stomach. Pete would grin as an unfathomable light shone from his eyes. Again, Metro saw enjoyment and expectancy in the other children's eyes. And when Pete would order him to sit down with, "You don't even know what's going on," he saw disappointment, for the children knew no better and truly enjoyed seeing him beaten.

He also suffered because of Gertie and Vincent's, boorish manners. At lunch, when Johnny complained he was hungry, Metro pushed a plain brown cake forward and Johnny greedily stuffed it into his mouth. Suddenly a boyish voice came from behind Metro.

"Don't eat that, Johnny. Metro's mother made it!"

Johnny immediately vomited the cake onto his desktop, the half-chewed food sitting on the varnished wood, sticky and unwanted. Metro felt the waves of laughter come at him and also the hot tears of humiliation.

Pete looked up slightly annoyed but he said nothing for he was busy biting into a large sandwich he had taken from a brown bag. As the children turned to other things and Pete chewed convulsively, Metro sat quietly. His eyes were misty and bright as he gazed at the pile of uneaten cake that congealed on the desktop.

# Twenty-three

Another winter came, with the wind howling down from the arctic and driving all wild creatures south or deep within dens or thickets. The children switched from bicycles to a horse-drawn sleigh and occasionally, weather permitting, Gerard drove the ancient Chevrolet. The sedan needed constant attention and at times when it had been especially cold, a pan of glowing coals was set under the engine so it would start.

Gerard was well aware of the amused glances when they puttered down the village's main street and parked at the school. He was also aware of his family's standing in the community and he bore the resentment and frustration deep within.

At first, a few neighbors visited curious about the family that had joined them. But Gertie's agitated stories of her childhood soon discouraged them until she would look sadly out the window on a Sunday afternoon and exclaim, "I wish someone would come for a visit."

Whenever she complained how hard life was, Gerard would frown and his thin lips compressed even more. At times he vented his shame to Arlene or Allen.

"Don't encourage her to tell those tarned stories. Don't even listen. They're not even true anyway."

At other times when she mispronounced a word, Allen would taunt her and demand, "Say it!" When she tried, he and Gerard would laugh and demand again and again that she say the word correctly. Gertie bore their mockery silently although her face would whiten and at times glisten.

Arlene was treated roughly too but it was due more to Gertie and Vincent's own childhoods rather than a deliberate attempt to humiliate.

When the warm spring sun had turned the snow to slush and after tender green grass sprouted, Arlene and Metro played with a new batch of kittens near the shop. Suddenly Vincent slammed the screen door and left the house, walking purposely toward them.

"Arlene!" he ordered. "Catch a bunch of them kittens. Leave about three and put the rest in a pail."

As they struggled with the kittens Arlene and Metro cast apprehensive glances at their father.

"Bring em here!" Vincent snapped. "One at a time."

He grabbed an old axe and stood by the chopping block splattered with dried chicken blood.

"Here!" he said and motioned to Arlene as Metro watched from the pail, a tight knot in his stomach.

"Hold that darned cat!"

Arlene held the squirming kitten on the block, her face chalk white.

Whoosh! The axe came down inches from Arlene's face. Bright, red blood squirted from the headless kitten and onto Vincent's pants.

"Throw it away! Get the next one!"

The axe fell again and again as Arlene held the squirming kittens on the block. In an instant, and with a single stroke of the axe, each one became a blood squirting, headless corpse. Arlenes face was chalk white and she wept openly through the nausea and fear.

Metro stood very still, gasping for air. He face was white too and he wrung his hands in agitation but he and Arlene were as powerless as the Mother Cat who mewed sadly and sniffed the inert bodies.

If anyone had told Vincent that what he did was cruel, he would have retorted that the kittens died quickly and didn't suffer. To him, killing unwanted kittens was a chore he didn't like but someone had to do it.

During this time Metro developed yet another disadvantage. When he was tired or tense and his stomach knotted his vision blurred, making reading impossible. He saw fuzzy lines in his left eye and when he closed it the blurriness switched to the other. After the migraine began, he felt a sharp penetrating pain, like a steel band being tightened around his temples. Then came nausea and the only remedy was to lie down in a cool spot, away from the bright sun or lights.

It occurred when they had visitors, Helen, Vincent's sister and her husband. Jack was a man of average height and mind and who constantly wore a bleak expression as if growing up in the depression had marred him for life. Once he had settled into a chair in the kitchen he sat, staring off into space with his hands folded in his lap. Vincent sat beside him and as the conversation died a lingering death both men stared off at totally different visions.

Metro sat at the kitchen table and tried in vain to draw a rabbit on an old piece of brown wrapping paper. Close by, Helen listened to Gertie's agitated complaints while they washed the dishes. Then, as Metro struggled with the pencil stub and worn-out eraser, he felt the familiar blurring of vision in his left eye. He closed it and it automatically switched to the right. Metro sighed and resigned himself to more blurred vision, nausea and a splitting headache. As the brown wrapping paper danced in front of him he gave up and turned to his mother.

"Mom! Can I have an aspirin? I got a headache."

He had learned that it was much easier to have a request granted when there was company. But the visitors were family and Gertie felt no need to act differently.

Her lips compressed for an instant and then she glanced at Helen and winked.

"That's because you draw so much. That's why you get them headaches. It's that tarned drawing."

Metro stared at his mother, his eyes wide.

Helen smiled down at Metro.

"Yeah! It's that drawing. That's what's causing those headaches."

Metro sat, puzzled and fearful. Then he slid down from the chair and left the kitchen quietly to lie down in the cool bedroom. He puzzled out the problem in his mind for he couldn't understand how drawing a picture could cause a headache. Still, why would his mother and aunt say it, if it was not true?


Over the years Gertie changed little, except for the gradual loss of some of her outrageous accent. Her stomach still knotted in inexplicable fear and she slid deeper and deeper into a superstitious faith evolving around the church. If she had been asked, she would have been unable to explain her faith for she knew little of the Catholic Church's origin or Christ's teachings. All she knew was that priests and nuns led a Holy life while hers was one of drudgery and searing guilt.

One day the family and relatives sat in the kitchen and watched the rain hammer down on the grass outside as lightening flashed and thunder rolled. Gertie wrung her hands in agitation and began rocking in her chair while the visitors exchanged amused looks.

Suddenly a roll of thunder crashed down, shaking the house. Gertie jumped up and ran into the bedroom where she grabbed a container of Holy Water that had been blessed by a Bishop. She ran quickly from room to room sprinkling Holy water in each corner with a quick flick of her wrist, her lips compressed into a thin line in her hard, white face.

The relatives laughed uproariously while Gerard sat by the stove, his face pinched and white and his eyes narrow. Vincent laughed with the relatives, his face red and his eyes watering. Arlene was busy in the living room with an old doll and Allen sat by the window and said nothing.

Metro watched his mother from a corner and again all he felt was guilt and shame

Gertie's inexplicable fears were never far from the surface. When they were outside and a distant roll of thunder made her face turn white, she pressed Metro against a granary with her right hand, holding herself flat against the wall. Metro felt confused amusement and shame as she held him against the logs, nodding her head rapidly and swallowing. At other times she would admonish him to never go into the pasture for a neighbor's bull roamed at will. To her even the word Bull was offensive and she referred to it as "The neighbor's ox."

Metro would look carefully about before wandering off into the woods. If he saw the bull grazing quietly with the cows, he ran quickly back to the yard, with the irrational fear clawing at his soul.

This caused an inordinate amount of anxiety for Metro who turned nine that summer. Two mares had fillies and he spent most of his days playing in the pasture with them, all the while casting apprehensive glances about for the bull. But there was one benefit from his fear. It helped him climb a tree.

He had found old rusty nails and a hammer and had placed poplar poles across branches in the trees in order to build a tree house. It took hours of work but finally he stood on tiptoe and pushed the last pole into place. Then he stood gazing up at the platform. It was barely higher than his head but his father's constant taunt of "Metro! You can't do that" surfaced in his consciousness and he looked forlornly up, wondering how he would ever climb to the platform.

Suddenly, through the trees, a large white, woolly head appeared as the bull plodded toward the trough of water in the corral. A spasm of phobic fear shot through Metro and he turned quickly and shinnied up a tree, until he could pull himself onto the poles. Then he gazed down at the placid bull who plodded slowly on his way.

At other times Metro wandered freely with the gentlest of the fillies, following the mares as they grazed. He spent so much time with the horses, the mares began to accept him as part of the herd. When they lay down in the hot afternoon, Metro lay with them resting his head on the fillys belly as she lay on her side. It made a soft and warm pillow, not unlike a reclining chair and Metro drifted off into a pleasant dreamless sleep. When he woke, he was lying alone on the grass with the colt grazing besides him a few feet away. He wondered how the filly could rise without waking him but she was gentle and accustomed to him.

One day Metro tied an old twine string around a mare's neck as she was grazing. Then he carefully lifted a leg and placed it over her head. When she felt his weight, she lifted her head and Metro rose suddenly. When she stood with her head high, Metro inched his way forwards along her neck until he was sitting on her back. He carefully and slowly turned around and then reached forward and grabbed the twine and kicked the mare in the ribs. She began walking slowly and eventually trotted with Metro bouncing and clinging determinedly to her mane. She was a heavy work horse and not built for riding but with enough kicking and urging she finally broke into a clumsy gallop with Metro hanging on grimly but still learning to move his body with the horse. At times he fell off but he kept climbing back onto the mare's back, via her neck until he fell less and less.

While Metro lived with the horses, barefoot and savage in appearance, Gerard continued his grinding but determined education. When he brought home a failing mark, Gertie's face went white for she dreamed of her son becoming a school teacher or even a priest. Gerard didn't feel any gratitude for her support, only shame and gradually, cold implacable hate.

While Gerard slowly and laboriously gained his ticket to freedom from the drudgery of the farm, Metro was picked on more and more at school for he had stopped fighting back. He was mocked, even by adults, until he longed for the freedom of the pasture and the gentle horses. Just before school began, Vincent brought home a rusty second-hand bicycle and Metro spent hours crashing into trees and onto the ground. But along with the cuts and bruises came a sense of balance. Then, the four children peddled to and from school with Metro struggling to keep up. If he fell too far behind and was late, he was condemned and punished for being lazy.

When he peddled unsteadily out of the school yard behind his brothers and sister, he had to run the gamut of children who tried to knock him off his bike. When his pants caught in the chain, he crashed to the ground and sprawled, the palm of his right hand bleeding due to his instinctively holding it out to break his fall. He tried desperately to pull his pants from the chain and then for an instant lay helplessly, watching his brothers and sister disappear in the distance without a backward glance. He didn't think to call out for help. Instead he turned again to the chain that held his pants.

"Let 'em lie in the dirt and get himself out. Serves 'em right for peddling so fast." A child's voice came to him as he lay on the ground.

The minutes dragged by tortuously as the children surrounded and mocked Metro. Then a great mental fog descended for it was the humiliation that made his eyes swim, not the pain in his hand that bled dark blood.

When he had finally figured out how to push the chain in reverse and free his pants he glanced up. A middle-aged woman walked by carrying a pail. She glanced down and sideways at the child in the dirt but continued walking for it was no concern of hers. In the school the teachers gathered over coffee and cigarettes and ignored what happened outside, for their day was done.

Eventually Metro freed his pants and peddled off after his brothers and sister. When he was home, hot and tired, Gertie railed at him for being late. He put his books away and wandered off outside, saying nothing for it all seemed so natural.

Metro continued to mature gradually in his child's world, learning from books instead of adults. He read *Black Beauty* and identified with the colt when his mother instructed him on behavior and that he had a place in life. Metro thought of the other boys who made a game of how far they could urinate or spit behind the school where no teacher ever went. He instinctively felt revulsion for such behavior but at the same time he knew, deep within his soul, that he was lower than anyone else.

At times at school the children would form a circle and mock him and he would lower his head until they tired of the game and left him alone. He rarely fought back even when he was beaten. To the teachers, that was further evidence that he was retarded, for what normal child wouldn't retaliate?

When he was still nine, Metro was moved to grade three and a new teacher. He sank lower with marks of five or ten percent but at times he would be unpredictable. It was the fashion then for the teacher to read the marks to the class, reinforcing those who scored high and further humiliating those who didn't. When it came to Metro, the teacher would laugh and remark that he had finally "Gotten a Big Fat Goose Egg," which is what a zero resembled. But one day she stopped suddenly.

"Hold onto your seats, everyone!" she said and laughed loudly. "This will come as a great surprise..."

"Metro! Sixty percent!"

Her tone was mocking and the class laughed uproariously. After that Metro filled in any answer, even when he knew it was wrong.

The same teacher who mocked him for passing, also took one of his sketches to the staff coffee room. It was of a steam locomotive and the perspective and lines were near perfect; the pencil used in shades to accent the shadows of the boiler. She took that as a compliment to her teaching but the label of retarded stuck nonetheless. Metro was later told by the same teacher that if only he could spell as well as he could draw, he would pass.

When he was home and the snow piled up in the yard, "Retarded!" was supplemented with "Can't be trusted" Gertie and Vincent, in one of their unpredictable moods, had promised a calf to be shared by Arlene and Metro. When it was sold, they each received nine dollars.

Metro eagerly flipped through a catalog until he came to a cowboy hat and boots. A month later when he tore away the paper and pulled out the boots and hat, Gertie laughed outright.

"So now! Now you'll see how long that junk lasts. I only let you pick it out so you'll learn a good lesson," she yelled. Then she remembered the green party dress she had bought when she was a teenager. But she pushed the memory aside and her mouth hardened into the familiar thin line.

"I told you so. Metro can't be trusted!"

When the snow melted, Metro gazed through wet eyes at the discarded boots that lay rotting by the house; mute evidence of his lack of judgment.

Later, Metro beat his Teddy Bear and threw it into a corner yelling, "You're not to be trusted! Good for nothing! Too lazy to work!"

Then he felt a, great unfathomable guilt. His face glistened as he picked up the teddy bear and held it fiercely to his chest, rocking back and forth on the edge of his cot.

# Twenty-four

When the warm winds of summer came, Metro rejoined the gentle horses in the wooded pasture for it was the best of times. The filly was only two years old but she let him sit on her back as she grazed, moving as gently as when she had risen from the grass with Metro sleeping with his head against her belly. Metro still went barefoot with the soles of his feet leather tough and dirty while his glasses were patched with white tape, barely holding together.

In the open fields he was not only free from school and the torment of the teachers and other children but also from his mother. She had taken to nagging Vincent with, "Cut his hair. Can't you see? He looks like a savage Indian."

Vincent would grumble and go to the cupboard where he kept an old barber shears. He would make Metro sit on an old jam pail on top of a chair, the pail's metal cutting sharply into his buttocks. But worse than the excruciating pain from the bucket was Vincent's impatient and careless handling of the shears, for he failed to manipulate the handles as fast as he pushed upwards at the back of Metro's neck. Small hairs were torn from their roots as Vincent contorted his face and grumbled about having so much to do. When Metro squirmed he would yell, "Hold up! Gosh darn it the heck anyway."

The words were no different from when he harnessed horses and they moved about.

All it took for Metro to feel a sudden phobic fear was for Gertie to nag that his hair was getting long. Then he would stay out in the pasture until darkness or hunger forced him in. At other times, when they were getting ready to go to Mass, Gertie would nag again and Vincent would summon Metro to the tiny washroom. He wrapped a thin face cloth around a wooden match which he dipped into cold water. Then he grabbed Metro by the neck and industriously dug into his ears with the match stick, contorting his face and snarling, "Hold up! Gosh darn it!"

One day, as Metro escaped into the pasture, Vincent and Gertie sat in the kitchen with Gerard for they had reached an important time in his life. There was a shortage of teachers and the government had offered, for the first time, a student loan for anyone enrolling in Teacher's College. It was a one year course and the five hundred dollars made the difference of attending college or being committed to a life of drudgery. Bzigniew who was retired in Saskatoon, along with his son-in-law, searched until they found a job for Gerard, building houses at a dollar an hour. When classes started, he was assured of board and room by the same uncle. All Gerard had to do was work hard in summer and study hard in winter and he would be given a career, or rather, an escape from the life of travail, in which his parents were trapped.

To Gerard, the time would remain in his memory as one of hardship for he hadn't lost his complaining and bitter outlook. College wasn't any easier than high school for all he had was a fierce determination fueled by the fear of having to labor with sweat in his eyes for the rest of his life. He stayed home on weekends and studied until he worried he might go blind. Gerard never told anyone about the trouble he had with the normally easy lessons. But when he was in class, he was embarrassed by his worn pants and frayed collar. When a female instructor called him into her office, he bit his lip and said nothing while the inner rage simmered.

"Gerard," the elderly woman began softly. "Why do you want to be a teacher?"

Gerard stood in front of the woman, his hands clasped tightly together behind his back. He knew he couldn't tell her the real reason.

"Uh, I want to teach kids so when they get odder they can make something of themselves," he finally mumbled.

"But you have difficulty in talking," she said quietly. She stared down at her desk for a strained moment and then looked back up.

"You also have a hard time talking in front of people." She paused as she remembered the instructions to pass nearly anyone due to the shortage.

"I know you may some day make a good teacher, but you seem to have difficulty with clothes."

Gerard's face whitened for it was true. He couldn't afford many new clothes but he also lacked the ability to pick out, at first glance, pants or a shirt that went well with a sweater or jacket. And anything he bought he had to wear even if it was out of style.

"If you like," the woman continued, "I can lend you some money for clothes."

The unexpected kindness cut like a knife. Gerard's face whitened still further and he bit his lip hard.

"Uh, no thanks, I can manage," the words came clumsily as he glared at his grey and tattered shoes.

Gerard struggled on, barely passing the courses that were lessons he would eventually teach to ten year-old children. And he suppressed the humiliation of being poor and blamed it on his parents. When he came home on weekends, he wasted little time in venting his frustration.

Metro, was growing rapidly. Despite his father's constant taunt of, "Metro! You can't!" his intellectual abilities expanded as he questioned events far from the farm. He also spent hours reading and the label of "lazy" was added to "foolish" and "can't be trusted!"

When he asked why the Russians had built an Atomic bomb, Gerard's face whitened.

"There again, you're talking about something you know absolutely nothing about," he yelled, his cheekbones pronounced and his face white.

Metro left the hatred in the kitchen and wandered outside, seeking company with the cats. At ten he had passed grade three and was moved to a class guarded over by a large and powerful woman. If the former teachers were mean, she was vicious. She had cut a strap from the webbed drive belt of an old threshing machine and it was two feet long, a half inch thick and three inches wide; heavy enough to knock the wind from a full-grown man.

At all times, the heavy weapon lay on her desk, ready for instant use.

In the fall, when it was still warm enough for the children to play outside during recess, Metro stayed indoors and read while the teacher knitted at her desk. A child suddenly entered from the rear door and ran up to the teacher.

"Teacher! Billy spit on me!" the child said out of breath.

"What! Send 'em down here. I'll show 'em to spit!"

Metro froze at his desk. In less than a minute Billy stood trembling before the teacher, who towered over him, strap in hand. She had worked herself up into a righteous rage and had begun to swing the strap back and forth.

"Did you spit at him?"

"But he hit me first!" Billy's face was white.

"Did you spit at him or not?" The teacher's words made a group of children freeze at the door where they had just entered. The room was deathly still as she rocked her two hundred pounds on the balls of her feet, hefting the strap in her right hand.

"Did you spit or not?" she demanded again.

"Yes but," Billy began.

The strap whistled down followed by a hollow thump. She hit him squarely on the head and Billy sank to his knees. She swung, again and again, the heavy strap hitting him between the shoulder blades and driving the wind from his lungs. Again and again, she swung as the child cowered on the floor and the strap made a muffled thump. Then finally, with sweat running down her cheeks and her breathing rapid, she stopped. The only sound in the deathly silence was her heavy breathing and a whimper from Billy who lay in a crumpled heap on the floor.

"Now, you'll know to spit!" she finally snarled after catching her breath. Then she walked ponderously to her desk, throwing the strap down.

"Recess is over! Get to your desks!"

A hurried shuffling sound of shoes on linoleum was over in seconds and every desk had an attentive and silent child in it, except for one.

Billy slowly rose and painfully walked to his desk his face white and glistening. The room remained deathly still with the children concentrating on their lessons until the teacher rose and began writing on the blackboard.

Later that day, Metro stared through the window at a patch of blue sky, daydreaming of the freedom of the woods and the company of the gentle horses.

Suddenly he sensed the teacher's presence behind him. Then the air left his lungs as he heard a muffled thump. Next came numbness and pain as the teacher swung the heavy strap until her breathing was heavy.

His crime had been not paying attention. For the rest of the period he hunched his shoulders painfully, trying desperately to see the blackboard through tear-stained glasses.

Later, Billy's mother complained that her child had come home with welts on his back. The teachers announced collectively that a strap was incapable of raising a welt and that any such talk would be met with a law suit.

Ironically, the same teacher recognized Metro's artistic talent and offered to teach him to paint with oils. When he was home, he flipped hurriedly through a catalog. The cheapest set cost three dollars.

Metro approached his mother with the catalog as she washed dishes and muttered, lost in her misty world of memory. She ceased muttering for an instant and stared down at him when he asked if she could purchase the set of brushes and paints. Then she stood, her head turned sideways with soap dripping from her hands while her square, sad face remained hard. Slowly, she straightened and spread her arms in the familiar gesture of helplessness and Metro's heart sank.

"Yuh! And I can't help you," Gertie said. Then she smiled as she snapped her fingers and shrugged her shoulders in a sign of helplessness.

Metro wandered off and drew with an old pencil stub on brown wrapping paper. When the teacher asked if he had been given the brushes he quietly shook his head and she never brought the subject up again.

A few days later Metro sat on the grass by the barn in the warm autumn sun while beside him the Mother Cat and her three kittens ate from a dish. Metro stared off into space, totally immobilized, his eyes holding a strange light. He sighed deeply and then looked down at the kittens who crowded about the dish. He reached down and gently picked one up, petting its soft fur. The kitten chewed rapidly and looked at the dish he had just been lifted from. Then, Metro's fingers, on their own, encircled the kitten's throat as it lay in his lap, trusting and fearless. And slowly, an urge crept up from the depths of his soul and his fingers tightened around the kitten's throat. He began to squeeze gently at first and then more firmly. The kitten stopped chewing and sat very still. Metro's fingers remained firm, around its throat as he fought the urge to squeeze; to throttle the kitten until its eyes bulged and it writhed and struggled until it breathed no more.

Then slowly, the urge slipped away, back into the depths of his soul and Metro loosened his grip. The kitten immediately sat up and swallowed, still trusting and fearless. Then it jumped down back to the dish and ate rapidly, trying to catch up to the others.

Metro sat very still, staring at the kitten, while an unfathomable fear clawed at his consciousness. He looked at his fingers and back at the kitten, trying to understand why; why he would have an urge to kill the one thing that was soft and gentle in his grey, foggy existence.

While Gerard was escaping the drudgery of the farm by studying long hours and enduring the shame of tattered clothes and nonexistent social graces, Allen was learning to improve his lot by other means. One early evening he stood in the middle of the kitchen and glared at his parents. Vincent sat by the window and stared down at his heavy callused hands while Gertie stood by the cupboard. Arlene and Metro also stood in the kitchen, Metro's eyes wide.

"Every boy my age gets the car," Allen began his attack.

Vincent kept his gaze lowered as Gertie nervously placed the dish towel on a hook. Allen glared at her, then Vincent who still stared at his hands. Then he pressed home the attack.

"I feel like we're the poorest of the poor. People laugh at us. I can't even go out and have fun." His voice rose and then he exposed Gertie's constant guilt.

"You don't even care what kind of life I lead!" Allen yelled and glanced through the window at the ten year-old sedan that Vincent had recently bought.

Vincent looked up from the floor, his eyes wet. Allen was seventeen and well built and Vincent no longer had any means of discipline. Gertie looked from her husband to her son, her square sad face agitated and pained. Metro stood by the table, his feet rooted to the spot for he had never heard anyone yell so loudly at his father.

"What kind of life is this?" the words kept coming.

"I milk cows, I work in the field and what do I get? Friday night and everyone else is out having fun and I got to stay home."

Finally, when he ran out of breath, Gertie turned to Vincent.

"Should we?"

Vincent stared at her for an instant and then slowly reached into his pocket and brought out the car keys. But Allen wasn't finished.

"What am I gonna do? Sit in the car while the dance is on?"

Vincent again stared at Gertie and then reached slowly into his pocket, bringing forth a frayed leather wallet. He took out three one dollar bills, money he needed to buy nails. Instead he would have to find old rusty ones and straighten them but he said nothing as he handed the bills to Allen. Gertie's face was grey and she bit her lower lip.

Allen smiled quickly and just as quickly pocketed the money. But he still wasn't finished.

"Now, I won't be able to have any fun. It takes a half hour of yelling to get the car from you and another half hour to get any money and now I can't even enjoy myself because of it."

Gertie bit her lip again and Vincent looked down at his worn boots. Neither parents said anything for they both knew they had lost control.

Allen drove the old car out of the yard without a backward glance, dust rising on the trail to the road. And he had fun, forgetting the yelling once he was in town. He used other methods besides yelling too, when he sensed he had gone too far.

"I just want to go to a movie and I'll take Metro. He should get out more because he looks like a savage Indian. What will the neighbors think?" Allen said quietly from the middle of the kitchen. Metro sat on a chair, watching the scene unfold.

Once again Gertie looked at Vincent and he once again reached into his pocket. The gas was meant to last a week but he was too tired to argue.

When Allen had parked near the theater, he was joined by friends. Metro sat in the front between his brother and another teenage boy as he looked straight ahead at the theater. It wasn't often that he got to see a movie.

"There's a dance at the lake," the boy next to Metro said.

"Yeah but I don't have no money," Allen answered.

"Don't worry. We'll pay your way in. We even got enough for some beer If we can get someone to buy it for us."

Allen glanced at the theater and then down at Metro.

"What about him?"

"Hell! Drive 'em home. He can see a movie next week," the teenager said. Allen smiled down at Metro.

"Would you mind?"

The other teenager looked steadily at Metro who sat very still. The theater doors were open and he could see people enter.

"Naw He doesn't mind," the boy laughed and poked Metro in the ribs. "You can see a movie anytime you want, eh?"

Metro fought back the tears.

"Okay!" he finally said and then looked down at the floor.

Allen drove Metro back to the farm, stopping the car on the road, three hundred yards from the house. He looked steadily down at Metro. Metro looked back, his eyes dry. Finally Allen smiled.

"I'll take you someplace else maybe. But don't tell Mom where I'm going or I'll never take you nowhere again."

Metro nodded quickly. Then he opened the door and walked slowly to the house. When he entered the kitchen, he was met by Gertie.

"What happened?" The words crashed down as he tiredly sat on a chair.

"The show isn't over yet. Where's Allen?"

"I don't know." Metro tried to be evasive.

"If you don't tell me I'll get the strap and lick you 'til you can only crawl!" Gertie snarled, her square, angry face fearful and threatening. She waited for an instant and then began to rise. "He went to the lake for a dance," Metro said quickly.

"What?" Gertie stopped and stared. "The lake's thirty miles. We needed the gas for church." She turned to the sink and dirty dishes, muttering to herself. Then she turned back to Metro.

"Well I'm gonna have a good talk with him once he gets home. So, that's what he thinks. Lie to me and then go running off where he wants."

Metro stared at his mother for a moment and then silently left the kitchen, sitting on the grass beside the Mother Cat who rubbed up against him. But it was little comfort as he wondered what the movie would have been like. As the tears finally came, he also wondered what his brother would do when he found out he had told where he had gone. But Allen had again got his way and Gertie didn't say much. It wasnt long before he was again standing in the kitchen, yelling at Gertie and Vincent for ruining his life.

Gradually as time passed, Vincent and Gertie beat Metro less but Gertie's hand would still snake out in a quick backhand slap to his head whenever he got in the way. And Vincent got immense pleasure from mocking him, constantly saying, "Metro! You can't do that!" whenever Metro tried helping with the work. The hurt in the child's eyes would make his grin widen, especially if relatives were present and they laughed. And if they mocked Metro too, Vincent would join in.

One wintery evening the failing light barely penetrated the frost-covered windows. The thermometer registered thirty-five below so Arlene and Metro played under the kitchen table as Gertie scurried about the kitchen and Vincent snored on the couch in the living room. Allen had taken the car to town.

"On no!" Arlene suddenly said and Metro froze in a sitting position.

"Mommy and Daddy are gone!" Arlene feigned fear. "There's no one else but us. We're all alone!"

Metro sat very still, his face white and then slowly the tears came. He stared at his sister, his eyes fearful and his breathing shallow.

"What're we gonna do?" Arlene persisted in the macabre game and Metro's face began to glisten.

Suddenly, Arlene laughed.

"Oh no! It's okay! Mommy and Daddy are here. They weren't gone after all. We just thought they were."

Metro stared at his sister and then out from under the table at his mother's feet as she stood by the cupboard, kneading dough. The tears stopped but a residue of fear remained in his eyes.

Gertie stopped muttering suddenly and glanced under the table.

"What you doing there?"

"Oh, we're just playing," Arlene answered.

"Oh, that's nice," Gertie said and then went back to kneading dough and talking to ghostly people in her mind while a loud snore came from the living room.

# Twenty-five

Allen continued to dominate Vincent and Gertie until he graduated from high school and joined the Air Force. Then he was gone, leaving his father's contorting face and his mother's incessant mutter. That left Arlene and Metro for Gerard had found a teaching position in a remote trapping settlement, three hundred miles north where his hatred simmered and he vowed to never be poor. Vincent spent more time sitting by the kitchen window with his head drooping and the lines deepening on his swarthy face.

A day after Allen had left, Gertie and Vincent sat by the kitchen table. Gertie's face was a picture of never-ending hardship, for the ancient Chevrolet was completely worn out. Then she rose, her mouth hard and thin.

"I guess we'll just have to sell some cows and buy another car," she said. "He runs off und leaves us with the mess."

Then she turned and glared at Metro who sat silently on a chair by the door.

"So now! No son off ours is gonna drive the car again."

Metro was eleven, and five years from a driver's license but he was the only son left.

One evening, Vincent started the car with the crank and then turned to Metro.

"Metro! You wanna go to a ball game?"

It was one of the many inconsistent things Metro's parents did, one time being callously cruel, the next almost kind.

Vincent drove to the hamlet, in the warm softness of an early summer evening, his face contorting and his heavy hands on the wheel. He sat stiffly and peered at the road, saying nothing to Metro for he only talked to him when it involved an order or mockery.

He parked the car on the grass behind a chicken wire fence that was the backstop. Metro wandered off, watching from a grey, sagging plank behind the home team. It didn't occur to him to sit next to his father. He still wore the battered cowboy hat that he had ordered with his share of money he and Arlene had been given. And as he watched the game, he was noticed by boys his age and older. Ivan poked him in the ribs.

"Hey! Metro! Your old man still start his car with that stupid crank?"

Metro stared straight ahead as a fog slowly engulfed him. A loud crack came as a line drive cleared the home run fence and the crowd cheered but Metro was unawares of the game. When Ivan saw he was getting nowhere he changed tactics.

"What's this?" He grabbed Metro's hat and held it in the air. "Look at this! He thinks he's a real Goddamned Cowboy."

Metro turned quickly, his face anguished.

Ivan's grin broadened and he continued relentlessly, "Hey! Let's stick this dirty old thing on top a tree. Then we can see if he can climb for it like, a monkey!"

Metro grabbed for the hat but Ivan was three years older and held it out of reach. Metro charged, humiliation turning to rage but three boys grabbed him.

"Look at this!" Ivan yelled and a few adult heads turned. A woman who attended Mass regularly in the same church, watched from a booth where she sold hot dogs.

"Look!" Ivan continued as Metro fought against the three boys. He could almost reach Ivan but they were too many.

"I'm riding Flicka!" Ivan mimicked a man on a horse. "That's that dumb horse of his."

The laughter closed in and Metro existed all alone, in a grey, foggy world of frustrated rage and pain. He saw his father sitting less than ten feet away but he didn't call out. And in the fog of humiliation he suddenly stopped struggling. Sooner or later they would tire of the game and leave him alone.

Ivan ran to a post and jammed the hat down. He could barely reach the top and he knew Metro couldn't. He yanked down as hard as he could, trying to ram the top of the post through the hat but the material was too strong.

"Leave it there! It's as useless as that stupid old horse of his," he said and the three boys let Metro go. He stood uncertainly then, staring at his hat on the pole.

As Ivan walked away, he saw Vincent sitting on a bench behind the screen and he grinned suddenly. He walked until he was a couple feet behind him.

"Vincent!" he yelled and then quickly turned and walked away.

Vincent turned and looked foolishly about and the boys laughed some more. Metro watched through the tears as his father was mocked. Then he went to the post and climbed until he could reach his hat. He stood and straightened the material while the same woman watched silently.

Metro held the hat in his hands, afraid someone would snatch it away. Then he walked slowly to the car and sat in the front, waiting for the game to end. Vincent suddenly looked in through the window.

"Turn the key and put your foot on the gas!"

He spun the crank as motors roared to life all around him. He didn't seem to notice the amused glances and he drove home glancing at his son who stared straight ahead into the gathering darkness. Vincent hurried for without a battery, the car had no headlights. But he turned to Metro again and for the first time noticed the glistening tears on the boy's face.

"Metro! What's the matter? What the heck you crying for?" His voice was harsh. Metro sighed deeply.

"They tried to take my hat away." He spoke quietly, staring straight ahead at the highway, avoiding Vincent's facial contortion.

"What! Why the heck didn't you tell me? Boy! If I'd a known I'd a fixed them."

Metro turned and gazed steadily at his father.

"You were right there. How could you not know?"

"Aw gosh darn it the heck anyway," Vincent's jaw trembled. "I got no time for kids. I was busy watching the game."

Metro gazed back at the road and the fog closed in until they turned into the driveway and he could see the yellow light coming from the kitchen window. Then he turned to his father once more.

"Don't tell them. It's bad, enough it happened. I don't want them to know."

"Okay!" Vincent said, his jaw twitching as he parked the car. Then he walked to the house with Metro following, still trying to straighten his hat. He was just in time to see his father jerk his thumb backwards as he entered the kitchen.

"Metro got beat up! A bunch of boys was picking on him."

Metro gazed steadily at his father. Seeing him break his word, minutes after he had given it was something he would have to work out in his mind for some time to come.

Gertie glared at him, noticing the drying tears on his face.

"That's because you're so mean. Now you got it. No one likes you!"

The words followed Metro as he sat wearily on the couch in the living room. He found a book he had read many times but in summer he had little chance of finding new ones. He turned the pages and tried to concentrate but his father and the scene with the boys and his hat kept crowding in. He laid the book down and went into the new addition to the house. It still had walls and a floor of rough greying planks. Metro lay down on his cot, against a tar-paper wall and stared at the ceiling. Then the tears came again and with them, a heavy congested pain that made his chest tight and numb. Words came too, in a barely audible whisper.

"Why? Why do they do it, God? Am I so different? Why? Why do they hate me?"


The humiliation drifted around Metro in a grey, misty fog and he withdrew into a world of dreams and events of his own choosing. He still drew pictures and even began writing short stories and in fall he had a new teacher.

"Good morning! I'm Miss Weems." A bright smile creased the young woman's pretty face as she sat at the desk. She appeared the epitome of youthful dedication and concern.

It didn't take Metro long to realize the smile and dedication were not for children like him. Still, there were paradoxes. When he wrote a story, he effortlessly let his mind wander in one of his day dreams.

He was lost in a desert, desperately searching for water while the broiling sun blistered his face. He wandered for days, eating lizards and sucking the juice from cacti, living in his dream world, his pen scratching quickly for half an hour.

The grammar and spelling were bad but when the teacher read the stories, she called Metro to her desk.

"Did you write this?"

Metro nodded quickly, his body trembling but she only smiled; the first smile, meant for him. She placed the story on top of her desk.

"You can sit down now."

Metro felt a small, strange feeling of accomplishment fighting the fear and confusion. The teacher took the story to the staff coffee room and showed it to the other teachers, taking credit for his being her student. But the teacher's fondness for the story didn't extend to Metro for she saw only a dirty youngster who appeared too lazy or dumb to wash. Later when she came to his desk she wrinkled her nose.

Suddenly Metro was yanked by the arm and dragged to a wash basin at the rear of the room. She lathered soap and then made him roll up his sleeves. The other students watched, delighted.

"Look at this!" She held up an offending elbow that was encrusted with dirt.

"What kind of lazy brat doesn't even know enough to wash?" She roughly scrubbed Metro's elbows as the angry words continued.

Finally she tired and threw the washcloth angrily into the basin. Metro walked numbly back to his desk, enjoyment in the children's eyes all around him.

On another occasion the teacher suddenly caught him by the arm and held him. Then she reached into the front of his shirt.

"What's this you got here? A string?" The mocking voice made the students look up from their desks and grin. "No, it's a Cross?" The teacher yanked forth the tiny Crucifix that Gertie made him wear.

"Well, of all the superstitious nonsense. I've never seen anything like it. Why you're liable to choke yourself, if you're not careful."

After that she concurred with Metro's former teachers, saying he was definitely retarded.

Later, Metro worked intently on a picture, for a contest had been announced. Then, his heart pounding, he gingerly placed it on the teacher's desk. As he sat down, she held it up for the class to see, along with another one.

"Okay! Let's vote on which one to send to the contest?"

A majority of arms were raised in Metro's favor. Paradoxically he was held in high esteem in art even though he was normally mocked.

"Oh, I don't know. I like the other one." The teacher gazed at both pictures for a moment. "You must have made a mistake. We'll vote again."

Again a majority of arms were raised in favor of Metro's picture.

"No. I like the other one better," the teacher said slowly as she gazed at the pictures, not mentioning that the other child's parents were well respected.

"I think I'll send this one in," she finally said. She gave Metro back his picture, telling him it was good and he should keep it.

Metro waited until recess and then threw the picture into the waste basket.

A few days later the teacher made him stay late and he waited at his desk, a cold shaft of fear gnawing at his soul. But when the teacher sat next to him, her manner was nonthreatening.

Metro gazed up at her, waiting.

"Metro! Why don't you have glasses? I can tell you can't see properly because you hold the book too close to your face."

Metro sat dumbly at his desk, hunching his shoulders and fighting the tears that came with the confused shame. The old pair that he had worn had finally come apart and he was forced to squint.

"Surely your parents could buy you a pair." Scorn crept into the teacher's voice.

"Your brothers in the Air Force. Surely, he could put a penny aside in order for you to get glasses."

Metro knew that Allen sent money home but he kept silent as the tears won against his determination not to cry. Finally the teacher lost patience.

"Well, what kind of parents are they, anyway? There sure isn't anything I can do if your parents don't care enough for you."

She stood and walked out of the room.

# Twenty-six

Time passed and seasons changed but the grey fog remained. Metro withdrew more and more, existing in his world of self-deprecation and books. Creativity and low self-esteem are contradictory and as he grew, they at times caused a dissonance in his soul. When in school, he kept as quiet as possible and the teacher normally ignored him. But if he irritated her she lashed out with whatever she had in hand.

Then at twelve, Metro's existence improved immeasurably, brought on by a rather insignificant event. The Public Library established a mobile unit for the rural areas and a large van began stopping at the school every two weeks, with each student allowed two books. Metro finished his in a couple of days and then waited impatiently for the next visit. But the mobile van was salvation for it gave him an outlet; a chance to read novels his rustic schoolmates hadn't even heard of and cared less about. He read about Pandora's Box and the careless Greek who had opened it. At other times he lived in the misty world of blue-coated Napoleonic troops pillaging their way across Russia or the desperate one of southern aristocracy in besieged Atlanta. The world was filled with hazy, imaginary men and women existing only in Metro's mind, but it was as real as the other world; the one where he despised school and feared his parents and teachers.

One late afternoon when he was reading a book in the living room Vincent demanded suddenly, "Metro, what you reading?"

Metro looked up surprised. It was the first time his father had appeared interested in what came in a book.

"It's about the Iroquois and the Huron," Metro answered self-consciously.

"What's that?" Vincent asked.

"The Iroquois and Huron were Indians," Metro answered. His father's ignorance always surprised him. "They lived in Ontario and they fought each other," he added.

"You're part Indian," Vincent said suddenly, grinning.

Metro stared at his fathers swarthy face and wondered if it was true. To him, being an Indian was a great thing for it meant he was, in a small way part, of the adventure he read about. Later he approached his mother in the kitchen.

"Mom," he asked, "am I part Indian?"

"What?" Gertie stopped short in one of her dashes from the stove to the cupboards. She glared at Metro.

"No!" she yelled.

"But Dad said I was."

"No, you're not. One of your Dad's uncles married an Indian. That's all. There's no Indian blood in our family."

"But," Metro began.

"Dont ever say that, or else!" Gertie yelled again.

Metro didnt bring the subject up again but he puzzled over why his father would tell him he was part Indian if he wasn't.

Later that week Allen drove proudly into the yard, wearing the sky-blue uniform of the Air Force. As Gertie dashed about the kitchen preparing a special meal, he showed Metro his car, letting him sit in the driver's seat and work the gear shift.

"See! All this comes from hard work. I got this car because I work hard. And that's what you'll get if you decide to work and not fool around with reading and drawing pictures."

Then Allen smiled in smug, complacent self-assurance.

"Ya know," he continued, "If they say you're retarded don't worry. You're just as smart as the rest of them. Oh, you're not brilliant, that's for sure. But in your own way you're just as smart as them."

Allen's smile became more self assured.

"Just remember. Reading and drawing just takes up time, that's all. Hard work! Now that's different. You work hard and you get something, like this car."

But Metro refused to quit reading and he drew pictures whenever he could find paper and a pencil. And he quietly bore his father's taunts.

"He's kinda foolish, that boy. Always foolin'," Vincent would say and make a face.

One evening, Metro rode the four year-old mare to the road and turned her around. She sprang forward into a lung bursting gallop while in the yard Gertie stood beside Vincent and Arlene, and watched.

Suddenly the mare shied and Metro lost a stirrup. He clutched the saddle horn but the horse shied again. Then he was flying through the air at twenty miles per hour. He hit the ground with a thud, digging a depression in the soft dirt. For an instant he blacked out and as pain spread throughout his body, he fought to get air back into his lungs. Then he became aware of a sound. It took a second to realize it was laughter, his mother's insane laughter. Loud guffaws shook her shoulders while Vincent's face turned red as laughter cut off his wind.

As the mare wandered off, Metro stood slowly and began dusting off the dirt from his clothes. He gazed at his parents and sister whose faces were wet from tears of mirth and then he looked down at the ground. He caught his horse and removed the saddle, his body stiff and sore. He had heard that insane laughter before but this time he understood. He had lain motionless in the dirt while his mother, father and sister had laughed until they cried. He wondered what they would have done if he had broken his neck. And it didn't take long for an answer. He wasn't worth the effort to check if he was dead or alive.


Gertie bent forward in the large garden, a hoe in her hand as she wiped the sweat from her forehead. She glanced at the long rows of potatoes with the tiny weeds poking their heads up for a place in the sun. The garden was way too large but to Gertie it was proof of well being. She sweated long hours, swinging the hoe with a vengeance while her lips moved steadily. At times like that, Metro stayed away for the hard thin line of her mouth was a warning.

But this time when she stood with the hoe clutched in one hand, her mind was on another matter. Gerard stood beside her in a pair of creased slacks. He didn't offer to help for, ever since she had hung his framed Teacher's Certificate in the kitchen, he had become an honored guest. He stood momentarily, his hands in his pockets, gazing at the potatoes. Then he turned to his mother, his eyebrows pinched together in concentration.

"It's the only chance she'll get," he said. Arlene had turned sixteen and he had decided that she should attend school in a convent. It didn't occur to him or Gertie to consult with Arlene.

"You mean stay there all year." Gertie blew her nose into an old dirty hanky and Gerard turned quickly away.

"But she helps so much in the kitchen. And Metro's so tarned stinky, lazy."

"If she doesn't go to the convent she might end up like some other girls, pregnant and no husband," Gerard snapped. Then he gazed south over the open field for an instant.

"I can send some money home to help with the cost."

"Well," Gertie finally said, the hoe still clutched, in her hand. "If you really think so." Then she stared at the weeds, her face filled with sadness and resignation.

Gerard stared at his mother as she began hoeing again, her shoulders rising and falling while she chopped viciously at the offending weeds. She paused for a second to wipe sweat from her forehead before bending to attack the weeds again. Gerard stood for a while, his hands in his pockets and his face white and pinched. Then he walked slowly through the garden and poplars to the house to where he saw Metro, barefoot and reading a book on the back step. Gerard's face turned whiter.

"Metro!" he yelled.

Metro looked up quickly.

"Mom says that you don't help her with the work." Gerard's cheekbones had become pronounced.

"You better smarten up and start listening to odder folk." The slight speech impediment showed when he was agitated.

"Or else I'll paste ya one in the nose!"

Metro stared down at his bare feet. Gerard was twenty-two and his senior by nine years. It would be senseless to fight back.

In winter, when the temperature dropped to minus thirty, Metro rode the mare to school with an old sheepskin tied to the saddle, as protection from the frozen leather. He endured the taunts of other students and hurried home to read *Moby Dick* and *The Prince and the Pauper*.

In summer he attended what Gertie called "Catti-Kissum, an indoctrination into the Catholic Church's laws and teachings. While he was supposed to be absorbing why Catholics were superior to other Christians, he wondered about contractors in far off Atlanta who made shoddy goods for the Confederate Army. He also wondered about man's inhumanity to man, and the harsh realities of an army pillaging and raping.

When he stood with another boy who was fifteen and two years his senior, he brought up the subject for he had no one to discuss it with. The boy looked at him uncertainly for a moment.

"Yeah times are tough all over," he said, quoting the adults in his life and he meant the immediate area in which he lived.

"It's always been that way," Metro replied earnestly. "During the American Civil War, Confederate businessmen made boots out of cardboard for the army and they made sure they were paid in Yankee Dollars."

The boy stared at Metro.

"What I mean is," Metro continued, "hard times are usually caused by someone's greed."

"Oh, yeah," the boy said dubiously and then grinned. "My Uncle was in the Second World War. Was that the same one?" The boy then shrugged his shoulders, turned and walked away, leaving Metro staring at his back and feeling puzzled and slightly foolish.

When Arlene left for the convent, Metro began to develop a nervous twitch along with an occasional head shake. Tension would build up until he couldn't stand it and the only relief was to twitch his nose or shake his head quickly. When he looked at his father's facial contortions, he fought the urge for an hour, but in the end, he lost out. The twitches were accompanied by a deep, dark depression and he would sit staring into space, his body gripped by an inescapable lethargy. With the lethargy and migraines gripping him, Metro existed with his parents in the cyclical drudgery that was their life. They seldom spoke to him and he read more and more with the reading becoming more sophisticated. During this, his father made faces and his mother nagged him about "That tarned reading."

When he turned fourteen, he helped his father, lifting the loose hay onto the rack with a pitch fork while his wrists ached and his muscles grew and hardened. Blisters broke and new ones formed but he gritted his teeth, struggling to keep up. That summer Vincent bought a fourteen-pound sledge hammer and they replaced the fence posts around the quarter section. Metro swung the hammer, sweat burning his eyes and Vincent grinned at his growing strength

Next, they worked for a neighbor and Metro drove a team of horses hitched to a rake for ten hours a day, his back aching as he slumped on the hard seat. Next he piled and smoothed the hay into a stack, sweat running into his eyes and his arms leaden while his stomach growled fiercely. He and the farmer worked until two pm without a break. When he finally demanded they stop for dinner, the farmer laughed and said he had been so interested in the work he had forgotten about the time.

Metro felt heavy and numb by supper, his face streaked with sweat and dust and his whole body covered with a fine dirt. He was too exhausted to wash and next, morning he was up at six a.m. But he stuck it out, proud to do a man's job.

When his father settled the account with the neighbor, he was given ten loads of hay for their labor and for Metros labor, thirteen dollars. As they drove home with Vincent contorting his face and gripping the steering wheel with his heavy hands, Metro finally asked for pay.

"I'll give you three dollars," Vincent said and Metro gazed at him steadily.

"What? You should be glad you got that!" Vincent yelled.

When they were home, he waved his arm.

"Metro! Go in the pig pen and pick up all them sticks."

"What for?" Metro demanded.

"How's it look?" Vincent snapped but Metro refused.

Later Vincent glared at the loose poles of the calf fence. "I can fix it," Metro said.

"You can't!" Vincent snapped and then grinned broadly when Metro's face fell.

"Get the hammer!" Vincent ordered suddenly.

Metro walked to the shop and brought the hammer. Vincent knocked a pole loose and stared at it for a moment.

"Get the saw!"

"Do you want the nails and the axe?"

"No!" Vincent snarled. "Get the saw!"

Metro again walked to the shop.

"Run! Gosh darn it!" Vincent yelled.

Metro refused to run but when he returned with the saw Vincent glared at him.

"Get the nails!"

When Metro brought the nails, Vincent demanded he bring the axe.

Next day Metro lay in the tiny cot with a deep, penetrating migraine. Slowly he drifted off into a fitful sleep but was jarred suddenly awake. His father stood over him, his foot raised. As Metro stared up at him, Vincent kicked him in the shoulder roughly.

"Metro! Wake up!"

Metro glared at his father.

"Don't kick me! You don't have to kick me!"

Vincent walked off laughing.

That day, Vincent drove the ancient Chevrolet to a neighbor's pasture for he had been given rusty, barbed wire. It was still nailed to the rotting posts, and in places had fallen with tall dry grass lying on top. Vincent ordered Metro to walk ahead and pull the wire free so he could roll it into a clumsy bale. Metro walked slowly, yanking the wire, trying to avoid the barbs which punctured his hands for he had no gloves. In a short while the palms of his hands were bleeding and by the time the hot sun shone directly down, his muscles and bones ached.

As they drove home for lunch, he examined the congealed blood mixed with sweat and dirt on his palms. When they were in the kitchen, Gertie dashed about in a particularly foul mood.

"Metro! You should help me more!" her voice rose to the familiar whine and Metro winced.

"Get the milk!"

Metro walked outside to the ice cellar, his vision dancing from the sudden hot sun. When he returned, Gertie glared.

"Set the table!"

Then she began the familiar singsong.

"I work and work. And for what? And dare and complain."

Metro glanced at the couch where his father lay and when lunch was ready he called him.

"Metro! Bring me water!" Vincent ordered from the table.

Metro and brought the dipper to his father with his hand under it so water wouldn't drip on the floor. Vincent blinked rapidly as he held it to his mouth and then begin to swallow. He drank deeply as Metro watched silently, his back aching. When Vincent finished, he made a face and wiped his mouth with his hand. Then he shoved the dipper at Metro.

"Maybe I should leave it here?" Metro asked.

"No! Take it away!" Vincent yelled.

After lunch Vincent lay down on the couch again, letting the food settle in his stomach.

"You should help me more!" Gertie whined to Metro in the kitchen and the familiar stab of guilt pierced his soul. He stood beside her and wiped dishes with a worn towel while Gertie washed.

"Hold over the cardboard!" she suddenly snarled.

She had spread cardboard so water wouldn't drip on the linoleum and Metro made sure he held the dish over it. As she washed and he wiped, Vincent rose and went outside to relieve himself. He returned with an armful of firewood just as Gertie turned and glared at Metro. Suddenly her right hand snaked out in a vicious backhand.

"Hold over the paper!"

"I am! What the hell's the matter with you?" Metro yelled.

Vincent grabbed a piece of firewood and attacked Metro, hitting him savagely on the wrist. Metro felt the quick stab of pain and then his whole forearm went numb. He clutched it painfully and stared steadily at his father.

After the meal they continued to pull the rusty barbed wire from the grass and neither spoke of the incident. Then, in the late, hot afternoon, they drove to the hamlet, the silence between them complete. Vincent parked beside the Chinese Café and entered without a backward glance. Metro followed and once they were seated on stools, Vincent rested his elbows on the smooth glass counter. An elderly Chinese man approached.

"What you want?"

"Gimmee one Ravel. And one Pepsi!' Vincent ordered.

"Is that all you want?" The Chinese man looked at father and son. Metro met his eyes for a very brief instant and then looked quickly away.

"Yuh! Bring it here!" Vincent contorted his face.

When the man returned with one Pepsi and one Ravel, Vincent bit into the cold ice cream. He stuck his tongue out and rolled the ice cream and chocolate against it. He didn't notice that it smeared all over his mouth. Then he drank from the Pepsi, his eyes blinking rapidly as yet another facial contortion came and went.

Metro silently watched as his father slobbered, his eyes half closed in the cool bliss of ice cream and Pepsi. When Vincent finished, he laid two dimes on the counter and walked out to the car, again without a backward glance.

Metro followed and when he was seated, he gazed steadily at his father in undisguised disgust.

"What the hell's the matter with you?" the words came quietly, his fear of his father evaporating for the moment.

"Is that what you think of me? Am I a dog Or a horse that you work for nothing?"

Metro's gaze was unwavering.

"Hell! You treat the horses better. And that's because they're worth money, right?"

Vincent sat in the car, his face contorting. Then he drove home, the silence between them, once again, complete.

Next day, he did buy a Pepsi and a Ravel for Metro but he bought two of each for himself.

# Twenty-seven

Metro stood nervously in front of the class, glancing down at the paper in his hand, then back up at the expectant faces. He cleared his throat and began to read his short story. Slowly the nervousness left and for a very brief time, he was master of his environment.

Art classes were the same. But at fourteen, Metro's sketches were bleak, usually a burned out forest with blackened, smoldering tree trunks, a sad black and grey picture of destruction. They were well done, the shading and perspective near perfect and his teachers could pick them out without his name on them.

They did however, portray his view of the world.

At the present though, in front of the attentive class, he read about Santa and his elves, how the elves were fed up with doing all the work, how they had gone on strike forcing Santa to fix his own sleigh, make toys and feed his reindeer. When Santa threw his hands up in despair, Metro stopped reading for he hadn't finished the story.

"Is that all?" A different, older teacher looked at Metro kindly. She encouraged him to draw and write and she would remain in his memory as one bright spot amidst a sea of grey.

Metro shrugged his shoulders.

"That's good. But why didn't you finish it?" she asked, after an awkward silence.

The power ebbed and Metro returned to his normal world.

"Uh, I don't know," he finally said, the nervousness returning.

"Well, I'd certainly like to know if Santa will ever get his presents out," the teacher said.

"Yeah." A voice came from the class. "We'd like to know too."

"I don't know." Metro mumbled and then walked back to his desk. He never did finish the story for he had begun to abandon them in the middle.

To the teacher he was talented but she couldn't understand why he refused to do homework, or his inability to solve even the simplest of mathematical problems. At the same time, in history, he read the text once and passed. She also couldn't understand why he wore filthy clothes that didn't fit or why he never bathed. At times, she would gaze at the boy, whose head shook and face twitched. Then she sent a message home asking to speak to his mother.

Gertie's mouth was hard and thin and her stomach seethed as she sat quietly and listened to the teacher in the staff coffee room.

"Metro has all kinds of talent. We gave him an IQ test and he scored higher than any student we've ever had. But he won't do his homework."

The teacher didn't mention his dirty clothes or unwashed hair for she noticed that Gertie wore a layer of face powder and had doused herself with perfume. She also noticed the stale smell of sweat.

"Yuh! And I don't know." Gertie spread her arms wide. "We give 'em the time. He can study all he wants."

"Well, there's definitely something wrong. He's bright but still he won't study," The teacher said and then paused.

"Can you tell me?" she asked quietly.

"Yuh! He can study all he wants. We don't stop him." Gertie spread her arms again.

"Well," The teacher circled the topic that was uppermost in her mind, taking care not to offend.

"There's got to be something, wrong in the atmosphere maybe."

"Yuh! He can study all he wants," Gertie repeated, her face deathly white as again she spread her arms in the familiar gesture.

"I think he's just lazy!" she added, her square sad face, hard."

The teacher took a deep breath and looked directly at Gertie, at her hard face covered with face powder and at the work worn hands. Then she looked directly into her eyes.

"Well, if I didn't know better I'd say Metro comes out of a disturbed home."

Gertie bit her lip, her face white and calm but her eyes telling of the inner turmoil.

"We tell 'em to study. And if he got trouble, why, it's of his own making." Gertie sat on the edge of the chair, her knuckles pressing into her hips.

"Well, I'm afraid there's nothing we can do," the teacher said. "He passes his grades because he's bright but what would happen if he got sick before June. We couldn't pass him on his average because he fails until the final exam. Then he glances at the books just enough to pass."

The teacher sighed deeply. She was from another reality, a totally alien world. She couldn't understand the woman who sat so stiffly on the chair. More importantly she couldn't understand Metro's reality.

"Yuh!" Gertie suddenly said. "There's nothing we can do. I think he's just a little bit lazy."

That evening she ordered Metro to sit at the table.

"I seen your teacher today!" she bit off the words, her square sad face, grey and angry. Metro felt the familiar stab of guilt and anxiety.

"She, give me good heck! She said there's nothing wrong with you, only that you're a little bit lazy." Gertie glared at Metro who sat with his shoulders hunched.

"You're just lazy. That's all!"

That was how the label of retarded shifted a bit to accommodate the one of lazy but it really didn't make much difference to Metro.

His world however still contained paradoxes. One Friday he walked rapidly home from school with a rare smile. He had been told that he would be a writer and he was lost in a dream, away from the drudgery of the farm and his father's contorting face. And in the dream he did what he loved, instead of the long hours of soul, destroying boredom that was manual labor.

Gerard sat at the kitchen table, home for the weekend. He turned white when he saw Metro. Metro brought out the worst in Gerard, which was the bitterness of someone who feels inadequate and humiliated because of lack of ability, and someone who seeks an easy target.

Gerard had joined the Air Force and was laboriously working toward a degree in History through the Recruiting Officers Training Program. But he still had to spend long grueling hours pouring over books that others skimmed over.

Ironically Metro was searching for the same respect and validation his older brother craved.

"When I get older, I'm gonna be a writer," he opened a window to his soul for the briefest of instants.

"What!" Gerard exploded.

Metro stared at Gerard. The window closed quickly.

"You can't be a writer! You can't even pass your grades!" Contempt dripped from Gerard's words and Metro examined a worn shoe. A heavy silence descended then as Gerard glared at him, his face white and lips, thin and compressed.

After Gerard had left, Gertie muttered in the kitchen, complaining to her sister-in-law that Metro was lazy. Helen wiped dishes and said nothing.

While Gertie muttered, Metro carried an iron pinch bar to the lean-to. Thoughts and images swirled while deep within his soul a simmering rage boiled. He held the bar carelessly as he walked barefoot past the cot against the tar-paper wall where he lay away at night escaping into his dream world.

Suddenly the images were scattered as hot pain blistered its way to his brain from his big toe. The bar had slipped through his fingers, dropping vertically and landing where the nerve endings were concentrated.

"God!" he swore, holding his foot and hopping about. He closed his eyes and groaned out loud for the pain was severe. He limped into the kitchen, agony etched on his face and tears in his eyes. Gertie stopped muttering and turned sideways, her square sad face, hard.

"What in the heck did you do now?"

"I dropped the bar on my toe," Metro gritted through his teeth as he sat by the table. He could see the nail turning black as trapped blood built up pressure and the pain intensified.

"Can I have an aspirin?" he finally asked.

"No! Serves your right! Next time you don't be so tarned stinky, lazy and it won't happen."

Metro fought the tears for an hour with the pain growing worse. He went into the living room where his father and uncle engaged in a desultory and fragmented conversation. He tried reading but the tears made the words blurry. He paced back and forth and then returned to the kitchen. Gertie glared at him.

"Serves you right!" she snarled.

Helen watched the boy hobble about with tears in his eyes and then she looked wonderingly at Gertie. But Gertie talked of how hard her life had been. It didn't occur to Metro to demand that she do something.

Finally Helen went to the stove, poked about and stirred the embers until flames began licking at the wood. She heated water while Metro paced from the porch to the living room and back again. It took a half an hour but finally she placed a basin on the floor.

"Here! Soak your foot in this."

Helen poured salt into the water as Metro gingerly placed his foot into it and then yanked it back. But eventually he was able to soak his toe and the pain lessened somewhat.

Gertie watched silently and when Helen had dumped the water outside she reverted to her story of how she had carried five gallon milk pails when she was fourteen, the same age as Metro.

A day later Metro stood beside a rooster, amongst the trees just north of the house, while a dull aching anger simmered just beneath his control. He glanced nervously about and then slowly raised a club, carefully herding the rooster to behind a straw stack and out of sight. As the rooster pecked unwarily at the ground, images and memories swirled in Metro's mind. His brother's, enraged white face, his father's taunts and Gertie's incessant mutter combined into a maelstrom of emotions with one feeling emerging triumphant: Seething white rage.

Suddenly he swung the club.

He swung again and again, viciously, until the rooster was a pulp beneath its flattened and quivering feathers. As his breath came in gasps and tears ran down his cheeks, the rage broke free from the chaos and he kept on swinging, long after the rooster had died and was a pitiful pile of crumpled feathers and flesh in the dirt by his feet.

Then, as his breathing slowed, Metro was engulfed with shame. He stooped quickly, grabbing the mass of feathers and bloody flesh, hiding, it into the straw stack, careful that no feathers showed. Then he threw the club away and walked slowly to the house, his face calm but underneath a whirlpool tearing at his soul.

He killed more chickens that summer, always with stabbing guilt and shame afterwards and he stuck the corpses into the straw or buried them in shallow graves. Then one seemingly small incident caused him to stop. Gertie blamed the missing chickens on coyotes but one afternoon she walked by the straw pile where he had stuffed the dead birds. Metro watched as guilt tore savagely at his heart.

Suddenly she stopped and pulled a corpse from the straw.

She examined the chicken carefully while Metro stood very still, his insides seething and his breath caught in his lungs. But Gertie never caught on, as she wondered out loud how a hen could get stuck in a straw stack, unaware that the killer was only ten feet away. Finally she threw the corpse to the ground and walked to the garden where she began hoeing offending weeds, in her own world of sweat, toil and anger.

Gertie's finding the dead chicken brought forth so much shame and anxiety that for the moment it won over the suppressed rage. The window that had opened to another reality closed and Metro remained in the two former ones; where he was worthless in one and at the same time read books in the other that the adults he knew couldn't fathom.

Metro quit killing chickens but the suppressed rage remained. At times when he read or sketched he knew a rare sense of serenity but the glimmers became rarer and he sank deeper and deeper into a morass of hazy, anxiety-ridden existence.

In school, in the basement where the teachers rarely went, he was picked on with older boys pushing him up against a wall or slapping his face. He endured the mockery for despite his growing physical strength Metro remained at the bottom rung of the student hierarchy. No girl would sit near him, not wanting to be mocked herself and Metro bore the humiliation silently, confused and hurting.

After one particularly bad day, he rode the school van to the road by the highway. Then he walked rapidly down the dirt road to the farm, the suppressed rage boiling near the surface of his consciousness, threatening to erupt. He discarded his books in the house and left through the back door, nearly running to the secluded south corner of the yard. He stood within the trees and stared at a club he had picked up. Then with his breathing rapid and shallow he hit a tree as hard as he could, swinging with the same rage as when he had beaten the chickens to a bloody pulp. For a very brief time the window to the third insane world of white rage opened a crack. But as he swung the club his breath became shorter and finally he stopped. Then he gazed anxiously across a field and at a farm nearly a mile away, fearing he had been seen.

They'd think I'm crazy, he thought wonderingly but that didn't stop the ritualized game. At times when he attacked a tree, he glanced anxiously over his shoulder for a deep sense of shame permeated his soul.

At other times the loneliness which closed in like an ice fog, made him play other games. He loved sports but only watched from the sidelines for the teachers believed that if a student did poorly in class, not allowing him to play sports would serve as an incentive. So, in the fog of loneliness and misty rejection he played his own game in the yard by the house, tossing an old ball into the air, catching it and running for an imaginary goal line.

At night, Metro lay in his cot against the peeling tar paper, playing a sad and lonely game with an imaginary but willing female. And after, when the sheets were soiled and sticky, he lived temporarily in a world of haunting, tantalizing love while he hugged a pillow.

In school, he came across a picture of a young man and lady, in gown and tuxedo, dancing a waltz. The lady's face was hauntingly beautiful, sensitive yet strong while the man's was aristocratic and assured. Metro stared at the picture for a long time, drawn to it inexplicably while a great void opened in his soul. He had no idea why he longed to be in the picture. All he knew was that he was immeasurably unhappy and wished fervently to be with people who appeared sensitive and refined.

When Metro was fifteen, his world was shattered momentarily. As he kicked the mare in the ribs, she burst into a gallop, her hooves digging up the grass in the pasture. Suddenly, a sparrow flew upwards and she sprang sideways. Metro was thrown through the air and hit the grass with a thump, digging a furrow with his hip. He lay gasping, his lungs fighting for air and he felt a deep, searing pain in his right side. He didn't realize it but the hip had been pushed into the vertebra and a nerve was pinched.

He lay until the pain lessened a bit and then went to the house and rested on his cot. From then on the pain would come inexplicably and vanish in a day or so. When he bent to leave the school van, a sudden pain shot up through his spine and he gasped. Then he bit his lip and walked home, gritting his teeth and forcing one foot in front of the other. His shoulders weighed down with an incomprehensible and nearly unbearable weight and his face glistened. Then when he swore he couldn't take another step, he was home. Sometimes the pain would last for days and at others it would disappear during the night.

Gertie and Vincent were aware of his labored walking but they did nothing. When Metro complained, Gertie glared at him.

"You're just clumsy, always hurting yourself!" she said.

Physical pain could be borne stoically but Metro had no defense against emotional anguish.

During one meal, Gertie stopped chewing suddenly and looked at him and grinned.

"Metro's sure growing!" she said. She had taken to speaking of him in the second person the way she would a dog or cat, even though he was in the same room.

Vincent stopped chewing, his mouth open and the food exposed.

"Yuh!" He waved his arm and then began chewing again as a contortion came and went. "He's gonna grow up big fat, lazy and good for nothing!"

When Metro felt the familiar stab of pain in his back, he bit his lip and said nothing for it had become normal, just another pain to be endured.

That autumn the same man who, had hired him for haying, hired him to pitch bundles while threshing. Metro waited anxiously for the grain to ripen for when he missed school for work he was doing a man's job. School only meant mockery and humiliation.

"Do you think we'll start tomorrow?" he asked as they ate supper one evening when the golden, red leaves fluttered to the ground and the air bore the tangy excitement of harvest.

"Huh!" Vincent let his jaw tremble and his tongue protrude. He knew the loud, rude "Huh!" bothered Metro and he used it whenever he could.

"You can't work yet!" he added, grinning.

"But I thought I was going to be a field pitcher," Metro declared.

"Well, maybe. We'll see." Vincent looked at Gertie and his grin widened.

"But you'll never last."

"Why not?" Metro, demanded. "I worked hauling bales this summer, didn't I?" The bales weighed eighty pounds each and Metro's shoulders had filled out.

Vincent looked at Metro and then at Gertie. The mocking grin stayed on his ruddy face.

"You can unload those bundles by the hay fence. If you can do that, then we'll see."

His mocking grin became mischievous.

"You're gonna be like a guy I knew trying to throw the bundles he was standing on and the machine was running empty."

"Why don't you show me?" Metro asked.

"Well, ya gotta kinda know," was all Vincent would say as he reached for more bread.

Metro unloaded the bundles, and then stood beside the empty rack as Vincent approached with his rocking bear-like walk. Vincent stared at the rack.

"Aw, it couldn't have been packed real good," he finally said, turning his back and walking away.

That fall it rained and rained until the stooks stood forlornly in the fields, wet and soggy. When the frosts came and finally the snow, the grain froze and could be threshed. The back pain that came and went was mercifully absent and Metro walked from team to team in the field, effortlessly throwing the bundles onto the racks. Due to the ice and snow they weighed close to twenty pounds each and had to be torn from the frozen ground by a blade mounted on the front of a tractor. Metro's wrists swelled and hurt but he didn't mention it and eventually the swelling was replaced by powerful muscles and sinew. As he worked, he felt a growing strength ebb and flow through his body.

When darkness closed in and the day's work was done, he played with the farmer's children, running about the yard in a rough game of hockey with an old stick and a ball.

"You'd think you'd be tired after a hard day's work," the farmer's wife said from the porch. Metro paused and stared at her.

What's she mean? Does she think I'm not tired because I don't work hard? The questions swirled in his mind and he quit playing to sit in the kitchen with the men.

Next day he threw the bundles extra hard. Still, he didn't feel any great fatigue.

# Twenty-eight

Dust rose from scuffed shoes as shadowy figures moved about in the gloom while now and then an exclamation or curse could be heard. The sun's rays barely penetrated the filthy basement window but a group of teenage boys could be seen playing marbles, using a steel mat made for scraping boots. The marbles were bounced onto the cement floor from ten feet away and onto the mat with the closest to the wall, the winner. The stakes were low, even for the farm boys, but winning for its own sake was very important. Countless fist fights were fought over the game with blood drying and mixing with the dust on the floor.

Outside the thermometer hovered at minus twenty Fahrenheit although it was early afternoon. It was warm in the basement but more importantly the teenagers were free from intrusive teachers, who preferred to drink coffee and smoke cigarettes in the staff room. And if the smallest of the children were cuffed about, they grew up tough and able to handle themselves.

In an adjoining room, two sawhorses with a sheet of old plywood placed on top served as a ping pong table. Instead of a net, a two-by-six lay on end, across the middle of the table. Rough bats were carved from one inch, planks and the ping pong balls were mostly cracked and had lost their bounce. When the children played their shoes scuffed, the dust at their feet and they were forced to breathe it, but it was preferable to freezing outside. Dust particles danced in the half-light from the high windows and the atmosphere was hazy and surreal, the figures appearing like wraiths. In the gloom, Metro stood by the table, glaring at another boy, who was two years his senior. The boy had grabbed a bat from a child and roughly shoved him aside. Metro had protested but the boy had shoved him aside too.

So he stood by the table, his fists in his pockets, and insides seething. The boy ignored him for Metro had never fought back before. But the seething maelstrom caused by seeing a child hurt, the way he had been hurt, slowly turned to silent white rage.

Metro stepped forward, his face white. Then he deliberately tipped over the two-by-six. The boy walked around to the other side of the table and righted the board, glancing sideways at Metro.

Suddenly, he rammed the board straight at Metro's groin. Metro sprang backwards on his toes and the wood stopped harmlessly, an inch from his pants. He gazed down at it for an instant and then up at the boy who glared from across the table. Then he walked calmly around until he was two feet from the boy.

"Ya wanna fight?" Metro said, the words silly in the sudden silence. The boy simply knocked Metro's glasses off, thinking he'd be blind.

And deep from within, in the fog of frustrated silent rage, Metro exploded. His fists flew on their own, catching the boy in the stomach, face and stomach again in a blurring combination.

Suddenly then, he was alone for the boy lay flat on his back on the collapsed ping pong table, his nose bleeding profusely. He rose and Metro advanced until his fists were flying again and the boy cowered against a cement wall. With the flowing blood Metro felt a quick satisfaction and then a sharp pain in his hand when the boy's teeth broke. Metro could feel the shock of the punches all the way up to his shoulders for he was beating his father, his brothers and mother, all at the same time.

Then through the red haze of rage and bloodlust he heard someone yelling his name. He stopped and looked about slightly bewildered. A crowd, of students were standing in a half circle staring at him. The boy slowly sank onto the cement floor and Metro stared at him in wonder and then at the blood on his fists. He said nothing as the silence deepened and then accepted his glasses from a boy younger than he.

An hour later, the boy who had brought his glasses sat beside Metro in the class room. His eyes were filled with admiration as he glanced at Metro who massaged his right hand and swollen knuckles.

"Hell! He didn't have a ghost of a chance. You could'a killed 'em," he said.

Later the principal came into the classroom with an announcement.

"You can tell your parents that there's an insurance company that'll cover you if you have an accident on the school grounds, or coming to, or from school," he said and then paused dramatically, a grin on his face.

"But it doesn't cover your victim in a fist fight, Metro."

Metro looked down at his desk in embarrassment. Then he looked up in wonder at the students and teacher who, instead of mocking him, looked at him with admiration. But what made his blood tingle was the smile from one of the girls.

Slowly winter lost its frigid grip with a soft wind blowing and the snow sinking. In the warm afternoon sun, the tinkling sound of water caused a quickening of the blood in all creatures. Calves frisked while old cows walked about in the sinking snow of the pasture, dreaming of green grass.

Metro slogged through the soft snow by the creek, near the tall spruce at the end of his father's pasture, whistling a nameless tune for he too felt the quickening life of spring. He walked effortlessly where once he had struggled as a boy, for he was sixteen and nearly a man. Then, after he had climbed a fence and passed under dark spruce he came to a neighbor's yard and saw him leaning on a pole corral, watching water run, into the creek from near the barn. The water was dark and stunk from cow manure but after seven months of winter, it was a pretty sight.

"Hi!" the neighbor called to Metro.

"Hi!" Metro answered and then got down to the business at hand. "Dad said you got some puppies. He said we could have one."

The neighbor nodded and led the way through the barn to his hay fence, walking with a slight stoop for he was a hardworking man. He carried a pan of warm fresh milk and placed it near a stone boat calling, "Here Puppy! Puppy."

He was also good with animals. He had tamed a wild dog by leaving scraps of bread where he had cut firewood in the winter and the half-wolf, half-collie bitch had followed him home. Metro remembered reading that a malamute was a highly intelligent dog but his attention was taken by a line of wobbly puppies heading for the warm milk.

"They've just been weaned," the neighbor said running a gnarled hand over his swarthy face. "You can take one home now."

Metro couldn't decide which one he wanted but just then the last puppy emerged from under the stone boat. He walked with wobbly legs like the rest but there was something definitely different about him. He was bigger by far and when he was near the dish, he nonchalantly shouldered the rest away.

"You mind which one?" Metro asked quickly.

"Naw, I got lots of dogs," the neighbor answered and Metro scooped up the large black and white puppy. The puppy growled, irritated at being yanked away from the dish. The man looked at the puppy and then at Metro.

"He's tough. He ain't scared-a-nothing," he said, scratching his stubbly chin, still bent slightly forward. His love of animals could be seen in his eyes.

"Theyre the best kind," he added and Metro smiled and stroked the puppy. He held him gently and his fingers brushed lightly against the soft fur. The pup settled down in his arms and Metro gazed at the large head. It was almost as big as the rest of his body and the pup's paws were huge.

Metro opened the old military tunic he wore and placed the pup inside, next to his shirt. He left a button open so the pup could breath and he kept his left hand under him so he wouldn't fall. Then he cast an eye at the red sun, sinking slowly into the west just above the tall dark spruce. The shadows had lengthened, dark and mysterious, under the heavy dark boughs. He shivered suddenly for a chill had crept into the air.

"Well, thanks. I better, be going," he said. He walked rapidly toward the spruce with the puppy snuggling into his tunic, for with the sun's descent the warmth left and the snow began to crunch underfoot. He came to the fence and held the top wire down with one hand, careful not to let the pup, fall out of his tunic. When he was over, he followed a path near the creek which ran between two huge spruce trees, their roots exposed where the water had washed away the soil.

Suddenly, he felt a prickly sensation and turned quickly. The mother was three feet behind for she had smelled the pup in his tunic. She leapt quickly away and disappeared amongst the trees. Metro felt a quick guilt for robbing a mother of her young and vowed to treat the pup well.

When he was home and in the kitchen he set the pup on the floor and set down a pan of milk. The puppy wobbled to the dish and drank thirstily. Then he urinated on the floor. Metro found a rag and cleaned up the mess and then sat and watched as the pup wobbled about on the linoleum, sniffing everything. It was the first time in Metro's life that he actually possessed something and his heart welled up and moisture formed in his eyes. He bit his lip to control the emotions and then wondered what to call the pup. Since all the former dogs had been called Buster, he decided on Buster the Third. And so the pup had a name and formally became part of Metro's life.

In the short years before he left the farm and even after, the dog would be more than just a pet. He would be all the good things that Metro knew.

As the days lengthened and spring turned into the lazy heat of summer, Metro spent all his free time with the pup, patiently training him to stay, to chase cattle and to return when he whistled. One afternoon, he sat on the lush green grass near the barn with the two-month-old pup beside him. A cow had solved the puzzle of the wooden gate and eagerly cropped grass, gradually working her way closer and closer. Suddenly, as the cow reached forward, her tongue extended to tear off more grass, Metro heard a tiny growl. Buster rose to his feet and advanced on the cow, who ignored him. Then the tiny growl grew to an enraged snarl and he began barking furiously. The cow stopped for an instant, staring in wonder at the strange and tiny creature in front of her. Buster, advanced farther, his hackles rising and his growl determined.

Metro rose quickly and the cow beat a hasty retreat with Buster barking triumphantly at her heels. Metro caught the pup and hugged him, his heart nearly bursting with pride. Then he again sat in the grass with the pup running in a circle about him. Suddenly Metro stuck out his hand. The pup attempted jumping over it but Metro raised it. Buster did a somersault and landed on his rear, yelping loudly. Metro laughed but the pup sprang to his feet and charged. Metro caught him only a couple feet from his face, his teeth bared and his eyes enraged. Instead of beating him, Metro petted Buster until he calmed down for he didn't want to break his spirit.

When Buster was more than two months, old Metro began training him to bring the cows in on his own. The pup at first instinctively tried to bite a cow's belly or hamstring her but with enough gentling and training Metro felt he would be a great cattle dog.

One day though, Metro watched his pup in puzzlement. Buster ran ahead to round up the cows who were lying down near a poplar bluff. Suddenly he stopped short as if brought up by a leash. Then he glanced back at Metro. Metro, tried again.

"Get the cows!" he called and waved. The pup ran for about twenty feet and then stopped short again. Metro, approached and knelt, laying his twenty-two caliber rifle, on the grass beside him. He took the pup's head in his hands and talked to him as if he were human.

"Buster! What's the matter? Don't you understand?" he said and petted the top of the pup's head. The pup wagged his tail and Metro tried one more time. Again the pup ran about twenty feet and then stopped short, glancing quickly over his shoulder. A terrible suspicion began to form in Metro's mind.

Next evening Vincent left the house, walking rapidly towards the pasture in that rocking manner of his. Metro followed and watched from a distance. When Vincent was close to the cattle who were all lying down near some willows, the pup ran forward and began circling the herd.

"Buster! Come back!" Vincent yelled, picking up a stone. He threw it and in landed right in front of the pup. The pup stopped instantly, glancing back over his shoulder. When he started again, Vincent threw another stone and the pup sprang sideways for it nearly hit his head. Then Vincent walked around the herd until he was directly behind them.

"Sic 'em!" he yelled. "By the heels!"

The pup sprang forward and the cows jumped to their feet, stampeding toward the corral. Metro thought of his parents' nagging that running made the cows give less milk. Then the confusion deepened as another attempt at something good, ended in failure.

Vincent made a face and grinned for he had played another joke on the boy who was "Kinda foolish."

The summer passed slowly with Metro still trying to train his pup. Vincent grinned more often as he played the joke, thinking Metro wasn't aware of what he was doing. So Metro wandered the woods with the ancient, scarred twenty-two and his pup while in the evening he reread books he knew by heart for there was no mobile library in the summer. He had barely passed grade seven and the simplest problems in math or algebra were insurmountable; for deep in his subconscious, lurked his father's constant taunt of "Metro! You can't!" As the summer slipped slowly by, he sank deeper into an emotional whirlpool that had become an inescapable morass. At times the imaginary reality of books became more real than the reality of his father's taunts and his mother's agitated nagging.

One sunny afternoon, Metro wandered in a neighbor's pasture crossing an open field and coming to a creek that was fringed with willows. He crossed the creek on stones with the pup right behind. Then he walked under a stand of towering spruce trees. Under the pleasantly pungent needles he felt a fleeting serenity and he sat on an old stump and sighed deeply, gazing about the little glade that had become a retreat.

The pup ran, quickly to beneath a tree and sniffed about. Curious, Metro rose and followed to where he was gazing down at the corpse of a calf. Its eyes were gone, with only empty sockets staring unseeing at the boy and dog. The intestines were partially eaten by scavengers and at first glance appeared to move. Metro starred at the maggots that crawled and fought for their morsels and a deep, dank depression settled into his soul.

That's how man is, he mused, fighting for a morsel that is nothing to another. Each one is convinced that his morsel of rotting flesh is a God given right, and the most important thing in the universe. Metro leaned on his rifle, deep in thought as the pup lost interest and wondered off.

If I were God or some other superior being that is probably how I'd see human beings, he thought and then smiled cynically.


In the winter, in the middle of the dark, frozen nights when timbers cracked from frost, Metro lay in his cot and dreamed of soft, tantalizing ladies. He never dreamed of the coarse farm girls who wouldn't sit next to him but rather of ladies of the highest born. He read of them and occasionally saw them in movies and his imagination did the rest. For a very brief time he lived in a misty world of warmth but as always the warmth was followed by wet sheets and searing, shameful guilt.

One night, when the wind drove snow devils across the open fields and the world was clothed in ghostly white from a silvery moon, Metro sat with his parents in the living room. They huddled close to the stove for the cold penetrated the log walls and the windows were heavy with frost patterns. They had gone to Midnight Mass, freezing in the ancient half-ton truck, for it was Christmas Eve, the holiest of all nights. Metro, had let the communion wafer lay on his tongue while he had cast his eyes about in abject boredom, for meaningless Latin and prayers recited by rote always did that to him.

In the living room, they ate roast pork and chicken for there was plenty of food. But Metro's mouth was dry and constricted, for food was the only commodity that was in abundance.

"Metro! Gimmee a drink of your milk!" Vincent suddenly demanded.

"I'll get you a glass from the kitchen," Metro replied quickly.

"No! Give it here. I just wanna swallow."

Metro watched as his father made a face before bringing the glass to his mouth. He blinked his eyes rapidly in his repulsive manner and then drank deeply with a loud slurping sound.

"Here! Take it away!" he snapped, handing the glass back to Metro. Metro sat it down and then gazed at his father who chewed pork and chicken, the food rolling about in his open mouth.

Finally Gertie smiled and looked at Vincent.

"Well! Are we gonna open the presents?"

Vincent played Santa Claus, laboriously reading a name on each gift and then handing it to Gertie or sat, it beside himself on another chair. There were few presents and finally he held a small package close to his face.

"Metro!" he called loudly and shoved the package at his son, adding "Here!" Then he wiped his mouth with the back of his hand before biting into a large drumstick.

Metro felt the package as a dark suspicion formed and he thought of the frozen fingers he had endured for months. He sat very still for a moment while Gertie and Vincent looked at him. Gertie's eyes were bright with a light he couldn't fathom.

"Well! Aren't you gonna open it?".

Metro lifted the package and slowly undid the string, pulling a pair of woollen gloves from the paper. He felt the softness of the wool and then pulled the gloves apart for a thread held them together. The price tag had been removed but he remembered it from the catalog. He thought of the fifty cents it had cost and also of freezing his fingers. He had asked for new gloves for months but Gertie had always smiled quickly, the unfathomable light in her eyes.

"Wait!" she had grinned. "Wait, and we'll see."

Metro had waited, walking to the school bus with one hand in his jacket pocket for warmth and the other carrying his books. He had to change often for his fingers would freeze quickly. When he had been in school it took over an hour before he could hold a pen properly.

"Well! What'a ya think?" Gertie demanded, the light still in her eyes. Vincent grinned broadly and he stopped eating for the moment.

"Thanks," Metro said quietly. "They're what I needed for the last two months."

Gertie's eyes slowly lost the unfathomable light and Vincent made a face and began cracking nuts with pliers, chewing rapidly while hefting the tool in his hand. Gertie looked steadily at Metro and then the thoughts came.

He doesn't even appreciate them.

Her mouth hardened but she resisted the urge to spread her arms wide. The next thought was, and what did he get me?

Metro slowly rolled a cigarette and then blew smoke into the air, staring at the frost patterns on the window, his eyes moist.

Gertie glanced at her son again and a final,bitter thought came. He can afford that tarned tobacco but he won't even buy me a present.

In late spring, when birds sang and the blue sky and green grass made the bitter cold only a memory, Metro sat in a classroom, moisture in his eyes and his hand massaging his jaw. He had an abscessed tooth and as he stared at the blackboard, his vision swam for the pain spread to the entire right side of his face. The teacher glanced up from her desk and wondered why there were tears in Metro's eyes but she didn't ask. To Metro, the toothache, like the recurring lower back pain or migraines, was normal.

Metro lost five pounds that spring but still he passed grade eight and at sixteen was ready to enter Junior High the following autumn. Later he sat in the kitchen at dinner while Vincent made faces as he ate with food rolling around in his open mouth. This time Metro didn't notice.

"Oh, why aren't you eating?" Gertie poked Metro.

"I got a toothache!" Metro snapped for he had told Gertie weeks before. She had spread her arms in the familiar gesture of futility. When he asked to see a dentist, she told him to wait for a while.

He had remembered that alcohol was a good pain killer and had asked for vanilla. That, Gertie had agreed to, sending Vincent to town to buy another bottle. Eventually though the 40 percent alcohol wasn't enough, for the gum had become badly infected.

"I can't eat!" Metro said and pushed his plate away.

"Huh!" Vincent snorted loudly. Then, as he chewed with his mouth open, he looked closely at his son who held his face in his hands.

"Just as long as you can haul hay," Vincent said. Metro lifted his head and glared at his father. Then as the pain came in waves and he rubbed his jaw, he had an idea.

"That's it! No dentist! No hay!"

"Huh!" Vincent exclaimed again and Gertie sighed. A heavy silence settled down upon the kitchen. Metro looked out the window at the gently rustling leaves and then back at his parents. Gertie sighed again and looked at Vincent.

"Should we?" The question was the same as when Allen had demanded the car. Vincent stared back at Gertie and then slowly capitulated.

"Okay! I'll start the truck."

The dentist cost three dollars and the gas, a dollar and fifty cents. Metro made note of the price and the event simmered along with the others, just below the surface.

One early evening when the sun still hovered over the bluff of poplars west of the yard, Vincent rose and grabbed the rosary box, rattling the beads. Metro felt a quick stab of anxiety and he glanced at the door. But he complied with his parents demand, kneeling on the hard linoleum and clutching a rosary in his hands. Every evening was the same. Vincent would recite the memorized prayers, and Metro and Gertie would respond with a chorus of repetitive words. Lately though, Gertie had become dissatisfied with Metro's mumbling. As he knelt by a chair, she turned suddenly to him.

"Metro!" Her whining voice made him wince. "It's time you learned to lead the rosary. All the other children do. So you should too."

Metro looked down at the floor for a brief while and then up at his mother.

"What for?" he demanded. He couldn't explain the total and crushing boredom he felt when praying meaningless prayers.

"Come on, Metro! We all pray too. So come on now! Lead us in prayer!" Gertie said.

Metro clutched the rosary in his callused hands and leaned forward until his elbows were resting on a chair.

"Why? Why do we have to pray every evening?"

"Because I made a pledge to Father Patten!" Vincent snapped. "He said people don't pray enough and I pledged that we would say the rosary twice a day. It's bad enough that we only say it once."

Metro glared at his father but Gertie's whining voice made him turn to her.

"Come on, Metro! We all pray. So why can't you lead us?" Her voice softened slightly. "Try Metro. Try to lead."

Metro gazed down at the floor again. He knew the prayers but he couldn't force the words. A heavy silence descended then and Gertie's face whitened. He was too big to beat with the strap so she tried a different method. During this, Metro kept his gaze on the floor and prayed silently.

"Dear God! Why can't my parents be normal?"

But the prayer went unanswered as his mother glared at him.

"Try Metro! Try!"

"I can't!" he blurted.

"Don't you know the words?" Gertie asked as Vincent impatiently shifted from one knee to the other. Gertie thought of Gerard's insistence that Metro was retarded. The silence deepened again and outside a crow cawed but Metro didn't pray.

"Don't you care, Metro?" Gertie's voice was innocent, contrasting with the whiteness of her cheeks. "All of us lead sometimes. So why can't you?" Then she turned to Vincent. "Show him how. If you say the words, maybe he'll be able too."

Vincent made a face and then began mumbling. But the words were jumbled and only a confused monotone. He had been saying them for so long he wasn't aware of their meaning anymore. Metro stared at his father.

"Those aren't the words. Why don't you say them like they're supposed to sound?"

Vincent turned slightly red. He tried again, and again all he could do was mumble, in a low singsong for the words' meaning no longer existed for him. He could only kneel and go through a ritual that sounded silly and filled Metro with a great shame. He thought of the crude saying about a man so stupid, he'd screw up the Lord's prayer.

He can't screw up the Lord's prayer any more than he already has, Metro thought disgustedly but Gertie's whining voice broke into his thoughts.

"Come on now, Metro. Try!" Her face appeared concerned and Metro felt a myriad of emotions. Suddenly Gertie began to sob.

"Oh why don't you care about the church? Oh why do we have to have a son who hates God?"

"I don't hate God!" Metro said softly, his throat constricted and his chest hurting.

"Then why can you not lead the rosary?" Gertie asked, her face glistening.

"Because, I don't believe like you do!" Metro blurted. "I don't believe mumbling meaningless words will get God's attention. I believe

God is outside amongst the trees and open fields. That's God to me, a God that creates beauty, not misery."

Gertie stared at her son, her face hard again and Vincent made a face.

"I believe God is good and, just and that he doesn't want people to make others do what they want just because they think it's right. I believe God is gentle."

Metro sighed deeply for he had run out of words. His eyes were moist as a heavy silence settled down again.

"But why can you not pray?" The question came again and Metro straightened.

"That's it! I've had it!" He rose and threw down the rosary. He took the twenty-two and went outside, calling his pup who sat up quickly and followed. Metro walked rapidly to the woods and then sat on a stump, absentmindedly stroking the pup's head, while a torrent of emotions swirled in his soul. He sat there until the sun set and darkness softened the contours of the earth. But in the gathering darkness there were no more answers than in the kitchen where his mother demanded that he pray meaningless prayers.

Metro wiped sweat from his eyes with a dirty hanky and glanced over the field of sweet clover stubble. Crows cawed from poplar trees and he wished he could join them in the shade for the sun broiled down, its intensity magnified by the grueling hours of loading loose hay with pitch forks. The dusty piles stood about the field, under the hot sun the green of the sweet clover turned a rusty brown. Metro stuck his fork into a pile, the weight making him take a quick step forward for balance as he lifted it shoulder high to throw it onto the rack. He glanced at his father who made a face and then wiped his mouth with his sleeve. When the pile was loaded he walked to the next as the horses pulled the heavy wagon, their muscles bunching.

Metro's mind wasn't on the horses or the hay for he had turned seventeen and still didn't have a driver's license. A vehicle was needed and he had no choice but to convince his parents to let him use the old truck for the test. He thought of when he had asked his mother.

"Mom," he had begun as Gertie's mouth had hardened. "I got an idea." He had paused and then plunged on. "You don't want me to smoke, well, I'll quit smoking if I can get a driver's license."

Gertie had bitten her lip and glared.

"I don't want to go out every weekend," he had added quickly. "Just maybe once a month. Everybody else can drive their father's car or truck. All I ask is once a month. That's not too much, is it?"

Gertie had glared at him some more, her mouth thin and hard.

"All you want is to drive that truck 'til it's broke!" She had suddenly blurted.

Metro had stopped, shocked. Then he had silently watched his mother's glistening face, the sobs more a whine than real crying and finally he had left the house. He had never asked her again. But he remembered the agitated conversation after his older brother had left and his mother's bitter words.

"So now! No son off ours is gonna drive the car again."

All this went through Metro's mind as he stuck his fork into another pile of hay. He also thought of his father's boast that he saved one hundred and fifty dollars a year by not bailing hay since he had a strong boy to work. The thoughts swirled as Metro stuck his fork into yet another pile and his pup chased a mouse. Vincent was his last chance for he would never ask his mother again.

"Dad! What about a driver's license?"

Vincent glanced at him for a second but said nothing as he contorted his face and then stuck his fork into the hay.

"Dad! I got to have a driver's license."

Vincent looked up from the hay and then, just as a grin was spreading, turned his back. He looked at the pasture and cows lying in the shade.

"Sure hope it doesn't rain," he said grinning broadly.

Metro stared at his back and then at the load of hay and rows of piles that still had to be loaded. Then Vincent turned around, the grin still on his face, and Metro thought about his conversation with his mother that morning.

"You think more of your cows and pigs than you do me, don't you?" he had demanded.

Gertie had turned from the sink and looked at him for an instant. Then, as a smile spread on her square face, she had spread her arms wide.

"Well, the cows and pigs, we can sell them for money."


Vincent parked the old half-ton ford fifty yards from the church with the high gothic steeple and cross. He contorted his face and rested with his heavy hands on the steering wheel. Beside him Gertie sat stiffly, her face white with powder but the hard lines of suffering still visible. Next to her was Metro with his shoulder pressed hard against the steel door of the truck, for the cab was small and just big enough to accommodate all three.

A few minutes passed as Metro looked about at the store that was open Sunday for that was when the owner did his best business, and at the empty parking spots between them and the church for there was still over a half an hour until Mass. Vincent liked to arrive early and wait until the spaces were full. At the end of the Mass he also waited until everyone else had left and Metro sat in the truck, shame winding its way into his soul for everyone could see the old battered half-ton when they drove past.

That morning, Metro sighed, rolled a cigarette and then turned down the window for fresh air. He lit the cigarette, blowing smoke out the window before looking at his parents. Gertie sat with her face, rigid and tired while Vincent made a face, wiping his mouth with his hand.

"Why do we have to be so early?" Metro finally demanded.

"I wanna make sure I got a good place to park," Vincent retorted.

"God! There's plenty of places. And why do you park so far from the church?"

"Because then I don't have to worry about leaving," Vincent snapped. "Besides you're supposed to wanna go to church."

Metro shook his head and stared at his father. Gertie sat in the middle saying nothing.

"Why don't you go every day?" Metro demanded.

"I would if I could!" Vincent snapped and Metro sighed and looked at the front of the church where a farmer parked a new car and then got out, slamming the door. As the minutes slowly passed, the small parking lot filled and finally Vincent and Gertie left the truck with Metro walking beside them. They entered and walked to the front and sat in the pew that Vincent paid a small rent for. All three genuflected and then kneeled on the hard bench, making the Sign of The Cross. Vincent and Gertie prayed for a moment as Metro picked up a small black book which he had read many times. But in the boredom of the church, he reread Christ's parable of the Prodigal Son and how his Father had welcomed him home.

Then he filed out of the pew to the confessional where he confessed sins he had been told to confess; That he had been angry at his parents and had been a bad son. After that he returned to the pew and waited. When the Mass had been celebrated, he again filed out of the pew with his parents and stood in line to receive the Holy Communion, the wafer tasteless on his tongue.

When most of the ritual had been completed Metro sat, resigned to yet another boring sermon. But this time a small balding man in a brown robe walked up to the pulpit and stared out at the parishioners. He was a missionary and was to present a guest sermon.

He began on a theme of respect, for your parents and authority. Metro glanced sideways at his parents, at Vincent who made a face and at Gertie whose white face was set in the eternal pose of silent suffering. But then the missionary took him completely by surprise.

"Respect your parents, yes! But you parents, where do you think that respect comes from?"

He paused dramatically and gazed down at the sea of faces.

"First you must respect your children, for what good are words alone? What good is it to tell your children that they must respect, you if you don't give them respect first?"

Metro glanced again at his parents but their postures remained the same.

"If your son wants to go out after working hard all week, let him. For that is part of growing up. Don't expect him to do as he's told all week and then be denied the opportunity to be with people his own age."

Metro stared at the tiny, balding priest and wondered what childhood he had known.

"If you've raised them right they won't do anything bad. But if you don't respect them, if you look at them as just free labor, don't expect them to respect you."

The missionary again paused and then ended his sermon with, "Demand respect from your children, yes; but first give them respect!"

When the Mass was over Metro sat in the truck while Vincent contorted his face, his hands on the steering wheel and Gertie sat in her customary pose. Finally Metro could contain himself no longer.

"Well, what did you think of the sermon?" He was still amazed that the missionary had voiced his exact concerns. But a silence deepened in the tiny cab as he gazed at his mother.

"So now!" she finally spoke, her mouth hard. "That's how they treated me. That's how the Blutes were. All they wanted was for me to work and work. But respect. No! They never gave me no respect."

Gertie's mouth was hard and angry as she stared out the windshield. Vincent turned the key and the truck motor sputtered to life.

As they drove down the dusty road, Metro sat in the cab, staring out at the passing scenery. He glanced again at his mother, at her hard bitter face and how she kept her hands, folded in her lap. Then he sighed deeply.

What was the use?

# Twenty-nine

A full moon rode high above the tree-lined dirt road, illuminating the gently fluttering leaves while close by, stood three grain elevators, the tallest stark white in the ghostly light. Right beside the elevators and parallel to the road ran silvery railroad tracks, gleaming in the moonlight and stretching off into the hazy distance.

Metro walked slowly in the warm soft night, barely aware of the night's beauty as emotions ebbed and flowed. He had turned eighteen, the muscles in his shoulders and arms hard and tough and his back strong except for the recurring and inexplicable spasms. But inside where it counted, a constant raging turmoil left him weak and vulnerable. As he walked, he thought of how no matter how hard he tried things always went wrong and the fog deepened with each passing year.

He had finally given up, dropping out of grade ten just before the final exams, coming home one sunny afternoon, and throwing his books on the floor next to the wall in the kitchen. Gertie had glanced at him as he sat on a chair, his shoulders hunched and his face resigned. Metro had looked at his mother and had sighed deeply.

"I quit school."

The statement had only caused Gertie to pause for a brief time as she rushed about the kitchen in her constant and harried attempt to do all the work at once.

"Oh!" she had said. Then she had voiced what was to her an already accomplished fact.

"You'll just have to work like the rest off us now, as a farmer, if you want to stay here."

As Metro walked beneath the poplar trees in the warm mid-summer breeze, the thoughts came and went and the moon didn't seem as bright as it usually was. He had sat in the kitchen, feeling uneasy because of his mother's lack of concern and he had thought of the grueling, mind numbing work without even being trusted to drive the truck. Then he had voiced his feelings.

"That's it! I'm not gonna stay home and work for nothing like someone who's retarded. I'm gonna get a job. I don't know where. But I'm gonna get one."

Gertie stopped instantly, in one of her dashes across the kitchen, her face turning hard and anxious.

"But you can't! Where would you get a job?"

"I don't know. But I'm not gonna stay here and work like a slave." Metro had been determined but deep inside, his stomach had churned in a hot ball of anxiety.

And what the hell good did it do, he demanded of himself? He glanced up to where the dirt road curved and crossed the silvery rails under the full moon as it rode high above the sleeping countryside. Then he glanced back down at the dirt under his worn shoes as the thoughts and anger swirled. The day after he had made his ultimatum, Vincent had driven out to the field where Metro drove the tractor under the hot sun.

When Metro had stopped the tractor, Vincent had wasted little time, placing a dirty hand on the tractor fender and looking earnestly up at his son.

"If you stay, I'll give you fifty cents a day, three dollars a week."

Metro had stared down at the worry in his father's eyes and his determination had evaporated. He had finally nodded his head and the deal was done. Metro had felt a twisted form of relief for being asked to stay and he spent long hours slouching on the hard tractor seat. But Vincent still didn't allow him to drive the truck, and every Friday evening Gertie would present him with three one dollar bills, her eyes bright and a brittle smile, on her face.

"And don't go and blow it now. You better save some."

The three dollars had been barely enough to pay for a movie and admission to a dance so Metro didn't save any and the guilt had deepened. With the work, he abandoned writing and found he couldn't draw the easiest of pictures. Slowly he sank into the world his family had created for him; where he was to labor in the fields like a dull beast, not even trustworthy enough to drive the truck.

Metro crossed the silvery steel tracks and glanced up at the moon as the warm breeze fanned his face. His chest was heavy and constricted and he sighed as he thought of the three miles yet to walk. He lengthened his stride for the next day was Sunday and no matter how tired he was Gertie would appear in his bedroom.

"Come on, Metro!" The words would crash into his sleep. "Come on! You gotta go to church!"

And he knew he would groan and dutifully pull on his clothes.

As he walked, he thought of the grinding boredom in the domed church, the meaningless prayers and the deep sense of shame when he watched his father make faces as he prayed.

Suddenly, he noticed a car approaching slowly from behind. He hoped someone would give him a ride but as the car slowed, he heard only mocking laughter.

"Hey Metro! Ya wanna good time?" The car sped up to just ahead of him and then slowed.

"Mary here says she wants to go out with you!" This was followed by a girl slapping the boy who was mocking Metro. Mary had been the girl he had approached during the dance that evening. She was unpopular and normally sat on the hard bench most of the night.

"You think maybe," he had stammered after standing at the door to the old dance hall and working up the courage. "You think maybe, you could dance with me?"

The girl had glanced up quickly, a deep frown on her face. She wasn't pretty, being thin with short brown hair and freckles. She had answered matter-of-factly, "I can't dance. Ask someone else."

"Sure you can. If I can try, you could," Metro had persisted.

"I said I can't! Get lost!"

The sudden angry words had made heads turn and Metro had retreated to stand at the doorway, his hands in his pockets and his heart filled with shame. Later, he had seen the same girl dancing and the humiliation had burned a spot in his soul.

"Hey Metro! Ya wanna ride?" The car slowed and then sped up just out of reach. The mocking laughter came at Metro in waves, breaking against his soul as he walked slowly, his shoulders hunched. But he knew sooner or later they would tire of the game. After a few more taunts the car suddenly accelerated, spraying gravel onto his shoes and pants. But he was left alone in the dust and humiliation.

Metro walked the rest of the way under the full moon and whispering leaves until he was home and in his cot. But sleep wouldn't come and the taunts remained in his mind. He wondered about his existence for he was capable of seeing himself and his parents in a realistic, if hazy way. And he knew there was something wrong with his father. Even when Vincent mocked him the knowledge was still there, festering like an open sore.

Suddenly though, Metro's world changed. Allen had written to his parents asking Metro to come to Calgary to finish school. And since

Gertie and Vincent knew that sooner or later he would leave, they told him and Metro had an escape.

Later, Gerard approached Metro who knelt by the hay fence playing with his dog. Gerard's face was pinched and white and his mouth thin. He stopped and glared at Metro.

"Mom told me you might go to Calgary to school."

"Yeah," Metro said warily.

"Well, ya gonna go?"

"I think so but I thought maybe I might join the Air Force."

"Well, if I was you, I'd just join the Air Force and get it over with." Gerard's eyebrows knitted together in concentration and Metro looked at him wonderingly.

"You'll just be wasting your time in school anyway. If I was you, I'd join up right now. At least that way you'll be able to do something you're capable of."

Metro stared at his brother's agitated white face for a few seconds, his mind confused. Then silently, he turned back to his dog.


Metro sat on a couch with his arms folded and his stomach in knots for he was in a totally alien world. About him were teenagers, some his age but mostly younger and an animated conversation came at him in waves.

After serious consideration he had changed his name to Mike. But if he thought that the mere changing of a name and a few hundred miles on a crowded Greyhound bus would make a difference, he was wrong.

As the conversation ebbed and flowed, Mike sank deeper into a personal morass of self doubt and emotional ineptitude. On one side sat a girl, two years younger than he but pretty with long dark hair. She turned suddenly and asked his name.

"Mike," he had replied slowly.

"You're not from here, are you," she said, her pretty face close to his.

"Uh, I come from Saskatchewan. I go to Saint Mary's," Mike answered, fearful she might ask what grade he was in for he was still two years behind.

Then, in the maelstrom of emotional conflict, Mike noticed that a game had begun. A bottle had been placed on the rug and spun. It pointed right to the girl next to Mike.

She smiled self-consciously as a pregnant silence deepened and Mike wondered what was to come. Then she stood, saying "I pick him."

Mike suddenly felt her hand in his. He rose slowly and then followed her to a bedroom for it was the teenage version of the ancient, but always new and at times frightening, game. When they were in a bedroom the girl sat right next to him on the bed and he was painfully aware of how she pressed against him. He turned sideways and looked down at the pretty, anxious face framed by long dark tresses. All the urges and dreams of the sad and lonely nights on the isolated farm collided in Mike's soul.

His arm was lead. Vainly he tried raising it to encircle her waist. But all the years of conditioning and mockery was there, simmering just beneath the surface and Mike twisted internally in a prickly feeling of anxiety and despair. He did nothing as the seconds ticked by and the girl's smile slowly disappeared, replaced by a frown. Finally she sighed and gazed down at her feet.

"You been here long?" she asked.

"Couple months."

Another painful and lengthy pause ensued with the girl glancing uncertainly at Mike and then down at her shoes again.

"Well, I guess we might as well go back," she finally said.

"Yeah." Mike sighed deeply. He tried desperately to do something, even a kiss. But it was too late. He rose obediently and followed the girl back into the living room where the other teens smiled knowingly at them.

Mike again sat on the couch, his arms folded while inside the turmoil raged. The girl sat beside him and wondered what she had done wrong. Mike covertly looked at her well, formed legs while inside the desperation raged. Finally then, came resignation. He straightened and stood, reaching for his jacket. He appeared calm and possessed but inside, he ached with a fierce pain. The girl stood too and followed him.

When he was at the door, she suddenly stood on tip toe and kissed him on the lips, gently. Mike stepped back quickly, his lips not responding while the turmoil intensified. His face lost its ruddy color but still he appeared calm and cold. The girl looked up, puzzlement in her eyes. Mike gazed back at her sadly.

Then he nodded, turned and was out the door in the cool evening. Along with the regret came relief and he sighed deeply, breathing in the night air. It felt good out in the open, where he was alone.

"What'a ya doing in here?" a tall, greying priest demanded suddenly, standing over Mike as he read in the library.

Mike looked up quickly, his face losing its color.

"I'm just reading," he said quickly but the priest only smiled and Mike became confused. The priest added to the confusion by placing his hand on Mike's shoulder.

"Why aren't you out playing football? Saint Mary's sure can use good men like you," he said quietly.

Mike had wanted to play but again the conditioning was so strong he had only watched from the sidelines as the football team practiced. Then he had retreated to the library and a book.

"Why don't you go down for a tryout? You certainly have the shoulders for it."

Mike put away the book and went down to the football field where he again stood by the sidelines and watched. Before he could practice though, he had to have a medical exam and the experience burned another searing spot of embarrassment in his soul. When the doctor had asked him to lower his shorts for the examination he had stared at Mikes penis for a moment. It was dark brown and if Mike had been the same color throughout the rest of his body, he would have appeared as dark as a treaty Indian.

"Been doing a bit of sun bathing, I see," the doctor had grinned and Mike's face had gone red with embarrassment. He had puzzled over what the doctor had meant for up until then he had not known that he was any different from anyone else.

He had passed the physical and the next day the head coach stomped about, yelling at the boys who wanted to be football players. Mike winced every time the coach yelled for in his experience a loud voice always preceded violence. The priest however had talked to the coach and Mike was soon in a practice uniform but still standing uncertainly on the sidelines. As he watched, an assistant coach approached.

Then he was on the line of scrimmage. The ball was snapped and someone slammed into him, knocking him backwards and bruising his arms with the hard shoulder pads.

Mike hadn't known enough to bend down and he paid for it with the pain in his arms. The second time the ball was snapped he took the punishment and rammed the opposing player backwards through the line, winning the shoving match that followed.

The coach and priest watched and exchanged glances. On the next play Mike slipped and was spiked on his left hand. He ignored it and they exchanged glances again. Mike's hand swelled but he went back into the line, more determined than ever.

The priest smiled and the coach shook his head. Tough boys who were willing to endure pain were hard to find. A little later Mike and another player were paired off by an assistant coach who wore a baseball cap and talked with a Southern accent. The priests believed in training boys through sports and even imported coaches. It showed in the nine out of ten city championships.

"I'm Jack! What's your name?"

Mike mumbled his name and the coach glared at him.

"Okay! I'm here to teach you some basic rules. Like how not to be stupid, so ya don't get bruises on your arms. Don't you know enough to get down on the line?"

Mike looked down quickly as shame and guilt immobilized him.

"Lookit your arms!" the coach continued. "They look like a rainbow. And don't tell me it doesn't hurt."

The coach then walked to where a white scrimmage line was on the grass.

Suddenly, Mike was slammed into by the other boy but he stood his ground and drove him backwards. The coach blew his whistle and scratched his head, holding his cap in the other hand. He was impressed by Mike's strength and determination but couldn't understand his lack of concern for personal safety. But after a few more scrimmages, Mike got down lower and slammed into the boy, driving him backwards.

"Now," the coach took Mike aside, "I'm gonna show you something." He placed both fists together and formed one. "When he comes at you bring up both fists into his chest. Understand?"

Mike nodded and got ready.

Then, as the other boy came at him, Mike drove both fists upwards with all his strength. Suddenly the boy stood upright on his toes, the wind knocked from his lungs. Mike's legs churned like pistons, his helmet aimed at the boy's groin.

"Hold it!" the coach yelled and then blew his whistle. "Stop! For Christ's sake!"

"Jesus! Mary and Joseph!" he swore again and then glanced quickly at the priest who was still smiling from the sidelines, out of earshot.

"This is practice! What'a ya trying to do? Kill em?"

"I'm sorry," Mike said quickly while the boy rubbed his chest, moisture in his eyes. Mike looked at him for an instant and then guilt spread for he would have driven his helmet into his groin, not thinking of the pain it would cause.

The coach scratched his head again, waving his hat about. Mike appeared to be blessed with great ability but still, there was a lack of concentration, almost confusion. The coach had known good athletes who didn't make a team, not because of inability but because they lacked mental aggressiveness. He wondered if that was Mike's problem.

Then he tried Mike as a tackle with the other boy running at him at full speed. As the boy approached Mike suddenly stood upright, catching him around the neck and hanging on. For a brief instant both were horizontal with the boy climbing an invisible staircase. Then they slammed into the grass, Mike's hands still about the boy's neck. Both lay with their helmets a yard apart and their bodies stretched out in opposing directions.

The boy got up slowly and massaged his neck, hurt in his eyes as he gazed steadily at Mike.

"What the hell was that? Where in hell'd ya learn to tackle like that?" The coach demanded, his hands on his hips.

"I don't know." Mike said. "We used to play tackle in the winter. You know, without any rules."

The coach stared at Mike. The boy still massaged his neck.

"Well, that's one hell of a vicious tackle, and great during a game when you want to take someone out. But for Christ's sake, this is practice. You do that in a game, not against your own players or we won't have a team left."

"I thought you wanted me to tackle as hard as I could," Mike said defensively.

"Well, that was hard all right!" the coach snorted and then laughed. "God! You keep that up and you're liable to make pro."

Mike stood for a moment, confused. He turned to the other boy who still massaged his neck.

"I'm sorry," he said quietly.

The boy said nothing. He just looked at Mike and then turned away.

"Okay! That's it for today," the coach suddenly said and then looked directly at Mike. "I'll see you here tomorrow right after class. Don't be late."

Mike left the field still confused. He knew the couch had been pleased but he had hurt the other boy. He thought of the words, "make pro." But that only deepened the confusion.

The coach walked to the priest and took his cap off, scratching his head again.

"Man, the kid's got talent. But still, I don't know," he said quietly.

# Thirty

The old oil heater's bright flame cast shadows against a darkened wall, trying mightily to keep the cold at bay. Still, the room was cold for the temperature had dropped to minus forty outside and timbers popped, sounding like muffled rifle shots in the old house while a cold, white moon hung over the silvery, desolate fields.

Mike looked at his father's contorting face as he cracked nuts with a pliers, crunching the meat in his open mouth. Mike was suddenly filled with nausea and he cast his eyes down to the cold linoleum floor. He shivered despite the heavy woolen sweater for he had grown used to city living. He shivered again as he thought of the frost-covered seat in the frigid outhouse and how he had recoiled when he had entered the barn and the stench had hit him with a physical force. He thought too how in the middle of the night when flesh would freeze in less than a minute and how he would use the barn instead of the outhouse.

Vincent's open mouth and smacking lips broke into his consciousness and Mike turned away for even in the house, away from the barn, he could smell cow manure on his father's clothes.

"Here! Metro!" Gertie suddenly held out a tray of nuts.

Mike took a nut and absentmindedly cracked it, ignoring his mother's refusal to accept his changing his name. He glanced about the living room at the picture of the Virgin Mary and the Crucifix hanging close by. Then he looked at the grate in the heater's door through which he could see the flickering flame.

He was the only one to come home for Christmas, so the family sat in the tiny, frigid living room close to the stove while the flame rose and flickered and the cold popped trees outside. Finally Gertie turned to Vincent and smiled, her square, sad face creasing in countless lines and wrinkles.

"Well, are we not gonna open the presents?" she asked.

Vincent stopped chewing for an instant and then put down the pliers and reached to a chair on which the presents were piled. He picked up the first and hefted it in his hand before laboriously tracing out the name written on it.

"Metro!" He handed Mike the present marked crudely "To Metro from Mom and Dad." Then he immediately turned to the others.

Mike opened the gift and pulled forth a cheap pair of woolen gloves. He stared at them for a moment and then placed them on the table and looked at his parents.

"Thanks," he said softly.

Vincent lifted a present and stared at the card, sounding out the words silently.

"To Dad," he finally read and then tore at the paper greedily. Suddenly his eyes widened in pleasure. Allen had bought him an electric drill and he turned it back and forth in his heavy hand, smiling and making a face.

"Boy! I sure can use this," he said as he gazed fondly at the drill. But Gertie grew impatient and he reluctantly put it down and picked up another present. He laboriously read the name and then glanced up.

"To Mom." He handed Gertie a present and then turned happily back to the drill.

Mike had wandered the stores in the city with only a few dollars and finally had picked out a plastic knife holder to be placed on the wall. He watched his mother tear away the wrappings, his eyes slightly moist.

"Thanks," Gertie said as her eyes lit up with childish pleasure and her face softened for a moment. "I sure can use that," she said suddenly. The lines creased on her square sad face and Mike felt a maelstrom of feelings for human warmth had that effect on him.

Then Vincent picked up another gift, hefting it for an instant in his heavy hand. Again the emotions ebbed and flowed as Mike gazed steadily at his father. And again Vincent laboriously read the writing on the present and then said suddenly, "To Dad! From Mike!" He glanced at Mike for a moment, making sure Mike and Metro were the same person. Then he tore greedily at the package and a soldering iron appeared. He stared thoughtfully at the tiny needle point.

"Aw, that's no good! It's too small!" he exclaimed suddenly. "I can't use it on heavy stuff."

"Here! Put it away!" Vincent held the iron out to Mike.

Then he turned back to the drill, gazing fondly at its shiny surface. "That tarned things too small. But this, Boy I sure can use this in the shop."

Mike gazed at the rejected soldering iron and then laid it on the table. His eyes held a strange light as he thoughtfully looked at his father who made a face for the millionth time.

He had failed again.


Mike sat across from Allen and his sister-in-law, his insides churning but his face cold and calm. Allen lit a cigarette, inhaled deeply and then blew smoke skyward in a ring. He placed the cigarette in an ash tray and stared at his younger brother, his eyes hard with the light of justification.

"Well, that's it," he said suddenly. "We've given you every chance we could but you just won't try."

"Yeah," Mike sighed. He had talked with the principal, a greying priest who had sat in his office gazing at the teenager he couldn't fathom. Then he had stated his opinion.

"You belong in school. You have more ability than anyone I've ever known. So what reason have you to quit? What are you going to do?"

Mike had squirmed under the priests steady gaze.

"I'm gonna join the Air Force."

"A lot of men become bums in the military. I used to be a padre and believe me, I know," the priest had snapped and then had exposed another topic. "Why are you really quitting? Is it your brother and his wife?"

"No! That's not the reason," Mike had lied quickly and the priest knew he lied.

That had been the end of the interview and as Mike sat in the kitchen he saw a familiar light in Maureen's eyes: Triumph.

"What'a ya gonna do now?" Allen suddenly demanded.

"I've been accepted into the Air Force," Mike said quietly. He didn't mention that he had lain awake most of the night, afraid he wouldn't pass the mental requirements for enlisted men. Although he was a natural athlete and possessed literary and academic talent he didn't understand, deep down he knew he was clumsy, unattractive and dull.

"How long before basic?" Allen demanded again.

"About a month."

"Well, you certainly can't stay here for a month," Maureen snapped.

"That's right!" Allen added. "We brought you here to go to school, not bum around. We'll give you bus fare to back home."

"Okay," Mike sighed quietly. Then he lit a cigarette as Allen changed the subject.

"Frankly, I don't think you'll make it. When I was in the Air Force, we had to get up at five-thirty. You got a hard time getting up at eight."

"Don't worry, I'll manage," Mike said softly. Again he didn't mention that mornings were a transition period from the safe world of dreams to total wakefulness, and that he would lie in bed wishing desperately that the day wouldn't come.

"Hell! You can't even make your own bed," Allen continued. "What'a ya gonna do when you get kicked out?"

"Well," Mike began. Then a rare glimpse of his inner being appeared briefly. "I still want to be a writer."

Maureen snorted derisively and Allen smiled.

"You better forget about that darned writing," he said genially.

"I know I can't write good now. But I need to grow, to experience life," Mike added.

"Well, I just can't see it," Allen snapped. "If you were a writer you'd be able to write good enough to get paid for it now. You better forget that silly dream."

As Allen spoke Maureen glanced at a Reader's Digest she read periodically. She smiled again, indulgently, at the teenager who had ambitions too great for his ability.

"Well, I'll wait for a few years," Mike said stubbornly.

"Hell's bells!" Allen snarled. "Why can't you see reason just for once? Writing's something people did in the past. Today everything's science. Just look around."

Mike looked steadily at his brother, bewildered by the sudden vehemence.

"Why don't you get into something like that? Then you'll have something. Not that darned writing. What the hell do ya get from that anyway? You'll only starve and wish you never even tried."

"Well, everyone's told me I should be a writer." Mike showed a rare stubborn streak.

"Who?" Maureen demanded.

"Well, my English teacher back home. She wanted me to write."

"What the heck does she know about writing?" Maureen snapped. "I've taught school for years and she's just a country school teacher." Then after a pause, she added, "I sent a story to Reader's Digest, and if I can't be accepted…"

A familiar look appeared in Allen's eyes and Mike saw the same triumph Maureen had displayed.

"Well, why did everyone tell me I was good, if I'm not?" he asked bitterly.

"He's got a point there." Allen smiled at Maureen and then added. "That stupid teacher told him he should be a writer. And now that he knows he got no talent, what's he supposed to do?"

Maureen sighed and then added, "I'd have a good long talk with that teacher." Then she picked up the Reader's Digest in dismissal. She had been engrossed in a tale of a black ghetto teenager in trouble with the law. Mike's problems paled in comparison.

Mike picked up a set of house keys which were attached to a ring and leather holder. He absentmindedly tried removing them but had trouble.

"There! There's a good example!" Allen said suddenly. Mike looked up, puzzled.

"Anyone else would be able to take those off in a few seconds."

"What's that supposed to mean?" Mike demanded.

"Well, I'm not saying you're retarded, like Gerard says, but there's definitely something wrong with you."

As Allen talked Mike saw an image of the old farm house, with the cold creeping in under the door and the frigid, frost-covered toilet seat in the outhouse. Next came the crowded Employment Office and an impatient counselor who had told him to return to school for there was no work. Images of the six months he had spent in the city drifted by along with the faint glimpses of a different world. Maureen and Allen had taken him to a production of Mikado and he had been enthralled, not only by the musical comedy but by the fine clothes and ladies in evening gowns. But his enjoyment had been tinged with an infinite longing and resignation.

As the scenes drifted slowly by, they were suddenly chased away by the pungent memory of his father's fetid barn. Mike looked steadily at his brother for an instant, then down at his hands.

"Yeah," he sighed. "Maybe you're right. Maybe there's something wrong with me."

He stood slowly and went to his room where he began packing.

An Airman wearing the flat top hat and sky blue winter uniform stared back at Mike from a mirror in the washroom. He forgot for an instant the screaming of the sergeants and the harsh unrelenting light at five-thirty a.m. He also forgot the ache in his legs as he stood for attention for, hours on parade, or gut clenching anxiety during inspection. Images of GIs with beautiful women on their arms came also, for he was about to leave on his first weekend pass. He had been paid thirty-five dollars, after a ten-dollar deduction he regularly sent home to his parents. He hid five in his locker, thinking thirty dollars was an enormous amount for a weekend. And it was, for in the spring of nineteen sixty-three cigarettes cost thirty-five cents a pack.

He had written home and had received a reply. He had stared at his father's barely legible scribbling and then had read the letter in the washroom away from prying eyes. He didn't write any more letters after that although he still sent home a quarter of his wages.

Mike suppressed all that as he stared at his reflection and for a brief instant felt a rare sense of pride and accomplishment.

"You ready?" a recruit suddenly demanded. Bob was taller and slightly bigger than Mike but, more important, he possessed the confidence of a seventeen year-old who had never known rejection. He and Mike had become friends for they complemented each other. When other recruits mocked Mike, Bob intervened.

"Yeah," Mike replied and then asked, "You think we'll find any girls?"

"Yeah! For the hundredths time, yeah!" Bob snapped and Mike was silent.

They rode an Air Force bus, through St. Jean and on toward Montreal, the city of countless dreams and beautiful women. When it traversed St. Catherine's Street, hookers waved and Mike craned his neck. Bob glanced at him.

"You dont wanna pay for it, do you?"

Mike didn't answer as he took off his blue flat top hat and stared at the shiny brass Albatross in flight.

As the bus rolled on, the streets of the big, wicked and magical city sped by as Mike's mind was again taken by images. He had arrived at basic training six weeks ago and when he had passed the batteries of tests he had come to a decision inspired by an impulse. There had been many trades to choose from but Mike had been intrigued by the Military Police. A sergeant had looked at him in surprise.

"But you can have any trade you want."

"What about electronics?" Mike had remembered his brother's admonishments. "I don't have grade ten."

"That's no problem for you," the sergeant had answered and Mike had become confused.

Finally the bus stopped at a depot and Mike looked for a washroom. When he returned his eyes widened for Bob stood talking to two girls. When he noticed Mike, he waved.

"Mike! This is Susan." The introduction was brief.

Susan moved imperceptibly until she stood close, looking up at Mike. Mike took a quick involuntary step backwards and the smile vanished from her face. As the girl looked bewildered, Mike's stomach churned in the familiar maelstrom. Outwardly he was calm and cold but his palms were sweating and his collar tight.

"What'a ya guys doing tonight?" Susan finally asked.

"I don't know. Maybe we'll go to the Legion dance." When Mike answered, he avoided her eyes.

"Boy! I sure would like to go to the Legion dance," Susan said quickly and brushed her dark hair absentmindedly. Mike suddenly wondered how Bob had managed to find two girls who spoke English in a French city.

"Yeah. There's lots of fun there," Mike heard himself say woodenly. He glanced frantically at Bob but he was busy with the other girl.

"I've never been to one of them dances," Susan said, biting her lower lip. She was slightly overweight but attractive none-the-less with young breasts pushing against her sweater.

"I bet you'd have no trouble getting in with your uniform. I bet you can sign anyone in too, eh?"

"Yeah, it's a private club but I can sign in three people. As long as I'm in the Military." Mike said, casting his eyes down and then looking at passengers lining up to embark on a Greyhound Bus. Susan covertly looked at Mike. He was handsome in his uniform even if he still looked to be no more than sixteen. She glanced at the passengers too and then back up at the young man who gave off such conflicting signals.

"Mind if I come along?" she suddenly blurted.

"No, no. Hell, I don't mind." Mike stammered.

His mind was numb, like a person who has undergone sharp, unfathomable pain and suddenly finds relief. Susan smiled up at him. She had her own past to live with and going out with strange young men in uniform was normal.

Two days later, after the dream had died a slow lingering death, Mike sat beside Bob as the same scenery rolled by, but in reverse. Bob exuded confidence as the memory of frantic coupling in the dark began to take on a more mellow, romantic hue. Then, as they were approaching the base, he turned suddenly to Mike.

"Well, did ya get it too?"

"Get what?"

"For Christ's sake! You don't have to hide it from me. Did you get laid?"

Mike took a long time answering as he gazed out the window. Then slowly he turned his head with the flat top blue hat.

"Yeah. I got it all right," he answered quietly.

Bob grinned and folded his arms, leaning back in the seat and closing his eyes. The scenes came back to Mike in a misty swirl. He saw the soft lights and women in close-fitting gowns and remembered the mind-numbing alcohol. He remembered also the slowly turning globe that had hung like a full, heavy moon over the dancers but most of all he remembered Susan's warm body pressed against his. When they danced slowly, he had tried mightily not to step on her feet as the past conditioning kept him in its icy grip. They had walked arm in arm down St. Catherine's Street past the countless bars and bright lights with teeming humanity all about them. Again Mike had been in a dizzying world of color and motion that nearly made him nauseous.

As they walked, Susan's arm in his, an elderly man had staggered from a bar, his grey hair rumpled, and his face red from alcohol. Suddenly he had stepped in front of Susan. Mike had stopped short, glaring at the drunken little man.

"What's this?" The man had asked. He fingered a cheap broach that Susan had worn on a chain around her neck.

"It's a new broach," she had answered while the little man looked at her unsteadily.

"Look fella! You better take a hike!" Mike had stepped between the two, alcohol washing away the normal hesitation. The little man took a quick backward step, and then disappeared into the bar from where he had come.

"He's my father!" Susan had blurted, her eyes misty.

"Oh! I'm sorry. I didn't know," Mike had stammered, confused.

"Forget it! I'm used to it," Susan had said quickly.

As they had walked on and Susan's face took on a sadness that he had thought he understood, Mike had squeezed her arm.

"Forget it!" she had snapped and yanked her arm away.

They had walked on in silence, the heady euphoria draining from Mike's soul. Then they had been in the abandoned lobby, for it was no luxury hotel that Mike and Bob had stayed in. When he had stood hesitantly, his hat in his hand, she had turned to him tiredly.

"Mind if I come up to your room?"

"Oh, sure. Sure," Mike had stammered again and then had led the way upstairs.

He had sat on the narrow bed with Susan on an old imitation leather chair. He had tried desperately to ask her to sit next to him but the words wouldn't come. So he had begun talking of other things with his hands, clammy and cold. Then finally, as the sounds of the city drifted in through an open window, Mike had found a rare courage that took more effort than anything he had done before.

"Do you think, maybe, if you want," he had indicated the narrow bed.

"No," Susan had said softly as she stood, looking down at Mike.

Mike had let his gaze drop for he had expected the answer.

"It's not that I don't like you. It's just that I don't feel like it tonight," Susan had said quietly. Then she gazed down at Mike, wondering why he didn't persist. Men were normally demanding, and Mike made her feel vaguely uneasy. But then she had felt a great fatigue and finally sighed softly.

"Well, okay. Just as long as we sleep and don't do nothing else."

So the two teenagers had lain on the narrow bed, fully clothed, and that's how they had remained. Susan had put her head on Mike's shoulder and he put his arm about her.

"Has your father been drinking long?" he had asked softly.

"I told you to forget it!" Susan had snapped and Mike had fallen into an uneasy silence as he had lain with his arm around her. He had been painfully aware of her warm body but the emotional paralysis had remained and they had lain quietly with the turmoil staying in his mind. Then all the foggy years of loneliness had engulfed him and he had turned and gazed at the sleeping girl. Slowly he had risen and gently kissed her on the cheek. She didn't waken, sleeping peacefully beside the young man she didn't understand. And as he had looked down at her, at the soft lines of her face, Mike had felt the warmth of her body while all the dreams of nocturnal, imaginary love came and he had thought he was in love. But deep down he had known it was as false as the lonely, misty dreams.

The next morning, Susan had risen and looked down at Mike, a vague sense of disappointment lingering in her eyes. As she had turned to the dirty, cracked mirror atop the scarred dresser, Mike had looked up at her.

"You wanna go to the Legion tonight?" he had asked softly.

Susan had turned quickly and gazed down at Mike for an instant.

"The Legion," she had said, turning back to the mirror and concentrating on combing her hair.

"No. I gotta stay home tonight," she had finally said.

Mike hadn't pressed for part of him had been relieved.

"We're here!" Bob suddenly poked Mike in the ribs, scattering the soft, cloying memories.

They passed through the guard house and were still in time for supper in the cavernous mess hall with propellers on the walls and pictures of famous war aces. The hall was filled with noisy airmen eating their Sunday evening meal and when they were seated at a long table a thin recruit with a rat-like face, stared across at Mike. Morris was one who took advantage of the confused and hurting.

"Well, Black Cock," he demanded suddenly, his mouth open as he chewed. "Did ya get laid?"

Mike had been forced to shower with the other recruits and it didnt take long for them to notice that his penis was dark brown and the name had stuck.

"None a your business!" Bob snapped.

"Aw, let Black Cock talk for himself for a change," Morris said, still grinning at Mike.

"I saw ya with that floozy Susan on Friday night. Jesus! If you didn't get fucked by her, you must be a Goddamn Gear Box."

"Susan's not a floozy! She's a nice girl!" Mike blurted.

"Jesus H. Christ!" Morris exploded into loud guffaws, food dropping from his open mouth.

"Ya hear that, guys?" He looked up and down the table. The other recruits stopping eating and grinned at Mike.

"Black Cock says Susan's a nice girl. Shit! I screwed 'er in the bathtub Saturday night. Ain't that so?" Morris turned to another man sitting next to him.

"Yep!" the man grinned. "And when you got through with 'er, I fucked 'er up against the sink."

"Huh! I didn't know that." Morris glanced sharply at the man.

"Jesus! A piece-a-tail's a piece-a-tail, eh. Besides, you passed out on the bed, and I didn't see your Goddamn brand on 'er."

Laughter ebbed and flowed about Mike, breaking against his soul like waves against a shore. He couldn't believe that Susan was a slut, for when he had gazed down at her sleeping face, he had only seen an innocent seventeen year-old girl.

# Thirty-one

Shimmering heat waves rose from the asphalt parade square as the sun bore down with a relentless, midday heat. With the heat came humidity, for Camp Borden was near two great lakes and with the humidity came hot, sweaty sores in the armpits and crotch. To the recruits the parade square was a short definition of hell.

Mike and the other Military Police trainees ran six miles a day and marched the same. The marching was the hardest for they swung along at one hundred and eighty strides a minute; three a second, and Mikes shins felt like they were on fire. The dividend was in the hardening muscles and stamina that made Mike a man, if only in physical things. Along with the running, marching, callisthenics and unarmed combat there was classroom time dealing with the National Defense Act and the Criminal Code. Mike's day began at five-thirty and rarely ended before six p.m. when the trainees had to run three miles back to the barracks, change and shower before they could line up in the mess hall for the leftovers. The mess hall closed at six-thirty and they normally had less than fifteen minutes to eat.

Mike passed the physical part with high marks, along with scoring ninety-four out of a hundred with a submachine-gun, for sweat and guns he knew. But now he was engaged in something else, human relations and how to curry favor with superiors, something he would never truly learn.

Mike and two other trainees stood by a station wagon with the Air Force logo on its door. They gazed across the shimmering asphalt at the driving instructor who approached with quick, short strides. He was a small man, but he thrust his shoulders back and his head forward for on his sleeves were newly sewed corporal's hooks. He stopped sharply and glared at Mike and the two other young men. They were to be his students for the next three weeks.

"What's your names?" he barked, his arms akimbo and his head thrust back.

"Langley! Smythe!" the two other men barked back. All three snapped to attention. Then the corporal glared at Mike

"Bronski," Mike mumbled.

"Huh!" the corporal snarled. "Speak up! Goddamn it!"

"Bronski," Mike said raising his voice.

"Brown Skin?" the corporal asked and then grinned.

"No! Bronski," Mike said pronouncing the name carefully.

"Jesus H. Christ! What the hell kinda name's that?" the corporal laughed and turned his back. The two other men snickered and Mike felt his skin turn clammy and hot. The corporal walked around the station wagon, and stood by the passenger's door, glaring at him.

"Well," he demanded and then got in. Mike opened the driver's door and sat behind the wheel. The two other trainees jumped into the back seat, still snickering.

The corporal glared at Mike and then handed him a key. Mike put it in the ignition carefully.

"Jesus!" the corporal grinned. "Don't tell me you don't even know how to start it."

Mike wordlessly turned the key and the motor roared to life. He shifted to low and popped the clutch, at the same time slamming his foot down hard on the accelerator. The car jerked forward and he yanked it back. The car slowed. Then he slammed his foot down again. The corporal's head snapped back and forth, his hat coming down over his eyes. He grabbed it in both hands and glared, his face scarlet.

"Jesus! Mary and Joseph!" He gazed skyward in mock prayer, rolling his eyes.

"Why me? Why me, Lord? Why do I have to get stuck with some stupid Polluck who hasn't even seen a car yet?"

Then he grinned outright.

"Is that how you drive in Poland? Or do you only have jack asses there?"

Mike could see the two other trainees in the rear view mirror, holding their sides and gasping for air. Then, inside Mike's head, a mocking voice took form. The voice was his father's.

"Metro! You can't!"

The mocking whisper exploded inside his brain. The car lurched forward with the corporal swearing and yanking his head back and forth in mock whiplash.

Mike grimly bore the mockery for three weeks, driving up and down a four-lane highway and then dusty country roads. When the course was finally over, the same corporal sat next to him with a clipboard and pen and paper.

As they left the compound, Mike turned a corner and the corporal grinned gleefully.

"That's five points right there!" he laughed and wrote feverishly.

"What for, Corporal?"

"For turning too sharp."

Mike sighed and concentrated on driving. When they returned an hour later, he parked the car and turned off the ignition. The corporal stared at the clipboard and then counted quickly, his head nodding as he calculated the score. Then he turned and grinned.

"Well, that's it Polluck! You flunked!"

Mike hurried to the sergeant's office, ready to demand another test with a different instructor. But when he was in the office, the sergeant read the test's results and then looked up, puzzled.

"What the hell ya want another test for? You passed with 60 percent. I know it's the minimum required but what the hell's the difference? All you need is to pass."

Mike left the office confused and slightly deflated. But when he met the corporal he saw disappointment in the man's eyes. The corporal knew that if he had failed Mike and Mike had scored high on a retest, it would have looked bad for him.

Eight months later, Mike sat across a desk from a different corporal, his 9mm semiautomatic pistol in the black holster at his waist. It hung from a heavy black belt and a cross strap that went over his left shoulder. Over his left breast hung the heavy, gold Military Police badge and on his right, a pass with his picture for he was stationed at a top secret base in northern Ontario. He remembered the pride when he had been posted to North Bay; the underground complex that was the brain for the radar systems strung across northern Canada. It was the first defense against Russian bombers for in nineteen sixty-three the cold war was in full force. But as he listened to the corporal, he mused wonderingly how the pride had died a slow, agonizing death. And as he looked down at his boots he thought how nothing had really changed.

"Moike." the corporal spoke with a Cockney accent. "Moike," he sighed and shook his head. "What am Oi to do with you?" He gazed at Mike for a moment and Mike cast his eyes downwards again.

"All Oi can say is you better shape up or you'll get de boot. The Warrant's pretty pissed off as it is."

The "Warrant" was the Warrant Officer First Class, the man who made everyone jump to attention and cry "Morning Warrant!" in unison every day around nine a.m. The Warrant usually snarled a reply sounding like "Arrgh!" before slamming the door to his office. He was a drinking man and mornings were bad for him.

"What in 'ell 'ave ya done so far?" the corporal demanded. "You've been here eight months and all you've done is a couple of dammed good security checks."

Mike said nothing but his mind quickly went to the tunnel, just beneath the guard house, which connected it to the underground bowels of the base. He had gone on foot patrols in a top secret area where twice he had discovered coded messages left in the open; easy prey for an enemy agent. He had been commended for thorough work but the corporal's question of "What ave ya done?" was of a totally different nature. It was peace time and what mattered most was simply how much a superior liked you.

"Well?" the corporal demanded. "What 'ave ya done?"

Mike remained silent as his mind slipped quickly to his first day at the guard house. His first assignment had been to make coffee for the Warrant and bring him in a paper as soon as he arrived in the morning. Mike had thought of the grueling training he had gone through to wear his badge and that the task was demeaning but he had said nothing.

"Put it down! Gimmee the paper!" the Warrant had snarled, his eyes bloodshot. Mike had done as he was ordered, a small knot of anger growing deep in his consciousness.

The next morning when the Warrant had slammed the door and stomped off to his office, Mike had turned and began cleaning his pistol. An agitated sergeant had nearly bowled him over in his haste to make coffee while a different corporal ran to the office with a paper. Then in a few minutes, the guard house shook with an enraged bellow for the paper had been a day old. The Warrant had noticed the pen marks when he began the crossword puzzle.

Mike had kept his back to the commotion, only vaguely aware that he had made an enemy of the corporal who had been the target of the Warrant's rage. He had also been told to join the bowling team for the Warrant loved bowling. But Mike hadn't bothered. There had also been the matter of the bed sheets. Mike had forgotten to change them. Then he had been too ashamed for they had become dirty and soiled. As time had passed, the sheets had become an obsession. The longer he had waited, the worse it had become, until he had been reported and had to appear before the Medical Officer. He had been disciplined and put on three months probation.

Mike suddenly became aware of the corporal's angry stare and he was jerked back to the present.

"Now! For Chroist's sake!" the corporal snapped. "You've been given three months to shape up or else."

Mike had been given three choices; "Shape up" and remain a Military Police Officer, remuster to another trade or leave the Military entirely.

"Really! You're not so bad a bloke." The corporal's tone softened. "But if you don't do something soon, you'll get de boot. What the 'ell ya gonna do? There ain't much work out there, is there?"

Mike thought again of the elite training and how erect he had stood at attention. He didn't mention that he had resented having to do domestic chores, like making coffee for the Warrant. He also didn't mention the commendation he had been given, for deep inside where it really counted he had already given up.

"Well, at least you could remuster to another trade," the corporal finally said.

"No," Mike said slowly. "I don't think so. I've had enough of the Military."

"That's it!" the corporal yelled, slamming his chair backwards and standing. He turned to the coffee pot and then snarled over his shoulder.

"Jesus H. Chroist! That's an 'ell of an attitude ain't it?"


Not long after the conversation with the corporal, Mike was on a trans-continental train westward bound. As he rocked with the train's motion and stared out the window, his mind and soul lost in a deep fog, he wondered what he was to do. He had a grade nine education and the only jobs for him would be heavy menial labor. As the train rocked along the track, through the Canadian Shield. Mike stared out at the rocks and trees as the fog deepened. Then gradually he slipped into the hazy, wistful world of daydreams as his mind sought an escape from the harsh, unrelenting agony of reality.

He was still in the Air Force or he had inherited wealth and at other times he traveled to far off, romantic places like Greece or South America, where always by his side were beautiful young women, willing and soft skinned. But his favorite was when he revisited the base he had just left, as an important man who found the security lax and the men cowering before him. He would send back a scathing report and then yell at the Warrant Officer. And always, in the dream, he was in control, a winner.

On the last night, when the train left the Canadian Shield and bounced and rocked across the prairies, Mike fell asleep in his berth. In the hazy warmth he dreamed a slow and tortuous dream where he drifted down a wide, muddy river. The water was warm and the current sluggish, while all about and bobbing on the gentle waves were ivory brown skulls, their eye sockets empty and unseeing. A cruel sun blazed down as he slowly drifted down the river, eventually coming to a ramshackle house boat. Then he lay on a cot in the shadowy, steamy interior, watching the people who lived there, for there were all manner of men and women: brown, black and white. All wore expressions of hopeless resignation, having lost even the will to live, their faces blank and uncaring. And then came the horror of bed wetting for Mike felt the familiar moisture spread. He shivered, as he slowly drifted down the river of skulls with the zombies who waited to take their place amongst the skulls.

Mike thrashed about, crying out, before lying still again. As he lay on a filthy cot, a grinning black man, baldheaded and skull like told him quietly that he would get used to it. Slowly then, as he drifted along with the bobbing skulls, he felt total resignation and evaporation of all hope. As the cot became wetter he didn't care any more and he sighed deeply. And in the dream he listened to the black man who had become a talking skull, and who told him that all things can be gotten used to.

Mike woke with a start. He lay in silent panic as he felt the wet sheets. Then slowly in a daze, he opened his eyes and realized that only the upper part of the cot was wet. The moisture was from anxiety induced perspiration and, as the train rocked over rough tracks, he felt a faint sense of relief.

He rolled over and stared out the window of his berth, at a full moon and wondered if dreams come true.

Again Mike stood in the farmyard, looking at the rising smoke from the stove pipe and at the barn and cattle grazing in the pasture. When he had told his mother that he had simply quit the Air Force, she had looked at him steadily and then finally spoke.

"So now! Now you can work just like us, like a farmer."

So Mike once again drove the tractor with its hard metal seat, in a cloud of dust. The dust infiltrated his clothes and boots until he was black from head to foot except for sweat streaks on his face. And since there was no shower or even running water, washing became a chore again and he went to bed, filthy and itchy. While the tractor slowly traveled from one end of the field to the other, he wondered what he would do. He had no money and it didn't occur to him to demand any from his parents although he had sent money home.

When they ate, he again saw the food rolling around inside his father's open mouth and heard the familiar smacking sounds. He wondered how it had all seemed so normal not that long ago. His parents still called him Metro and as he ate dinner or rode the hard tractor seat, his shoulders slumped in resignation for the image of the skulls stayed with him.

He remembered his pride when he had come home on leave in the Winter Blues of the Air Force and how his mother had boasted about her son being in the Military Police. He also remembered how, when it had been time to go, he had to carry his bags to the highway to hitchhike, for his father had gone hunting. A neighbor had passed, grinning from his half-ton, and as he had struggled with the heavy bags, Mike had averted his eyes.

Once again, despite his getting older, nothing had really changed.

# Thirty-two

The mine's Head Frame stood stark and bleak against the countless miles of unbroken Manitoba wilderness, a lonely sentinel to man's insatiable craving for minerals and profit. A raven flapped by the shaft and over the outskirts of the small city, croaking hoarsely. His harsh, deep throated cry was loud in the frigid air for the bright, midday sun provided only light and little warmth. It was December and north of the 55th parallel, snow was two feet deep and the thermometer dropped to minus sixty at night.

The muskeg swamps and jack pine forests stretched in every direction, north to frozen tundra and south to farmland. And in the swamps was an inexplicable loneliness with the raven and hungry wolf in search of sustenance to ward off the implacable cold. In single men's barracks, there too was an inexplicable loneliness for men are not made to live without the company of women.

In Thompson there was one theater, one indoor shopping mall and one bar where the men gathered to drink away the loneliness and their wages earned deep in the bowels of the earth. They were the ones who came up in the cages after every shift, their faces blackened with only their teeth and eyes showing and their clothes encrusted with dirt.

The city evolved around the mine shaft, a tiny island in the unbroken sea of primeval forest. And in the island there were the necessities for survival and rarely any pleasure. There was only the bar where alcohol flowed so fast it took a freight train to keep the supply coming. There were no dances for single men because there were no available women. The few women who did live in Thompson stayed at home after dark and avoided the rough men who sat around a table in the bar. So on payday, the men went south to the Pas for what comes in panties; and for a price, has a soft, willing body.

The shaft went down two thousand feet beneath the frozen earth and employed more than five hundred men. And anyone who worked on the surface was employed directly or indirectly by International Nickel. If a private contractor wished to build a house, he first had to get permission from the company. That was why it cost twenty-five cents to ride the decrepit and freezing Blue Bird school buses to work when the fare was a dime in the south. And the taxis had no meters, charging a dollar a head no matter the distance. If a driver could squeeze eight passengers into his cab he made eight dollars, even if the trip was a couple of blocks. When the charge for room and board was fifty dollars a month in the south, it was a hundred in Thompson for the men had no choice. They were paid two, to two-fifty an hour, a goodly wage in nineteen sixty-four for a man who labored with his back, but after board, alcohol and cigarettes, he was lucky if he saved any money at all.

It was in the company's best interests that he saved little, for hopefully he would make a life around the mine shaft and continue mining the nickel which made the owners rich. The company sold houses for only a two hundred dollar down payment, knowing that if a man paid off part of a house, he would be reluctant to leave.

The soft men in the cities to the south who owned the mine couldn't fathom why there was always a shortage of workers. But the men, who went down every day to the bowels of the earth where they couldn't see their hands in front of their faces knew. The noise was so deafening a man couldn't hear a shout from a foot away. The racket bounced off the solid rock walls and intensified and men became deaf for there was no protection for the ears. And there was the damp. The drills used water to keep down the dust which caused miners lung and a slow lingering death. It ran down the rock face as the diamond bit punched into the hard ore and a man became soaked and clammy from the water and his own sweat. In the Stope, which was a blasted out area in the rock, it would be seventy to eighty degrees Fahrenheit and men gasped for air, while on the surface it was minus fifty. When the shift was over the men sometimes had to walk for miles along a tunnel that was called a drift. There it would only be forty-five degrees and colds and flus were common. At times they had to run through a solid sheet of icy water that poured down into the drift from a Stope above for a "Sandfill" operation was underway. Sand was used to fill a mined out Stope for the next level of drilling and blasting. The sand was forced through heavy steel pipes with water and at times the water escaped.

If the sweat and shivering cold in the drift wasn't bad enough there was always danger for no matter how safe the company tried to make the mine, accidents happened. Man wasn't meant to labor deep beneath the earth's surface as human moles who rarely saw the light of day. And when an accident happened it usually was a fatality for ore rock weighs an inordinate amount and man is puny. There were many who thought they were the lucky ones, for when a man wasn't killed but severely injured, he would exist in a wheel chair, remembering a time when he had felt his muscles ripple. There was no safe way to remove an injured man for the rules changed when underground. If there was danger of more rock falling the injured man was moved, even if he had a broken back. When a stretcher was brought down from the first aid room the man was strapped to it and if he was in a Stope, pulled up by hand to the next level. Or he was lowered, again by hand, to the one below. Then a grimy, grim-faced group of men would gather in the eerie light cast by their lights and gently lift the man onto a stretcher all, the while assuring him that going up or down, strapped to a stretcher with the pain coming in waves, was the only way he would live.

Whenever an accident happened, the mine would lose from seventy-five to one hundred men.

Mike walked along a drift, keeping his boots in the middle of the tracks that carried the ore trains. He wore a helmet with a light, attached to it. An electric cord ran from the light to a battery on his belt and the battery had to be charged every day. When it went dead, a man had to wait wherever he was, until he saw a pinprick of light approaching along a drift and then be guided to the lunch room. If it happened in the Stope he had to have his partner guide him and if his partner wasn't there he sat and waited.

As he walked along the tracks, Mike remembered the hard rock miners he had read about and he remembered a tale of tough men who risked their lives deep in the bowels of the earth. He tried to ignore his sticky cold feet for socks only lasted a couple of days. He thought of the romance in the book compared to the actual reality of working underground. And he thought too of how reality was never romantic, only grimy and dangerous. Everywhere he went, there was water and his rubber gumboots had cracked. He used blasting wire to tie them for the leather laces had rotted. He wore rubber gloves and his hands were wrinkled and pink from the constant moisture.

Two men worked each Stope for hourly wages plus a bonus which was a percentage of their wages. The harder a man worked the more he earned and it was said that the bonus killed more men than anything else. With the incentive, they took shortcuts in the chase for the dollar.

Mike looked for a small sign with the number thirty-nine on it for he had been assigned to that Stope to help timber. He wondered when he would be assigned to a permanent Stope with a partner for he was still a mucker who went from Stope to Stope, whenever someone was sick or lumber or other supplies were needed. The planks were used to cover the sand which the mined out Stope was filled with and on which to stand as a man handled a "jack-leg" or "stoper."

After a month, Mike had learned the alien words by heart. A jack-leg was a drill run by compressed air from a hose which came from a large pipe. The drill also had a water hose and hydraulic leg. All together it weighed a hundred and twenty-five pounds. The stoper was slightly lighter and the leg was stationary for it was made to drill into the roof, or "back." It weighed more than a hundred pounds and the first time Mike had tried to carry it he could barely get it off the floor. A miner, who weighed no more than one hundred and sixty pounds, came over and hoisted it onto his shoulder, walking rapidly away as if he hardly noticed the weight. Mike had watched in wonder but within a month he could climb a ladder using one hand for the rungs and the other to hold the stoper. But his fingers felt like they were being torn from his hand for he had to swing it away from the rungs so the leg wouldn't catch.

He had been shown how to collar a hole, which was lifting the hundred and twenty five pound drill with his left arm while his right hand was on the handle, propping the leg against rock so it wouldn't slip. Then he had to cradle the drill in his left arm and press a small switch forward with his right hand. The drill had roared to life, full throated and dangerous and Mike had held it steady while the diamond bit pounded into the rock. When he had thought it was deep enough, he had turned up the pressure.

Suddenly, he had been thrown into the air, landing ten feet away, nearly unconscious and his light gone. When he had turned up the pressure, the bit had bounced from the hole and the machine had jumped straight upwards. He had lain for a moment on a pile of muck and then got up and tried again, a new respect for the machine burned into this soul.

Mike smiled as he remembered the old timers who had boasted about the rigors of pitching bundles during harvest and how weaklings faded away. Compared to mining, pitching bundles was child's play.

He turned his head and with his light he could see a sign, number thirty-seven. He wasn't far from the Stope whose leader had asked for help. Mike wished he could help in blasting instead of doing dull labor work. He had watched as a different leader had stuck the blasting cap into the sticks of dynamite. Only it was called "stelgel." The man had rammed it into the drill holes with a wooden stick so he wouldn't strike a spark and ignite the cap while he was two feet away. They had climbed the ladder to the next level and waited for the "shots" to see if all had ignited. If they didnt, they were called "miss-holes" and the next shift was warned so they could wash out the dynamite and cap with a water hose. One miner had drilled out a miss-hole instead. The cap had ignited and it was said he hit the opposing rock wall at two hundred miles an hour with the hundred and twenty-five-pound drill, rammed right through his chest.

There had been another miner who had laughed at those who climbed to the next level to wait for the shots. He had gone too just behind a crib set made of timbers piled like match sticks to keep the back from sagging. But he had grown impatient for the blast and had stuck his head out. The man had been found headless for a rock had hit him with uncanny accuracy.

Mike hadn't been present during any of the accidents but he had his own harrowing experience the first day. He had been walking down a drift, worried that he might get lost when he came upon a miner standing by the tracks and nonchalantly smoking a cigarette.

"Chute blast," the man had said laconically, bending his head slightly so his light wouldn't blind Mike.

"Yeah sure," Mike had answered for there were so many foreigners he had a hard time understanding them. He didn't realize that the man was a guard and that the ore had caught in the chute above them and that only dynamite could shake it loose. The miner had chuckled and dragged on his cigarette as Mike turned to go.

Suddenly, Mike had been lifted off his feet and for a frenzied blood freezing instant he had thought the mine was collapsing. The walls had reverberated with the explosion and he had dropped to his knees with his arms over his head. For another frenzied instant, he had cowered in mortal fear and then as the dust settled with the blast still vibrating in his ears, he had looked up at the grinning miner.

As he passed the Stope where he had been taught respect for instructions he grinned too for in retrospect, it was funny. In the short month he thought he had learned a fair bit for at twenty, Mike was still naive enough to think life could be an easy game. With the adventure of being a hard rock miner the emotional fog had lifted a little.

He had also learned that what appears extremely dangerous was at times not, and what appears innocent can kill you. He had gone to a

Stope to help a miner, standing beside the man while he had manipulated the controls on a "slusher", another machine run by compressed air. It had three cables attached to the walls by rock bolts and then to the drums. Next the cables went through the pulleys and to a bucket at the end. One cable pulled the bucket forward while the other two pulled it to either side. The slusher's bucket was used to scoop and push ore to the chute, which went to the drift below.

"Here! Take this cable and tie it around that rock," the man had ordered.

Mike had gazed uncertainly through the dust at a pillar of rock that hung from the back and was wedged against the floor. Other rocks hung from roof bolts, while others were still others loose and waiting.

"Aren't we gonna scale first?" he had asked.

"What the hell for?" the miner had snapped for scaling took time and was hard work. What he was supposed to do was walk slowly with a long steel bar with sharpened and flat ends. He was supposed to poke the rock with every step and knock down any loose that hung from the back. It could save your life but there were those who considered it a waste of time and money.

"Well, I don't wanna go under that rock," Mike had said for he feared the rock more than the miner's scorn.

"Jesus H. Christ!" the man had sworn and then had taken the cable himself and climbed over rocks and debris to the pillar. He clumsily wound the cable around it and then tied it. Once he was back at the slusher, he had pushed down on a lever and air roared through the hoses and out the exhaust which turned white when cold mixed with warm. Mike had watched as the slusher bounced and the pillar shook. But it held as the miner swore and pushed down on the levers. Then, as the choking dust billowed and the pillar shook, Mike saw and heard a large rock hit the floor. Dust thickened as more fell, each coming closer. When a large rock had landed less than six feet away, Mike had spun and run to the "manway" cover leading down to safety. Then he had turned and glanced back. The miner had still stood, barely visible in the dust, still pushing down on the levers and swearing. The pillar had finally fallen then and as the dust had settled he had grinned at Mike's fear. After a few uneasy minutes they had climbed forward through the debris and he had shown Mike how to stick dynamite into a blast hole and pack wet sand on top for tamping, for the rock had been too big to fit through the ore chute.

Mike stopped and chuckled at the memory of his fear. He bent forward and let the light from his lamp fall on the tiny sign. It read number thirty-nine and he knew he was at the right place. As he stood he could hear, or rather feel the staccato reverberations that traveled through the rock from miles away, telling him that miners were hard at work in some distant Stope. He also knew that in the Stope a rifle shot wouldn't be heard.

He began to climb the ladder, wondering why he didn't hear the sound of a jack-leg or stoper from above.

"Maybe they're timbering," he mused.

As he climbed the hundred-foot ladder with its ten foot flights, the silence deepened. He pushed the steel manway cover aside. Then he sniffed for the smell of rotting onions, the warning of gas and a silent death. A sudden shaft of anxiety pierced his soul but he shoved it aside for he had been wrong before. As he walked through the eerie dust filled silence of the long Stope, he thought of the safety meeting that same day. Old hands resented the meetings for it took them away from their Stopes and the bonus. The Mine Captain had talked of how close Christmas was and how they were to be extra careful. As Mike peered through the surreal light of his lamp and the dancing dust particles, he remembered the seriousness on the Captain's face.

Then, as he walked and sniffed the air, he thought he heard a sound. He spun around and stared through the haze to a corner where the back was only four feet high. He thought suddenly of the legends of Stope rats that were bigger than small dogs and how they crept up to the lunch room when the miners were gone. It was even said that if a man fell asleep it would be his last glimpse of this world for the rats would clean his bones. One man had quit because of the legends and Mike had laughed. But in the silent and eerie Stope, his laughter was gone as his stomach twisted into a tight, painful knot.

Maybe Luigi went to get powder, Mike thought. But, his partner would still be here.

Mike whirled again for he had heard the same tiny sound. As he stared at the dancing dust in the corner, he thought he saw a movement and the hair on the back of his neck rose for he had a phobia of rats. He approached slowly, his skin prickly and damp.

Then he stopped and stared, horrified. Luigi and his partner lay, nearly covered with rock and a low moan came from Luigi's lips.

In the stale, weak light Mike thought he had lost his mind. Luigi lay with blood oozing from his nose. He was covered from the waist down where his bones were mush. But more macabre was his partner's head and arm, all that could be seen from under the rock. Through the head, a scaling bar protruded, rammed up through the mouth to the ears. It had jammed on the rock on either side with the ore hitting the man on the back of the head. Mike stared petrified at the dead man staring up at him with unseeing eyes and with a bar sticking through his head.

Mike turned and fled, running down the ladder to the lunch room where he found the Shift Boss and told him of one man dead and another still alive. Then he sat and tried to smoke but the trembling wouldn't go away. The Shift Boss looked at him for a instant as he rang the surface for the emergency crew.

"Take a deep breath! Stay here for a while and then take the rest of the day off. We'll look after Luigi."

Mike nodded and drew heavily on the cigarette, his fingers trembling and his face chalk white. He drew on the cigarette until the coal was bright and glowing but the trembling wouldn't go away for he knew what "look after Luigi" meant.

The safety team would have to strap him to the stretcher and haul him up by hand through the manway, with the screams burning a spot in their souls for Luigi's legs and hips were crushed; nothing but blood and broken bones and muscle, flattened and useless. His partner would be hauled up by hand too but the safety crew would be spared the screams.

Later, the Stope would be closed with a large stop sign nailed to planks at the entrance. But it wouldn't really be necessary. No miner would ever work a Stope where a man had been killed for it was felt that the ghost should be left in peace. A full investigation would also come with the police going reluctantly underground and finally a statement would be issued from the company. It would state, as usual, that the men had been at fault; their carelessness was to blame for the accident.

The next safety meeting the Mine Captain demonstrated the proper use of a scaling bar and how it had to be longer than four feet. That was one meeting when the Old Hands weren't impatient to get back to their Stopes.

A day later Mike was in the Dry where the men changed and showered. He was approached by a man for a contribution and he gave all he had in his wallet, five dollars; for it was for the dead man's family. It was all they could do; collect money for the widow and children.

Two other young men sat beside Mike on a bench and slowly pulled on their street clothes. Mike stared straight ahead for he could still see the bloody bar sticking out of the man's head with unseeing eyes. He had told himself, when he had gone down underground, that if he was to die, he was to die, so why worry? But that was a poor defense against the image of the unseeing eyes. Mike chain smoked cigarettes as he listened to the men talk.

"Ya know the funny thing is Luigi was gonna go home to Italy, for the first time in ten years," one said quietly.

"Well maybe he'll go some day when he heals up," the other answered softly. They didn't mention Luigi's partner who would go quickly, in a coffin.

Mike's shoulders slumped and he felt a weight pushing him down into the muck he worked in. He thought of writing a poem but then shrugged the thought aside. As the talent was pushed deeper and deeper into his soul, he became more and more a shell, reacting to his world and never controlling it.

"That's it!" the first man suddenly said, taking Mike's attention from the unseeing eyes and crushed bodies.

"I've had it! I quit! And there's a hundred others who're doing the same. To hell with Christmas and saving money. If I come home broke, at least I'll be coming home alive, not in some Goddamn box."

"Yeah! Me too!" the other agreed.

Mike looked first at one and then the other. He thought of the cold and hostile drift but he also thought of the farm and his father's contorting face and the cloying smell of cow manure in the barn. Then he remembered when he had come home after working on a construction job. He and his brother Allen had stood talking, not far from the outhouse.

"I don't care what reason you had. You quit and that's that. Boredom's no excuse," Allen had snapped, glaring at him. "Why'd ya come home anyway?" Then Allen had hit upon his favorite topic. "Besides, I don't know what you got to complain about. You probably had it a lot better than the rest of us."

The memory was interrupted suddenly.

"Well! What're ya gonna do?" the first man asked. "Ya gonna stick it, or quit? You know the company don't give a Goddamn about your life."

"I know," Mike said slowly and then added, "But hell, the odds are the same now as they were two days ago. Christ! They must be better because we've had our quota of accidents for this month." He meant that to be funny but neither of the men laughed.

"I guess I'll be staying. At least 'til spring. There's no jobs in the south now anyway."

"Suit yourself," the first man said for it was Mike's business.

That was the second Christmas Mike spent away from home. An inexplicable loneliness closed in like the ice fog on a frozen lake in the evening; chilling even the very essence of his soul. He didn't send any gifts home, not even a card. Instead, he bought a case of rum and two cases of beer. He spent Christmas Eve at the boarding house, after he had been carried to his cot in the basement, for he had slipped on the stairs and lay unconscious on the cold cement.

That was one Christmas Eve he wouldn't remember.

Days blurred into weeks and Mike rose, went to work and returned as the cold deepened. For six weeks the temperature hovered between sixty-one and sixty-nine below at night. Mike worked days one week and evenings the next, so for a week at a time he never saw the sun, going down in the cage when it was pitch dark and coming up when the stars had come out. He lived in a basement with a cement floor and frigid cement walls and slept in a cot with extra blankets. His roommates were Joe and Steve. Joe was a youngster who had left home for the first time and although they were the same age Mike felt immeasurably older. Steve was seven years his senior and a thickset farmer who needed cash to pay debts. He had a coarse face with thick lips and heavy eyebrows but he didn't take long to fathom that Mike could be taken advantage of.

As the grinding boredom descended and Mike went down into the ground every day, an image came and stayed. He was a beast chained to a pole and endlessly circling a well, goaded by a whip. Mike gritted his teeth, when the alarm rang at six a.m., for he rarely got enough sleep. The tram that ran on the tracks in the drift had a loud sharp horn that was similar to the one on the furnace that sounded whenever it started. When Mike was in the drift and he heard the loud beep and saw the blinding light of the tram, he flattened himself against a wall for the clearance was only eighteen inches. At night in the dark, when the furnace beeped, he would waken, rigid. It normally took a half hour before his breathing returned to normal and he could sleep again.

He didn't dream of the man with the bar sticking through his head but at times he would waken with an inexplicable and paralyzing fear. He would struggle to open his eyes and then stare into the darkness, as slowly the pounding in his chest subsided.

Despite the image of crushed bodies and unseeing eyes, his greatest fear came from knowing that he was condemned to labor like a beast for the rest of his days.

At times he would try writing but it never came out the way he wanted for the talent simmered very deep. At other times he felt guilt for deep down he knew he shouldn't be laboring like a beast. But whenever he looked up at the company offices with their bright lights and central heating, he knew that the distance to them was greater than that of Luigi's last place in life and his home in Italy.

One day he forgot an unfinished poem upstairs on the couch. His landlady smiled as she placed supper on the table.

"Who's the poet? I found this on the couch."

Mike felt an inexplicable embarrassment and he looked down at his plate. But Steve felt no such shyness.

"Who in hell's gonna write junk like dat?" He glared up from his plate. Then he laughed with food dropping from his mouth.

"I got no time for dat crap. I gotta earn a living, like a man."

"It must have been you." The landlady turned to Mike.

"Yeah," he said softly and then was silent as Steve glared at him. He ached with a burning desire to know what she had thought of it but he couldn't ask. Instead he ate and listened to the conversation, as the turmoil once again raged deep within.

That New Year's Eve Mike sat in the rear of a car with Steve. In the front was Wayne along with one of the rare women who would go out with a miner. Between Mike and Steve were two dozen beer and again Mike let the conversation ebb and flow about him while he drank. He wished he had bought a bottle of rum, for rum got a man drunk a lot faster and didn't fill his bladder.

Suddenly the girl turned in the front seat and gazed steadily at Mike. The interior light was on and Mike felt all eyes on him.

"What about you?" she asked.

"Huh!" Mike said.

The pretty, young face was framed with dark hair. Mike kept his eyes on his bottle.

"It's New Year's Eve. Isn't it customary to get a kiss?"

Mike looked at the girl in surprise.

"You want to kiss me?"

"Sure! It's New Year's Eve, isn't it?"

Mike woodenly leaned forward and allowed the girl to kiss him. She opened her mouth quickly and he felt the tantalization of a woman's tongue and he knew instinctively that it carried a message.

Wayne glared at Mike but his fear was unfounded. Mike hadn't yet found the confidence to ask a girl for a date.

As spring finally promised to break winter's deathly grip, Mike still labored in the mine without being assigned a Stope. He had gone to Stope School but lacked the desire and drive to make a good miner so he remained a mucker, working alongside men with half his experience.

One day Steve called to him after they had eaten supper. His eyebrows were knitted together as he brushed his coarse black hair from his face. Mike followed him downstairs where they were alone.

"I gotta problem," Steve said as they sat on opposing cots. Mike looked into the eyes of a worried man.

"Is there anything I can do to help?"

"Naw you wouldn't want ta get involved in another man's problems. I only mentioned it because we're friends."

"Sure I would, if we're friends," Mike said sincerely.

"Well, okay. I'll tell ya. But it don't mean ya gotta help," Steve said just as earnestly and then added quickly, "I just got a letter from home. If I don't come up with a hundred and fifty bucks they're gonna take my tractor."

"Don't you have any money?"

"No! I paid off taxes and now I'm broke 'til payday," Steve sighed deeply. "But that's over a week away. And they said that if I don't mail the money right away, the tractor's gone."

Mike had forgotten he had told Steve that he had saved a hundred and fifty dollars over the winter. He looked down at his shoes, sighed and then looked up at Steve.

"Well, I guess I could lend it to you."

"Naw, it's not your problem," Steve said quickly. Mike never thought of asking to see the letter.

"No. It's okay, I got the money," he persisted.

"I'll figure out a way," Steve suddenly dismissed the offer, helping himself to beer Mike had bought. "It's my problem and a man's gotta figure out a way for himself."

"But I wanna help," Mike insisted, the familiar feeling of rejection making his stomach churn.

"Well, okay then," Steve finally said. Then he added quickly, "but don't tell nobody about this, eh. It's bad enough I gotta borrow money. It'd be worse yet, if people said I can't even pay my debts."

"Okay," Mike said. "I'll go to the bank tomorrow."

He didn't appear to notice the second beer Steve helped himself to. And he also appeared not to notice that in the mine, Steve worked hard with sweat running down his face whenever someone watched. But when they were alone, he sat on a plank and let Mike do the work. Mike would have been surprised and deeply hurt if he had known that Steve made fun of him behind his back.

Mike lent Steve the money, telling no one but as the weeks passed and Steve quit, he began to wonder why he had trusted him. And when he didn't receive a letter he was angry, but more than the anger was a deep sense of shame for having been duped.

During lunch he gazed at the two cheese sandwiches and apple his landlady had packed in his lunch bag. He thought of the small bowl of cereal for breakfast and only one serving for supper. When he worked evenings, he had to get by on two sandwiches and an apple as his main meal. At twenty, Mike was still growing and when he lifted timbers or a jack-leg, weighing more than a hundred pounds, he nearly passed out. He only needed a thirty-two-inch belt despite being one hundred and ninety pounds of bone and muscle. He felt no pride in his strength, for the image of the beast hitched to a pole endlessly circling a well came with it.

Suddenly he rose, throwing his lunch into the garbage. He walked to the door, picking up his bronze tag from a board. The tags had numbers on them and if one was missing at the end of the shift, it meant a miner was missing too; possibly injured or dying in a Stope. Mike remembered the commotion caused when someone had forgotten to leave their tag on the board.

When he was at the door, he glanced at the shift boss, back to the lunch room and then out at the drift, leading to where he had found the man with a bar through his head.

Mike hefted the tab in his hand for an instant and then nonchalantly tossed it into the garbage pail, tipping his hat to the shift boss.

Then he turned and walked out the door. It was a boyish attempt at bravado but Mike had his fill of the mine.


Mike sat in the old kitchen once again, watching his mother run about, trying to do all the work at once for Gerard had come home with his wife. But if it was shameful not to have a well-prepared meal for honored guests, it was sinful not to attend Mass on Holy Easter. Once again Mike had knelt in the confessional and confessed sins of indecency brought on by wistful, nocturnal dreams. He had filed down the isle in the old church and had allowed the priest to place the Holy Communion on his tongue. He had felt hunger again for the Church still did not allow food on the morning when he was to allow Christ into his soul. Mike saw no sense in standing in a church, mumbling meaningless prayers while deep within lurked, the image of death's apparition, two thousand feet beneath the earth.

But Gertie had seen it differently.

"Come on Metro!" she had yelled from the bedroom door. "You gotta go to church!"

Mike had put off the confrontation and had gone to receive the tasteless communion and had mumbled the meaningless prayers. Beside him had sat Gertie with her square, sad face, hard and determined.

As Mike sat in the kitchen with his back to the window, Gerard suddenly broke into his thoughts.

"You had a steady job. Why did you quit?"

Mike sat, for a while longer, as the crushing boredom and the skull with the bar sticking through it came and went quickly.

"I wanted to see what the rest of the world looked like," he finally said. "Thompson's pretty isolated, you know."

"I talked to a guy who was in Thompson," Gerard snapped. "He sounded like he knew what was going on in the world."

Mike didn't answer. Instead he thought of the blindfolded beast hitched to a pole. Then he became aware of Doreen's steady gaze. The light in her eyes was the same as in his brother's and Mike wondered how Gerard could have found a wife so suited to him. Earlier she had laid three pennies on the table and had insisted he solve a simple riddle. Mike had woodenly complied, ignoring the bright look of anticipation in her eyes and then reward, when he didn't get the right answer.

Gertie stopped suddenly in one of her mad dashes, and glared at Mike.

"Never mind the job! He didn't even go to church once while he was away."

# Thirty-three

The late morning sun filtered through the dirty window, illuminating the peeling varnish on the dresser, the grey walls that were once white and the sink, with the smudged mirror above it. A closet, one chair and a small bed were all the furniture in the room while, under the blanket, lay two prone forms. As the light penetrated the filthy windowpane it passed through countless fingerprints of countless occupants who had been in the three dollars a night room. And the fingerprints had been left by the countless men who had sought surcease, from the endless drifting, with a partner who drank their booze and gave their bodies in payment. All the frantic couplings in the dark, the forced and determined attempts at gaiety had passed before the window. The smudged fingerprints were the signatures of the Damned.

Mike moaned and rolled over in the narrow bed throwing his arm across the sleeping form next to him. His mouth was dry and acrid for alcohol has its own price for the brief oblivion it gives. He raised his head and gazed into a female face covered with smeared makeup and wrinkles advertising a speedy end to a once youthful bloom. She was no more than thirty but she had lived a thousand years, in countless three dollars a night rooms and with countless partners who gave her booze in exchange for coupling in the dark. The closed eyes had blue shadow and the eyelashes were messed. Mike gazed for a moment and then rolled over, pulling the cover over him as he tried to recapture an image in the nether world of a dream.

He had been in a far off place standing before the Acropolis, the remnant of Greek glory and had gazed at the straight and simple, beautiful columns that rose on a hill. A ghostly full moon rode high and in his hand he felt the warm softness of the Greek girl who gazed too at the beauty her ancestors had wrought. The warmth of her hand promised delights way beyond anything Mike had ever known and all the more tantalizing because of it. In the Nether World a woman never snored, never nagged and was forever beautiful and young for that is the beauty of dreams. And in the dream he was a writer, a man who strung words into sentences and paragraphs, capturing the beauty of a moonlit night or the savagery of battle.

But the dream stopped there, for Mike knew no way to string the words together. All he knew, was to hide in the warm dream that was a world of soft, shimmering beauty.

The bed creaked suddenly as the bundle next to him turned and began to snore, chasing away the image of the sweet heart shaped face. Mike opened his eyes and lay still for a while longer with the snores awakening a vague memory of the night before. He had gone to the "Jungle," a bar that was a hang out for ironworkers. He had drunk draft beer until the room swirled and his lips were numb. The woman had materialized from out of the chaos and he vaguely remembered paying three dollars in advance for a bed and four walls. But the drunken fumbling beneath the cover, accomplished nothing. When Mike was with a woman, who had forgotten how many men she had bedded, guilt played about in his subconscious. Alcohol fogged his brain enough that his shyness evaporated but it did nothing for impotence.

If Mike had been told that he was an alcoholic he would have denied it vehemently. Alcoholics were little old men on park benches, in filthy brown raincoats and who drank from bottles hidden in brown paper bags. A man drank because he was a man, he would have said and it took a man to control alcohol. It never occurred to him that he was the one who was controlled.

He turned painfully and looked again at the young, old face; at the wrinkles and smeared makeup and he wondered who she was. Then he thought foggily how she had become another nameless face in his dream, four years before, when he had drifted down the River of Skulls. He imagined all the flesh gone from her face with only the yellow, white bone left, while her exposed teeth grinned a welcome to her world. Mike shook his head violently. Then he grimaced before rolling back and drawing the cover over him, trying to recapture the soft, sensitive face and warm promising hand of the maiden in his dream. But the snores kept driving away the beauty and replacing it with the face that was a grinning skull.

Then, as he lay with his eyes shut, he heard a sudden loud pounding on the door.

"Come on! Mike! Wake up! What'a ya gonna do? Sleep all day?" Walter's voice crashed through the door.

Mike blinked, took a deep breath and glanced quickly at the snoring bundle before rising and searching for his pants.

"Yeah! Just hang on! Goddamn it!" he yelled. The bundle started in the middle of a snore. Then the woman opened her eyes, blinked and rubbed them with a pudgy hand, all the while looking about in a bewildered manner. When Mike had found his pants he opened the door and Walter stuck his head inside and grinned. He didn't say anything but the grin was enough. The woman dressed hurriedly under the covers, awkwardly pulling on her panties and then slacks. Walter's grin widened as she rose and looked uncertainly at Mike who was busy buttoning his shirt.

"Uh, maybe I'll see you tonight?"

"Yeah sure, maybe," Mike mumbled, as he finished the last button, keeping his eyes from the tired and smeared face. She turned then and hurried from the room, not forgetting to grab her purse.

Walter collapsed on the bed, making the springs groan. His grin widened until he was laughing outright.

"Boy! Ya sure the hell can peek 'em. At least ya can't be accused of robbing de cradle."

Mike kept his eyes downcast as he sat on the chair and yanked on his socks and then tied his shoes. When he glanced up, Walter had lost interest in the departed woman and was instead examining the fly specked wall.

He was Mike's only friend. Together they followed the construction boom across Canada and down into the United States, working as ironworkers and drifting aimlessly in their quest for the perfect job and final bankroll. Their kind was contemptuously called "Boomers" by the family men who stayed in one union local, for the Boomers gave them a bad name.

Walter's parents had come from Eastern Europe and although he had been born and raised in Canada, he still spoke with an accent. Mike ignored the fact that Walter was lacking in any social graces, for Walter and his family had accepted him. Walter's brother was known as Clampett, after the Beverly Hillbillys character. When he talked, he waved his arms and when he had a few drinks he "played the roll," pretending to be rich. He was also lazy and known for the drunken, unattractive women he picked up in bars. The ironworkers tolerated him, for he was someone they could laugh at. Mike tolerated him, for without friends he was totally alone and he feared that more than the danger on the steel.

When his creative soul had shone with a tiny flame, Mike had sketched with a pencil. He had left the sketches in Walter's car and the next day had asked where they were.

"Aw, I threw 'em out!" Walter had snapped and Mike had tolerated that too.

Once, in a bar and with enough beer in him, Mike had invited two attractive young women to their table. But when they had seen Clampett, with his protruding beer belly and his hand around a beer bottle, they had stopped short. Clampett had belched suddenly.

"Don't be shy!" he had announced. "We'll have a couple beers and then head for the hotel."

The women had left in a hurry and Mike had tolerated that too. Emotionally he was listless and dependant on acceptance from those he thought were friends. But his friends didn't know the meaning of morality and deep within his soul simmered an abiding shame.

After he was dressed, he took the key and went downstairs. Walter still grinned at him and Mike tried changing the subject.

"How long will it take?" he asked. They sat in a booth in a run down café with dirty, grey walls and wrinkled and torn menus.

"I don't know. Maybe two or three days," Walter snapped as he stared at his menu. He scraped at a tiny bit of food on the paper with his fingernail and then continued, "The Bennet Dam's in northern British Columbia. That's over a thousand miles."

Once again they had quit a job and together they were driving to another, filled with dreams of three-eighty-one an hour and a big stake. In nineteen-sixty-six a thousand dollars was a small fortune.

Walter was taller than Mike but his front teeth were rotting and his long black hair was lanky and unwashed. The two had become like the fox and the cat in a fable. One was lame and the other blind, with the blind supporting the lame and the lame pointing the way.

A tired waitress approached their booth with an order pad and pencil stub. She wore a soiled apron over a yellow dress. Greying blond hair had escaped the elastic band at the back of her head and hung down in grey listless strands. Mike glanced at Walter, wondering if he would order the inevitable meal, a hot beef sandwich. He wondered how anyone could exist in so mundane and boring a fashion. But Walter grinned suddenly at the waitress.

"What does Confucius say about a girl, who fly upside down?" he asked suddenly, exposing his decaying front teeth.

"How the hell should I know?" the waitress snapped.

"Confucius say she has, crack-up," Walter laughed.

"Look! If ya wanna eat, order something, or shut the hell up and leave," the waitress snapped, glancing quickly at her husband who watched impassively from behind the cash register. Walter's grin vanished and he looked quickly down at the menu.

The waitress took their order and left, disappearing into the kitchen.

"For Christ's sake! Why do you have to do that?" Mike demanded.

"Aw, I don't give a shit!" Walter grinned, glancing quickly at the owner who still stood impassively behind the register. "I don't care what people think. That's me, boy. If they don't like it, why that's their problem."

After the waitress had brought coffee, Walter drank with a loud slurp. Then when she had brought their meals, he ate with loud smacking noises, opening a door to a lurking memory in Mike's soul. For a very brief instant he saw his father and the food rolling around in his mouth and his contorting face.

"Well!" Walter demanded suddenly. "Did ya get eet last night?"

Mike tried to ignore him, gazing out the window at a parking lot. But Walter persisted.

"Come on, Mike! Eef ya can't tell a friend, who can ya tell?"

Mike stared out at the parking lot for a long time. Walter grinned from across the table but then he grew impatient.

"Well?"

"Yeah. I got it last night," Mike lied.

"One a these days, you're gonna get a dose, just like Clampett. Screwing all them sluts." Walter didn't let up.

"Did ya go down on 'er?"

Mike glared at Walter.

"Did ya chew it?" Walter demanded and Mike scowled. Then, he did what his father had done when mocked. Slowly a self-conscious grin came and he looked out at the parking lot again. When he showed no anger, Walter lost interest. Instead he concentrated on his fork as he dug into a lemon pie. He ate with his mouth open for he had a cold and as he chewed he smacked his lips and emitted a loud "Ah Hem" in appreciation. Then he wiped his mouth on his sleeve and shoved in another forkful.

Mike kept his eyes on the parking lot. There didn't seem to be much he wouldn't tolerate.


A grey ribbon of shimmering asphalt stretched off to the horizon, over hills and down through green valleys. At times it wound through solemn forests of spruce and poplar and at others, through open fields while a warm sun beamed benignly down. In the fields farmers cut hay and the air bore the soft, tantalizing scent of sweet clover.

A car sped down the highway past the dusty farmers on their dusty tractors in the aromatic hay fields. The farmers sweated and cows contentedly chewed their cuds in the pastures, unaware of the car or the occupants. But inside a controlled excitement simmered, for the two young men were going to the Bennet Dam in the Peace River country, the last frontier for those looking for money and adventure: Three eighty-one per hour and free board and room and they would be rich in a year.

Walter drove and Mike sat besides him, his eyes on the trees and farmyards where children played. He wondered if they noticed the cars whizzing by and then a memory came.

He had been with his father, sweating in a hay field with blisters breaking out on his palms. His father had paused, made a face, and then had stared at the highway a half mile a way.

"Look, at all them cars!" he had exclaimed. "Boy! They're heading for the lake." Then he had spat, bent and jabbed his fork into another pile of hay. Mike had stared too. And he had thought of lying in the sun by a cool lake, instead of laboring like a beast in a field.

And then, as the image faded Mike thought of writing and wondered why the urge never seemed to leave.

Walter drove the car with one hand on the wheel, thinking of how girls were impressed by chrome. Mike glanced at him for a second and then back at the road. He remembered Walter's boasting and he felt a twinge of shame. He knew vaguely that Walter's sole pretense at manhood was the owning of a powerful Oldsmobile, even if it was seven years old.

Walter and his family were bums but they always supported each other when there was a need. Then, as the car began a descent into a broad valley, Mike remembered a confrontation with Gerard because of fifteen dollars he had borrowed. Gerard had glared at him in the farmhouse demanding payment and when Mike didn't have the money, he had contemptuously called him a bum.

As Walter drove and hummed a nameless tune, Mike's face grew dark with the memory. Then, as the car sped on, more memories flooded into Mike's consciousness. He had met his sister for the first time since she had left for the convent. She had smiled condescendingly at him and he had known more confusion. Once again, he, his sister and parents had knelt in the small kitchen reciting the Holy Rosary with the meaningless words, a repetitious blur.

When they had eaten dinner, Arlene had suddenly turned and glared.

"Metro! You should let Daddy serve first." She had also refused to call Mike by his chosen name. And what she had meant was that he should hand the meat tray to his father and let him pick out the best pieces.

Mike had glanced at his father who had made a face with his tongue protruding. Then he had looked back at his sister.

"Why?"

"Because the father's made in the image of God!" she had blurted.

During all this Vincent made faces and ate with loud smacking noises with the food rolling around in his open mouth. Arlene had seen the faces too. But she had chosen to ignore them for she too was given a choice; see her father as he really was, or cling desperately to what the nuns had taught her. The latter was the least painful.

"Metro should work for a farmer," Gertie had said suddenly. "At least then he'd have a steady job."

"Jesus Christ!" Mike had snapped. "I'm an ironworker."

"That's enough!" Arlene had suddenly begun yelling. Her face had turned scarlet and she had slammed her hands down on the table. Mike had stared in confusion.

"That's enough!" Arlene had screamed again. "These are your parents. You should show them respect. But you won't even let your father serve first. You never did nothing for them. Your mother cooks and sews for you and is that all you can do?" The nearly incoherent words had tumbled forth. Mike had stared at his sister.

A brittle light of triumph had shone from Gertie's eyes and then slowly changed to one of suffering and pain.

"What have you ever done for them?" Arlene had demanded.

"What about the two hundred and forty bucks I sent home?" Mike had asked quietly.

A sudden silence had then settled down upon the kitchen. Vincent had made faces and Gertie's face had remained a picture of suffering. Arlene had looked from one to the other.

"Did he?" she had finally asked. Her voice had lost its insane pitch and her color was returning to normal.

Gertie had stared at her daughter for an instant, her face hard.

"Yuh! But he only sent home one hundred and twenty dollars," she had finally answered.

Mike had stared at his mother. Then he had wondered if he had made a mistake. Arlene had turned to their father then.

"Did he send money home?"

"No!" Vincent had laughed as he chewed with his mouth open. Mike had remembered him saying that the money had been peanuts and that he had hardly noticed it.

Mike had gone outside and had sat on a bench in the cool evening, staring out at the driveway and petting his dog. As Buster shoved his nose under his hand, he had wondered if he had indeed sent the money home.

Walter glanced at Mike suddenly, taking his eyes off the road for an instant. He laughed nervously.

"Jesus Christ! What the hell're you so mad at? You look like you could kill somebody."

"Oh nothing. I was just thinking of my family." Mike replied after a moment.

"Shit! I never go home no more. All they ever want is for me to be just like them," Walter said. Then he too glared at the road. Mike remembered Walter telling him how his brothers had lent him money whenever he asked.

The miles sped by beneath the Oldsmobile as they came closer and closer to the Bennet Dam and the big stake. Then Walter glanced at Mike again.

"How come you always say `mouse' instead of `mouth?'" he asked mockingly. "You're always slurring your words. You sound like a Goddam Indian."

Mike remained silent.

"Open your mouse! Close your mouse!" Walter mocked Mike, as the car sped by a farm truck. Mike glanced at the farmer and then back at Walter.

"You need a pressure teekit to get Een!" he said quietly, mocking Walter's Ukrainian accent. Walter's face fell suddenly and he glared at the road.

"Once we get to the dam," he said slowly. "You'd better get someone else to bum rides off of."

Mike looked steadily at Walter for an instant, remembering that he paid for half the gasoline. Then he looked back at the road.

"That's the best idea I've heard all day," he said quietly.

# Thirty-four

Thundering, boiling, foamy water cascaded down between two hundred foot limestone cliffs hurrying on toward the Peace River country of Alberta, where it joined with the Saskatchewan in its headlong rush to Hudson's Bay. The Peace River was mighty, bearing all before it, smoothing boulders and rolling them along the floor while wearing new channels in the rock. All that had stood before the river had perished for its power was beyond comprehension.

Then one day, a man named Bennet had a dream and engineers began poring over desks late into the night. The dream became reality and the river that had once swept away all before it was treated with the same scorn by the men who had harnessed a much greater force, technology. The river was tamed and a dam spanned the cliffs, channeling the water into penstock tunnels. The water's power turned into electricity and the dam was named after the man with the dream. Power lines stretched southwards, over mountains, spanning chasms and valleys. Electricity hummed with a force that mocked the fears of the men who had originally looked upon the river in awe. On the side of Portage Mountain a large plaque proclaimed the spot where Alexander Mackenzie had stopped in his explorations and a large dinosaur track was etched in stone for eternity. Tourists came and looked at the track and read the plaque, stopping momentarily to wonder about the courage and vision it had taken to challenge the mighty river in only a canoe. But they gave little thought to the perils that had long ago disappeared.

A restaurant was perched four hundred feet above the thousands of men who labored in the hot sun. Engineers pored over blue prints and the men sweated while the tourists gazed down in awe at the immensity of the creation. All three were as distant from each other as Mackenzie had been from the man who had dreamed of the power project. The tourists knew and cared nothing for the sweat below and husbands told their wives how they envied the construction worker and the freedom of working a huge job and leaving with a stake. But their wives and they both knew they would never leave the soft confines of the office for the rigors and loneliness of the bunkhouse, a thousand miles north of Vancouver.

While the engineers dreamed of harnessing a mighty river, something they would talk of for years to come, the men who sweated in the heat dreamed a different dream: Three eighty per hour with free board in the bunkhouse. The money piled up in the bank and they were getting rich. Single men dreamed of soft willing women, while married men dreamed of freedom, or of a new house and the talk ebbed and flowed about the mighty job and mighty wages. They came from the four corners of the earth; Spaniards, Portuguese Frenchmen, Americans, Eastern Europeans and Britishers, all lured by the same siren call of making it rich for a man could save more than a hundred a week. In the days when a beer cost less than forty cents and a pack of cigarettes half a buck, that was money and something to keep a man awake at night.

A story was told of a man who came from Greece and who worked for ten years in the construction camps and then returned with sixty thousand dollars, never having to labor again. And there were those who saved their money and started businesses or returned home with a stake for a car or a house. But there were others who didn't. They were the Boomers who drifted over the land, constantly seeking the one big stake, but rarely staying long enough for the dream to come true. They were the ones who couldn't resist a hooker's soft body: Twenty bucks and they could enjoy for a very brief time what married men took for granted. And they gathered in the bars and boasted of making forty bucks a day, while the hookers, at times, gave more than three hundred to their pimps. With the onslaught on Friday night, a girl was kept busy from sundown until the sun broke over the mountains.

The Boomers came and went, boasting of their pay and blowing it in the first bar or poker game, for the determination of the immigrant was not in them. They had never heard a starving child cry in the night and they always knew there was another job just around the corner, at least while the boom lasted.

Beneath the restaurant where the tourists gathered and gazed down in wonder, Mike sweated with the other men. Occasionally he looked up at the tiny figures four hundred feet above, wondering what the men and women were like. At times he was proud for the dam was the last frontier where a man could be part of something big, something that would live on in his memory for the rest of his life.

But gradually the newness, and the immensity of the project wore off, replaced by the familiar grinding dull, boredom. Then came the image of the blindfolded donkey endlessly circling the well. When the sweat ran down his forehead under the blazing sun Mike felt it burn slowly into his soul and he envied the men and women who gazed down in wonder from the mountain top. But he knew of no way to join them so he stayed, day after grinding day, until the boredom became a living enemy. He rose at six a.m., ate breakfast in the mess-hall, rode a bus to work, returned for a brief midday meal and then glanced at his watch until four thirty p.m. Then, after a shower and supper, the boredom would crush down with a tangible force. There were no recreational facilities except the bar, fifteen miles away in Hudson's Hope, the small town that had been suddenly thrust into the boom.

One evening Mike bought a magazine and gazed in wonder at the pictures taken by a man, who had stepped from a plane one day and had left the next. The story described the job, the one hundred and twenty-foot high Powerhouse that was the length of three football fields, hollowed out of the rock by diamond bit and dynamite. He saw himself there, laboring in the dust. He had moved inside, under the rock and tourists but still a hundred feet in the air on the steel. He read on, how the men were leaving in droves and how nobody understood why.

Why in hell don't they ask us? Mike thought bitterly and wondered what to do until bedtime, four hours from supper. He thought also of the danger and how men quit because they felt their luck had run out. He wondered if it was time to draw his pay and find the nearest bar where he would forget for a while the clutching fear that woke him with his sheets drenched. He had three close calls on three consecutive days and he wondered if the number was significant. He had become superstitious like the old hands who believed that if a man came to camp with money in his pocket it would be bad but if he came broke, it would certainly be good.

The first close call had occurred when he was working on the jumbo, a contraption of iron that was ninety feet high and on which the rebar was tied outside in the open. Once the steel was intact, a caterpillar was hitched to it and the five foot, solid steel wheels would turn slowly as the "Cat" pulled the jumbo inside the tail race tunnel. Then the rebar was welded to the rock bolts and was ready for the cement to be poured.

Mike had stood on the jumbo, ninety feet above the rock, when it was still out in the open and just outside the tunnel. As he had bent forward, he had lost his balance and began falling. But he had let the momentum carry him until he grabbed a bar, swinging with the weight of his body. He had saved himself from falling, ninety feet onto solid rock.

The foreman had laughed, trying to break the tension.

"If you're gonna fall, at least gimmee back my tape measure. You'll smash it all to hell."

Mike had laughed too and breathed deeply, trying to forget the sudden gut wrenching panic.

As work and boredom blended, the image of his brother's angry words and his sister pounding the table came and he began to take unnecessary chances, climbing the steel like a monkey until he gained the grudging respect of the other ironworkers. Some might have said he had a death wish but Mike hadn't heard the expression and never thought of it. He only knew that when there was gut churning danger, the time passed quickly. When he was on the ground and safe, he chained smoked cigarettes and glanced at his watch every few minutes.

The second close call had been inside the tail race tunnel which was more than ninety feet high and would eventually carry the water from the penstock tunnel that turned the turbines. He had stood on the jumbo and looked thirty feet away to a row of rebar that was tied close to the rock wall. Between him and the rebar had been open air except for two bars which were welded together and laying on top rock dowels that stuck out of the rock about six feet apart. Together the bars were barely more than two inches wide and were more than two feet from the rock face. Mike had a choice of climbing down nearly ninety feet and then up again on the rebar, or walking across on the bars. He hadn't hesitated, for an inexplicable force urged him on. He had walked slowly, careful to touch the rock with his fingertips every second step for it offered a psychological safety. Beneath and coming up from the cement had been upright bars and he knew that if he had fallen he would have been impaled. But the thought had passed quickly as he had ignored the amateurish advice to never look down. If he looked, he could treat the danger with disdain.

Suddenly he had lost his balance and swayed with outstretched arms like a tightrope walker. He had teetered for half a couple of heartbeats, and then had slowly regained his balance and continued walking. Another quarter inch and he would have been hanging, impaled on the rebar with the life leaving him in bright red spurts.

The third close call had come when he had thought he was safe. He had been standing on a bundle of rebar which rested on the rock dowels between the jumbo and rock face, thirty feet from the floor. He had pulled up a vertical bar and placed it against a horizontal one with the bar grazing the ancient and loose stones, above him. Unknowing, he had bent sideways for a tool.

Suddenly a tremendous weight hit his left leg. The rebar bent and then rebounded and he had grabbed a rock bolt with his stomach knotting painfully.

A large rock had grazed his calf and tore his pants but leaving only a bruise. If he had been standing upright, it would have hit him on the head and left shoulder. It had bounced off the rebar and hit the jumbo, bringing together two large V-shaped, half-inch steel plates which were joined by a bar. The rock had weighed more than five tons.

Mike had slid hurriedly down the steel and had finished out the shift, apprehensively glancing upwards at the tunnel walls while he had mentally added up the money he had saved. Then came the image of the miner with a bar sticking through his head and Mike had decided it was time. Still, the inexplicable force had beckoned and he had decided to wait until payday.

He worked in the powerhouse, hefting the heavy bars onto his arms and then climbing a wall of rebar with four other men. They ran up the wall, stopped and hooked their safety hooks onto a vertical bar and tied the one they were carrying to it. Then they hurried down and repeated the climb, stopping occasionally for a quick smoke break. Sweat ran down their faces and they gasped for air, for they were working at an altitude of more than five thousand feet. But the wall went up, one foot at a time and Mike reveled in his strength for he had the stamina to outlast the other men. At times like that he forgot the grinding boredom and the days that were an eternity.

Suddenly, a siren burst into life with a screaming urgency, the wails rising and falling for an ironworker was down. Mike jumped from the wall and ran with the crew to where a connector had been walking a beam thirty-five feet above the rebar that stuck upwards from the concrete. The connector walked no more.

He lay on the cement, on his back, his face the color of death. Slippery, slimy intestines hung from his stomach cavity to the bar, dripping with dark, red blood. Mike stopped, rooted to the spot, a paralysis clutching at his soul.

The glistening intestines hung, slippery and wet while the man screamed and screamed and his partner held his head and tried to comfort him.

"It's okay! Buddy! Just hang on. The safety crew'll be here any minute. Once we get you onto the stretcher you'll be fine." His eyes were moist while he clutched Buddy's head and Buddy screamed and screamed.

Mike stood very still, his breath coming in gasps while the screams of the dying man blended with the harsh wail of the siren.

Then the man's mind left him and he stopped screaming.

"Just grab it!" He lifted a bloody hand and pointed to a long and slippery, bloody intestine.

"Can't you just grab it? Stick it inside my gut. That's all ya gotta do!"

The words became a hoarse whisper as the siren subsided and a brief silence hung over the dying man. He had lost all reason and in the few brief seconds he had left, he couldn't accept the encroaching death that crept through the pain and growing numbness. His partner still held his head in his arms, gazing a far way off while tears cascaded down his cheeks.

"It's okay Buddy! It's okay! We'll get you outta here right away," he said softly and then was silent.

Blood suddenly bubbled from the man's mouth and he raised a hand and smeared his hair with his own gore.

He began screaming again, the high-pitched wails burning into Mike's mind. He stood still, numb and calm and he knew he would once again be contributing money to a dead man's family. The screams slowly faded as the safety crew ran and stumbled over the muck and debris with a stretcher. When they were near, they slowed for there was no more need to hurry. The screams had quit and the man stared upwards at his partner with the still, glazed look of death. His partner bent and cradled his head in his arms.

"It's okay Buddy!" he crooned softly, rocking slowly back and forth. "We'll get you outta here real quick. Just hang on!"

The DC3 droned on as Mike stared down at the sullen, frozen rock of the mountain peaks, wondering how long he would live if the plane crashed and was scattered about the frozen snow and rock. Then he looked toward the front of the plane where a pretty stewardess waited on passengers. He sighed and lay back in his seat as the plane droned on toward the pleasures of soft women and mind numbing alcohol.

Mike had drawn his pay right after the accident for he had lost his nerve. He didn't think of it, but in the dream world that haunted him at night, he couldn't suppress the screams of the dying man and he'd waken, fighting to open his eyes, and then lay in cold sweat while the pounding in his chest slowly subsided. At other times he dreamed he was on a beam, two inches wide and thousands of feet above the earth with fleecy white clouds between him and the ground. In the dream he would slowly and nonchalantly step off the beam and then begin falling. Again he would wake in cold sweat, with his chest pounding as he stared at the light from the window. He wondered about the belief that if you landed in the dream, you died.

Mike lay back in the seat and left his belt buckled as the plane gained altitude. It was strange that sleep in the afternoon rarely carried the terror of the night.

The pretty stewardess walked down the aisle and noticed the seat belt still buckled around Mike's waist. She bent slightly in order to undo it without waking him.

Suddenly, she was in an empty seat across the aisle, a painful bruise growing on her jaw. Mike's fist had shot up, catching her with a glancing blow. She sat stunned for a moment. Passengers stared at the young man who still slept but who had nearly broken her jaw. She rose slowly, carefully and reached her hand to Mike, intending to wake him.

The same fist shot upwards again but this time it missed. The stewardess still fell backwards into the empty seat while passengers stared in puzzlement. Mike woke then and stared too, first at the stewardess and then at the other passengers, wondering why they were staring at him. Then slowly came a foggy memory of her falling backwards and his fist returning to his side. Mike shook his head quickly to clear the cobwebs as the stewardess turned and beat a hasty retreat to the front of the plane. Not a word had been spoken and the other passengers looked away for they couldn't meet the wild look in his eyes.

Mike stared at a spot just above the stewardess's head and wondered what had happened. But he got no answer, only the confusion and fog that closed in while he felt a deep, unquenchable thirst. He wondered how much longer it would be before he could find the nearest bar, where the alcohol beckoned in tall, cool bottles and the liquor would slide down his throat.

Then he would know a peace-giving numbness and a dreamless sleep.

# Thirty-five

Snow devils played about the grey frozen asphalt, whipped to and fro by a cold, freezing wind. The daytime temperature hovered around minus twenty Fahrenheit, and except for the snow devils all was still. On either side of the frozen ribbon of asphalt stretched a great white wilderness; open fields interrupted by the odd frozen poplar or spruce bluff, standing stark and stiff. And all around the snow piled high in hard drifts.

Suddenly, a Greyhound bus blasted through the snow devils, its tires humming. It rocked and bounced whenever the highway was uneven, its back draft making the snow devils dance crazily in small circles. Then they settled down and all was once again, frozen and still.

As the bus rocked and bounced, the driver gripped the steering wheel and stared grimly ahead. He wore gloves for the temperature inside was barely above freezing. While he stared into the blowing snow, he occasionally used a metal scraper to laboriously scrape frost from the inside of the windshield. But he was careful to keep one hand on the wheel and an eye on the road.

Near the rear, and in the smoking section, Mike sat with his head against the back of the seat and turned toward the window while a cigarette dangled from his mouth. He stared unseeing at the lunar landscape with the blowing snow and dead, brown grass by the fence. His mind filled with memories of a very brief, soft time. He had stayed in a good hotel in Vancouver and had spent most of his money on a Call Girl called Terri. She had been gentle and refined, her body and hands soft. She seemed to understand Mike's confusion and aching loneliness. But when his money was nearly gone, she had quietly slipped out of his room early one morning. Mike bore her no resentment, feeling only a deep, sad melancholy. Any thoughts he may have had about alcoholism were quickly suppressed and replaced with hazy, bitter sweet memories of a woman who had appeared warm and understanding.

As he drifted amongst the hazy day dreams he remembered the Cave, a nightclub where people were polite and wore fine clothes. He had bought a suit and had taken Terri there, enthralled by the gentile surroundings. But when he had asked Terri about the older men with young women, she had laughingly told him the women were Call Girls and the men were clients.

As the images of a happier time appeared and slipped away, Mike finally slept fitfully, his body rocking with the bus' motion until suddenly, it stopped. He woke, smelling oily diesel fumes as passengers hurried off the bus. The driver stood, stretched and then announced laconically, "Edmonton! Twenty minutes rest."

Mike rose quickly and then stood shivering by the baggage compartment until he saw his green suitcase and canvas equipment bag. Then he quickly shouldered his way through the crowd of people who were hugging and shaking hands.

"Where to?" the cab driver demanded, a cigarette dangling from his mouth.

"A cheap hotel."

The driver took him to the York, not far from 97th street and Jasper Avenue, the center of the city and the place where construction workers and hookers gathered. Mike rented a three dollar a night room without a bath. For that, he had to walk down the hall to a communal washroom with a bathtub. He threw his suitcase and equipment bag down on the floor and locked the door. Then he gazed at the narrow bed, along with a closet and dresser and one chair which didn't match the bed or the walls. The leather was cracked where too many patrons had sat and the window pane was smudged with the signatures of countless drifters before Mike.

He hid one hundred and twenty dollars in the suitcase, taking fifty for the evening. Then, impulsively he opened the dresser drawer and looked at the inevitable Gideon Bible. He idly flipped through the pages, noticing where parts had been torn out for handy note paper.

When Mike left his room, he hailed another taxi to the Hub Hotel, kiddie-corner to the Coffee Cup Café and across the street from the Rainbow Theater and Dance Land Ballroom. As he gazed at the city streets from the back seat of the cab, a fleeting image passed through his consciousness. He saw the grinning, bobbing skulls of the dream from long ago. In the dream he had drifted down a great river, sinking slowly to the slime at the bottom. And, as he gazed through the cab's dirty window he felt a numb, detached sense of sinking too.

Mike shook his head, ridding it of the image. Then he saw only the magnet of bright lights and heard the siren call of empty laughter, which comes when a bottle is drained and friends materialize quickly from out of the haze. The dense fog in his soul became denser as he walked into the Hub Hotel's beer parlor.

In those days there were still men only beer parlors; the last refuge of married men who could drink fifteen cent draft beer and for a brief time, escape the cares of a family. There were others, like Mike, who were there for different reasons. They didn't notice the dirty floor, the overflowing ashtrays and the soiled cloth on the tables, or the stale smell of beer blending with the more pungent odor of urine from a flooded urinal.

As Mike sat, a waiter came over with a tray full of draft, for whiskey was not yet legal in a beer parlor. If a man craved whiskey he had to buy it at a liquor store and then secretly pour it into his glass when the waiter wasn't looking. Even if he was caught, the management didn't really mind, just as long as he paid hard cash for the draft.

Mike drained one of the glasses before the waiter had gone and then he looked about at the shabby clothes of the customers and soiled dirty rug under his shoes. Through a door marked "Ladies and Escorts" he could see men and women, for that part of the bar was for women who had partners. If a man didn't have a woman with him, he couldn't sit there. It was the last dying gasp of the "Bible Thumpers" who had forced prohibition and morality on a reluctant population many years before.

Mike watched the bums who came in with items for sale: shoes, watches or wallets. Anything that would bring fifty cents or even a dollar so they could sit amidst the gloom and hurriedly tip a glass. In those days there was no Welfare. For single men the only help was the Salvation Army or the city hostel, but there was a three-day limit. Then he was given a transit token and told to move on, to the next city. In the summer the bums slept in abandoned cars or down by the Saskatchewan river but in the winter they were forced to seek shelter in the "Sally Ann." When the temperature dropped and the wind blew, the custodians normally were not quite as strict.

An old man, who couldn't have been more than thirty approached Mike. His face was lined and his pants shiny from grime while his overcoat was a wrinkled yellow grey from sleeping in it too many times.

"Mind if I sit?" he asked.

Mike looked up and hesitated briefly. The bum sat down quickly for in order to survive a bum had to think fast. He looked longingly at Mike's full glass and was about to beg for the price when the changing look in Mike's eyes stopped him. He changed tactics quickly, pulling forth a worn leather wallet that had originally been black, but was now a sad grey, with wrinkles where it had been folded.

"This is a good wallet," he said but Mike didn't answer.

"See here. It even has a slot where you can put your change. And the leather's not worn too much. It should last for maybe a year If ya don't use it too much." The bum looked questioningly at Mike, his eyes pleading.

Mike's lack of response was misleading, for when he smelt the body odor a sudden flash of anger came.

"How long will it take you to walk to the door?" he asked calmly.

"I don't know. Why?"

"Because that's the only thing that'd save your Goddamn neck."

The bum looked up quickly. He gazed for the briefest of instants into Mike's eyes. Then he said softly, "Oh!" He rose quickly and nearly ran to the door, bumping into a table with two men who glanced up, cursing.

Mike waved to the waiter and held up two fingers. When the waiter brought two more drafts, another bum entered. He was older than the first, his face, wrinkled and grey, a worthless old man who had succumbed to alcohol. Nobody knew he had once been an ironworker, who had fearlessly walked a beam, hundreds of feet in the air. Nobody cared and if they had known they would have cared even less. A man's future lies in his own hands and those that are threatened feel less sympathy, for they see a reflection of themselves.

The old man stopped at the table with the two men and smiled, exposing rotting teeth. He held up an electric clock, with a price tag of twenty-three ninety-five. It could fetch as high as five dollars in the bar, if he handled the bargaining right.

"What'a ya want?" one of the men demanded.

The old man shakily held the clock at shoulder height with the price tag prominently displayed.

"It's a clock," he said. "Brand new. I can let ya have it for say, just fifteen bucks." He was an old hand and knew what he was doing.

"Lemmee see!" the first man at the table said and stood, grabbing the clock from the old man whose toothless grin widened.

He held it to his ear and listened.

"I don't hear no Goddamn ticking. Say, just what the hell kind a clock is this anyway? No Goddamn ticking."

The bum's smile vanished. The general hubbub suddenly subsided as the second man at the table grinned from his chair. All eyes were on the old man who trembled from enforced sobriety.

"It's an electric clock! There's no ticking in an electric clock!" he said urgently, looking quickly at the door.

The first man held the clock to his ear again and then held it out at arms length. He paused for a moment, grinning at his partner and then spread his fingers. The clock dropped to the stone floor with a loud clang, the face cracking. He stooped quickly and snatched it from the floor before the old man had a chance. He stood, again holding the clock. This time he glared at the old man.

"Say! Just what the hell ya trying to pull off? Selling me a busted clock?"

The old man glanced quickly at the door again.

"You deserve a good shot in the mouth. Who the hell do ya think I am anyway? Some dumb asshole who just got off the boat?"

The crowd laughed uproariously as the old man stood still, momentarily lost and confused. He reached forth a tentative hand and the first man gave him the clock. Then he gave him a hard shove on the shoulder, nearly knocking him down. The old man staggered and half fell over the back of a chair, his eyes terrified.

"What kinda place is this anyway?" the first man demanded, in mock rage. "Bums trying to sell me busted clocks."

The bar rocked with laughter as the old man clutched the ruined clock to his breast. His eyes were wet for the clock had been an escape from the "Snakes" that would surely come in the wee hours of the night.

As the first man sat down amidst the laughter, the old man clutched the broken clock to his ancient and greasy coat. He opened the door to the street and a gust of frigid air blew in. Then he was gone, leaving only a faint odor and the laughter from those more fortunate than he. He staggered down the street against the cruel wind, pulling the filthy coat about his thin shoulders. He was an old and useless piece of humanity and nobody cared, for caring never made you rich.

Mike finished his beer and pushed the image of the sad, old man from his mind. Then he wondered where he could find a woman. A woman was soft and warm, not wrinkled and grey like the old man and her breath didn't reek.

A woman was everything Mike longed for.


The Coffee Cup Cafe's walls were peeling and grey, and the floor filthy. But the customers didn't mind, for it was the last stop on the slide to oblivion that is euphemistically known as "The Street." The building was round and had round windows with a part for the customers who only wanted to eat, and another for the ones who were looking for a different service. The first sat on stools and ate greasy hamburgers while the second sat in booths and drank from large, plastic Coke glasses. One of the windows had been broken when a man had thrown a bottle through it. The owner had never bothered fixing it, and dirty brown cardboard kept the cold December wind at bay.

Mike sat in a booth next to the grey, brown wall, and watched silently. Young, old girls with tight miniskirts sat in booths, exposing their legs and smiling brittle smiles. Meanwhile, their pimps sat at different tables and kept a watchful eye on their property.

A large man in a grey overcoat suddenly approached.

"Wanna Micki?" he asked in a low monotone, his hands in his coat pockets. Besides his hands, the pockets contained twelve ounce bottles of cheap rye, still in their brown paper wrappings. The man was the bouncer who had the bootleg franchise and who also had a couple of hookers. Mike paid five dollars for the bottle which cost two fifty in the liquor store and then dumped part of his coke onto the floor beneath the booth by his feet to make room for the rye. The owner didn't mind for he got a percentage of the bootlegger's profit. The owner also paid the man minimum wage to keep the undesirables away. An undesirable, was anyone who didn't have money for the varied wares sold in the café. It was said the army once tried to clean out the place but what the young men in uniform didn't know was that pimps are not average adversaries and that the Coffee Cup was their home and their business. The young men in uniform had left, battered and bruised and some had to be treated in a hospital for the pimps carried switch blades. It was said that an assault a day was average in the four block area surrounding the Coffee Cup, the Hub Hotel and the Dance Land Theater and Ballroom. The police only came when they were called, and then never was less than three. They were content to contain the sub-world to the small area just as long as the hookers and pushers didn't move up town.

Mike shuddered when he swallowed the abrasive rye for he had dumped nearly all the coke onto the floor. He moved his feet so his shoes wouldn't get soiled and sticky and then he looked about. When his gaze again fell upon the hookers, they smiled back encouragingly. Then he looked through a door and into the kitchen at the cook, a heavy woman who was more than two hundred pounds. She fried the greasy hamburgers for the customers who only had money for a meal, and who sat in the other part of the café.

In one booth, close to Mike, four B&E men sat, their clothes almost as flashy as the pimps for they had a good deal with the owner. Any money they stole, they left in his safe. He charged thirty percent and everybody was happy. The pimps had their hookers, the bouncer his bootleg franchise and the B&E men had a safe bank for their money. The owner made a fast profit and it mattered little that some of the hookers were only thirteen or fourteen years old. He shrugged his shoulders for since when was he, his brother's keeper? Besides, no one made the girls come down to the Cup searching for a pimp to look after them.

The girls didn't have to search for the pimps though. The pimps found them, sensing the bewildered hopelessness that comes from having abusive, uncaring parents. To the pimps the girls were merely pieces of merchandise, a commodity to be sold and resold until the value was gone and then to be abandoned in some flop house with only a needle for solace. To the pimps, the girls were not human, for neither were they, having sunk to the level of predatory animals a long time ago. But if the pimps were inhuman and treated their girls like trash, abusive parents made the trash available.

Mike looked at a hooker who was no older than fifteen. She was pretty, with firm thighs that she expertly exposed by hitching up her skirt without using her hands. She had experienced a lot of men and knew the hungry look. Mike saw only a pretty young girl, for he desperately craved the softness only a woman can give. But the only softness the hooker had, was in her thighs and breasts. There was no softness in her heart.

The hooker owed loyalty to no one, except her pimp and only because she feared him. Within her breast there was no more compassion than in a female cat, and also no more cruelty. She stalked her prey with the only tools she had, and in the manner of a cat. And she hurt men whenever she could, like a cat playing with a mouse. She didn't understand the nature of cruelty any more then a cat for it was in the natural order of things.

Mike looked at the girl again, his eyes lingering on the soft thighs and firm young breasts pushing against her white blouse. He debated whether he could afford the twenty buck fee. He knew where he'd end up if he ran out of money but as he struggled with conflicting thoughts, he also knew he was fighting a losing battle.

Suddenly a figure materialized, from out of the smoky chaos, to stand over his booth. Mike looked up into the hard, cold eyes of a woman barely into her twenties. She was thin, her shoulders emaciated and her face beginning to show the ravages of drugs.

"You got thirty bucks?" she asked, for she recognized the bewildered air of a man looking for something he couldn't find.

"I'll be real good for you," she added tiredly.

Mike stared up into the cold eyes and his expression hardened.

"I need a fix real bad," she added quickly.

"You don't look like you need a fix," Mike snapped.

The woman savagely tore at her sleeve, pulling it back and exposing tracks, dark blue and leading in every direction. Triumph gleamed in her eyes, as Mike's anger turned to confusion. Wordlessly he reached for his wallet and then gave her twenty dollars. He didnt even know why he did it, only that he didn't have the strength to say no.

The woman didn't say a word, turning and walking unsteadily toward the door. Then she was gone, leaving Mike with guilt playing about in his mind. He glanced quickly about, hoping no one had seen him give the woman money. They'd think I'm real stupid, he thought wonderingly, shaking his head. Then he glanced back at the hooker who stood and stretched, exposing more of her firm thighs. She walked seductively over to his table, her hips moving rhythmically.

"Wanna go?" The question was the same one all hookers used.

Mike glanced up at the beauty of the teenage-aged hooker and he felt a deep, dark depression.

"Yeah. Why not?" he sighed.

He took her to his room and when they sat on the cot he passed her the Micki. She took only a quick sip for it wouldn't do to get drunk while working.

"What's your name?" Mike asked softly. It was debatable who was the more tired, the hooker or the trick.

"Vicki," she said tossing her hair.

"That's a nice name." Mike held the Micki in both hands and tried to smile.

"I'm Mike."

"Yeah, sure," Vicki snapped. Then she stretched out her hand. "Pay me!"

Mike hesitated for a moment and then gave her twenty dollars. It disappeared quickly into her purse and then they sat for a few more minutes, until she grew impatient.

"Well! Do you want to or not?" she demanded. "We only got half an hour."

Then she lay back on the narrow bed and pulled down her panties. Mike lay besides her and began to unbutton her blouse.

"I don't strip for twenty," Vicki snapped and Mike stopped. He lay for a while on his side with the fog closing in.

"Well! Ya gonna fuck me or not?" Vicki demanded again. Mike sighed and rolled over and undid his pants, desperately trying to salvage some warmth from the sad and ludicrous moment. But the sight of the young hooker, lying on her back with her legs spread was too much. Mike was again impotent. He tried but the dark, deep, depression made the young girl appear old and ugly. He lay back down on the bed, gazing at the ceiling, his arm resting on the pillow. Vicki's head was just beneath it and together, the hooker and the lost young man lay resting for a few moments. Finally Mike tried to start a conversation.

"Were you raised here?"

The question startled and confused Vicki. Tricks never asked about her.

"Well, yeah. Sorta. I grew up in a small town west of here."

"Do you ever go home?" Mike asked.

Vicki turned her head quickly and stared at Mike, trying to determine if he was mocking her. But his face was serious.

"I phoned home a couple times but my mother always hangs up. I got one sister who talks to me."

"Why don't you go and see her?" Mike asked.

"I said she talks to me! I didn't say she and her man want me around," Vicki snapped suddenly. Then she turned and glared.

"What're ya, a Cop? Or ya writing a book?"

She sat up and pulled on her panties. Then she stood and grabbed her purse and walked to the door. She didn't say goodbye and neither did Mike. She only glanced at the young man who was attractive enough to not have to pay for sex. Then she slammed the door and was gone.

Mike lay on the narrow bed, wondering why he had paid a hooker a days wage so she could lay on his bed and remove her panties. Then came more guilt and he thought of other things, trying to capture a day dream that would momentarily take him from the dingy room and lumpy mattress. As Mike lay with his arm thrown over his eyes, as a shield from the single light bulb, he realized he had sunk as low as he ever had.

He also realized there were lower places still.

# Thirty-six

A cold December wind howled down from the arctic, whipping the snow along Jasper Avenue and making the sidewalks slippery and treacherous. Only those who had no choice hurried along the street, hunching their shoulders as they faced the vicious wind. Even the hookers and bums were mostly inside for it was cold enough to freeze exposed flesh in seconds. The bums found a lobby where the desk clerk wouldn't call the police, or they circulated the bars trying to cadge drinks. The braver ones walked from store to store looking for unwary clerks who didn't notice their quick hands. The hookers woke in the early afternoon and sat about in the cafes, drinking coffee and waiting for the sun to set. Then they would once again freeze on street corners, hoping for a John to take them to a warm place for a brief time. The hookers owned the clothes they wore, some cheap jewelry, a purse and little else. The pimps drove new cars and wore three hundred dollar suits with shiny rings on their fingers. Despite the cold December wind, business was good.

When the sun's dying rays cast a gloom along the street the hookers gathered while the potential customers fortified themselves with booze. Many were construction workers who had come south, from where there had been no bars or willing women. They bought bottles of rye at liquor stores and slyly poured it into beer glasses in the beer parlors. The owners said nothing, just as long as they kept buying beer and a profit was made. Profit was the key and nobody cared if the men were blowing hard earned wages. It was their problem if they couldn't handle money or didn't have wives and children to go to. Some did have wives and children but still they came to the bars and Coffee Cup in search of the Pimp's wares, for there is no explaining some men.

Mike sat in the Cup, his hand around a large plastic glass with only Coke for he was down to his last twenty dollars. He watched three construction workers at the next table who were busy drinking bootleg whiskey and boasting of money made. Mike noticed how it was always obvious when new men had just come to town with a stake. They always wore dress pants that hadn't yet been scarred with cigarette burns or ashes and coats or jackets that still had the sheen from the rack. But most importantly was the air of confidence, of simmering excitement for they kept casting their eyes about, looking occasionally at the hookers and then drinking from their plastic glasses. Beneath the booth the floor was wet and sticky with spilled Coke for the men dumped it on the floor in their eagerness to make room for the whiskey.

Over at another table three hookers sat watchfully, their conversation muted. Mike looked from the hookers to the men, idly wondering about the nature of things. The scene in the Cup never changed. The hookers came and went, staying for only a couple months, and while Mike had been there for barely four weeks, a few new faces had appeared. The men, who the hookers contemptuously called "Tricks," came and went much faster but the only thing that changed were their faces. The talk was the same, of money made and jobs worked, while their clothes rarely varied, with the new dress pants and jackets a clear advertisement to the hookers.

One of the men at the table spoke loudly.

"Hell! We worked six days a week, ten hours a day. That's sixty hours, at three bucks an hour. Boy! With the overtime, that's two hundred and ten bucks a week. Jesus! I stayed there six months."

"You going back after Christmas?" another man asked.

"Naw, the rig's shut down 'til break up," the first man answered. Then he grew quiet and pensive, adding, "It's a good thing I got Pogey to fall back on."

Pogey was Unemployment Insurance and it only paid a hundred dollars a month. A man could drink that in a few days.

"I stayed eight months with the rig I was on," the second man said. "Christ! I saved three grand. Well, actually more when you count the back pay when I quit." He glanced at the hookers and then added, "I'm gonna give 'er shit for a few days. Then I'm heading home."

"Where's home?" the third man asked.

"Just south of Calgary. Parents got a farm?"

Mike listened quietly, the words "home" and "farm" opening a great void, leaving only a deep melancholy. He lacked the bus fair and the blowing snow and cold made him hesitate when he thought of hitch hiking. Every day he stayed he spent at least ten dollars. In two days he would have no place to stay. Again the fog engulfed him and anxiety tied his stomach in knots. He couldn't make up his mind whether to stay in the Cup or go back to the hotel.

Then, as his mind drifted through the haze of desperate longing, he saw his mother's face without the hard, complaining look and his father's without the faces. Next he saw his dog frisking about in greeting.

Mike looked at a smeared and ancient painting on the wall, left over from more gracious days. The grain stooks and open field beyond, filled him with a, dark lethargy, as he gazed inwards at the roast beef on the table, boiled potatoes and a crew of hungry men who had just come from the threshing machine.

Every once in a while, Mike's private world was shattered by loud voices from the men or a laugh from one of the hookers. He remembered his dream of saving three grand: Return home with three thousand dollars and live well for the winter. Now, he would come home broke, with not enough money for tobacco until he received a check from the Unemployment Office.

He thought too of the job he had in the city and how he could have lived well. But again the fog had descended and he had sat in a bar after work, unable to decide whether to go to bed early or stay for another beer. He had sat in the fog while his money vanished and his thirst increased. And in the morning a deep, dank depression filled him so that he couldn't rise.

Mike drained the glass and idly wondered why Coke never quenches a thirst for beer or rye. He looked at the brown paper bag at the next table and the thirst increased. But he had not yet descended to where he would beg a drink from a stranger. He ordered another Coke and shook his head when the bouncer with the bootleg franchise looked at him inquiringly.

He sat with hunched shoulders, occasionally sipping from the glass. The hookers had all taken their turn, looking at him with a question on their pretty lips, but it was met with another sad shake of his head. They ignored him after that. Mike took another drink as the place began to fill and he realized it was getting late. Around him the people were almost disembodied as they drifted in and out of his vision. Some approached and then faded away as the memory of the dream and the river of skulls came. Mike wondered if that was where he was, in a place where humanity had died, leaving only grinning skulls.

If he had more money, no matter how much, he would have drifted to the Cup every night. He had lost the drive, the incentive that makes a man a man, and not a mindless animal. Mike's world had become a kaleidoscope of the grotesque.

Suddenly his attention was taken by two men. They walked toward each other in the narrow aisle, neither willing to step aside. They appeared to move in slow motion in the grey, yellow light of the Cup. One stepped back slowly and then lashed out with a Karate kick. Blood and teeth vomited forth for he had caught the other full in the mouth with the hard tip of his street shoe.

Blood spattered forth and down the man's shirt, mute testimony to hours of practice and the killer instinct. The man fell, in slow motion and landed on the floor next to Mike and then lay in his own gore, spitting out broken teeth. He slowly wiped his chin, his eyes glazed while the other stood over him, grinning.

"Ya want more? There's lots more where that comes from." He posed in the classic stance of the Martial Artist, his fists in a fighting position while a bright, brittle light gleamed from his eyes. The man on the floor didn't want more. He rose slowly and then ran for the door, staggering slightly. Mike watched the retreating figure for a moment and then looked down at his Coke. During the brief but vicious fight he hadn't moved.

"I'll fight anyone!" the man boasted, still standing victoriously with his fists, ready. He was ignored for, who wants to fight for no reason? Then he looked down at Mike and grinned.

"Mind if I join you?"

He sat down before Mike answered. When he was across the table, his hands held forward, he grinned again, satisfied and confident.

Mike knew that the man would become one of the skulls, floating down the river for that kind of aggression rarely went unnoticed. It needed only for someone to have a reason before the man would die with a knife in his ribs.

"If ya think I'm fast with my feet, ya ought'a see my hands. That's one thing everyone says. I sure got fast hands." He glanced at the Coke glass in front of Mike. "And I'll fight anybody. I don't care who he is. I'll fight him, cause I sure don't back down from nobody."

Mike remained silent as the man appeared to talk in slow motion with his words sounding like scrip from some pathetic gangster movie. But Mike didn't laugh for humor had died along with the humanity.

"Is that rye ya got there?" the man finally asked.

"No. Just Coke."

The man picked up the glass, sniffed the coke and then placed it back in front of Mike, looking quickly about the café. He grinned again.

"I'll fight anybody," he said and then looked directly at Mike.

"You wouldn't wanna fight, would you?" The question was more an attempt to include Mike in the conversation than a call for battle. Mike shook his head and the man finally tired of the game.

"Scuse me," he said. "I gotta go talk to somebody." He stood in slow motion and then left with the "Scuse me," sounding ridiculous, just after he had kicked out a man's teeth.

Mike sat alone, again and watched the people, through the yellow, grey haze as his thoughts turned inwards. He dreamed of returning home to the respect of his parents for surely they must welcome him if he had money and a car. But money was something to be spent while it lasted, with the desperate enjoyment of trying to forget its passing, with more booze and hookers.

He thought again about the job he had quit after a week, and of going to work without breakfast and not having any lunch until he was dizzy. He hadn't been able to get an advance on his salary and had desperately gone to a bar in the evening. He had met a woman he knew slightly and had joined her table. She was thirty but looked much older and he had tried to ignore the way she gulped beer.

Mike was a young man and whenever she looked in a mirror she was reminded that young men would soon become a memory. She had invited him to her room and there, Mike had performed the sex act. He couldn't understand why he wasn't impotent despite the smeared make up and faint body odor. When they were finished, she had stood naked over the sink.

"Who the hell wants to get dressed just to go to the John?" She had grinned and urinated.

"Oh for Christ's sake!" Mike had muttered. "Don't you have any class?"

"What the hell's class? Men do it all the time."

Mike had said nothing more, for he had needed a favor.

"Do you think," he had finally said and then, hesitated. "You think you could lend me five bucks?"

The question was the same he had heard from the floozies who lacked the confidence to ask for money outright. "Lend" really meant "give."

"Sure," the woman had said as she had come back to the bed. "My old man leaves me lots of money." Then she had stopped and gazed down at Mike, her hands on her hips and her breasts sagging.

"My old man goes outta town a lot. I'll lend ya money, just as long as you promise to come see me afterwards."

Mike had promised, thinking how the woman knew he really didn't mean it. Mike had finally gone back to his room and tried to sleep with the shame, for what was the difference between a hooker and what he had done.

He had lived for a day on the five dollars, buying breakfast, a light lunch and a cheap supper along with cigarettes. But when hunger again made him dizzy, the woman's old man had returned. Then in a few days he had felt panic and pain while urinating, and he had faced the added humiliation of going to a VD clinic for a needle in the buttocks.

As he sat in the Coffee Cup, his shoulders hunched, and idly sipping from his Coke he remembered the people who had tried to help him. He had met a man who was living with the cook whom he could see through the kitchen door. Laverne weighed well over two hundred pounds and had a moustache but she worked steadily and Dick could always count on a hot meal and a supply of beer money. Mike had met them in a bar and had gone to their suite with a dozen beer. The suite was two and a half rooms with the kitchen and living room combined. The bathroom was down the hall and the linoleum was worn and scarred and the walls a dirty blue.

When he had run out of money he had come to the door and waited until he had been invited to eat. But when he had owed Laverne twenty dollars, a belated sense of pride had made him stay in his room with hunger turning to pain and then a numb feeling, while he had wondered how long he could last without food. The muscles in his arms became knotty and he lost weight. Finally he had been paid and approached Laverne with five dollars.

"That's all I can give you," he had said guiltily, thinking of his brother's tirade when he hadn't paid him back immediately. "I'll pay you the rest next payday," he had added quickly.

Laverne had looked at Mike in surprise, while she thought of the men she knew and how they rarely repaid a loan. Then she had put the money in her purse and smiled.

"I'm gonna buy a turkey for Sunday dinner. You better be there, too. We can play cards in the afternoon and then eat." She had made no mention of the fifteen dollars he still owed her.

Mike had thought again of his brother's ranting about him being a bum because he hadn't paid him back and the confusion deepened. What a brother wouldn't do Laverne had, but she was fat, smoked, drank and swore steadily. And more important, she never went to church and never preached to others.

Mike had blown his pay and had borrowed more. And in the confusion he lacked the courage to approach even her again.

As his face masked the turmoil within, he sat hunched over his Coke and watched the pimps as they began arriving for the day's business. There was a wary comradeship among them that lasted as long as it was mutually beneficial. The tallest wore a black Stetson and was known as Cowboy and another was Joker but the most dangerous of all was Willie, a heavy set black man. It was said Willie could hit a fly on a wall with a switch blade, and his eyes had the wild and savage look of a man who had begun to shoot drugs into his veins. Mike had gone to the bathroom once and had walked into Willie, who had stood in front of the streaked mirror, his sleeve rolled up and his eyes glazed. Willie had stared at Mike, the veins in his eyes standing out against the white and Mike had left hurriedly. Tangling with a pimp "strung out" on Junk was madness.

A girl, no more than fifteen, walked by Mike's table then and he could tell she hadn't been a Hooker for long. She belonged to Willie and Mike wondered idly how long she would retain the bloom on her cheeks and air of ladylike beauty.

She wore white gloves, a new green overcoat and high Cossack boots, while her miniskirt exposed firm white thighs. The other pimps looked at Willie in envy, for she would bring in thousands of dollars. The girl had the face of someone who lived next door, the kind a man could fall madly in love with. Her skin was creamy white and dark brown curls flowed down onto her forehead. She even walked like a lady, the moral decay not yet breaking through the soft, warm beauty. As she passed Mike's table, she talked to Willie.

"I'm not going with that trick. He's mean and he beats women."

"You'll do what I say," Willie snapped, for he was in danger of losing face.

"If I go with him, I know exactly what's going to happen," she said, her sensuous mouth in a stubborn pout.

Suddenly Willie grabbed her arm and yanked her roughly to him.

"There's gonna be a happening!" he screamed and the café went deathly silent. He hurled her forward, with her head snapping back and her eyes opening in terror. Her shoulder hit the door and she spun and fell in a heap, her skirt rising and exposing pink panties. Willie stood over her and glared, his fists clenched and breath coming rapidly. Slowly she rose and squatted, the lady-like quality replaced by primeval fear.

As Mike watched, Willie and the hooker again appeared in slow motion as if in a hazy, yellow dream.

Willie yanked her to her feet and she stood, her head hanging sideways and her breath rapid, with her eyes dilated and round. Then Willie shoved her through the door and outside to where Mike could see them through the round window. Willie grabbed her coat and slapped her across the mouth, hard. Her head snapped backwards and then forwards, a red welt rising on her cheek. Suddenly sobs bubbled forth and tears streamed down her face. As her chest heaved and she gasped for air Willie paused, his hand poised, ready for another blow. But the girl was new and he hadn't yet tired of her soft white body so he hesitated. Besides, if he beat her too much, the Johns would turn away from the bruises.

Willie yanked her forward and held her to his chest, her sobs rising and falling, as she cried out her terror and pain to the man who had caused it. To her, crying in the pimp's arms was in the natural order of things.

Mike watched silently through the window and part of him felt the girl's pain and demanded he do, something. But the rules had changed. He knew that if he had tried to help her, he would have died, or would have been beaten to a pulp. The pimps may not have trusted or liked each other but someone interfering with a man's stable was a threat. That action could spread, and lead to all manner of trouble.

While the girl sobbed piteously in Willie's arms, Mike stared pensively at his Coke. He knew it wouldn't be long before Willie tired of her body and then he wouldn't hesitate. The girl would either obey instantly, or wear dark glasses and turn tricks with bruises on her body.

As soon as Willie quit beating the girl, the people in the Cup turned back to more pressing matters. In a short while the hubbub rose and fell and it was business as usual with the bouncer selling his booze and the hookers smiling at the Johns. Above them the hazy blue smoke hung in the air, darkening the walls and ceiling while outside the cold December wind howled down Jasper Avenue.

# Thirty-seven

The dingy, dark café was only one block from the Coffee Cup. But it was a world away, for it only had two booths and a row of patched and unsteady stools. And it stunk. Years of body sweat and stale grease had permeated the air until it hung heavy and nauseating. The walls were greasy and flyspecked and dirty hand prints remained where they were, unnoticed by the owner or customers.

Mike sat on a stool that had scotch tape where the imitation leather had torn, and he was careful not to lean for fear it would collapse. He was also careful not to touch shoulders with the wino who sat next to him, chewing loudly with his mouth open. The wino wore a shiny suit jacket that had accumulated years of grime and he smacked his lips, enjoying his sandwich, the first meal in days. Mike leaned in the other direction, careful not to tilt his stool too much, and he tried not to breathe too deeply for the body odor filled him with revulsion. But hunger boiled in his belly and he picked up the greasy hamburger with both hands, forcing himself to chew slowly. He had bought it with his last dollar.

A fat woman with a faint mustache had brought it and then had glared at Mike.

"That'll be ninety cents!" she had snapped.

Mike had reached for the chunk of fatty ground beef, between two slices of plain bread.

"That'll be ninety cents!" the woman had snarled, yanking back the saucer.

"Jesus Christ!" Mike had sworn. "Normally you wait until a man's eaten before you demand money."

"Not here, we don't!" the woman had snarled again. Mike had stared at the moustache on her upper lip. Her apron was filthy and grey with accumulated grease and she stunk. He could see lines of imbedded dirt in the folds of fat on her neck.

"Oh hell! Okay! Here!" Mike had said tiredly, giving the woman his last dollar. She had given him a dime which he had carefully put in his pocket, checking if there were any holes through which it could escape. The woman had slapped the greasy meal on the counter and had turned back to the kitchen. It didn't matter if Mike was young. She had been ripped off before.

Mike tried to chew slowly, although his stomach cried out. He was angry too that the woman had treated him like the other bums. The insult simmered as he chewed and tried to avoid touching the wino who smacked his lips and then wiped his mouth on a filthy and shiny sleeve. Then with the insult came the realization that he was really no different from the filthy bum next to him, a bum that couldn't be trusted to pay a ninety cent bill.

The greasy meat sat queasily in his stomach for he hadn't eaten in two days. He rose slowly and left, hunching his shoulders against the biting wind as he walked back to the hotel. He owed a week's rent and he had been walking carefully, guiltily past the desk clerk to go upstairs. He walked slowly along the frozen sidewalk, in no hurry to face an irate desk clerk who would demand twenty-one dollars. The bus fare home was only eighteen and he wondered for the thousandth time why he hadn't left when he had the chance.

As Mike walked he thought wonderingly. This can't be happening! But he could feel the lone dime in his pocket, and he knew that no matter how desperate the thoughts, or sincere the remorse, he was faced with one undeniable fact. He was a bum, hunching his shoulders on a wintry street at night while the snow swirled and he could feel the frost through the soles of his thin shoes. There was a place for bums like him but he had stayed too long at the Cup and the doors to the Salvation Army and the city hostel closed at ten p.m. No one was allowed in after that, even when it was forty below and timbers cracked with frost.

Mike turned a corner and stopped by a store window. A jolly, smiling Santa Claus advertised the season of love for all mankind. But the love wasn't for bums on the street. Mike felt the moisture on his cheeks freeze as he stared through the window. Inside, there was all manner of food, nuts and candies and farther back he could see a meat counter. The rest was in gloomy shadows for the owner had closed and gone home to his family. Mike thought wonderingly how in three days it would be Christmas Eve.

He hunched his shoulders and stared at the food, while the greasy hamburger was a heavy weight in his stomach. It would have been easy to smash the window and fill his pockets with nuts and candies and then gorge until his stomach bulged. But as he shivered by the window, the urge slowly faded and he turned and walked to the hotel where the desk clerk waited.

Suddenly, he was aware of another human on the cold and frozen sidewalk; for from out of the chaos and haze, appeared a little man, not even four feet tall. Mike recognized Little Badger, the retired Midget Wrestler who wandered from bar to bar.

As they walked, both their shoulders hunched and their faces down, Badger glanced up at Mike.

"Cold, eh?"

"Yeah," Mike answered.

They walked a way farther with the little man turning his head occasionally. He still wore the Iroquois hair cut that he had been famous for when he had fought in the ring.

"You got a place to stay?" The question surprised Mike.

"Yeah, I got a place," he said quickly. Then he hesitated before continuing, "Well, sorta."

Badger looked at him steadily. Then he stopped on the frozen sidewalk.

"Well, actually no," Mike finally said, stopping too and casting his eyes on the frozen cement.

"You can stay with me," Badger said slowly and Mike stared down at him. Badger certainly couldn't plan on rolling him, Mike thought. Maybe he was queer. But if he was he was taking a grave risk, for he was tiny.

"Okay," Mike heard himself say and then together, the man and midget walked to a seedy building. Badger led the way upstairs to a single room, four walls, a hot plate, a bed with a small table and one chair. A fridge was down the hall and had a padlock with each tenant carrying a key. For water and bodily functions, the bathroom was five doors down the hall.

Badger sat on the creaky bed and Mike on the scarred chair. A silence deepened, as Mike waited wary and tense.

"Here!" Badger finally said, bending down and pulling a cardboard box from under the bed. He gave Mike some old newspaper clippings.

Mike stared at the faded, wrinkled paper. Badger smiled from a picture, an Indian Headdress sitting proudly on his head, while a promoter presented him with a belt. Mike glanced about the room at the peeling wallpaper and the worn linoleum and then at Badger. It was the same person all right, but then it wasn't. In the pictures he was smiling, confident, but in the single room with the glaring light bulb, he had the same air of dejected bewilderment as Mike.

"I was the best," Badger said quietly as he neatly folded the faded newspapers and placed them lovingly back in the box. Then he carefully pushed the box back under the bed and looked up at Mike.

"You know, I made sixty grand one year. I even went to Japan and Europe. I was in demand, you know."

Mike gazed at the little man whose eyes were moist with memories. Then slowly, the dull glazed look of humiliation returned.

"What happened?" Mike asked quietly.

Badger stared at Mike for a moment.

"Well, what happened to you?" he answered just as quietly.

"Sorry!" Mike said quickly.

"It's okay," Badger said just as quickly. Then he stared down at the floor for a moment before talking slowly, "Booze, women, drugs. Well, you know." Then he looked up.

"I had a lot of expenses too. I had to pay my own way to all them countries." He sighed deeply and gazed back down at the floor.

"Well then, I quit." he said wonderingly, and then paused.

"I don't know…" The last words were barely audible.

Mike moved uncomfortably on the chair, sorry he had asked.

"I wrote a letter to a promoter," Badger said suddenly. "I think maybe I'll make a comeback. Heck! Lots of guys are wrestling at my age."

Mike noticed the greying hair and wrinkles under his eyes.

Then Badger stared at a point a long way off in the distance, over Mikes left shoulder, and the silence deepened.

Mike stared down at his worn shoes, wondering what to say next.

"Do you believe in Jesus?" Badger asked suddenly.

The sudden question startled Mike and his eyes narrowed.

"Well yeah, I guess so. Why?"

"Well, I go to church every Sunday now. It's the only way. When I had lots of money I didn't give a shit. But now…" Badger gazed about the dingy room.

"Now I don't know. It's the only way," he added softly.

Once again the silence deepened until Badger looked at Mike.

"You could come to church too, you know. It might help."

"No! No! I don't think so." Mike shook his head quickly. "It never did nothing for me." He couldn't explain his father's contorting face, or the crushing boredom of reciting meaningless prayers.

"Well it's up to you," Badger said. "I don't like to force no one. A man's got to make up his own mind." Then he began humming a tune that was vaguely familiar. When Badger broke into a line, Mike recognized it.

"Swing low Sweet Chariot, Swing Low, " made Mike suddenly want to cry as a great weight settled on his shoulders.

Little Badger had invited him in from the cold, to a dingy room with only one bed. He had taken a great risk, for there is no telling what manner of man you meet on the street. Then, the image of Mike's family came again. He saw the cold, implacable hatred in Gerard's eyes and his mother's complaining, sad face while his father made faces and recited the meaningless words of the rosary.

Badger lay down on the bed, then making room for Mike. Both sought sleep, fully clothed, careful not to touch each other with an elbow.

Mike's last sight, before he drifted off into a dream-filled sleep, was the dirty and cracked ceiling, while beside him the former wrestler who had made sixty grand a year, began to snore softly.

Maybe Badger was right, he thought wonderingly. Maybe the church was the only answer.

Next morning, when they rose, Mike stood hesitantly by the door.

"Well thanks," he said, a sudden shyness coming over him.

"That's okay. If you're stuck again, just come here. And maybe we can go to church sometimes."

"Okay," Mike said quickly and left. He forgot the address and that night, after wandering the streets and hotel lobbies, he turned his steps reluctantly toward the Salvation Army Hostel. Then he stood shivering, cold and humiliated before a grill. He was told it was full and the only hope on a bone chilling night, was the city hostel, forty blocks away. Mike walked rapidly, the cold cutting through his suit jacket like a knife.

Finally, his face red from the cold and his ears frostbitten, he stood before another grill. An unsmiling and uncaring man glared down at him.

"Name?"

Mike hesitated and then told him. In the icy fog and confusion, he even had a hard time remembering that.

"You're late for supper," the man snapped and Mike looked up for the briefest of instants into the icy stare.

"That's okay!" he said quickly. Then he was shown to a dormitory where he was to sleep on a single bunk. Mike sat down wearily and sighed but the man wasn't finished yet.

'You can't sleep for another hour. What's your rush anyway? You bums always got lots of time." The man laughed and turned back to the grill. He was tired of bums, always looking for a place to sleep and then drifting off without so much as a "Thank You."

Mike sat in the lobby, on a hard wooden bench. He reached into his shirt pocket for he had bummed fifty cents from Badger. He had bought a pack of cigarettes, idly wondering at the wisdom of a hardened man of the street.

"Ya know it's funny," the man had said. "When you're down to your last fifty cents and ya needs smokes or food, ya always buys the smokes."

Mike wondered why, as he noticed that only ten cigarettes were left. Vaguely he saw a bum rise quickly from a bench against the opposite wall. He approached in quick jerky steps.

"Gotta smoke?"

Mike wordlessly held up the package. The bum quickly grabbed a cigarette and turned back to his bench with the tailor-made. His eyes flashed triumph for a man had to know how to score a cigarette and he had to ask right.

Mike smoked his cigarette slowly, staring down at the dirty floor beneath his scuffed shoes. Then one of the double doors, down one flight of stairs opened suddenly. A small, wizened gnome-like man entered, letting in a cloud of frost. He had just beat the curfew and he walked slowly up the steps, keeping his left hand over his suit pocket. He turned slightly away from the man in the grill as he walked carefully, staring straight ahead. The man behind the grill stood and glared at him.

"You got a bottle in that coat?" he yelled and the lobby became deathly still.

"No! Honest ta God! I don't got nothing here." The little man's face turned white.

"Bullshit! You Goddamn bums think you can fool me." The man turned and left the booth, slamming the door.

"Gimmee that coat!" He grabbed the little man by the arm and reached for the pocket. The little man's eyes were pleading as he stared up at the enraged clerk. The clerk yanked and then held up a half empty wine bottle.

A bottle of wine was a major score. The little man looked sadly at the bottle with the red liquid swishing around inside, and his eyes were wet.

"Okay! That's it! You know the rules."

"No!" the little man exclaimed, his eyes wide.

"That's it! You bastards know that if you're caught sneaking in booze, you can sleep on the street." The clerk grabbed the little man by the scruff of the neck.

"Okay! Move! Get outta here!"

"For the love-a-God. Gimmee a break, will ya." the little man pleaded. "It's forty below out there!"

"No Goddamn way! You know the rules. You get outta here, or I call the cops."

The little man refused to leave. He twisted his neck quickly and escaped the clerk's grasp, walking jerkily to the bench opposite Mike. He sat down, pulling his greasy jacket about him. He had no hat or gloves and the temperature had indeed dropped to minus forty. He looked up at the angry clerk, his eyes wet and pleading.

"That's it!" The clerk turned and went to his booth where he picked up a phone and began dialing.

The silence gradually gave way to a low murmur of voices as the bum stared straight ahead with the clerk glaring at him occasionally.

Suddenly the doors banged open, letting in a gust of frigid air. Two police officers, both more than six feet tall and wearing fur coats, stomped ponderously up the steps. Billows of steam came with them as the warm air met the cold.

"Which one?" the first demanded.

The clerk pointed to the sad, little man with the white glistening, face. The two officers stomped angrily over to the bench and glared down at the tiny remnant of humanity. Rousting bums wasn't real police work.

"Please! For the love-a-God!" the little man pleaded.

The police officers wordlessly reached down and grabbed his jacket, yanking him to his feet. Then they spun him around and pushed. The little man spurted forward and then stopped, still refusing to leave the warmth of the hostel. Suddenly the larger of the two cops grabbed the bum by the arms. At the same time he brought his knee up with terrific force. The blow propelled the little man forward. He tripped and fell down the stairs, ending up against the door where he could feel the frost coming through the crack at the bottom. The police officers walked ponderously down the steps and stooped, picking up the little man. Then they opened the doors, letting in more billowing white frost as they roughly shoved him outside. The doors slammed shut and they were gone.

A gnarled wino, sitting on the same bench as Mike, turned to another.

"Did ya see that? He whispered. "They kicked 'em right in the ass, right down the stairs."

The second wino shook his head sadly but said nothing. Bums weren't welcome anywhere.

The cold, damp haze closed in around Mike. Then he thought he was losing his mind, for faintly at first and then louder, came a sound. A group of bums, sitting on the steps just outside the dormitory had started singing, their coarse rusty voices, a mockery of the sweet music of the just and righteous.

"Silent Night" came then and the clerk behind the grill laughed outright.

The bums had a warm bed for the night with porridge, toast and coffee in the morning. Everything was relative.

That night Mike slept in a large room with twenty bunks lined up with the heads touching a wall. If a man had money he slept with his wallet under his pillow or clutched in his hand. But Mike had no money and as he lay in the dark, his stomach burning, the nauseating odor of unwashed bodies came at him in waves. It was there even when he turned and pulled the blankets over his head. Then he thought he was losing his mind again for he could smell food. He sensed someone walk by his bunk and he heard whispering.

"Want some cheese?"

"Yeah. Sure. Where'd ya get it?"

"Aw, I boosted it from that store with the blind girl on 97th. I got some bread too."

Mike kept his head covered but he heard smacking lips and could almost see cheese and bread on a plate. Then he heard, whispering again.

"Mmmmm, that sure tastes good. I missed supper tonight."

"Oh! Why?"

"Hell! I was sitting in the Cecil and I had twenty drafts in front a me. Some guy from up north was buying rounds."

"Jesus H. Christ! That's Heaven you're talking about."

"Yeah. But I looked up at the clock and it said twenty to ten. Jesus! I got up and beat it across the tracks. To hell with the beer. It's not worth it. Shit! It's forty below outside."

"Yeah." A sigh was followed by more whispering.

"In summer you can find an old car or something to sleep in. Even the river bank, but not in winter, it's just not worth it."

"Yeah." Another sigh, then, "It's just not worth it."

Suddenly the whispering and smacking of lips ended and the bunk creaked. The dorm was filled with snoring and Mike lay in his cot, the blanket still over his head and sleep a long way off. Then the thoughts came unbidden.

This can't be happening. But the stench and raging fire in his belly didn't belong in a dream. Other thoughts came and for the first time in his life, Mike truly prayed.

"Dear God! Help me!" He lay still, feeling the prayer from his soul and then came a question.

"Dear God! Why?"

His mind wandered to the farm and his frisking dog and a small but firm resolve formed. Tomorrow! Tomorrow I'll hitchhike home. He forgot his father's contorting face and his mother's nagging voice. He forgot also the mind-numbing hours spent in the church beside his parents who prayed to the Crucified Christ and Virgin Mary. He even would confess his sins to the unseen and bored priest on the other side of the grill in the confessional.

Again, everything was relative.


Mike pushed his frozen street shoes up against the car heater and rubbed his hands together. He massaged his ears and felt the sharp sting of frost as the flesh begin to melt. Although it was mid-afternoon, the temperature was still minus twenty and he had stood on the frozen asphalt for hours, praying a car would stop. It was Christmas Eve but that didn't mean anyone would give a bum a ride.

The previous night, the cold had made his lips too numb to talk and he had been afraid he'd freeze to death. A trucker had finally stopped, and he had ridden the remainder of the night in the warm cab. Then he had stood once again on the frozen asphalt, clapping his hands together to keep the circulation going. A bright orange sun had risen slowly over the frozen fields before a car had stopped and he was on the last leg of his journey.

He had left the hostel after the clerk had brought up an ancient coat from the basement. Mike had tried it on.

"There's a hole in the elbow," he had said.

"Jesus H. Christ! What the hell more ya want? Maybe a Goddamn Christmas gift too," the clerk had yelled and Mike had bitten his lip. He had no hat or gloves but there was no point in asking.

He had eaten a breakfast of oatmeal and skim milk and hard toast, jamming the food into his mouth for he felt faint and wondered if he would make it through the day. Then with a token clenched in his hand he had shivered at a bus stop and then asked the driver to let him know when they were at the last stop on the city's outskirts. The driver had stared at him for an instant but had said nothing. As the bus rolled along the frozen city streets, daylight claiming the city from the night. Mike had gazed out a window, seeing the Hub Hotel and the Coffee Cup Café. He had wondered idly if the pimp had tired of the soft white body of the lady hooker who had still retained enough assurance to demand things from a man.

He knew that in less than a year she would be just another whore tricking with Johns in filthy flop houses. And in a couple of years, if she was alive, she would be just another piece of human garbage, floating on the concrete sea of the city.

As the young man beside Mike steered the car with both hands, he felt drowsy from the sudden and unaccustomed heat. The driver glanced at him occasionally and finally said.

"I'm Fred. What's your name?"

"Mike."

Then when the silence deepened, Fred asked, "Going far?"

"Yeah. North of Prince Albert."

"Hell! I can give you a ride right to where you're going."

Mike looked quickly at the driver.

"Okay. I'm going to my parents farm. It's only a mile from the highway."

He sighed deeply for it meant no more standing on the frozen road and wondering if he would become just another statistic, a bum that frozen to death.

"What happened?"

"Whatta ya mean?"

"Well, you obviously don't have any money or luggage. Something must have happened."

"Oh!" Mike hesitated. "Uh, I had three hundred dollars and I was going to catch a bus home, but last night I stayed in a hotel and someone stole my wallet."

"Oh yeah," Fred said and didn't press any more.

As the car sped along the winding highway, Mike's eyes grew heavy, and finally his head nodded. He dreamed of traveling a mountain road with high granite cliffs. Suddenly a monstrous boulder, the size of a house appeared, rolling along beside the highway, keeping pace and threatening to bounce and crush him and the car. The boulder sped up and slowed with the car staying to Mike's right, and suddenly there was an image of the miner, crushed to death in the mine in Thompson. Mike moaned and Fred glanced quickly at him and then back at the road.

Mike moaned again as the boulder bounced alongside the car and then suddenly he saw the Lady Hooker. She was lying on her back, broken and smashed, her bones shattered while blood seeped from her wounds. From an upright bar hung her intestines, ripped from her soft white belly, slimy and glistening. The Lady Hooker opened her dainty mouth and screamed. The scarlet lipstick suddenly turned to bright foamy blood as she angrily demanded to have her intestines back.

Mike woke with a start and gazed about bewildered. Then he was aware of Fred's eyes. He shook his head and stared out the windshield an instant.

"Bad dream?"

"I guess so."

"I get them sometimes. Anyway, isn't that the road you told me about?"

"Yeah! That's it!"

Mike once again hunched his shoulders against the biting wind and trudged the mile to his father's farm. The familiar scene of pasture, woods and field unfolded slowly and he remembered where he had hunted with his dog. But the wind whipped about him and he forgot about hunting while he clapped his hands to his ears to keep them from freezing. When he felt the familiar sting in his fingers, he jammed them into his pockets until his ears began to freeze again. Then came an image of when he was fifteen and had frozen his fingers because his parents wouldn't buy him gloves. He remembered how he'd sworn to leave the farm and never return. The blowing snow ended that image and he hunched his shoulders and tried to tuck his chin into the collar of the ancient coat.

Finally he came to the frozen creek where the trees blocked the wind and he turned into the driveway and could see the house with the grey smoke billowing from the stove pipe. Snow was piled on either side of the driveway from a snowplow and the scene was pristine and clear.

Suddenly, his dog burst from the yard, running flat out. Buster, growled and barked but then stopped. He sniffed and a great metamorphous took place. His tail began wagging joyously and he galloped to Mike and sprang forward, his paws on Mike's chest nearly knocking him down. He barked happily and licked Mike's face and Mike threw his arms about him as he fought back the tears. Then he knelt for a brief moment hugging him while Buster's tail whipped back and forth. But Mike's knees began to freeze and he stood and walked rapidly to the house with his dog frisking about beside him. Then, he stood at the door and knocked loudly.

Suddenly, his father stood in front of him, staring for an instant. Then, as an embarrassed silence deepened, he turned slowly. He didn't say "Come in!" He just made room for Mike to enter.

Mike was in the familiar kitchen then, with its slippery linoleum floor which he had dreamed about in his most melancholy of dreams. Gertie stopped short, in the doorway from the living room, her breath caught in her mouth and her eyes hard. She didn't smile like she had in the dream.

"Where have you been?" she demanded. "And where's your suitcase?" She noticed the ancient coat with the torn elbow and also that he had no gifts.

"Uh, I left it in Edmonton," he answered slowly and then repeated the lie. "I had three hundred bucks but someone stole my wallet."

"Oh!" Gertie said, her mouth hard and thin. Then her face took on its familiar complaining look.

"You got to be more careful."

Mike gazed down at the floor and his shoulders slumped from an inexplicable weight while his eyes bore an infinite sadness. Gertie and Vincent went into the living room then, leaving him alone. He glanced outside at his dog. As he looked through the window, he heard his mother's agitated, nagging whisper from the living room. Buster, wagged his tail furiously but Mike looked back down at the floor. Then he glanced at a small book, used in the Catholic Mass. He idly flipped the pages and stopped at an illustration.

A father ran out onto a road to welcome home the Prodigal Son. Mike stared as tears formed in his eyes and he felt a great frozen lump in his chest.

# Thirty-eight

Grey, wintry skies hung low over the farm while the cold east wind piled snow banks hard enough for a horse to walk on. The cold hung over the earth too, an invisible shroud making iron stick instantly to exposed flesh, and chains break if yanked too hard. At times the sun shone brightly from a pale blue sky, an orange orb that turned blood-red as it sank slowly into the western sky, giving the earth back to the frozen darkness. It was January, the coldest month of the year when the sun rose at nine a.m. and set before four, the brief few hours in between more a respite from the dark, frozen netherworld than a full day. During this time, Mike pulled on heavy clothes to help his father outside in the snow, or in the frigid, cloying barn whose presence stayed with him, even in the house. At other times he read old books or watched TV for Vincent had bought a secondhand set.

At times Mike tried engaging his mother in conversation. Gertie would listen, the words seldom making a dent in her mental armor.

"But Mom," he would begin. It would be early evening when the cold and dark gathered about the house, with the wood stove and bare light bulb keeping them at bay. "I've seen too many things to truly believe like you do."

That was all he would say about the mine and the Bennet Dam, where two men had died; one under the ore and the other ripped apart by a steel bar. But Gertie had her own memories. Mother and son talked to each other, for they were the only company available, but they existed in two solitudes, worlds apart.

"I don't believe you have to be in a church every Sunday," Mike said one evening while Gertie sewed and appeared to listen. They were alone in the kitchen for Vincent snored loudly on the couch.

"What! Are we cattle?" Gertie demanded suddenly in the eternal argument, neither could win.

"No! But what do cattle have to do with it?" Mike answered patiently. At twenty-three he was beginning a slow and painful metamorphosis, or rather a mental and emotional renaissance.

"God gave man intelligence so he could use it, not just follow rules. Look! Most of the laws of the church were set down thousands of years ago. But then everyone thought the earth was flat at the time."

"But Metro!" Gertie snapped. "We don't think of such things."

Mike was beginning to understand. No matter how hard he tried he would never break through, but the loneliness of a wintery evening with the wind moaning about the old house bore relentlessly down. He tried desperately to make his mother understand that he was a man, capable of forming his own faith. But always, the result would be the same. He was also having resurgent memories from his childhood and occasionally, when he was trying to sleep or daydreaming, a scene would suddenly appear. He remembered the toys he wasn't allowed to bring north when he was only seven; the time his head had been rammed down into a tub of water on Halloween, and also his mother's insane laughter.

I must be imagining all this, he thought at times, for he had been told that none of it had happened.

His mother's vehement statement of "hard times of his own making" also came and he felt more confusion and guilt.

When he asked her why he had never been allowed to get a driver's license, Gertie snapped, "Well you would of started going and going, and next thing we knew, you would have been gone all the time."

It meant he couldn't be trusted and he said no more. At night he lay in the cold, dark house, wondering if he was indeed imagining all the events of his childhood. Mike's intelligence was only a hazard for it wouldn't let him accept everything he was told.

He tried again and again, attempting to penetrate the fog surrounding his mother.

"What is Christianity to you?" he asked one evening. His father snored from the living room, at times drowning out the wind moaning about the eaves.

"Huh!" Gertie looked up startled.

"I mean, how much do you know about Christ's teachings?"

"Well..." Gertie took awhile answering. "He was left on a river and drifted in a basket. Then some good people picked him up and saved him."

It was Mike's turn to be startled, shocked by his mother's ignorance.

"That was Moses!" he exclaimed. "You mean, you don't even know about Christ's teachings, and you insist I go to church every Sunday and go to Confession and Communion."

"Well, you're our son. So you gotta go."

"But what if your son believes differently?" Mike demanded.

"Well then you gotta knock 'em on the head so he don't," Gertie laughed.

The conversation would continue with Mike trying to explain his beliefs to a doubtful Gertie. He even told her of some of his experiences.

"There was this woman. She was fat and ugly and she drank and swore all the time. But she helped me, and I owed her twenty bucks. I paid her back only five, and she invited me to dinner," Mike looked down at his woolen socks before continuing.

"That's more than my brother ever did. And, she never went to church. So how can you say that going to church makes you a better Christian?"

Gertie's answer made Mike grit his teeth.

"You got no business hanging around with low people like that."

"Low people! Jesus!" Mike swore and Gertie glared.

"She saved my life. Low people! Hell! What about Gerard? He's my brother and he hates me. Now that's low!"

"Can you blame him?" Gertie snapped, her sewing unattended in her lap.

"What? What the hell do you mean by that?"

"Well," Gertie began. "He lent you fifteen dollars and you didn't pay it back right away."

"Jesus!" Mike swore again. "That's a really good reason to hate your own brother? I sure the hell hope his family doesn't go hungry over a lousy fifteen bucks."

Gertie's eyes widened. Just for an instant, Mike had found a chink in the armor. But it was only a chink and it closed quickly.

"Well, he had to peddle you to school when you was eight."

Mike was suddenly speechless and Gertie returned to her sewing. He never had an answer for statements like that.

After conversations like that he would read. Gertie would sew or watch TV and Vincent would snore loudly. Sometimes for days, neither would speak. When Mike could no longer stand the solitude, he would try again. Vincent slept through most of this but when he was awake he would automatically take Gertie's side. Mike was caught between denial and constant emerging memories. At times he wondered if he was losing his mind.

Even when he tried to retrain his dog, Vincent interfered, holding Buster when Mike called, or calling him when Mike sent him after cattle.

One day Vincent drove the old Ford truck into a snow bank and stripped a gear in the transmission. Instead of getting it fixed he drove with only second and third and no low gear. A few days later, they stood by the barn.

"Metro! Take those logs and drag them to the house for firewood," Vincent ordered suddenly.

Mike stared at his father.

"Why can't I use the truck?"

"The truck's broke and it got lumber on it," Vincent snapped. "It stays were it is."

"I can unload it."

"You leave that darned truck alone!" Vincent suddenly yelled, waving his arms. His angry shout startled a flock of sparrows, who rose into the air and flew off toward a poplar bluff.

"You touched it once all year, and now it's broke."

Mike stood dumbfounded. His father had lied many times before but each time he did, it was always new.

As the winter wore on, Mike slipped more and more into dreams. The soft confines of a nightclub would become reality and the soft, white body of the lady hooker would be there, so real he could feel her satiny skin. When the morning came the harsh cold reality would crowd in and he would feel ashamed for dreaming such things. Then his mother would stand in his bedroom door and yell.

"Metro! Wake up! Come on now. You gotta go to church."

During this time the desire for all things artistic simmered and occasionally he tried writing. He would sit at the kitchen table but the words wouldn't come. Gertie would glance occasionally at her son and then interrupt. Mike would lose his patience and sit on the couch in the living room with a pen and pad.

Gertie then began running into the living room with the words, "Metro! Hold your place!"

"What do you want?" Mike demanded once.

"Uh," Gertie turned and gazed back into the kitchen. "Do you think I should make potatoes or maybe use up that rice?"

"Oh for the love of God!" Mike threw the pen with such force it shattered against the oil heater. He had just found a line, feelings caught in verse, when Gertie had run into the living room.

Gertie stared at the anger on her son's face and then wordlessly turned and returned to the kitchen.

It was during, this time, when poverty was a living enemy, that Gertie had an idea. The government had begun removing neglected or abused children from their natural homes and placing them with Foster Parents. The government paid ninety dollars a month for the care of one baby, a decent sum in the mid-sixties.

Gertie nagged Vincent until he fixed the transmission, and together they drove to the city in the ancient Ford half-ton to see a social worker. When they sat in an office, Vincent had a hard time suppressing faces and his jaw trembled whenever the worker looked at him. But there always seemed to be more unwanted children than foster parents. When Vincent and Gertie were back home, she took out a scribbler and pencil and figured out how much they would have to spend on clothes and baby food and the difference left over each month. They were also lonely and a baby would help pass the long, cold evenings.

During this brief period, Mike worked on a sawmill, standing on the deck in minus thirty weather and using a cant-hook, rolled logs onto a carriage. As fast as he worked, so went the mill and he fought the image of the slowly circling, blindfolded beast, by driving his body. Still, at the start of each day he wondered if that was to be his life, until he was too old to work. Then he would work himself into a lather, despite the cold.

When the job was done, he returned to the farm and was surprised at Gertie's smile. A baby was in the house; a four-month-old, warm, living human baby who cried and demanded all manner of things. He was the center of attention in the lonely old house with the wind howling about the eaves. The baby's name was Benny and he gave more than he received.

Mike experienced more conflicting emotions when he saw his mother hold the baby in her arms. And when his father held him Mike felt a deep, unfathomable feeling, both revulsion and alien warmth. The baby was easy to love and Gertie knew that any mistreatment would cause Social Services to take him away.

At first Mike was irritated by his crying and by his mother's words of, "So Metro, this is what I did for you," whenever she changed a diaper. But as time passed he gazed wonderingly at Benny. Benny was partially bald at the back of his head for his mother had rarely held him. He had spent the first four months of his life on his back in a dilapidated crib, seeing the world from upside down.

One day, Mike was standing close to the heater in the living room and close to the crib. Benny sat, gazing up at the stranger just above him. Suddenly, he held up his arms in the universal signal of all babies, who wish to be picked up. Mike was confused. He glanced quickly at the kitchen where his mother worked and muttered, then back to the baby. Then, in slow motion, he bent and grasped Benny just under the arms, noticing how light he was. As Mike held him awkwardly, Benny gazed about from the unaccustomed height. He suddenly reached with a tiny hand, trying to grasp Mike's glasses. Mike moved his head, just enough so the baby couldn't reach. He held the baby by the warm heater for a few moments, his emotions a raging current just beneath the surface. Then he walked to the couch, placing Benny on his lap, crossing one leg with his ankle resting on his thigh. He sat, the baby in the area where his left knee protruded. Benny fit perfectly, as he sat still for awhile, gazing about and up at Mike. Then he tried to grasp Mike's glasses again with his tiny hand and Mike held his head just out of reach. He held the baby like that for half an hour until Gertie came and gazed down at them.

"That's nice," she said. She was puzzled for Benny had cried when she had first picked him up, yet he seemed so content in Mike's arms.

As Mike sat on the couch with Benny he wondered why; why when he held a baby tears formed in his eyes.

After that he played with Benny for hours, holding and bouncing him on his knee. Benny's eyes would fill with joy and he would laugh and wave his tiny hands in the air. Finally his eyes would grow heavy and his tiny head nod. Mike would look down, filled with wonder at the sleeping baby. He would rise slowly, lifting Benny with his hands under his arms, and gently placing him in the crib. Mike took care to never make a sudden movement as he held the baby, his tiny feet poised just above the mattress. When Benny's toes touched, he would lean him backwards and gently, slowly, lay him down. Benny would sleep through all this, and then lay in his crib, unawares that he no longer was in Mike's arms.

Gertie would stare down at the crib and then up at Mike.

"I can't understand why he don't wake up," she would say. When she tried doing what Mike had done Benny would always wake and cry.

One afternoon, when Mike held Benny on his knee on the couch, memories and bitter thoughts of his oldest brother suddenly came. The bitterness made his voice harsh as he glared up at his mother.

"Why when I'm supposed to be such a bum, such a bastard, mean and everything, why does a baby go to sleep in my arms?

"Aw, go on with such talk," Gertie snapped.

But all things must come to an end. One day, when the grass was turning green and calves frisked in the pasture, a new car with the words "Social Services" on its doors, came into the yard. Inside was a determined young nurse with a difficult job to do.

"Come in! Come in!" Gertie did her best to control her anxiety.

"Sit down! You want some coffee?"

Just then Mike entered with a smiling Benny in his arms. The nurse looked up quickly and then back down. She toyed with her cup, mentally preparing herself. She had been through this before.

"Well, you might as well know why I'm here."

Gertie's face lost its color. Both she and Mike stared at the Nurse. Vincent stopped in the doorway, his face frozen in a contortion and his hand in mid-motion.

"The judge decided to give Benny's mother another chance."

"What does that mean?" Mike asked still holding the baby.

The nurse sighed and took a sip of coffee before answering.

"It means, I'll have to take him back with me. The judge ordered that he be given back to his mother. He said to give her another chance."

"What about him?" Mike demanded, holding Benny who smiled happily. He thought bitterly of a faceless judge, who had ordered a baby back to a mother, who hadn't bothered to even pick him up when he lay in his crib.

"What happens if she doesn't look after him again?"

"Then we'll have to take her to court again. It's her last chance," the nurse answered and then looked out the window.

"But what about him?" Mike demanded again. Then he gazed into Benny's eyes. Benny smiled back.

"What chance does he get?"

The nurse looked down at her coffee for there was no answer. Who can argue with a Judge, even if his decision was based on facts existing in his mind only.

"It's not up to me," she finally said, noticing the moisture in Mike's eyes.

Gertie sat, staring at the nurse, her knuckles pressed into her hips and her lips drawn and tight.

"I have to take him back with me," the nurse added quietly.

There was nothing they could do. Mike watched through the window as the nurse turned the car around. Benny sat in a tiny seat, gazing about, his eyes wide. Since he had begun falling asleep in Mike's arms, he had begun to trust adults.

A couple weeks later Gertie found out that he had cried steadily in his mother's apartment and that even if he had wanted to, he would have been unable to sleep. The apartment was small and there were constant parties with a steady parade of men and women and alcohol. Eventually the same tired old judge reluctantly ordered the baby taken away for good, and sent to different surrogate parents.

After that the silence once again deepened in the kitchen with Vincent making faces and Gertie siting very still, her face hard and bitter. At night, when Mike tried to sleep, the dreams came and in one Benny reached with his tiny hand and brushed against his chin. And then came others. He was standing in the yard beside an ironworker. Suddenly, blood spurted and the man knelt, beheaded. His head rolled on the grass before Mike, while from the stump on his shoulders spurted scarlet gore. Mike woke rigid, and drenched in sweat, his breathing rapid.

At other times he would drift off and then suddenly waken, a nameless horror lurking just outside his vision. He could sense, a breathing, faceless terror just a few feet from his bed. He would quickly turn and face the window, where some light came from the stars. Then, when his breathing slowly returned to normal, he would drift off again, only to waken again to the nameless horror.

In the morning Gertie would appear in the doorway, her face hard and angry.

"Metro! Get up! There's three of us in this house, not two. You should be helping more."

Mike would rise, more exhausted than when he went to bed. At times his anger would snap and he and his parents argued often.

# Thirty-nine

When spring passed into full summer, a Social Services vehicle once again appeared in the yard, but with a different nurse at the wheel. Beside her were three young children: Heather, Tommy and Ethel. Heather was five and a half years old, Tommy three and a half and Ethel one and a half. Their behavior was abnormal for they were not normal children.

They had lived their entire short lives in a shack tent one hundred and fifty miles north, surviving the cold and snow for six months and the flies and bugs the rest of the year. They had been abandoned for a week at a time, living off anything they could find, while their mother sought the insane happiness of partying with men; any men, just as long as they provided mind-numbing alcohol. At times she had brought men home, and the children had grown wary of strange adults.

When they ate, they used their hands and food clung to their mouths and faces. For clothes, they wore tattered and too big cast offs and their shoelaces were untied and filthy. The eldest had already learned the foulest of language, for human anatomy and fornicating had been a common sight.

At first they meekly did what they were told. But in a few days they began testing Gertie in what would become a never-ending struggle. As the days passed, the silence was shattered by the anguished cries of children who were punished for doing what had been normal a short while before. Ethel was beaten savagely for throwing off her clothes and running naked through the house. Heather was beaten for swearing and Tommy because he refused to pick up toys.

Mike came into the living room as Vincent stood over the child, his right hand raised and ready to strike again. Tommy sat on the floor, paralyzed by Vincent's enraged, contorting face and his shoulders shuddered in uncontrollable, terrified sobs.

"Pick 'em up!" Vincent yelled hoarsely.

"He can't!" Mike stepped in front of his father. He stooped quickly and placed a hand on the tiny and shuddering shoulder.

"Look, all you have to do is try." He knelt and gently placed a toy in Tommy's hand. Then he guided Tommy's hand to the box. "See! It's easy."

The shuddering sobs slowed somewhat and Tommy reluctantly let Mike guide his hand. Finally he began picking up toys on his own.

"See! You don't have to yell." Mike stood and looked steadily at his father. Vincent looked back at Mike and then down at Tommy, who was slowly placing the last toy in the box.

"You're lucky you did what you were told boy. I'd a given ya one!"

Then, he made a face, wiped it with a heavy hand and left the room.

---

At the time the children appeared, Mike was experiencing a resurgence of artistic longings. At first the sketches were not much but with practice and determination he was able to make the moose, elk or deer he copied from a Wildlife magazine, look almost real. When he sketched the image of the blindfolded endlessly circling donkey slowly faded and a dream began to form. In the dream he painted and wrote stories, feeling the tantalizing and melancholy victory of receiving his first check. Then quickly, in the dream, he was making thousands of dollars and his parents were giving him grudging respect.

He even sketched his mother, unintentionally capturing the hard, thin mouth and fatalistic demeanor. Gertie hated it and Mike kept it in his room.

When summer was deepening, he hitched a ride to the city and waited for hours in the Employment Office until he was called into a tiny office. A counselor, no older than he, looked at him from across a desk and wondered why Mike was there. He glanced down at the employment record before him, a hodgepodge of jobs, stretching across six provinces and two states, none held for more than six months.

"Why do you wanna take art?" he demanded, massaging his temples for his head ached and his eyes were bloodshot.

"Well," Mike began slowly, searching for words, "I just think it'd be a good idea."

"Ya gotta have a better reason than that," the counselor snapped.

"Well I always liked to draw pictures," Mike said quietly while within the turmoil raged.

"Well, there isn't much call for artists," the young man said, glancing up at the clock. It was only eleven a.m., a long way to quitting time.

"Hell!" He glanced down at the file. "You got a pretty sketchy job record, you know. What makes you think you'll stick to commercial art?"

"If I was given a chance," Mike began and then gave up. It was another lesson in his slow, tortuous education. Whenever he attempted to improve his lot, rarely would there be anyone willing to help.

"Besides!" the impatient young man snapped. "You're registered in Saskatoon. Why did you come here?" He snapped Mike's file shut.

Mike left, his mind churning. He hitchhiked to Saskatoon, leaving the farm early so he would be back before dark. He had no money and ate nothing for dinner. When he sat in another counselors office, he was asked the same questions. Why did he want to take an art course? Again he felt the same emotional paralysis. Then he was told to return north for that was where he was from, and maybe they would help him there.

Mike walked tiredly into the farmhouse and to his cool bedroom. He lay down on the bed, and with anxiety churning his stomach he thought, I'll just lie here where it's cool. Tomorrow I'll figure out what to do. Slowly he drifted off into an exhausted sleep.

Gertie appeared suddenly in the doorway.

"What the dickens!" she screeched and Mike was up in one motion.

"What the hell's the matter with you?" he demanded. "Couldn't you see I was sleeping?"

"All I saw was a strange man lying on the bed," Gertie said and turned back to the kitchen, a faint smile playing about her hard, thin mouth.

Mike went outside where he watched the three children playing. Tommy held a cracked toy car in his tiny hand. He wasn't sure what it was, for he had never seen cars in the shack tent and bush that had been home. He laid the car down and picked up a doll, holding it by an arm and looking at the cracked face.

Suddenly, Heather lunged.

"Mine!" she cried, yanking the doll from Tommy. He tried to hit her but he was too little. Heather rained down blows with her tiny fists and then kicked him.

Mike was by the children in a stride. He yanked Heather by an arm and smacked her rear soundly. With the numbing blows, his frustration was suddenly released and he swung with a grim rage. Heather's wails of fear and anguish joined Tommy's as Mike beat her savagely.

When his hand hurt, he looked down at the children. They huddled together in fear, their eyes wet and faces streaked. Suddenly, an emotional shaft shot through to Mike's soul for the terror on the little faces opened a window to his childhood. He retreated to a bench and watched the children, who subsided to pitiful sobbing. Finally they returned to the broken and cast off toys.

"What the heck's going on out here?" Gertie suddenly demanded, from the step.

"Heather was beating up on Tommy."

"Serves her right then!" Gertie snapped and returned to the kitchen. Her words did nothing to ease Mike's guilt. If anything, they made it worse.

Next morning he placed his best sketches in an ancient, cracked briefcase and once again hitchhiked to the city. The anger that had boiled over when he had beaten Heather stayed near the surface, for the more he heard no, the more determined he became. When he rode in a car, answering the driver in monosyllables, his mind drifted back to the previous evening.

He had sat in the kitchen with Vincent and the same neighbor who had given him his dog. Outside, the gloriously setting sun turned the entire sky pink but neither Vincent nor Joe had commented on it. It had only meant the end of another day.

"Sure was hot today." Vincent had leaned forward in his chair, clasping his heavy hands together, his face contorting slightly.

Joe had sat next to him, his hair grey and middle bulging, for he had aged since Mike had carried the best of his puppies through the spruce to the farm.

"Sure hope it don't rain tomorrow," Joe had said. "I got lots a hay out yet."

"I heard they had a real soaker over near town," Vincent had replied as he rocked slightly forward.

Then Joe had looked at Mike.

"You gonna help with the hay this year?"

"Yeah, I guess so. But I don't know about harvest. I'm going back to school."

"What for?" Joe had demanded.

"I'm going take an art course." Mike had aired his ambition reluctantly for a few days earlier Vincent had yelled, "Go sit on a snow bank with your darned writing and art!"

Joe hadn't yelled. He had only laughed quietly, his shoulders rising and falling quickly.

"Whats so funny? Do you think its a bad idea?" Mike had demanded.

"I think you're made for hard word," Joe had answered seriously. "And the sooner you forget about that foolishness, the better."

Mike had said nothing, looking down at his hands while the anger simmered and Vincent grinned.

"I knew this guy once who used to draw pictures," Joe had said then. "He could draw your picture so fast, and it looked like you, none of this stuff about fields or something."

Mike had earlier shown him a sketch of hills and a stream.

"But he never charged for it. He was an elevator agent, 'cause you can't make money at something like that. But he sure could draw that guy. Two, three minutes and he'd do your picture."

"Funny how some guys can do that," Vincent had said, while Mike's stomach had hurt.

Joe had shrugged his shoulders. He had run out of philosophy.

"I guess you gotta be kinda handy," Vincent had finally answered his own question. "Like some guys can drive a Cat."

His mind skipped then to other matters.

"Remember that guy, Henry?" he asked Joe. "Well one day he was bragging that his brother was so good on a Cat. He said that he's so good, why he can make that Cat jump."

Next morning as he rode in the stranger's car, Mike's anger burned and boiled. There's no such thing as no, he thought grimly. When he entered the Employment Office, he walked rapidly, his head and shoulders thrust forward, in the newly forming manner of a man determined to get his way.

When he was seated across from a new counselor, he took his sketches from the cracked briefcase and threw them onto the desk. The counselor looked at the paper and then up at Mike in surprise. He was used to meek men and women who came in to find work.

"Look at them!" Mike ordered.

The counselor gazed down at a near-perfect fawn.

"Now look me in the eye and tell me I have no talent."

The counselor looked up into the eyes of the angry young man and then said softly, "Sit down. Take it easy. No one said you don't have talent."

"Well, the last time I came here, the guy refused to even let me fill in an application. He had a hangover and I guess I must have bothered him. He said I had to go to Saskatoon but when I was there, they told me to come back here." Mike glared steadily at the counselor.

"Don't worry," the counselor laughed nervously. "I can see that you got some talent. I'll get an application going for you to take an upgrading course."

Mike stared in surprise.

"Well, you can't take a commercial art course until you have grade ten."

Mike sighed in relief as he carefully placed the sketches back into the old briefcase. It seemed so easy, too easy.

"But," the counselor cautioned him. "I don't know when an art course will be open." Then he added quietly, "It was good that you came in here, determined. But don't do it too often or it'll cause a negative attitude."

"Okay," Mike said wondering how a meek demeanor would help. But that was the future. The first step had been taken and for the first time in his life, he had changed his situation instead of being changed by it.

He didn't know where the determination came from. It just simmered naturally, vented by anger and frustration. All he knew as that when he saw a young man and woman, sitting close together in a new car he felt instant rage and frustration and he hated the young man with a passion.

---

Mike sat painfully on the hard chair, dinner noises all about him. His back ached and his ribs felt like they carried all the weight of his upper torso. Once again, inexplicably, his vertebrae had arched in his lower back and he knew the searing pain that made standing, or even sitting a test of will. While he ate, he tried to ignore his father's smacking lips and his brother's cold, implacable stare from across the table.

Heather, Tommy and Ethel ate at a tiny toy table near the door and Gertie cast an occasional watchful glance in their direction. They still ate with their hands but she pretended not to notice.

As Mike chewed he thought of the evening before.

"Well, what are you gonna do?" Gerard had demanded suddenly.

He had told Gerard about the art course and Gerard had gone through a fast period of internal confusion. If Mike was suited only for dull, brute labor, why would he constantly try to improve his lot? For a very brief time Gerard had mentally wrestled with the disturbing image.

"You should be a carpenter," he had finally said. "At least that way you'd have a job."

"I don't want to be a carpenter," Mike had explained patiently. "I always liked art and writing. Why can't I do that?"

"Aw that!" Gerard had waved his hand in dismissal. "I guess you're pretty well forced into art," he had added after a momentary silence.

"What the hell does that mean?" Mike had demanded.

Gerard had crossed his ankles and had looked at his brother from across the kitchen. They had been the only ones there but they had sat at opposite ends of the room, as if distance would keep them mentally and emotionally apart.

"Well, Mom and Dad are getting old. They might retire and then you'll have no place to stay."

Mike had stared at Gerard. Surely Gerard couldn't mean that he stayed on the farm because he couldn't do anything else.

"Well, you shouldn't have any trouble with the upgrading," Gerard had finally said, easing some of the tension and Mike had felt a faint, alien sense of acceptance. "But I doubt, if art will ever do you any good." The faint feeling had faded quickly.

"I still think you should be a carpenter," Gerard had finally said and laughed. Mike had risen and gone to bed, where he tossed and turned for hours.

As Gerard sat across the table from Mike the next day, Mike painfully straightened his back and a calculating light glimmered from Gerard's eyes. It had rained the night before and the roof leaked.

"You could go up on the roof and fix the leak," he said innocently. Gertie looked at Mike.

Mike painfully straightened his back again, trying to ease the muscle spasm.

"How the hell can I?" he demanded. "I can hardly sit, let alone climb a ladder."

Gerard said no more, his thin cruel mouth curving into a slight smile.

After supper Mike lay on the couch trying to ease the pain. Suddenly Gerard's wife appeared in the doorway with their baby.

"Sorry Metro! But you're gonna have to move. I gotta change the baby," she said gleefully.

Mike painfully left the couch and lay on his cot in his room, letting the pain slowly drain from his consciousness. Suddenly he heard his name mentioned in the kitchen.

"Is he going to that school?" Gerard demanded.

"Yuh!" Gertie answered. "He's gonna get thirty-seven dollars a week to live on."

"Thirty-seven dollars!" Gerard snapped. "You mean he got no money, and has to mooch off the government."

"Well, that should be enough," Gertie said.

"Enough for nothing!" Gerard's wife snapped.

Mike lay on the cot, his stomach churning. Then he heard his brother's cold voice.

"I don't think he'll ever amount to anything in life."

"Why?" Gertie asked. Mike was surprised to hear his mother question the statement.

"He's too lazy!" Gerard snapped. "I told him he could go up on the roof and fix the leak but he was just too tarned lazy."

While the conversation continued in the kitchen, questions flew rapidly through Mike's mind.

"God! How could I? What if I'd have fallen?"

# Forty

Mike's intellectual growth continued, and he experienced more and more of a personal renaissance. During this, Vincent's boorish manners and Gertie's complaining, bitter demeanor became more obvious.

On a wintry afternoon, Vincent watched TV from the couch, leaning forward with his heavy hands clasped together while Gerard stood by a cupboard. Mike was by the oil heater, with one leg up on a wooden chair, as he rolled a cigarette.

"They're all Niggers!" Vincent suddenly exclaimed, making a face and waving his hand. He grinned at Mike and then at the TV. He had been watching a documentary about racial intolerance in South Africa.

"Good God! How in hell can you say that?" Mike demanded. Gerard looked on, his eyebrows drawing close together on his white face.

"They're all Niggers!" Vincent laughed loudly, grinning at Gerard.

"Jesus! How do you think a black would feel if he heard you?"

"Oh, I imagine they must be used to it by now," Gerard said suddenly, his lips thin and compressed.

"You can kick a dog all year , his being used to it won't help him any," Mike said emphatically. Gerard stared at him for a moment. Then a thin smile appeared briefly on his compressed lips.

The mental metamorphosis couldn't be halted, no matter what Gerard said or did. When Mike drove the tractor, endlessly circling the field in a cloud of dust, he learned to keep a very small part of his mind on the machinery and the rest on whatever he was thinking about. At the time, the Catholic Church had banned contraceptives, arguing that it was against natural law. Mike puzzled over this for a long time, sensing there was another reason. As the tractor motor roared, and the black earth passed slowly beneath its turning wheels, he sat on the hard seat and formulated an understanding.

The major reason they're against contraceptives, he mused in his hazy world, is because the Pope fears a lessening of control. If they allow birth control, next will come a relaxed attitude toward sex, followed by promiscuity. He remembered an article in the Catholic Digest written by a priest who had explained why newlyweds should not feel guilty on their wedding night. But he also had written of the horrific consequences, if the bride were to look forward to the marriage's consummation.

They would sooner see a young girl get pregnant and live in shame the rest of her life, than see her avoid it with contraceptives, Mike mused. He absentmindedly smoked a hand-rolled cigarette, steering with one hand, as he sat slumped on the hard seat, deep in thought.

When he entered the kitchen for lunch, he played a mental game with Gerard. He was beginning to understand that his older brother purposely disagreed with anything he said.

"I don't believe in that darned contraception," he said sitting in a chair by the window. Gerard hunched, forward in his seat in his anxious manner. Suddenly his face whitened and eyebrows joined.

"What! Good grief! What the heck do you know about that?" he demanded, clenching his hands together.

Mike was surprised at how white Gerard's face had become.

"You got no business talking about something you know absolutely nothing about," Gerard continued.

"You mean, contraceptives are good and should be used?" Mike asked quietly.

"Yes!" Gerard yelled. Then he stopped in sudden confusion, clenching his hands until the knuckles whitened. He bit his upper lip, and glared about the kitchen and then back at Mike. Mike glanced out the window, suppressing a smile.

It was a victory for Mike, but Gerard was resourceful too. That evening, Mike sat in the kitchen by the window. Gerard stood wiping dishes while Gertie washed.

"Heather came out with a couple fancy words," he began. Gertie's mouth hardened, boding ill for the offending five and a half year old. Then Gerard glanced obliquely at Mike.

"I doubt she could have gotten it from Metro," he added quietly. Gertie stopped washing for an instant, her soapy hands suspended in mid-air.

Mike was silent, staring pensively through the window at the three children playing in a sand box.

Next day as the children played in the yard, Tommy looked up suddenly at him.

"Catch with me?" he asked, standing by the house with a rubber ball in his tiny hand.

"I can't! I have to haul wood," Mike answered. But as he looked down at Tommy, a memory stirred of a time when he had played in the same yard with imaginary friends.

"Throw it in the air," he said slowly. "When it comes down you can catch it. That's what I used to do."

"Can't!" Tommy's face lengthened with the tears waiting, ready to flow.

"Sure you can!"

"Can't!" Tommy repeated and the tears started.

"Okay! Show me," Mike said quickly. He sat on a bench to watch.

Tommy looked down at the ground for a moment and then at the rubber ball in his tiny hand. He took a deep breath and threw the ball straight away from him. At the same time he raced forward, trying to catch up to it.

Mike exploded into laughter for Tommy's tiny churning legs and look of fierce determination was hilarious, but only for a second. Once the ball landed, Tommy slowed and then slowly retrieved it. He looked up at Mike, while Mike avoided the look in his eyes.

"Here! I'll show you." Mike stood quickly and took the ball from Tommy. He threw it straight up into the air and then caught it. He repeated the throw a few times so Tommy would understand. Tommy's eyes were round as he watched, and Mike's misty as another memory quickly came.

He had been eleven years old, standing in the same spot with a worn glove and baseball, while he had asked Gerard to teach him to throw a curve.

"Aw, you can't!" Gerard had snapped but Mike had persisted.

"Okay! But if you wanna throw a curve, you gotta learn how to catch one first," Gerard had finally snapped, walking to the center of the yard. Mike had squatted in a catcher's position as Gerard had gone into a windup. Then he had thrown a slow curve that had missed Mike's glove by six inches.

"Aw, you can't!" Gerard had waved his arm in dismissal. Mike had begged for another chance and Gerard had thrown the ball again. That time it had missed the glove by a foot and Gerard had grinned triumphantly.

"See! You can't even catch a curve. How the heck do ya expect to throw one?" He had waved his arm contemptuously, walking to the house and adding over his shoulder, "You might as well forget about Little League. You can't play!"

Mike remembered the hot tears and then as the memory faded, he looked down at Tommy and gave him the ball.

"Here! Now you try. I'll watch."

As Mike was leaving with his father to haul wood, Tommy still played by himself, throwing the ball into the air and holding his hands out. Mike looked away for Tommy evoked all manner of emotions.

That evening, Ethel wet her pants and Gertie spanked her long and hard. The child didn't resist. She just leaned forward and grasped Gertie's calf for support while she endured the blows. Mike watched silently from the chair by the window and the same uncomfortable emotions came. This time he had an idea.

"Why don't you try something different?" he asked later that evening, when the sun's rays slanted into the kitchen, turning everything golden.

"When she wets herself, don't let her sit on your knee or the couch. Just make her sit on a hard chair. Tell her it's because she'll get you, or the couch, dirty. Maybe that way she'll learn not to do it."

Gertie looked at Mike, her eyes narrow.

"At least it'd be better than beating her," he added lamely.

"Oh! Maybe," Gertie finally said and then went back to washing the dishes, her mouth moving in the never-ending whisper.

Mike tried. When Ethel wanted to climb onto his lap, he asked quietly, "Did you wet your pants?" If she had, he made her sit on a hard wooden chair, with a newspaper on it. He never raised his voice. He just explained patiently that she would get his pants or the couch dirty. Ethel had sadly sat on the hard chair, her little face long and eyes wet. But in a couple days she climbed up onto Mike's knee, smiling and saying, "None wet!"

Mike hugged the child, again fighting back inexplicable tears. Gertie watched, her eyes hard and she exchanged glances with Vincent.

After that they both deliberately held Ethel whenever she wet herself, and once again the house was filled with the harsh sound of a palm striking bare flesh.

Mike began to intervene more and more. One evening as he watched TV, Vincent went into the bathroom. Gertie had gone to a neighbor's and they were alone with the children.

Suddenly the quiet was, shattered by a shout, followed by deathly silence. Mike was off the couch in one motion.

"Who left the water on?" Vincent yelled, just as Mike entered from the kitchen. Heather and Ethel stood side by side fear immobilizing them.

"Ethel did it," Heather lied suddenly.

"What!" Vincent bellowed coarsely. He bent and swung with an open hand. Ethel was propelled backwards, out of the bathroom and into the kitchen. She rolled and got to her feet, screaming in terror as she ran. Vincent's enraged face was horrible to behold, as he stood in the doorway, his heavy arm raised. He pointed an accusing finger.

"Darn you!" he yelled and took a step forward. Ethel's breath caught in her throat and she stood still, too terrified to breathe.

"What the hell's going on?" Mike demanded, stepping in front of her. He felt a familiar gut wrenching fear as a scene from the past sped by, but he stood his ground, his fists raised.

"She left the tap on," Vincent finally said.

"She's not even tall enough to reach it," Mike snarled.

Vincent said nothing. He just lowered his arm and turned back to the washroom. Mike's chest heaved and he gasped for air, for he had been ready to fight his father.

Vincent merely shut off the water and then went into the living room, through a different door. In a little while Mike heard his heavy snores from the couch.

Mike continued to experience a maelstrom of emotions, with suppressed memories and new experiences intertwining. He easily passed upgrading, wondering why grade ten math had been so hard just a few short years before. But that was the only area of progress. He was still immobilized by anxiety whenever a girl approached, and he would take a quick involuntary step backwards. Mike appeared aloof and cold while inside emotions seethed and he felt sick. The only exception was when he was drunk.

One thing definitely didn't change. On a Sunday morning, when he was home for the weekend, Gertie stood in his doorway.

"Come on Metro! Get up! You gotta go to church," Gertie yelled. The words were never "Will you go?" They were always "You gotta!"

"No!" Mike said from his bed as Gertie entered his bedroom.

That was the first time he had openly refused to attend Mass.

"Oh no!" Gertie wailed, turning and running into the living room. Mike heard her agitated voice while Tommy looked into the bedroom, his tiny face frightened.

"He won't to go to church! Vincent, do something!"

Vincent made a face and then yelled, "Come on Metro! Get up. See how you feel."

Mike knew that once he was up, they would insist he attend Mass.

"No! I'm twenty-four years old and I think I can decide for myself if I want to go to church or not. I'm not going."

"Gettup!" Gertie screamed, running into the bedroom. Her face was ashen white and her mouth, a thin compressed line.

"Come on! You gotta go!"

"Jesus Christ!" Mike swore and jumped from his bed.

"What the hell's the matter with you?" He hopped on one foot as he struggled to pull his pants on. "Why can't you be like other parents, for the love of God? Why can't you be normal?"

"Oh why can't you be like other children?" Gertie wailed and then bit her lip until it was white.

Mike hurriedly buttoned his shirt, his face angry and determined.

"No! I'm not going," he said slowly, emphatically, as he left the bedroom. Then he stood in the kitchen facing his parents, his fists clenched.

"Other kids go with their parents, so why can't you?" Gertie whined.

"I just don't believe in it, and you have no right to demand I do," Mike tried reason.

"Just like Walter!" Gertie screamed as a faint memory of Vincents cousin appeared. "He was like that. He didn't care if he never went to church."

Mikes stomach hurt while his skin was hot and clammy. He thought for a minute that he was in a nightmare. But Gertie's ashen, agitated face and Vincents enraged stance were real.

During this, the children stood close together in a corner by the door, maintaining a tense terrified silence. Gertie's or Vincent's rage could very quickly be turned on them.

"Sweet Jesus!" Mike swore softly, the words more a sigh than a curse. He looked at his father's contorting face and then his restraint broke a little.

"Go to hell! And leave me alone!"

"You say go to hell!" Vincent said slowly, his jaw trembling. "You're the one that's gonna go to hell if you don't go to church!"

"Just leave me alone," Mike finally said, sighing deeply.

"There's the door!" Vincent suddenly shouted, waving his arm toward the porch.

"Oh no! Vincent no!" Gertie interrupted, her face shaking with the words as tears streamed down her face. Then she turned to Mike.

"Youre just like Walter. Other children go with their parents, so come on now! You gotta go!" Her body shook and her face glistened.

Mike stared at his mother, as the nightmare unfolded and he felt totally numb.

They're crazy, he thought. They're both totally insane! Then he quickly suppressed the thought.

"Just go and leave me alone." He walked slowly back to the bedroom, his shoulders slumped. Gertie stood beside Vincent, her hands on her hips and her lips twitching. The children huddled closer together, their eyes round and bodies tense.

"So now! You wanted more children! See what we got now!" She turned on Vincent. The agitated words came to Mike in the bedroom and he bit his lip.

"I never wanted no more children!" Vincents voice came then, as Mike sat on the bed, a great weight on his shoulders. As the moments ticked by, the words "There's the door!" still echoed in his mind.

Finally he heard a door slam and then the truck motor roar to life. As Mike slumped on the bed, fighting the guilt, he hunched forward and clasped his hands together.

But what's the use, he thought finally? Then he slowly rose and packed his bag. He walked from the house telling his dog to stay and feeling the disappointment on Buster's face. Then he walked slowly to the road, changing the bag from hand to hand when it got too heavy. He had walked the road a thousand times, and he had sworn a thousand times that life would improve. Idly he wondered why he kept returning, like a moth to a flame.

Mike stayed away from the farm, studying in the tiny room he rented and passing the upgrading courses with ease. One day he received a letter and there was no mistaking the childish scrawl of his father. There was also a black and white photo inside. He stared at his parents and the children and the barely legible words were "Maybe you'd like a picture of us." Then he slowly deciphered his father's scribbling, telling him how the harvest was and how his dog missed him. He knew they must have spent an hour at the kitchen table, Gertie dictating and Vincent laboriously writing. He knew also, that the children would have stayed as far away as possible, for whenever a new task was before her, Gertie became agitated and unpredictable.

Mike went home the next weekend and volunteered to attend Mass. He even went to confession, making up a list of sins, for he had committed no evil. But he was once again doing what he was told. After the upgrading course, he continued going to the Employment Office and was told over and over that "Sorry, the course's full." But he kept coming back, until he became familiar to the counselors, and they tired of telling him to come back in a few months.

Finally, after two more years of wandering and dreaming, Mike at twenty-six, was accepted into a ten-month commercial art course. During that time, he was a lumber jack, farm laborer and horse wrangler on a ranch in the Cariboo Country of British Columbia. There he had lived alone in a tiny log cabin, experiencing an alien peace among the animals. But always, a small unease would surface in his consciousness and he would try again to write or paint.

Then, when he had been told he was enrolled in the course and when the crows flocked and grass once again turned brown, he sat on the couch on the farm and sketched. He had a few days before he would again pack his bag and hitchhike eastward. As he sketched, his mind wandered off into a daydream where he sold his first story. Then he sold another, until he owned a new car and good clothes. And in the dream, his parents no longer demanded he go to church.

At times the grim reality would break through the curtain of dreams and he would be painfully aware of his circumstances. Hate is a good thing, he would think wonderingly, as he sketched. It can be very useful because it doesn't let you give up. Then suddenly he became aware, of a different and destructive hate which needs only an easy target.

Tommy had been playing on the floor near the stove and had rolled into some spilled water. Gertie stopped in one of her sudden dashes about the kitchen and looked down.

"What the heck are you doing?" She bent and grasped the child under the arms. "You shouldn't be playing on the floor!" She stooped suddenly and felt Tommy's shirt and pants.

"What! Are you wet?"

Tommy's face went deathly white.

"Oh no! You're all wet! You peed in your pants!" The words came in a torrent and Tommy went rigid, tears flowing freely down his ashen face.

Gertie yanked him to his feet and carried him to the basin, where she began stripping his clothes.

"Here!" she snarled, yanking down his underwear, away from his tiny hands. Exposed and vulnerable, he desperately tried covering himself with his tiny hands. Gertie dumped ice cold water in the basin and grabbed a washcloth. She washed roughly while Tommy's terrorized screams intensified.

Mike threw aside his pencil and paper and ran into the kitchen. He stopped dead in sudden confusion, gazing in horror as he felt Tommy's pain, in a different time, when he had stood naked and exposed in a different basin.

As Gertie washed, she quickly worked herself into a righteous rage.

"Dirty! Stinky! Lazy boy! Piss and shit in your pants!" As the words tumbled forth she began flailing with her hands and Tommy cringed, keeping his tiny hands over his genitals. As Gertie's hands flailed and the harsh sound of palm on flesh mingled with the screams, the anger slowly cooled and she tired. Then she began washing again, the cold water and her rough hands making the child gasp.

Then quickly, her rage gained momentum and she began flailing, while Tommy's screams rose again.

"Lazy boy! Dirty! Stinky lazy! Piss and shit in your clothes." Gertie's voice rose in a singsong in time with the blows and her whole body shook.

In a corner, near the door Heather and Ethel stood transfixed, their eyes round, and faces white, their breaths caught in their throats.

The hate came at Mike in waves and his stomach tied in a painful knot. He violently shook his head and then stepped forward, between his mother and the child, grabbing her by the shoulders and shoving. His skin was clammy and damp and he thought he would throw up.

"That's enough!" he yelled. "What the hell's the matter with you? Are you insane?"

The wild, familiar light slowly faded as Gertie gazed into his eyes. They stood like that for a brief time as Tommy whimpered and cowered in the sink, his tiny hands still covering his genitals. Ethel and Heather remained by the door, their faces, white and their bodies rigid. The silence deepened, as a soft snore came from the couch where Vincent lay. Again Mike saw evidence he couldn't believe.

Then slowly, her face white and mouth thin, Gertie began dressing the child, all the while muttering.

"There. There. Mommy didn't want to lick you. But you gotta learn, not to pee in your pants." Tommy shivered and his chest heaved, as the sobs slowly subsided. Mike looked from him to the floor where the water had been spilled, and then slowly he walked back to the living room and began sketching, while he tried to find the dream where he drove a new car and wore expensive clothes.

Mike gazed down at Tommy and Ethel just outside the old house. Their eyes were solemn for they sensed something of importance was to occur. Mike's throat, was constricted and dry as he looked about the yard and at his dog, before gazing out at the driveway leading to a community college and Art course. He glanced at his father, who contorted his face as he waited in the truck.

Mike looked quickly through the window at Gertie who bustled about the kitchen. He had said goodbye to her so she stayed in the house, preparing dinner. Heather had started school so only Tommy and Ethel were left. Mike suddenly remembered the insane light in his mother's eyes. Then he swallowed and wondered how to say goodbye to the two children.

He knelt then and put his arms about them.

"Ethel! Tommy! I got to go now." He held the children tightly and then added, a mist in his eyes, "I won't be back for a long time."

His dog whined and he freed a hand to pet him. Then he turned back to the children.

"You be good now. Don't be bad and mind so you don't get beaten."

Tommy suddenly gazed into Mike's eyes.

"You go far away?" he asked haltingly.

"Yeah I gotta go. I don't have a choice."

Ethel put her tiny arm around Mike's neck. She was too young to fully understand, still she sensed the sadness.

"Are you going to be good?" Mike asked Tommy, not wanting to let go just yet.

"No!" Tommy fought a losing battle with his tears, his face glistening.

"No! I not good!"

Mike held the children, as the seconds ticked by and his dog shoved his nose under his arm. Then slowly, he straightened and released the children. They stood close together gazing upwards at one more adult, who had appeared suddenly in their short lives, and who was leaving just as suddenly.

Mike turned quickly and climbed into the truck, slamming the door. Vincent looked at him, at the moisture in his eyes and then turned to the road.

"Nice day!" he said, contorting his face for the millionth time.

"Never mind the Goddamn weather! Just drive!" Mike snapped.

# Forty-one

A hot, relentless sun burnt down from an azure sky as heat rose in shimmering waves from the grey concrete. Even the pigeons sought shade for the mercury rose above one hundred degrees Fahrenheit. And on the grey blistering sidewalk, with sweat burning his eyes, stood Mike. Streets stretched in four directions away from the downtown core, the oldest part of the city and where the winos staggered.

Mike used his hand to shade his eyes from the shimmering glare as he watched the light change from red to green. He was slow in moving, for he had all day to make the endless round of bars asking the endless question, "Need any waiters?"

"No! Not right now," the same answer would come from a sweating bartender.

"Think you might need someone in a few days?" Mike would ask.

"No! We don't need nobody."

Mike would then wander to the next bar. He craved a cigarette more than food and the churning in his stomach came from more than just anxiety. He had been in a place like this before, rundown hotels, seedy rooming houses and countless hookers. And always there were lonely men blowing their cash with the hookers paying special attention until they were broke. The city was Calgary, not Edmonton, but the faces were the same. The same sad, desperate fear was there too, for he was broke and owed a day's rent on his room.

Mike thought of the old joke: Two weeks 'til payday and no job yet. The joke had no humor for deep within the recesses of his soul was the failure of the art course. Maybe that was why he was turned down in the bars, for nobody wants a loser.

He had lasted six months. Instead of learning landscaping or anatomy, there was only hand lettering and the course had been a kaleidoscope of young men in long hair and sandals and girls who refused to wear underwear. Mike had at first contemptuously called them Hippies but once he had known them, he had felt ashamed for having called them names. The confusion had deepened and he had quit, silently stealing away with one more defeat sinking down to the depths of his soul. So he had headed west on a Greyhound bus with the vague plan of seeing the Calgary Stampede.

Maybe if I check the Carlton again, Mike thought as he crossed the street, squinting against the sun. He nearly bumped into a wino who staggered and cursed. Mike ignored him. Maybe they'll need someone, even for a few hours, he thought. But he had been there only the day before.

He felt the dime and nickel in his pants pocket, just enough for one draft beer. He wondered about the confidence that even a little money can give, but it was the desperate, forced confidence of someone who won't admit he is on a slow slide to oblivion. Mike saw evidence of the slide every time he passed a wino.

As he turned to enter the hotel, he pulled his light jacket closer about him, even though he was sweating. His shirt was torn and dirty and he hoped the bar manager wouldn't notice the wrinkled pants and worn dusty shoes.

He walked slowly by the round tables, occupied by old men in dirty unpressed, shiny trousers and patched shirts. It was early afternoon and the pensioners crowded into the bar, counting their change for their daily one or two beer. Mike passed the last table as he felt the hard stone floor through his thin shoes. It would be hard on the feet to work here, he worried. But the worry was a wistful dream. He glanced into the mixed part of the bar, where men and women sat, for in nineteen-seventy-one some establishments still maintained the men only Beer Parlor. The men's part had a stone floor and there was the faint smell of urine, while the mixed section had a stained, worn rug and the Terri cloth on the tables wasn't quite as patched or dirty.

As Mike reached the bar, the washer made a squeaking, irritating noise as the glasses passed slowly through the scalding water. He waited, his eyes downcast until the bar manager, a red-haired Italian, finished drawing ten draft. Danny looked up from the glasses and saw a drifter who needed work badly. He had seen many before, for if this wasn't the worse bar in town, it didn't have far to go.

"Yeah! Can I help you?" he demanded.

"Do you," Mike began slowly, "do you need any waiters?"

Danny gazed at the young man, his eyes squinting slightly. He didn't see any difference from the other men who came and went in the endless cycle.

"I've got experience," Mike blurted suddenly, a stubborn, desperate light in his eyes. "I worked in a bar where we sold hard liquor. If I can handle that, I sure as hell can handle draft and bottles."

"Where'd you work?" Danny demanded, removing the plastic wrapper from a sandwich and biting into it. Mike desperately tried to keep his eyes from the food but Danny noticed for he had seen that look too.

"In Brandon. In the Beaubier Hotel."

Danny put the sandwich down and looked at his schedule.

"Well, looks like you in luck." He grinned suddenly, brushing back stiff red hair and displaying brown, tobacco stained teeth.

"Don no feel so good today. You can work his shift."

Mike felt a weight lift from his shoulders.

"It's only four hours," Danny added quickly.

Mike thought quickly. Four hours times two and a quarter an hour came to nine dollars. That wasn't counting tips and he felt his mouth curl in a faint smile.

"When do I start?"

"Let's see, come back at four," Danny said. Then he wiped his hands on a dirty towel and turned to draw more draft, as a waiter approached with a tray load of empty glasses.

Mike nearly ran back to his room, where he smoked a short butt he had left that morning. Then he sat on the squeaking cot and gazed at the peeling wallpaper.

Maybe if I can get on full time, maybe I can stay at the hotel he mused as he blew a lung full of smoke heavenwards.

Then as he lay back on the lumpy mattress he pondered the past two years. In two weeks he would be twenty-seven and all he had to show for his struggle was more yearning and wistful dreams. But he would think of that later. He glanced at the ticking alarm clock on the scarred dresser and then closed his eyes and catnapped until the alarm woke him.

He was up in one motion and out of the rooming house walking rapidly for it was ten blocks to work. As he passed the Empire hotel, a place that was lower than the Carlton, he stopped suddenly. Two drunks staggered out the rear door to the gravel parking lot where they squared off. One threw a slow, overhand haymaker and the other charged forward and grappled, throwing him to the ground. He tried kicking him in the face but missed and his shoe sailed ten feet into the air. A crowd of pimps and hookers laughed uproariously at the two drunks who couldn't even fight properly.

That evening Mike carried trays of draft beer to the men gathered about the tables in the Men's section. There were no tips for most could barely afford the beer. He could feel the hard stone floor through his worn shoes and his feet ached. He had worn the same socks for five days and the encrusted dirt grated against his wet and sticky feet. He had been given a ten-dollar float and he immediately bought cigarettes and a sandwich from the tray on the bar. He forced himself to chew slowly and then smoked a cigarette, as he eased one foot and then the other. Danny noticed but said nothing.

Slowly the bar filled but Mike didn't take orders. Instead he filled his tray with twenty drafts and ran from table to table. At each table, he put the glasses down and picked the money up, careful to drop the nickels and dimes into the changer on his belt. Then he moved on. The job took no intelligence, except the ability to count and to carry the twenty-pound tray. It wasn't long before Mike felt his arm grow leaden and tired.

As the evening wore on the customers faded into the night and finally he stood by the bar with little to do. The men who had stopped in after work had all gone home and the pensioners had spent their daily quota of thirty or forty-five cents. Mike laid his tray on the bar and again shifted his weight from one foot to the other. Blisters had broken and his socks stuck to his feet. To pass the time, he thought of the bar's simple rules. As long as a customer was dressed so clothes covered him, he was allowed in, just as long as he had money: But no Hippies, no long hair, or sandals or men without shirts. Danny had been specific.

"You smell some a ting funny! It gotta be dope! Kick dose bastards the hell outta here! And if dose damn faggots come in from across da street, make sure dey know dey not welcome."

When Mike had seen two men in fancy red shirts and tight white slacks sitting in a corner, he had made them wait twenty minutes. When he had finally got to the table, he spilled draft on one of them. It didn't take long for them to leave.

Danny had smiled from behind the bar.

"You catch on pretty good. Maybe there be a steady job for you yet."

"I sure as hell hope so," Mike answered and Danny turned back to the tap.

Then as the evening stretched into night, a huge hulking man in filthy, baggy pants and a dirty shirt walked ponderously in. He was at least six feet tall and about two hundred and fifty pounds, while his face was florid and fleshy. He didn't stop at a table but walked right up to the bar.

"You dirty bastard dago!" he yelled and Danny stiffened.

"Take off! You sonna bitch!" Danny yelled and Mike quickly put his tray down.

"You gonna make me! You Goddamn spaghetti bender!" the man yelled, his fists ready. Mike took a deep breath, his stomach knotting and his mouth, dry.

Danny ran around the bar and tackled the man. As the man cocked his arm for a mighty haymaker, Mike caught his forearm and hung on. Then he grabbed him around the neck with his other arm and Danny did the same from the other side. Neither said anything, saving their breath for the fight. Together they ran the man to the rear door, knocking over a table. But he grabbed the door frame with two ham-like hands and hung on grimly. Mike drove his fist into an elbow and Danny hit him in the back with his shoulder. The man tumbled head over heels into the alley, his baggy trousers coming undone and tripping him. He landed face first in the gravel, rolling about and cursing wildly for a few seconds. Then he sat upright and tried to pull up his trousers with his left hand while shaking an enraged right fist at Danny and Mike. Just then a taxi whipped down the back alley. The driver slammed on the brakes, skidding to a halt a couple feet from the man and spraying him with gravel. Then he slowly drove around, grinning from his window.

The man pulled up his pants and charged at Danny like an enraged bear. Mike stepped in between and hit him with a perfect right cross to the nose. Blood splattered across his face in two streams and the man staggered backwards. Then he turned and disappeared into the shadows of the alley. Mike slammed the door and he and Danny went back to the bar. Mike let the air slowly from his lungs and controlled his rapid breathing, marveling at the strength a sandwich can give.

"You jump to fight real good, eh!" Danny said, grinning from behind the bar.

"You needed help." Mike shrugged his shoulders.

Danny turned then and looked at the schedule on the wall behind the bar

"Ya know, maybe we need a waiter. But you gotta work straight nights."

"No problem!" Mike said quickly and looked away, embarrassed at his relief. Danny noticed but said nothing. Anybody could be out of work.

Later Mike helped clean tables and then counted the money in his float. He had made only thirty-five cents in tips and he was short.

"You got money in your wallet?" Danny asked.

"No."

"No problem! We just take from your pay."

Mike nodded and then took a deep breath.

"You think I could stay here in the hotel?" he asked haltingly.

"Sure! Why not? They just take from your pay. I tink its twenty-five bucks a week for staff. And you get half price on meals."

Again Mike nearly ran to the rooming house to get his suitcase. He resolved to never back down from a fight in the bar, no matter who it was. Sleeping on the streets was a lot worse than a bloody nose.

The days once again spread into weeks with Mike rising at noon and starting work at four. The endless customers told the endless tired jokes, discussing the endless vitally important matters: sports, politics and women. The easy answers to all problems were there too. If a man lost his job, it was the government's fault, or if the world was going to the dogs, it was the hippies.

Mike carried trays of draft beer to thirsty men and women who didn't care what he thought or who he was, just as long as the beer kept coming. He worked right through the Stampede, perspiring freely in the oppressive heat of mid-July, for he and the other waiters were kept constantly on the run. At times the beer became warm and flat.

It was a time of abandon for all manner of men and women. There were cowboys with wide brimmed hats and high heeled boots and men from up north in town, for booze and hookers. There were also educated young women who came to see the stampede in the daytime and to find entertainment of a different sort at night. There were men who asked, "Where can I find a woman?" and Mike would answer, "Down the street to the Vic's." Business was so good the hookers were content to wait for the tricks in the beer parlor of the Victoria Hotel.

Mike kept his section clear of the homosexuals who occasionally tested the climate. He also kept it clear of long, haired hippies, except for the hippie girls in hot pants who sold long stemmed roses for a dollar a piece. Nobody cared if they were hippies, just as long as their legs were long and curvy and nobody cared either if the roses were stolen from a mall.

On Mike's first day, he had ordered fourteen drafts, laying two dollars and ten cents on the bar. When Danny had drawn fifteen, he had shrugged and placed another dime and nickel on the counter.

"Never mind," Danny had grinned, pushing the money back across the counter.

"Just make sure you stand behind the pillar. It don't look so good if you drink in the open."

After that Mike would disappear behind a pillar with a full tray of twenty drafts. When he appeared in a few seconds there would be nineteen full glasses and one empty, with traces of foam on his lips. Patrons would buy him a beer just to see how fast he could drink it.

There were evenings he couldn't remember but Danny never mentioned them the next day, so he assumed he had worked his shift without mishap. But he had to come down to the bar at least an hour before his shift began, so he could drink himself into a proper mood.

When he began working the day shift, eleven a.m. to seven p.m., he overslept just making it down in time to open the doors. Immediately a customer entered and held up two fingers. Mike shakily carried the tray to the man who sat near the door. The trembling was so bad, he spilled the beer on the man's pants.

"Oh for Christ's sake!" he swore. "Wait! I'll get you two more and you don't have to pay for it."

"Don't do that," the man grinned. "Here! Get me two more and two for yourself. You look like you need it more then me." This time Mike carried the tray with two trembling hands. He carefully set it down and then downed the two beers before the man had a chance to wet his throat.

"Can't stand to see a fella hung over that bad," the man laughed.

Mike laughed too. Being hung over was always a joke, for who wanted to admit what he was doing to his body.

There were times however when thoughts of art and writing would appear unbidden. When he was alone in his room with a six pack of beer and time to kill, he tried sketching again. At other times he read, buying secondhand paperbacks from a pawn shop. The dream hadn't died but it had become foggy and unreal, blurred by the beer and kaleidoscope of the bar.

Mike knew he was only one step from the winos who sold cartons of cigarettes for half price in the bar. He saw how they staggered to the back alley and threw up from too much wine or rubbing alcohol. In his sober moments, in the morning when he hadn't yet had a chance to obscure his vision and reasoning, the question was how long will it take?

One night after the rodeo, Mike, Danny and another waiter, with four cases of beer played poker in a tiny room. The cards and money were on the narrow bed for there was no table. There was enough beer for the night and two each on Sunday morning, before they looked for a lounge that was open. As Adam dealt the cards, Mike sat holding a bottle, musing out loud.

"This ain't much of a life, is it?"

"What'a ya want?" Danny snapped, picking up his cards and then throwing them down. "Shit for luck. I never get no cards."

"Well, all there seems to be here is booze."

"What the hell more ya want?" Adam demanded. Then he too threw down his cards.

"Well, I'm still young enough to still have ambition. I mean, I want something out of life, not just an existence."

"Shit! You got a room. All ya wanna eat and drink," Danny snapped his face red. "And you could get all the fookin you wanted too, ya know."

"There's more to life than that. I think I'm gonna see if I can get back into the art course."

"What if you can't?" Adam demanded.

"Well, I heard they're accepting mature students now in the university."

"What's a mature student?" Danny asked.

"People who don't have grade twelve," Mike answered.

"Bullshit!" Adam yelled, his face suddenly white. "Once you quit school, that's it. You're finished."

Mike stared at Adam's sudden anger. He looked out the window at the bright neon lights flashing on and off. Then he looked back at Adam.

"If you really want to, you can start again," he said quietly.

"Bullshit!" Adam yelled drunkenly. "I can't go to college and neither can you. Besides, who'd want to? It's full of dirty hippies anyway."

"How do you know there's dirty hippies?" Mike asked.

"Jesus H. Christ!" Adam screamed. "Who the fuck do ya think you are? You're no Goddamn better then me."

Mike stared at Adam, puzzled at why a dream could cause so much anger.

"You got steady job," Danny interrupted patiently. "And you're not scared to jump to fight." He was in his forties and had developed patience over the years.

"Why in hell you wanna leave?"

"I got talent," Mike said slowly, his stomach hurting.

"You can shit on your talent!" Adam yelled and grinned at Danny.

"I'll show you," Mike said quickly and rose. He was back in a minute with a sketch he had done of a Mongol Warrior. He had taken special care in expressing the wild savagery of the face. Adam stared at the sketch drunkenly.

"This is what I think of that shit," he snapped and threw the picture on the floor.

Mike stared at Adam. Then he picked up the sketch and left with a case of beer. When he was gone Adam, grinned.

"I sure in hell told him, eh? Christ! He's no Goddamn better than me!"

"You don't think he quit, do you?" Danny asked suddenly.

"Nah, he'll be getting drunk in this hotel as long as there's beer," Adam laughed and then added, "Jesus! My feet were killing me tonight!"

Next door Mike tried sketching but he was too drunk. Then, as he lay on his cot staring at the ceiling, a spark of anger began to burn brightly.

No Goddamn way! I'm not going to end up like Adam, just an old drunk who's grateful for a room and booze.

After that Mike constantly told himself that he would quit before it was too late. But he stayed in the netherworld of grey, drunken nights where all else, except the bottle, was of no importance. The dream made his sober hours miserable but he only drank more with the days and nights blurring. Then as always, there appeared a catalyst that broke him out of the drunken lethargy.

One evening, after he had worked his shift, he sat at a table with a woman in her early thirties and a large Paratrooper, sergeant with a brush cut. The woman appeared to like Mike and moved her chair imperceptibly closer while the sergeant's eyes narrowed.

Suddenly he sprang to his feet, knocking his chair backwards.

"Why you're nothing but a Goddamn son-a-bitching ass-hole!" he screamed. Red veins stood out against his neck and his face was white. Mike tensed, his legs coiled under his chair and his stomach knotting.

Suddenly, the sergeant swung, his open palm catching Mike flush on his left cheek. He heard the loud smack as his head rocked back and his glasses sailed across the room. His feet hit the floor and he exploded out of his chair in a football crouch with his head down. He charged forward, his legs pumping frantically and the sergeant was propelled backwards. Mike drove him over two tables, upsetting beer glasses and scattering patrons in every direction. The glasses shattered and the sergeant fell on them, his back cut in countless, deep places.

Blood sprayed from the cuts and Mike's hands became slippery and red as he held the man by the throat. The sergeant twisted and turned, trying desperately to evade the beating.

"You wanna fight! You son-of-a-bitch!" Mike yelled. He drew his right arm back but then something stopped him. He paused for a second, poised over the helpless sergeant who twisted and turned on the bloody floor.

"Mike! Mike!" Danny suddenly yelled and he and Adam pulled him from the sergeant. When they did, Adam's shoe slammed into the sergeants face and his rage grew. He was on his feet in an instant and charging forward like a demented bull. He tossed Adam and Danny aside, and grabbed for Mike. But Mike ducked a blow and lowered his head, catching the man in the stomach as once again he drove forward, his legs churning. The sergeant went down on the broken glass, the blood spraying and soaking Mike's hair. He heard a ripping sound as his shirt was torn off and he felt the sergeant's blood on his face. And again he held the man by the throat with his right hand cocked and ready. But he couldn't deliver the blow. The sergeant turned his head sideways and closed his eyes, waiting for the beating.

"Mike! Mike!" Danny yelled again and Mike stood dazed and confused. He looked down at the sergeant, who lay on the floor and broken glass, smeared with his own gore.

Danny gazed at Mike for an instant as two huge police officers walked directly toward them.

"Wanna lay charges?" one of them asked.

"Charges?" Mike asked, shaking his head and brushing his bloody hair back with a bloody hand.

"He hit you first didn't he?"

"No," Mike said slowly. He stared as two ambulance attendants carried the sergeant out the back door on a stretcher. He had lost so much blood he had fainted.

When Mike finished his shift that night, he washed the blood from his hair and discarded his bloodied and torn shirt. Then, alone in his room he lay awake, puzzling over why he couldn't hit the sergeant when he had him down, and helpless.

Later in the week Mike was tipped off that the sergeant planned to get even. Mike told Danny, who smiled grimly.

"Not to worry! I just call my friends and relatives."

That evening the bar was filled with determined Italians, and Mike knew the cold fear he had felt as an ironworker. But the danger from falling was impersonal. What he faced now was the anticipated insanity of all-out violence. His stomach churned and he threw up in the bathroom, ashamed to tell anyone. He stayed sober for a week, waiting for the sergeant and his friends but they never showed up. Maybe they too were warned of what to expect.

The fight and fear afterwards, along with the week of enforced sobriety, made Mike pack his suitcase and catch a Greyhound Bus to Brandon. He had no job to go to, not even a place to stay.

Still it was better than what he was leaving behind.

# Forty-two

Once again heat rose in shimmering waves from the grey sidewalk, while a blistering sun burnt down from a cloudless sky. Mike waited for a light to change, as the hard concrete bore up through his thin shoes and his socks grated against his feet. He had left Calgary but he couldn't leave the knot in his stomach and fear in his heart.

The rumor had been fact and the university was indeed accepting mature students who didn't have grade twelve. But that caused more anxiety, for it gave his dream a physical property and with it the reality of failure.

He wondered how he would pay the tuition but that was something he would deal with later, for at the moment he had a more pressing problem. He needed to find a place to live. He felt the five-dollar bill in his pocket and a faint smile came to his mouth when he remembered the night before.

He had sat in a bar, a small anxiety steadily growing into a full-blown fear. He had no money and no place to stay. But then from out of the smoky haze a woman had joined him. She was forty with sagging breasts and a protruding belly, and her eyes tired and slightly desperate. To her, Mike had been a chance, at least for one brief night to help keep the fear of aging at bay. She had invited him to her place and Mike had quickly agreed. Then, a man with balding grey hair and a beer belly had joined them. He had boasted about his Cadillac and had shown Mike and the woman a trunk full of beer and rye. Next the three of them had ridden, crammed into the front seat, to a two-bedroom house with peeling paint and tangled weeds on either side of a cracked front walk.

Once they had sat on a tired old sofa with a worn, patched cover Mike had looked about the room at the peeling wallpaper and used furniture. Then he had gazed at the woman for an instant, avoiding her eyes and then at the man who had placed a beefy hand on her knee. The woman had smiled, her make-up smeared as she held a glass of rye and coke in one hand and had then brushed Mike's knee with the other. Mike had wondered desperately if he could sleep on the couch. Then the man had risen suddenly and turned toward the kitchen.

"Come mere! I wanna talk to you," he had said to Mike over his shoulder.

Mike had rose tense, and ready.

"How much ya want?" the man had demanded when they were in the kitchen.

"Huh!" Mike had been surprised.

"How much ya want for me to buy ya out?"

"Buy me out!" Mike had stared at the man.

"Here!" The man had suddenly pulled out a leather wallet.

"I'll give ya five bucks if you'll take off," he had added and then had grinned, nodding toward the woman who still sat on the sofa in the living room.

"Okay!" Mike had said, as he grabbed the five-dollar bill from the man.

"She's all yours," he had said.

When the man had grinned back, Mike had wished he had held out for more. Then as he had left, he had marveled how a woman who filled him with revulsion could fill the man with such anticipation. Then he had walked hurriedly away from the old house, the five dollars tucked securely in his pants pocket. In nineteen seventy-two, five bucks could still buy a lot of things.

Mike shrugged the memory away, as he looked at a run down rooming-house, with a sign "Rooms" in the window. He ground out a cigarette on the sidewalk for he had bought a pack from the five dollars that morning.

The landlady was in her late sixties and a little strange, her head bobbing up and down as she hopped about. Mike looked about the tiny kitchen and into the lonely living room with the black and white TV and ancient bric-a-brac.

"Now I don't want no tough customers," the woman whined suddenly, her face twitching. "Only men who are clean and quiet."

"All I want is a room where I can be left alone," Mike said.

The woman stared at him for a moment.

"That'll be ten bucks, in advance," she said suddenly.

"All I got is two bucks," he lied meeting her eyes. She was the first to look away.

"But I got a job," He added, holding out two, one dollar bills.

"Okay!" The landlady grabbed the money quickly and crunched it in her clawlike hand. Then she paused and stared at Mike again.

"But you'll have to get a socket for the lamp. Otherwise, there's no light."

"How much is that?"

"Two dollars."

"I need the two dollars then." Mike held out his hand, again meeting her eyes. Again she was the first to look away.

"Well, okay. Since it's for the room," she finally said. Mike stuffed the money into his pants pocket, along with the other two dollar bills he had. Lying was something he was never comfortable with, but honesty had always been a poor substitute for food. The landlady held out two keys then, one for the front door and one for his room and Mike took them and left. He would wait until he got paid before he would buy the socket. He didn't need a light, just to sleep. But he was to begin work in a couple hours and as he ran his hand nervously over his chin he felt the two-day-old stubble. He walked rapidly towards a sign that read "Salvation Army Thrift Store" and entered, as a middle-aged woman looked up from behind a counter.

"Got any used razors?" Mike asked.

"On the table."

There were all kinds of shaving gear strewn about, even an ancient straight razor. Mike picked up a packet of blades, the paper wrappings, brown with age. Then he pulled his old safety razor from his shirt pocket.

"Can I use the bathroom, to try them out?"

The woman stared at Mike.

"Well, how do I know if they're any good?" he demanded.

The woman nodded toward a door barely discernible in the store's gloom. Inside, it had a bare light bulb hanging from a cord and it took Mike a minute to find the string. Then he locked the door and let the hot water run for a couple of minutes before lathering his face as best he could with a hard bar of soap. It took him a few minutes to shave for the blade hurt his face but there were only a few nicks and the stubble was gone. He opened the door quickly and walked to the table with the razors. He glanced at the woman who hadn't moved from behind the counter.

"I don't want them," he said tossing and open package of blades back onto the table. The woman opened her mouth but Mike was out the door before she had a chance to speak.

That night, he took ten dollars from his float and hid it in his wallet. At the end of the shift he claimed he had made a mistake and it would have to be deducted from his wages. It was enough for meals and cigarettes for two days.

As Mike walked to his room, he mused how some day he would laugh at what he had done. But when he lay on his cot in the darkness, sleep was a far way off. All he had to do was register at the university, but with that thought came the sudden painful, knot in his stomach.

The next night, a waitress twenty years older than he and someone who had known the battle with the bottle, talked casually while they stood at the bar.

"You know booze kills brain cells."

"Oh! Really! Come on." Mike laughed in disbelief.

"Really! Believe me I know," she insisted. Mike remembered how drunk she had been the night before.

"I've sobered up ten times, but I guess one of these times I just won't bother," she said quietly, looking deep into Mike's eyes. "But if I was twenty years younger..."

Mike quickly looked away.

"Every time you get drunk your brain cells die and there's no way you can ever replace them," she added.

Mike tried not to think of what she had said, but he quit drinking the next night. He did it in the manner he lived, suddenly, on a whim and not really knowing why. A week later he was in the bar with a bottle of beer in front of him. As he was tipping it to his lips, his eyes met those of the waitress. They were not condemning, they just said, "I know what it's like, believe me."

Mike sat the bottle down hard and left the bar. After that he bore the thirst and trembling in his hands, like a frightened desperate animal. While he held the booze at bay, he still carried trays of liquor and beer. The smell assailed his nostrils, making his head dizzy and one day he threw up in the bathroom. The next his nose bled but he stuck to it grimly.

Then one morning, after a sleepless night, he walked from the downtown rundown bar to the university. His stomach churned and all the reasons why he should turn and flee crowded into his mind. He was too old, had been out of school too long and had only a grade nine, with upgrading to ten. The anxiety was so great, he thought he would vomit and he stopped at a light for a moment, breathing deeply, forcing air into his lungs. A voice deep in his soul stridently urged him to flee, back to the hotel and to the booze. Then the familiar shadowy image of a donkey, blindfolded and hitched to a pole, circling a well for eternity flashed by and he forced his feet to walk.

Finally Mike entered the registrars office and waited, his hands sweaty and his head and stomach aching.

"Okay!" A man finally stuck his head out of a door.

"What education do you have?" he asked when they were seated in his office.

"Uh, grade nine," Mike replied, the roof of his mouth sticky. He couldn't keep from leaning forward in his chair and clenching his hands. "But I took an upgrading course once. It was for grade ten."

"Oh! Well, you'll have to write a short biography of yourself, your work history and education," the man said glancing at Mike's hands and how he crouched forward in his chair. The university had built new facilities, anticipating the enrolment to continue increasing. But the expected five thousand full time students had only become one thousand so mature students could now enrol.

Mike was given his first break because of an error in planning and the written history was the only obstacle the man could place in front of him.

Mike nearly ran to his dingy room with the cracked molding and dirty wallpaper. He set a rented typewriter on the table and began typing furiously. Within twenty-four hours the man in the registrar's office read his history, noticing the typos and misspelled words. But there was something to the story and he passed it around to the secretaries. When Mike phoned the following Monday he was informed he could enrol. The university needed students as badly as he needed an education.

Mike walked down the same streets as before, under the same trees and on the same concrete, but his step was immeasurably lighter. He was just as short of money and his clothes just as worn but he was a university student. At times when he woke at night, he would lay staring at the ceiling and he had to reassure himself over and over that it was real and that he was indeed in a Psychology class. It seemed strange that no one noticed that he was twenty-eight years old and that he had been out of school for ten years.

Beside Mike walked Al, who was two years younger and nearly a hundred pounds lighter. Al walked in a quick manner, his body leaning slightly forward, as if he was about to break into a sprint. They had worked in the same bar and when Mike had told him he had enrolled, Al had enrolled also. While Mike was consumed by the knot of worry in his stomach, Al exuded the confidence of someone who meets life head on, with a forced sense of self-assurance.

"God!" Mike mused out loud, as they approached the academic building. "I hope I can pass."

"What the hell you worrying about? If these eighteen year olds can do it, we sure the hell can."

"Well, I don't know," Mike said slowly but Al interrupted him impatiently.

"The trouble with you is you don't got no confidence," he snapped, keeping pace with his quick walk. As they turned down another street, the student residence could be seen, framed by two rows of trees with golden, red leaves.

"Yeah," Mike answered. He glanced at Al whose moustache and large head were thrust forward, as if he meant to meet the challenge of college in a physical way. When Al had found out where Mike was living, he had immediately offered him a place to stay. When Mike had told him that he had no money, Al had only shrugged.

"Just give me what you can," he had said and Mike had thought himself lucky to find such a good friend.

When they were seated in registrars office, waiting for their class schedules, Mike turned to Al.

"They lost that biography I wrote," he said quietly. "Then yesterday one of the secretaries said they had found it. They were passing it around so they all could read it."

"Aw, they don't know what the hell they're doing," Al snapped and Mike changed the subject.

"I don't understand this," he began looking at the course schedule. The anxiety was so intense that only a small part of his mind was able to concentrate.

"Gimmee that!" Al grabbed the schedule. "Look! I'll explain it, so even you can understand." He rustled the paper, reading off the course titles.

"Intro-Psyche! Right! Well, it's from ten-thirty to eleven-twenty on Monday, Wednesday and Thursday. Religion's on the same days only at eight-thirty and Representative English Works is on Tuesday, Thursday and Friday. What the hell's so hard about that?"

Mike took the schedule, saying nothing. Al had also corrected him for mispronouncing registrar and he had mocked the way Mike dressed but Mike felt no anger, only embarrassment.

He worked in the bar until two in the morning and when he had an eight-thirty class, he struggled to stay awake. At home he studied long hard hours in the sparse kitchen of the basement suite they shared. Al had demanded to know why he was taking Psychology since he had more problems than anyone he had known. Mike had shrugged off the question but when the results of the first exam were announced in class, he nearly quit. He had scored 58 percent on a multiple choice test, and he spent the entire weekend alternating between grim determination and wanting to flee back into the bottle.

The following Monday, the professor announced that he had purposely marked hard to discourage those who wanted to take Psychology as a filler. The highest mark had been sixty-two and Mike spent the rest of the day between nervous relief and fighting the urge to vomit.

The golden days of autumn passed quickly. At times they played with an old football in an empty lot, at others they argued over politics in the cafeteria with other students. Mike was caught between a burning desire to be heard and a near emotional paralysis, leaving him in a constant state of anxiety. When alone he concentrated on his courses, reading Chaucer's Canterbury Tales and saw reality in the corruption of the church. He felt compassion for the Prioress; a nun who appeared unhappy in the convent and a fleeting memory of his sister came quickly. He read John Milton's Paradise Lost, empathizing with Satan's will to never yield.

The course in Introductory Psychology was a matter of applying new terminology to past experiences. When he read about superstitious behavior and how it's reinforced, he immediately thought of his mother.

One time, when he walked home in the autumn evening, his mind filled with new concepts, he suddenly stopped for he had walked right past the house where he lived. He was embarrassed that he had been so preoccupied, and he said nothing to Al.

Then one day, an English essay came back with the words "What source?" scrawled in red ink all over the paper. Mike turned to Al who condescendingly explained what footnoting was. After that Mike spent hours of frustration, trying desperately to fetter his creative mind into the straight-jacket of formal essay writing.

Next day when they sat in the cafeteria, Mike's English professor walked by.

"Hey! You wanna coffee with us?" Al called and Mike's stomach twisted and knotted. The professor smiled and then returned with a coffee.

"Mike here tells me you gave him a D minus on his paper. Why?" Al demanded, as soon as the Professor sat down.

The professor glanced about quickly but it was too late. He passed a hand over his balding head and stared at Al warily. Then he sat his styrofoam coffee cup down and sighed.

"I can't remember. There's so many papers to mark."

"Well for Christ's sake!" Al snapped. "Mike's only got grade nine, you'd think you'd give him a chance."

Mike felt the flush grow on his face as the professor looked at him, slightly puzzled. "Well, as far as I'm concerned," the professor finally said, "I don't see how anyone with only grade nine can pass my course."

Mike slowly let the air from his lungs, ashamed and angry. He glared at Al, but he knew Al would only say he was trying to help. Then the professor excused himself and left for a different table.


One professor, some students, a couple of middle-aged women and Mike sat around a long rectangular table. As the others talked or glanced down at poetry or short stories, Mike sat stiffly, his hand hiding a poem he had written the night before. Anxiety fluttered in his stomach and his palms were sweaty. He bit his lower lip and wondered why he was there in the bright, academic room. But the desperate, sad need for acceptance of his writing forced him to be there, no matter how hard the knot in his stomach.

He was conspicuous, although he dressed the same as the rest, in jeans and a T-shirt. He had even grown a beard but he resembled a lumberjack more than a poet.

"Well," the professor turned to Mike, chasing away the swirling thoughts. "Have you brought anything you'd like to read?"

Mike swallowed and slid the piece of paper across the table to the professor.

"Aren't you going to read it?" the professor asked, smiling indulgently. He wore a pinstriped, black, double-breasted suit with a canary yellow vest. From his mouth hung a Sherlock Holmes pipe and on his head was a Holmes hat, with a beak at front and back. He appeared the epitome of deep intellect, with just the right trace of rebelliousness.

"Well," Mike stammered, the knot in his stomach growing more painful. "I'm not very good at reading in public." Anxiety, made his mouth constricted and dry, while his face felt hot and flushed.

The professor looked dubiously at the young man, who appeared unafraid of anything in his lumberjack beard and face. Then he took the paper, a slight condescending look in his eyes, before reading silently. But his attention remained on the poem for more then a cursory few seconds.

"If you like, I can read it for you," he said the patronizing look gone.

"Sure. If you want," Mike answered and then sat in pained silence, anticipatory, yet fearful.

The professor lay his cold pipe on the table, adjusted his hat and rustled the paper. The silence settled down, deep and pregnant, with some eyes on the professor but most on Mike who sat hunched forward, his eyes, downcast.

"Apocalypse! That's the title, is it?"

Mike nodded and the professor began reading, his voice deep and resonant, weaving a soft, sad spell:

I once Dreamed a Dream
Shrouded in Mists
While Humanity, In a Stream
Drifted slowly by

The professor glanced upwards at Mike, a new light in his eyes. Then he cleared his throat and returned to the words:

Bones and Skulls: Skulls and Bones
Rock upon Rock, With Head Stones

Caricatures, Hulks of Former Men
And I wondered What
They were When
They knew Love and Grief

Bones and Skulls: Skulls and Bones
Rock upon Rock With Head Stones

Dull, Ignorant Ape-men
Masters No More
Of the World When
Man had become God!

Bones and Skulls: Skulls and Bones
Rock upon Rock With Head Stones

The professor stopped reading, staring pensively down at the paper, as the silence deepened. Mike sat, very still for he had bared his innermost soul.

"Oh! I like it," the professor said suddenly. And when he looked at Mike, there was respect in his eyes. Then others joined in.

"God! I could almost feel myself by a cemetery, with the graves of all mankind," a young woman said softly and Mike glanced at her, his pulse quickening.

"It seems kinda morbid though, doesn't it?" a middle-aged woman added, pursing her lips.

"No way!" the professor snapped and Mike stared at him, surprised at the vehemence in his voice.

"The destruction of the world by nuclear holocaust has to be morbid by its very nature," the young woman added and Mike felt his face flush again. They were discussing his work, his innermost thoughts. Mike gazed down at his hands, disbelief fluttering in his soul.

"You're going to write more, aren't you?" the professor asked suddenly.

"Yeah. Sure. If I get the time," Mike answered as he thought of the previous night. He had sat on the edge of his cot with a pen and pad, anxiety raising havoc with his intestines. But the words had come nevertheless, an emotional cry from the heart. If he could write a poem like that in twenty minutes, surely he must have talent!

As Mike walked home in the swirling snow words, sentences and verses came unbidden, and he imagined he was in front of an audience, reciting his poetry. As he walked, he didn't notice that his ears were beginning to freeze.

Next evening he sat at a table with Al, a typewriter and paper in front of them. He nervously read a sentence from a story he had written that afternoon.

Al vehemently shook his head.

"No no! That won't do!"

Mike gazed at the words, "The gentle, soft touch of a woman," He couldn't understand what was wrong.

"Shh!" Al said suddenly, gazing at some imaginary scene, his eyes bright. Then he raised his hand and opened his mouth. He placed his fingers on his right cheek and smiled.

"Al, you're a genius," he exclaimed and then looked at Mike.

"Quick! Write this down. The sexual, titillating touch of a female.'"

Mike stared at Al. He had asked him to help in spelling and grammar, but Al was re-writing the story.

Mike gave up in disgust, slamming the typewriter carriage so hard, it knocked a cup off the table.

"Well. I was only trying to help," Al said. "If you never get published, don't come crying to me."

Mike's slow, painful climb upwards out of the emotional morass continued. There were those who would help, but he was beginning to understand that there was always a price.

# Forty-three

The leaves shriveled and died while the snow muffled sound until all was buried under the great white. Christmas came and went, a mere break in the classes as Mike existed in the new, and at times alien, world of books. Gradually, he began to see himself as a student, whose mind is occupied by problems of the intellect, not the immediate one of sustenance and shelter.

He scored in the top ten percent in a reading test for first year students. But he was still a paradox, an intellectual one moment and then lapsing into street slang the next. Then came boredom for most courses was just a matter of memorization and regurgitation, and his marks slipped. He was angered by a Psychology professor who declared that it was impossible for anyone with a grade nine to obtain a degree and become academically successful. It would take Mike years to understand how both he and the professor were right.

He wrote more poetry and learned to play chess, at the same time discovering classical music. He read Othello the Moor, marveling at the genius of Shakespeare, wondering why he enjoyed reading it only after he had dropped out of the course.

One evening, he and Al sat hunched over a chess board placed on a coffee table. Mike was two moves to mate and while he waited for Al to move he placed an LP on a cheap turn table. When the needle touched the disc, a Chopin waltz came into the room. Al glanced up quickly.

"You playing that highfalutin crap again?" he demanded and moved his Knight.

"It's not crap," Mike answered and moved his Bishop. "It's a waltz, by Chopin." He picked up the record holder and gazed at it for a moment.

"I didn't know you liked French music!" Al said, keeping his eyes on the chess board.

"Chopin was Polish," Mike said.

"No!" Al snapped. "He wasn't a Polluck! He was French."

Mike gazed at the holder again, reading the composer's personal history.

"It says here that he was born and raised in Poland and that he adapted Polish peasant music to classical," Mike said. "That makes him Polish."

"Gimmee that!" Al snapped, grabbing the record holder from Mike. He read quickly and then threw it on the floor.

"Well, I'll be dammed," he said incredulously. "I sure the hell never thought the Pollucks had composers."

When Mike studied Wolpe's Reciprocal Inhibition, he begin to understand how a person could slowly be de conditioned from a phobia. He thought of the unreasoning stab of anxiety he felt whenever he was near a girl and he began to understood why. He also felt a great unreasoning fear, breaking into a sweat every time he was near a rat cage in the lab, but he didn't remember being bitten when he was a child. At times education only caused confusion, for he was knocking on doors to his soul he had kept locked.

One afternoon, Mike and Al were in the cafeteria, when they were joined by two girls from one of Mike's classes. Both were first year students and still in their teens. Mike craved their acceptance as much as he did an education.

"You know, I think I'm finally beginning to understand infatuation," he began slowly. "If a girl likes Clint Eastwood, someone she admires and who turns her on she'll be receptive to a fella that has the same mannerisms. I guess that's why so many guys want to be macho."

One of the girls looked at Mike, a light in her eyes he couldn't fathom.

"Bullshit!" Al snapped suddenly. "If a girl loves a guy, that's it! She loves him. I don't believe all that Psychology shit."

Mike looked quickly at Al. It was apparent that once again, he was quickly outgrowing a friend. Then the conversation moved on to another topic.

"What do you think of capital punishment?" one of the girls asked. Mike looked at her innocent face, framed by soft blond hair and eager eyes. He noticed how her blouse strained whenever she pulled her shoulders back. But when he thought of asking her for a date, a quick stab of anxiety tore at his stomach.

"Well, I'm in favor of it," he heard himself say.

"No way," the girl replied quickly. "God is the only one who has the right to take a life."

"But if you've ever lived with a murderer," Mike countered, "you might have a different opinion. I mean, it's easy to feel sorry for some criminal who claims he's a victim but when you're in close contact, it's a little different."

"How do you know?" the girl asked.

"Well," Mike began slowly. Then he shook his head and stopped. He thought bitterly, how it always seemed to be criminals who got sympathy from pretty, young women, while those who worked hard to change their lives, rarely were noticed. During the brief time when he hesitated, he thought of the rough men he had known, especially the one who had boasted about doing nine years for murder. Then Al suddenly killed the topic.

"Aw, if a guy kills someone he deserves to be hung up. To hell with him. Those Bastards got no rights anyway."

Mike noticed the amused glances between the two girls and his stomach knotted more painfully. Then the blond girl turned to him.

"I hear you're a poet."

"Well yeah. I write some poetry," Mike answered, glancing down at his cup.

"Why don't you write porn?" she asked innocently. "There's a big market for it, you know. All you have to do is write at least three Fuck words into every sentence and it'll sell."

"Hell!" Mike laughed self-consciously. "How can I write about it, when it's been so long. I forgot how to do it?"

"Whose fault is that?" the girl asked, looking directly into his eyes.

Although Mike was beginning to break some of his emotional chains, he was still unable to obtain what most men with half his intelligence took for granted. He began to identify with the Wizard in the Taro Cards, frozen in his own wisdom and unable to apply it to himself. Most of the nights he tossed and turned, his stomach in a hard knot, rising in the morning nearly numb with fatigue.

He began to drink again, telling himself it was so he would have the nerve to ask a girl for a dance. Again, if asked if he was an alcoholic he would have denied it vehemently. He decided to see a psychiatrist, telling himself it was only to help his sleeping problem. Within a week he was in a cluttered office with a grey-haired man who wore a red sports jacket, red pants and a red turtle neck sweater.

The first thing the psychiatrist did was set a large alarm clock. Then with the clock ticking loudly in the tiny office, he leaned back in his chair and regarded Mike, all the while puffing heavily on an ivory colored pipe.

"Well, what seems to be the problem?" he finally asked from behind a cloud of blue smoke.

Mike hesitated, clenching his hands and leaning forward, until the psychiatrist shifted impatiently in his chair.

"I'm not sure really," Mike finally said. "I got a hard time getting to sleep at night. It takes two or three hours, no matter how tired I am."

"Oh!" the psychiatrist said and puffed more blue smoke. Then he looked through the smoke, right into Mike's eyes.

"Have you ever thought of committing suicide?"

"What?" Mike said surprised.

"Don't worry!" the psychiatrist said. "I've tried it six times myself."

"Oh!" Mike replied, glancing at the ticking clock. He still had forty-seven minutes to go. "Well, I guess I've thought of it," he finally said.

Then finally when the alarm had gone off, he left the office with two bottles of pills. The first was filled with an anti schizophrenic drug, and the other, sleeping pills. He was to take one of the anti schizophrenic pills in the morning and two at dinner. What he didnt realize was that the labels had been mixed up. He dutifully took the pills, but he began falling asleep in the afternoon. The more pills he took, the more sleepy he became. After three days, he quit taking them. He phoned the psychiatrist, but he was told by the receptionist that the doctor had been successful on his seventh suicide attempt.

Mike always seemed to be vulnerable, needing advice or a counselor, always dependant on someone else's dedication or concern. Going to the wrong psychiatrist, or taking advice from Al, it really was the same.

Despite all this, he passed his courses with a C average and became a regular student after one term. Al however failed, and as spring came and went, Mike felt more lonely than ever.

Mike sat in a Sociology classroom, surrounded by three regular students and a majority of middle-aged school teachers. The students were there to pick up courses they had missed, the teachers in summer school to upgrade their qualifications, and therefore their salaries.

At the front, behind an oak desk and a pile of books, sat an ex-professional football player-turned professor, due to a pinched nerve in his back. He gazed at the class from his thickset face and leaned backward, his chair protesting with a loud squeak. He had been a linebacker and it showed in his bulging muscles and broad shoulders, for he was not yet thirty years old. He gazed for an instant at the students, who sat waiting patiently at their desks, their note books and pens at the ready.

"Good afternoon," he finally said. "I'm John, your instructor which you already know." He smiled faintly.

"But you can call me Woody."

The middle-aged teachers watched the professor intently, pens poised.

"After the class," Woody continued. "If any of you want to get to know me I'm buying the first round at the Red Oak Inn."

The attentive expressions remained the same, and a pained look crossed Woody's face.

"Okay! I can see most of you like life in the fast lane," he said and then laughed. "You're taking the right course, eh, the Sociology of Deviance."

The majority of students still waited, pens poised and ready. Woody sighed deeply.

"Nobody here does anything deviant. Right? So how in hell can I teach deviance from a text book? All you'll do is read the material, memorize it and then pass your exams."

The middle-aged students still sat, their faces attentive except for a couple who glanced dubiously at each other.

"What I propose to do," Woody continued and then shook his head. "I can see everybody's got their pens ready to write down everything I say, except for one or two that is." His gaze fell on Mike and Mike shrugged his shoulders.

"What I propose to do," Woody started again, "is to give you a real life lesson in deviance. Not just some boring crap from an antiquated text book."

Two days later, the students filed through the city jail, gazing quickly at inmates in the cells and then, just as quickly away. The school teacher/students maintained a single file, remaining as far away from the steel bars on either side of them as possible. A couple of the students exchanged the odd glance with each other.

Suddenly, an electric shock went through the single line of students.

"Hey! That's Fred! And Bill!" one of the students exclaimed, and then immediately averted her eyes. In a cell to her right and on a bunk, sat two students from class, one with what appeared to be a blood soaked bandage on his head. The rest of the students immediately filed past the cell, keeping their heads straight ahead.

The next class Fred and Bill sat in their regular seats and Fred had even brought his ketchup stained towel, that had served as a bandage.

"By now you must know it was all just a hoax," Woody finally said, when the class was full and the silence pregnant. "Either that or they've got the best lawyers money can buy." His shoulders shook with silent laughter. None of the older students laughed.

"Oh well, back to the grind," Woody said then. "What I want you to do is write your term paper on what you saw and how you felt," he said slowly, glancing around the class.

"Remember! Ending up in a cell was a deviant act all right, but what's more important is your reaction to it."

Mike looked forward to the term paper, for it was a challenge. But later, he walked into the cafeteria and saw most of the class sitting at a long table. One of them waved and he joined the group.

"Well, what do you think of that professor?" a bald man demanded vehemently.

"What do you mean?" Mike asked, his stomach knotting.

"Well!" a silvery-haired woman, with worry lines about her eyes snapped, I've been teaching for thirty years, before he was even born. Who does he think he is? A young man like that trying to tell me."

Mike met the malice in her eyes for a brief instant. He wondered what it was that Woody was supposed to have tried to tell her. He wondered why they would take the course if they didn't want to learn. Then he became aware of the bald man pushing a paper toward him.

"Here! Will you sign this?"

"What is it?" Mike looked down at the row of signatures.

"It's a petition!" the silvery-haired woman said, her eyes still spitting malice. "We don't want him teaching university courses. At least this way, if we fail, maybe we can still get passing marks if we stick together."

"But why would you fail?" Mike asked.

"I can't write a paper on how I feel," the woman snarled. "Papers are supposed to be on what you've learned in class, from the text book."

"But didn't you learn something?" Mike asked the infuriated woman, wondering how her students fared when they went against her wishes.

"I've been teaching thirty years," she snarled, ignoring his question. "That's certainly not teaching. I don't know what that is."

"Are you going to sign this or not?" the bald man demanded, laying down a half-eaten doughnut and handing Mike a pen.

"No!" Mike rose, leaving his full coffee.

"No! I can't sign that." He shook his head and then turned to go, leaving the icy stares and a deep, deep silence. When he was twenty feet away, but still within hearing, the silvery-haired woman spat out her feelings.

"He drinks with the professor. Every afternoon they go down to that Red Oak Inn. God knows what goes on there. That's why he got a B+ on the first exam. He drinks with the professor."

After that Mike, Bill and Fred sat in one corner of the classroom with space between them and the rest. Woody taught the rest of the course with a sardonic look in his eyes, for the petition did him no harm. And the schoolteacher/students grimly bore the unorthodox teaching, for with a passing mark their salaries were increased.

Mike was beginning to understand the nature of deviance, and not just the kind committed by criminals.


Once again Mike gazed about the tiny living room, at the old flowered wallpaper, the framed pictures of the Virgin Mary and Joseph with the child Jesus, then at the oil heater mightily trying to keep the cold at bay. He stared at his mother's sad, fatalistic face for an instant, before his attention was taken by his father who made a face as he cracked nuts with a pliers.

It was Christmas and he had felt the inexplicable desire to be home with his parents. He had shown his mother a Psychology textbook and had watched her covertly, as she had looked at it. Her expression had been hard and she didn't appear pleased that he was in his second year of college. Mike felt the familiar tightening in his stomach, only now he knew what it was.

The three children had been taken away, with the explanation that Vincent and Gertie were too old and the old house was once again cold and silent. Mike's mind wandered back light years to the campus and the world he couldn't explain to his mother. He glanced at her again and then went to the bathroom with his father's ancient scissors. When he was standing before the mirror, trimming his moustache, he heard voices from the living room.

"Metro's trimming his moustache!" Vincent said quickly and grinned at Gertie. The last time Mike had heard his father use that mocking tone of voice was when he had been making fun of a mentally disabled man.

As the maelstrom of emotions ebbed and flowed, Mike calmly finished trimming his moustache, although his stomach ached. He thought of the psychological concept of cognitive dissonance, and how a person cannot keep two opposing concepts in his mind at the same time. And then, his father's mocking voice won over his emerging self-esteem. While at home he slept little.

The next day, Christmas Eve, Gerard drove into the yard alone, for his wife refused to come in the winter. He stood by the ancient cookstove, gazing at the Christmas cards on display near the red plastic radio on a tiny shelf in the corner. His face pinched and eyebrows drew close together, as he turned to Mike.

"Mom tells me that you're going to college, part time!"

Mike sat on a hard wooden chair, bending slightly forward as if to ease the knot in his stomach.

"No!" He heard his own voice, cold and emotionless. "No, I'm going full time."

Gerard's eyebrows knitted closer together.

"Oh! I see!" he said and then paused and gazed out the window and back again. "Well, I guess you're just in arts," he added quietly.

"Well yes," he said. "Obviously I can't get into science because I don't have grade twelve. Besides, I'm interested in Psychology."

Gerard's thin lips formed into a quick smile for a very brief instant.

"There's too much rats in Psychology," he snapped suddenly, the words accompanied by a quick wave of dismissal. Mike gazed out the window at the barn and at the cows gathered at the well for water. Then he stared at his mother, who dashed about trying to do all the work at once. He sighed deeply and looked down at the floor.

Gerard had been thrown into confusion when he had heard Mike was in college. But as he stood by the stove, glancing occasionally at his mother, who ran about preparing a special meal just for him, he felt more at ease.

"I don't suppose you've run into Piage," he finally said, the faint smile coming and going quickly.

"Sure I did! In first year Psych. He pioneered development in children," Mike answered quickly. Then he continued, the game a faint smile, now on his lips.

"Have you taken any Festinger? You know cognitive dissonance."

"No!" Gerard's curt answer made Mike smile again.

Then Mike told Gerard of the Social Psychology course he had started in September and how the professor had at one time worked with B.F. Skinner, the pioneer of behaviorism.

"There were thirty of us enrolled at first but now there's only eight left," Mike said. "The B I got for the first half was the highest in the class."

Gertie suddenly stepped between them and held up a roaster for Gerard's inspection, her back to Mike. Mike noticed for the first time, how she sought Gerard's approval, and for the moment he was at loss for words. Then he gazed again through the frost-covered window, at his dog who was trotting to the barn, followed by the large mother cat.

"I guess the standards in Brandon University are pretty low," Gerard suddenly said.

"What!" Mike snapped.

"I talked to a guy who was a professor there," Gerard added quietly, the cold smile playing about his thin lips. "He said he left because they were allowing people in without grade twelve and the standards were being destroyed."

"How can that be?" Mike countered. "When I enrolled I took the same courses as regular students and when I passed I became a regular student."

"Of course you took remedial training," Gerard asserted.

"No! I just took regular courses."

Gerard's eyebrows joined again, and Mike wondered about the whiteness of his face.

"Who the hell is this professor?" he demanded.

"Henderson."

"That was the guy who was fired because nobody would take his courses. All he ever did was read from a text book," Mike laughed and then added, "I'm surprised he got a job at U. of R. though."

Gerard glared angrily at the floor and then back up at Mike. His eyebrows were still joined and his face white as he contemplated the cigarette Mike had lit.

"Well the standards are so low anyone could pass," he finally said.

An oppressive silence settled down upon the frigid kitchen. Mike felt a chill from under the door and from Gerard's face. Finally he broke the silence, staring pensively at his shoes.

"That commercial art course. It didn't turn out. I had to drop it because they taught us stuff that hadn't been used in years."

At the words "drop it," Gerard's ghostly smile suddenly blossomed into a wide grin. Then as the silence settled down again, his face reverted to its normal pinched, complaining look.

As the red sun sank slowly into the west, over the frozen poplar trees, the rays cast shadows in the kitchen and the cold increased its silent attack. Gertie held up a pie for Gerard's approval and Mike watched.

It all seemed so natural. So right.

# Forty-four

Tiny spruce trees stood, lonely and stark, growing from the muskeg swamps stretching in all directions under a pale blue, cloudless sky. The trees were the highest points, for this was the Land of Little Sticks, the vast stunted forest that preceded the wild, untamed barren grounds. It was broken occasionally by a small river that had cut through the tundra, down twenty feet or so. The banks were lined by spruce trees whose tops were the same height as the banks of the ravine and safe from the freezing wind.

Mike stared out the small window of the Twin Otter, down at the countless lakes and muskeg inhabited by caribou, wolf and black fly. The plane droned on as the land met the sky in a never-ending portrait of primitive purity; green and blue, the colors of the earth.

When they finally landed on a gravel runway, Mike stepped from the plane, once again entering a different world. The T-shirt that was warm at six a.m. in Winnipeg, wasn't enough to keep the chill at bay at four in the afternoon, for Gillam was north of the 58th parallel.

As he shouldered his equipment bag, walking to the small trailer that was the ticket office, it occurred to him that he felt at home. Once again he was a drifter, a "Boomer" following the construction boom to the Land of Little Sticks. Within the hour he was in camp dumping his bag onto a cot in the bunkhouse. Then he was in the bar looking for familiar faces. Around him buzzed the languages of the world, for the northern camps were still the places of dreams, of making it rich quick. It didn't take long to slip back into the old routine.

During his first shift Mike met Dennis, whose hair was greying around the temples and his middle bulging a little. They had worked together on the Bennet dam and he remembered Mike. They spent their lunch break together talking over old times.

"Me, I don't give 'er shit no more like I used to," Dennis said, for he was in his early forties, old for an ironworker. "I just do the rigging." Rigging was slinging the cables onto the steel and signaling the crane operator.

"I don't blame you," Mike said, thinking about the years of wandering and sweating Dennis must have done. Then he had another thought.

"You remember that guy, Willie? He used to sing real good. I wonder where he is now."

"Willie," Dennis said and then thought for a moment. "He was half Cree, wasn't he?"

"Yeah," Mike answered. "But he sure could sing."

"Oh yeah. I remember him now," Dennis chuckled, and then was suddenly serious.

"The last time I seen him was in Vancouver on Hastings Street." Dennis paused to scratch his neck. "He used to drink a lot but I never expected to see him like that."

"Like what?"

"Like a Goddamn Wino! Shit! As soon as he sees me, he comes running. Christ! Then he asks me to borrow him twenty bucks." Dennis shook his head and then sipped coffee from a thermos top. The beating blades of a helicopter could be heard overhead as both men were silent for a while. The sun bore down and shimmered off the Nelson River, flowing only a quarter of a mile away. Over the river seagulls flapped looking for unwary minnows near the surface.

"I guess it happens to some guys," Mike finally said, his voice soft.

"Yeah. I guess so." Dennis cast his eyes upwards to the top of the rebar, eighty feet above where they sat.

"But it's funny. He couldn't remember nothing about singing or iron-working but he sure the hell could remember my name and to ask for twenty bucks. Guys like that they lose part of their brain it seems."

Mike looked down at the dirt beneath his boots. He wondered what makes a man become a wino, and then quickly suppressed the uncomfortable thought that he too was vulnerable to the hidden disease. He gazed upwards at the steel, swaying slightly in the wind. He wondered why when the work wasn't dangerous, the image of the blindfolded donkey still lurked just beneath his consciousness.

The foreman appeared suddenly and waved from the tiny office where the blueprints were kept. Both Dennis and Mike stood and stretched, before placing their lunch buckets in the lunch shack.

Suddenly Dennis stopped and stared at Mike's T-shirt and at the words, "Brandon University."

"What the hell's this?" he laughed.

"A T-shirt! I got it at the university."

"How?" Dennis, demanded.

"I bought it! Jesus Christ! I go to college now. I only work on steel in the summer."

"I'm sure!" Dennis laughed. Then he turned to the steel, his broad back receding.

Mike's stomach knotted and he glared at Dennis. Then he pulled himself up on the steel using his hands and legs as if he were climbing a rope. The steel was size eighteen, the circumference of a beer bottle and too big for his safety hook. When he climbed, his stomach muscles bunched and hurt and he rested, hanging from his hands. It was more than sixty feet down to the concrete but he feared the other men's scorn, if he had to slide to the ground. Instead he hung on grimly until his stomach relaxed and then he pulled himself up the rest of the way to a two-by-four tied horizontally with rebar wire to the vertical bars. He stood on the plank and kept an iron grip on a bar, musing how a pair of pliers couldn't tear his fingers from the steel. Then as he inched along the two-by-four to where it stuck out and away from the vertical bars, he glanced at the "Whirly." The crane sat on top a hundred and twenty foot iron frame, high enough to move steel to where Mike was. The vertical bars Mike hung onto had been joined by weld, forty feet down and to the bars coming from the concrete, for the pier was built forty feet at a time. It was ten feet across and forty feet long and when it was finished a concrete slab was to fit on top. Once the cement had been poured to forty feet the next cut of bars was lifted by crane and welded onto the ones sticking from the cement. A sleeve was fitted onto the ends of the bars and a pot placed over the splice. The welder lit a powdery substance in the pot which burned intensely, melting the ends of the steel into one. Mike's job was to stand at the end of the two-by-four and hold onto the bar as it was lowered by crane so it was steady for the welder.

He had been given a safety line but the steel didn't always weld properly and if it ever broke he would be tied to it. Without the safety line he could at least jump and hope for the best. Mike preferred to trust in his reflexes rather than a weld by a man he didn't even know.

He moved to the outside of the pier, above the concrete and assorted junk lying eighty feet below. On the inside he would have only had thirty-five feet to fall. But on the inside there were bars coming from the concrete and he preferred the sudden death from a long fall than the slow agonizing one from being impaled. If he closed his eyes he could still see the dark red blood and hear the screams of the man impaled on a bar years before at the Bennet Dam.

He and Dennis had discussed it during lunch.

"Ya know," Dennis had said, eyeing his thermos philosophically. "When it's your turn, that's it. There's nothing you can do."

Mike vowed it wouldn't be his turn, as he held a vertical bar with an iron grip while steadying the other being welded.

Suddenly a gust of wind swayed the steel and he found his dinner nearly in his throat. It wasn't bad when he swayed forwards and could see where he was going. But when the wind blew from in front and he swayed backwards, he prayed silently that the day would soon end. Still he climbed the steel, seeking something even the obvious danger couldn't, discourage.

Early that morning he had been told to find a hose for a tugger hoist. There were hoses on the next pier and ladders went down forty feet and up. But stretching across the twenty-five feet of open air had been a wooden beam, six-by-six inches. Mike had looked quickly at the ladders and at the beam. He hadn't hesitated, placing one boot down and trying his weight to see if the beam gave. Then he had begun walking, his arms hanging nonchalantly by his sides. The foreman had glanced from a blueprint to Mike and back down again. Then he had looked up quickly, his eyes narrowing. As Mike returned on the beam, carrying the thirty pound hose slung over his shoulder, a faint smile had creased the foreman's tanned face.

"You, you don't mind heights?" he had asked quietly, as Mike had stepped from the beam to the pier. Mike had shaken his head.

"Wanna go up?" the foreman had nodded to the steel swaying slightly in the wind. Mike had again shrugged his shoulders and began climbing. He had stood on the outside of the pier on the side that was above an area blasted out of the rock one hundred and fifty feet below. Again there were bars sticking out of the concrete, ready to impale any man falling on them.

That day an event occurred that made the other men view Mike with both awe and scepticism, for they figured he had to be slightly crazy. A cement bucket was used to carry the wet concrete from the trucks to the pour just below Mike. It swung on the end of a one inch cable from the Whirly and normally poured the concrete over the rebar where the Portuguese cement crew swarmed with shovels and strong backs. Suddenly a gust of wind caught the bucket and it swung toward Mike's pier. Mike was unaware as the operator desperately hauled on a lever. But the wind won against the crane and men suddenly began yelling from below. Mike didn't pay any attention for men were always yelling. But when he saw his foreman waving his arms and pointing, he glanced over his shoulder. In a heart beat, he was clambering nimbly like a monkey up over the steel and hanging nonchalantly from a horizontal bar on the inside of the pier. The bucket which weighed five tons had been only a yard away.

"Jesus H. Christ!" the foreman yelled. "Be careful! Because you know it's not the Goddamn fall, it's the sudden stop."

From then on Mike kept a wary eye on the cement buckets and whenever he heard shouting, he looked about quickly. But when he stood on the two-by-four and gazed down at a low flying helicopter, the pilot waved and he waved back. At times like that Mike felt truly alive.

His days were not without humor. The job was so big and at times so disorganized that it was not uncommon for men to be left in a group until a foreman found something for them to do. A group of carpenters, who spoke little English, milled about on the ground. Once in awhile they looked skywards at Mike but normally they stood in a confused group, directly beneath the welder. The welder ignored them, only yelling "Fire!" after he lit the powder.

Suddenly molten metal spattered down, hitting the concrete and bouncing back up four feet in a shower of bright sparks. The carpenters ran in all directions and some were burned. After that when the work slackened, some of the ironworkers on the pier amused themselves by occasionally yelling "Fire!" The carpenters ran at first but when no molten metal cascaded down, they came back to stand bunched by the concrete base of the pier.

Then the welder lit the powder once more and yelled "Fire!" And again the white, hot sparks flew and a couple more men were burned. After that the carpenter foreman complained vehemently to the ironworker foreman who only shrugged and laughed.

One day Mike gazed from his perch atop the steel, toward where a blast was being readied. Laborers placed heavy rope mats, made of hemp, four inches in diameter over the rock that was to be blasted. The mat was supposed to prevent rock from flying into the air and landing on unsuspecting men a half mile away. One time a stone, the size of a kitchen table, had landed right beside a crew of carpenters. There had been fewer men after that, for a half a dozen had gone south on the next plane.

Another time, the Whirly crane operator had pulled the brake lever instead of the clutch when he was lowering a load of lumber. A pin, eight inches in diameter, had been sheared and the sixty-foot boom had come crashing down. It had lain twisted and broken, like a tinker toy some child had angrily thrown away.

The sudden shriek of the siren made Mike tense and grasp the steel bars in preparation for the bone jarring bang. Faintly he could see thousands of seagulls wheel in a flock and then land on the rope mat. The sudden crash jarred his teeth and made the steel tremble. Mike closed his eyes and when he opened them he could see a cloud of dust along with countless white feathers floating in the breeze. Later, in the bar, the men laughed about it over their beer.

As summer slowly slipped away, Mike thought often of the seagulls and how little they meant to the men. And as the wind made the steel sway and men refused to climb, he also wondered how much, a man's life was worth.

One morning the men went on a wildcat strike. The foreman insisted they go up even though it was raining and the steel slippery and treacherous. They demanded that scaffolds be built at the halfway point where the bottom half of the pier was joined by the top. That way if a man fell, he had a chance of grabbing the scaffold. It wouldn't necessarily save a life, but it would make the odds a little better.

The general foreman stood before the men, his face tough and angry.

"Well, go back to work and tomorrow we'll start on the scaffolding," he said. His face creased in a sudden smile but no one was fooled.

"No way!" Someone yelled suddenly, "You'll only put it off and hope we forget about it."

The general foreman glared but said nothing more. The foreman suddenly demanded again who was going to climb the steel that day. All the men shook their heads until it was Mike's turn.

"I'm sick and tired of freezing in the rain. It's someone else's turn," he said. He would have gone up but he feared the men's scorn more than the bars coming from the cement, eighty feet below.

The strike was settled with the scaffolding in place, and the men going back to work. The summer continued to slip by as Mike resumed his customary place, standing on the two-by-four and swaying with the gusts of wind.

The morning's coolness heralded the end of the short interlude in winter's grip north of the 58th parallel. The leaves on the stunted poplar and willow in the ravines turned to orange and then began to shrivel while flocks of geese honked overhead in their preparation for their long sojourn south.

On a large bulletin board in the mess-hall, a notice announced a weekend Beer Garden in the tiny settlement, thirty miles from camp. A three-sheet curling rink had been rented and three railway cars of the Polar Bear Express had been loaded with booze and was on its way from the south.

Mike stood in the lobby, beside an RCMP Constable and watched through the dirty glass as the harried waiters ran with full trays of twelve percent beer bottles. The thirsty men didn't care what brand was on the tray, just as long as the booze kept coming. They sat on metal chairs around large wooden drums that had been used to wrap cable around for shipping. A dance floor had been built out of fresh lumber and on it a drunken man and woman shambled about the floor while a band played a desultory tune. Tiny spruce trees had been stuck into the sand surrounding the dance floor and a small mongrel dog ran about barking. Nobody noticed the dog, for amid the hazy blue cigarette smoke and drunken humans he could barely be heard.

As Mike watched through the dirty glass, the Mountie expressed his feelings.

"This is crazy! It's a potential riot. Putting thousands of men and booze together like this. All they can drink and nothing to do but pick fights. It's a Goddamn potential riot and only three of us."

Mike glanced at the Mountie and then back to the men arguing and drinking at the tables. The only thing that could have relieved the tension would have been a trainload of hookers but the authorities preferred to ignore the reality of man's urges.

Suddenly, a young man rose shakily and then climbed onto a table, kicking beer bottles aside. He began to sway to the music in a grotesque mimicking of what the men really wanted. Loud raucous laughter rocked the curling rink and the men began to chant, "Take it Off! Take it Off!" The young man began a strip tease, as the band quickly switched to slow bump and grind music. Then amidst the shouts and music, an enraged voice could be heard.

"You Goddamn fookin bloody queer!"

A grey-haired man stood beside the table and gesticulated. The men roared with laughter at the new and unexpected entertainment.

"Get the hell outta here!" he screamed. The young man grinned down at him and begin to undo his belt.

Suddenly the gray-haired man lunged, grabbing the young man by an arm, and yanking him down to the sandy floor. In an instant, he had him in a hammer lock, pushing him to the door. The young man's face was shocked and filled with pain, but if he yelled no one heard because of the laughter.

"Go get 'em Gramps!" a large man yelled, as the two disappeared out a side door.

Mike glanced at the Mountie beside him, wondering if he would do anything. But the Mountie stood very still.

"Goddamn potential riot!" was all he said.

The party continued until the wee hours of the night. All that happened were a few assaults and one knifing by an irate wife, not a bad night for the Mounties to handle.

Back in camp, Mike sat on a bunk drinking beer with a crew of ironworkers who had grown weary of the noise and smoke in the curling rink. Amidst the ruckus he thought of College and a fear wended its way into his consciousness. If he didn't pass, he would have to return to this world for good.

Then he forgot the fear for a short fat man stood in the center of the room, gesticulating.

"The hell with this shit! I'm gonna phone my old lady. Jesus H. Christ! But I miss that bitch!" He turned and stomped out of the room, going to a pay phone in the hall. The man next to Mike turned and grinned.

"Sure nice to see true love, eh?"

Mike laughed, but inside he wondered about the loneliness that made a man call long distance at four a.m., just to hear his old lady's voice.

Suddenly the man slammed down the phone and came storming back into the room, his face white with rage.

"How soon I get my pay?" he demanded of the foreman.

"Couple days! Why?"

"I just phoned the bitch, and there's no fuckin' answer."

"Maybe she was sleeping and didn't hear it," the foreman said quietly.

"Bullshit! Not at four o'clock in the Goddamn a.m. The fuckin slut's out whorin' around," the man yelled. Then he sat on a chair and opened a beer with his teeth, spitting the cap onto the floor. He glared straight ahead, his face grim and his hand gripping the bottle so tightly the knuckles stood out white.

Suddenly another commotion was heard from a room down the hall. Men were beginning to line up outside the door, grinning and laughing and digging into their pockets for change.

"What the hell's going on?" Mike asked the man next to him.

"Aw, the Portuguese got this Indian girl drunk. They brought her on the bus and I guess they were screwing her."

"Piece a tail! Fifty cents!" a man yelled from the doorway. Then he ran off to line up at a door down the hall.

"Christ! Was that the kid on the bus?" Mike asked. "She can't be more than fourteen!"

"So!" the man grinned. "Old enough to bleed, old enough to butcher! Besides she's passed out anyway."

The man stood then and dug into his pocket for two quarters. He juggled them in his open hand for an instant and looked down at Mike.

"Coming?"

"No!" Mike said shaking head. "Who wants to skate on a wet rink?"

The man grinned and ran out the door, stopping at the end of the line that was nearly the length of the hallway. All manner of men waited from Europe, the African continent, Canada and the United States. Mike stared down numbly down at his beer bottle. There wasn't a thing he could do, so what was the use of getting beaten up? But deep inside within his soul which he kept hidden from the rough men about him, he bled for the young girl.

Again Mike pondered how much a life was really worth. The answer was in the beer garden, on the job and the swaying steel. It was also in the bunkhouse where the unconscious fourteen year old girl unwittingly serviced more than fifty men. Mike put aside his beer and reached for a rye bottle. He needed a real drink, bad.

The next day, the company announced they had run out of booze and the beer garden was closed. The fourteen-year-old girl had to walk nearly thirty miles back to her mother's shack beside a muskeg swamp. Mike settled back into the routine, climbing the steel in the daytime and drinking in the makeshift bar in the evening. He couldn't shake the image of the girl, who was really a child, resignedly leaving the camp with her shoulders slumped and her eyes on her worn sneakers, while the men grinned at her departure.

Mike remembered his conversation with Al before he had flown north.

"You know it's funny, but I got a gut feeling that I'll come back in a cast," he had said, half in jest.

On the steel and in the small hours of the night when he tossed and turned in his bunk, there was a deep sense of foreboding. But he couldn't quit just because he was afraid.

# Forty-five

Heavy, grey clouds scudded across the sky as a fine rain settled down upon the earth soaking everything. By two p.m. Mike was wet to the skin with his leather boots a sodden mass. The steel was cold and damp and he shivered uncontrollably, but the steel kept going up regardless of the weather. Finally though Gary, the new foreman, waved from the ground cupping his hands to his mouth.

"Time to dog It! Boys!"

"Dog It!" was slang for quitting early or taking the easy way out.

Mike gratefully slid down the steel and sloshed through the puddles to where Gary and the rest of the crew waited for a Bluebird bus to take them back to camp. Then they headed straight for the bar, shedding sodden clothes on the floor. When the table was full of beer bottles the party began, for what good was it to "dog It" and not get drunk? The crew drank the rest of the afternoon, staggered off to supper and returned to close up the bar. But the party still wasn't over. Mike, Dennis and Gary, along with his son and a waitress from the coffee shop went to his trailer where he lived, for a foreman had privileges.

When they were seated in the tiny living room Gary set his bottle down hard on the varnished coffee table and grinned.

"Young punks these days, they can't cut it with the old timers."

It was Gary's favorite theme and ordinarily Mike laughed it off. But he was drunk and suddenly all themes were serious.

"Bullshit!" His voice was thick. "I'll work with any of you old farts."

He had been in that argument a thousand times, about who can work the hardest, pack the most steel or tie the fastest.

"Aw hell! You probably won't make it to work tomorrow just because you'll be hung over. Punks these days you're all the same." Gary was in his mid forties and his greying hair and lined face was all he had to show for a lifetime of iron-working: That and the bragging rights to tell younger men how tough times had once been.

As Mike drunkenly tilted his bottle, Dennis grinned. Gary's son was busily convincing the waitress to go to one of the bedrooms.

"Jesus H. Christ! I'll work with you any day, any time, any place!" Mike snarled.

"We'll see," Gary grinned and the argument continued. By four a.m. they had drunk the last of the booze and stumbled off to bed, Dennis back to the bunkhouse and Mike to one of the rooms.

At six a.m. Gary was shaking Mike's shoulder. Mike violently shook his head, trying to clear his vision. Then he slowly sat up. When he did, his vision darkened and he nearly fainted. But it was six a.m. and time to go to work. His angry words of the night before came flooding back and Gary's grin meant he hadn't forgotten. Mike dressed clumsily as a steel band tightened about his temples and the room swam. He could have refused to go to work, for there were only three more days before he was to return to college. But a dare was a dare and Mike determinedly pulled on his boots, which were still soggy from the day before.

When they were in the mess hall he gulped scalding coffee, burning his tongue and throat. He shakily sat the cup down and then wearily rubbed his eyebrows, pinching his nose with thumb and forefinger. He closed his eyes for an instant and when he opened them he saw Gary grinning from across the table.

"You getting burnt out? You said you could work with us Old Farts." He didn't mention that his son had stayed in bed with the waitress.

"I'll be there!" Mike said grimly. He shook his head again, trying to rid it of the vertigo. He thought of the steel's damp, coldness for in early September the frosts left the grass white in the morning. He wondered how it took five times the nerve to climb steel in the cold and damp, than in the afternoon when it was warm.

Then he rode the bus to the site, and determinedly belted his reel and pouch, with pliers and cutters around his waist. He gazed up at the forty foot wall of concrete. Pins stuck out at intervals from the wall and vertical bars were tied to them. There were also two horizontal ones, onto which the rest of the verticals would be tied. They would be lifted by a "Cherry Picker," a yellow mobile crane. Dennis stood ready by the crane as Mike sloshed his way through a puddle and then grasped a vertical bar. Again he could have stayed on the ground and slung steel but when he glanced at Gary, standing by the crane with his hands at his sides, he remembered his boast.

He pulled himself up, climbing the bar like a rope and when he was near the top, forty feet above the bars sticking out of the concrete, he hooked his "suicide hook" to the horizontal bar. A suicide hook was one without a spring operated catch that kept it from slipping from a bar. Mike had been beside a man who had used such a hook and he still remembered his scream when he had fallen twenty feet. New hooks had been ordered but had not yet arrived. Next to Mike was Rocky, an apprentice who liked to boast about his strength. Rocky pulled himself up on another vertical, and then hooked onto a horizontal with his feet on one below, careful to hang in the same manner as Mike. As Mike leaned backwards with his belt around his waist the cold, hard bar began to hurt his feet, for all his weight was on an inch and an eighth of steel. He shivered as a deep, desperate thirst came over him, for his sinuses were plugged and he had to breathe through his mouth.

Dennis signaled to the crane operator and three bars came rapidly upwards held by a choker, the short cable with loops at either end. The choker was attached to a large iron hook at the end of the main cable that ran from it along the length of the boom and then around a spindle on the crane. Mike and Rocky quickly untied the bars, letting them lean against the horizontal. Then they both grasped one and with the help of the men on the ground lifted it so it spliced with a bar sticking five feet from the concrete. Mike tied the bar and unhooked his belt to move over and do the same with the next. Then he watched impatiently as Rocky clumsily finished tying the third one.

"Just hold the Goddamn bars in place. I'll tie," he growled.

"No way. I can tie too," Rocky snapped stubbornly, as he held the pliers clumsily with two hands and twisted.

"Jesus Goddamn Christ!" Mike swore softly. "Hung over like you wouldn't believe and I get stuck with a friggin rookie who won't listen."

He glared at Rocky.

"Just do as you're Goddamn told, eh!"

Rocky grimaced as he finished the tie and Mike signaled to Dennis. Another bundle of steel rose rapidly upwards and he grabbed the bars, leaning them against the horizontal and then undid the choker.

He ignored the looped end, which twisted lazily behind the horizontal, dangerously close to the tip of his suicide hook. He glanced quickly down and noticed that Gary had started to climb the steel, to see why he and Rocky were taking so long to tie.

"Grab that Goddamn bar," he yelled at Rocky, whose face was wet from exertion. As Mike glared at Rocky, the choker looped and twisted lazily again.

The sudden thought that it could catch the tip of his hook came, but he ignored it, still glaring at Rocky.

Mike signaled to Dennis, who signaled to the operator to lift the cable and swing the boom away from the steel. Mike didn't notice that the cable had wound around a vertical bar two feet above him. He waved impatiently and the operator pulled on the lever. The tension in the snagged cable above Mike increased, just as the choker wound lazily around for the third time. Then the loop barely caught the tip of Mike's hook.

Suddenly the cable snapped free like an elastic band. Mike was instantly yanked skywards, his fingers grazing the steel as he desperately lunged forward. Then he was falling to the upright bars, waiting to impale him.

As he hurtled downwards, Gary who was halfway up the steel, instinctively reached outwards. He caught Mike's heel, flipping him over backwards. Within a heart beat, Mike was facing downwards, falling toward the bars that were a foot apart.

For the briefest of eternities, Mike heard a coarse, full-throated scream. Then suddenly, the scream was snuffed out. He was impaled with one bar through his right thigh and his left leg smashed in four places. It took a millisecond to realize that it had been he who had screamed. Then he went limp, with his shoulders caught on two bars sticking out of the cement at a forty-five-degree angle. He closed his eyes, his jaw sagging open as he calmly thought that he must be dying.

So this is how it feels, he wondered. And quickly, unbidden came the image of the man who had screamed his life away, his guts torn from his body. At the same time Mike became aware of a gurgling sound, like a beer bottle being emptied on cement. Then came a great sadness and a grey fog of loneliness closed in. He saw the campus; the pretty, intelligent young women and the professors. Then he felt the damp, depressing loneliness of the early morning.

"Dear God! Not here!" he prayed silently.

Even in his agony Mike could feel the cold, damp of the steel and the immovable hardness. Then a new thought came, small at first but growing in intensity and determination.

"No way! No Goddamn way!"

He opened his eyes and again heard the gurgling sound. Then he wonderingly reached out and grasped the next row of forty-five-degree angle bars, surprised that his arms obeyed the mental order. Slowly he pulled himself upwards as still another thought flashed by.

I'm not dead yet!

Wonder filled his soul, as he became aware of his blood spurting in a high arc and landing eight feet in front of him in a spreading, scarlet pool. So that had been the gurgling sound. The bar had cut the main artery in his right thigh and the blood spurted with each heart beat, splashing in the bright, sticky pool.

Behind Mike, the crew stood immobile, staring at the spurting blood, frozen in horror, for they thought he was dying.

But suddenly Mike grasped the next row of bars, pulling himself upwards until his body hung nearly horizontal. The bar in his thigh was forced against the torn artery and the spurting arc of blood slowed, splattering toward him, until he merely bled severely.

"Get me off here!" he demanded. Something stopped him from screaming "Help!"

"Hit the siren!" Gary yelled. The piercing wail made men all over the job stop and glance about apprehensively.

"Jesus! Sweet Jesus!" Mike swore softly. He turned his head to Rocky, the apprentice, who stood beside him, his face ashen.

"Lift my left leg forward. I can't hold on much more. It'll help me balance." Mike didn't think of the torn artery. But he knew instinctively that he couldn't fall forward again, for his mind was razor sharp, despite the pain that washed over him.

"Stand on your other leg," Rocky suddenly said and turned, the half digested breakfast coming from his mouth in a stream. A quick rage boiled inside Mike and if he could have, he would have hit Rocky.

"I can't! It's fucking broken you idiot!" he snarled.

Rocky turned his back, as Dennis grabbed the leg and pushed forwards and upwards. A great new wave of pain washed over Mike, as the broken shards of bone ground together. Instead of a scream, all that came from his mouth was a dry rasping sound. Then a great misty, blackness threatened to overwhelm him and he shook his head violently.

"Dennis! Hold me! I can't hang on much longer," Mike gritted through his teeth. His head drooped and the blackness closed in, as he grimly willed his fingers to hang onto the steel. In a second, Dennis squeezed his two hundred pounds through the one foot clearance and reached across Mike's chest, gripping a bar. Mike leaned forwards, letting Dennis support him as he closed his eyes. He heard voices behind him, as Gary seized an acetylene torch and began cutting the bar Mike was impaled on. As the white flame bit into the steel, Mike's blood spattered down and Gary's face became streaked with gore. He shook his head and concentrated on the torch.

"Has he passed out?" Mike heard a voice ask.

"I fucking hope so!" another voice answered fervently.

But Mike didnt pass out. He lifted his head and the men exchanged wondering glances. His mind was still clear and he stared straight ahead at the scarlet pool of blood on the cement that was a yard across. Then he saw his blood-splattered hard hat two feet from the pool.

"When this is over Dennis, can you get my hard hat and gloves?" he asked. He had removed his gloves and dropped them on the cement so he could get a better grip on the steel.

"Yeah sure. Just hang on!"

"And don't forget my gear in the bunkhouse. I got a new pair of pliers too. Don't let anyone take them."

"Sure. Just leave it to me," Dennis said. He exchanged glances with Gary who looked up, his face smeared and bloody.

Then as the blood ran into Mike's eyes, his world became a red haze, and the man dying on the Bennet Dam with his guts ripped out came again. He thought he was dying too, as his mind began to play tricks on him.

"Dennis!" he cried hoarsely from a frothy mouth for he had swallowed his own blood. "Why don't you just tie a choker around me and lift me off with the cherry picker?"

"Just hang on! It won't be long!" Dennis said quietly.

A sudden, sizzling came from where the torch burned Mike's pants. Gary had almost cut through the bar.

"Won't be long now," he said. Then he passed a hand over his face, smearing the blood farther until it looked like he had been injured severely.

Suddenly a spark burnt through Mike's pants. A red hot pain shot upwards to his brain and he instinctively moved his left leg. The broken shards of bone ground together and his mouth opened for a scream.

Again, all that came was a dry rasping sound. Then Mike's mind left him.

"Dennis! For Christs sake! Just tie the Goddamn choker around my waist and lift me up."

"That's okay! Mike! That's okay! We'll get you off here right away," Dennis said softly. The same familiar vision as Mike's of a man dying with his guts ripped from his body, danced before his moist eyes.

"Okay!" Gary suddenly said for he had cut through the bar.

Then as the siren's insistent screaming wail rose and fell, Mike was lowered onto a stretcher. The whole crew, even Rocky, helped and gently they held him with their work-worn hands. The bar remained in Mike's thigh, sticking out between his legs and up past his shoulder. The jagged bottom end where Gary had cut with the torch, stuck out between his ankles and was still smoking hot.

The men struggled and slipped as they carried Mike and the stretcher fifty yards over steel and debris to the waiting ambulance. With the bar and stretcher, he weighed more than two hundred pounds and suddenly one of the men slipped. The stretcher tilted with Mike nearly rolling off. The bar swung and he thought his right leg was on fire. His body arched upwards and he wrung his hands together with the knuckles, white and pronounced.

"Sorry!" Gary's said, his face chalk white where it wasn't smeared with congealing blood.

As the stretcher lurched, Mike clenched his teeth, his jaw muscles standing out in bold relief. No Goddamn way will I scream, he told himself, as he wrung his hands violently and his back arched.

As he felt the men place him and the stretcher through the rear door of the ambulance, he surprisingly felt a sharp pain in his thumb where it had slammed against the steel. He looked up at a white-faced medic and laughter bubbled from his frothy mouth.

"Jesus H. Christ! I hurt my thumb. Can you believe that?"

The man bent for a closer look.

"You hurt your thumb?" he asked seriously and the laughter left Mike as quickly as it came.

"Never mind!"

He could see the grim-faced crew staring through the rear doors of the ambulance and he raised his right hand in farewell. Then the doors slammed shut just as he heard a shout.

"Hey! Get the hell out'a the way of the ambulance."

Then a rocking motion made the bar bounce, and the jagged edges of bone rub together. Inside him the familiar voice spoke grimly again.

"No Goddamn way will I scream!"

A low moan escaped his lips as he saw the medic bend low again, holding out his hand.

"Grasp! Hang on! Squeeze as hard as you can!"

Mike squeezed but his strength had drained with the bright, red blood in the pool on the cement. All he could do was hang on. The medic bent his head still farther, gazing at where the blood seeped through Mike's dirty pants, where the bar left his body, inside his right thigh.

"Don't spare the Goddamn horses! He's bleeding like hell!" he yelled to the driver.

The ambulance rocked and bounced over the holes left by heavy equipment. The broken shards of bone ground together while the bar bounced and white flames of pain swept over Mike. Still, he refused to scream as groans gritted through his clenched teeth. Then another thought sped through his mind.

I can't stand it. I can't stand it anymore. But he stood it for he had no choice.

The ambulance sprayed gravel as it finally came to a skidding stop at the First Aid station. Medics ran to the rear door and Mike was pulled and then lifted as they carried the stretcher inside and laid it on a table. A large needle was jammed into his arm and the medics fussed about, tying his legs to the stretcher so they wouldn't move. Again, Mike heard the hiss of a cutting torch but this time he smelled scorched wool. Somebody was holding a blanket by his side so he wouldn't be burnt by flying sparks. The medics cut the bar where it went past his right shoulder for it was too long for them to fit him through the doors of the ambulance plane.

Finally, at first slowly and then faster, Mike felt the blissful, soft and warm lassitude of morphine weaving a magic spell through his body. Then he saw an RCMP Corporal standing right beside his stretcher.

"Can I have a drink of water?" he asked. "I swallowed a lot of blood and I sure the hell am thirsty."

The Mountie glanced quickly at a medic who shook his head. Then he looked down at Mike and shook his head too.

"Jesus Christ! I'm hurt in the legs not the Goddamn guts," Mike growled. Then he felt a great sorrow when he saw the look in the Mountie's eyes.

Suddenly a door slammed.

"Jesus! Mary and Joseph!" a loud swearing came from the pilot who had just entered and saw Mike for the first time.

"Shut the fuck up!" someone yelled and there was silence.

Mike raised his head to see his legs but a medic stopped him with the words, "It won't do you no good to see."

But Mike saw the bar sticking out between his legs on the stretcher, with his left foot turned completely, around and the toes pointing downwards. Both boots were drenched with blood.

Then as his eyelids drooped, he felt the stretcher lift and he knew vaguely that he was being carried to the Aztec, the swift ambulance plane. As the medic trotted beside the stretcher, he lifted Mike's hand and let it drop. It landed limply back on the stretcher, for Mike didn't have the strength to hold it up.

"Jesus Christ!" the medic swore. "I only wanted to kill the pain! Not knock him out!"

Mike knew he should tell the medic that he was okay. But he was too tired and he let his eyes close. The medic would find out that he was fine soon enough.

The plane trip would be burnt forever into Mike's mind, for the morphine wore off and the pilot kept hitting turbulence, with the plane bucking and dropping every few seconds. Again, the jagged edges of bone ground together with the bar, a white hot burning flame in his thigh. The medic's face was deathly white as Mike's fingernails dug grooves in the leather upholstery on either side of him.

I won't scream! The silent vow shouted inside his head as his jaw muscles stood out and a low moan escaped his lips. Then he glared at the medic.

"What the hell's he doing? Can't he fly right?"

"That's okay! Just hang on!" The familiar words came again.

I can't stand it anymore! The agonizing thought came again, and again he stood it, for he had no choice.

"Did you radio that we're coming?" the medic called to the pilot, who kept his eyes on the horizon trying to coax as much speed from the plane as possible.

"Yeah, yeah! In a moment!"

Then Mike felt bumping and rocking as the plane touched down on the gravel runway. The bar stayed a white hot, burning force in his leg as he stared upwards. Then he felt the stretcher move.

Men in white uniforms carried him to another ambulance with the pilot running alongside.

"Hurry up! He's got a chunk of iron in him this big!" he yelled, his arms wide.

The ambulance swung around and bumped onto a paved road as the trip continued in a kaleidoscope of white hot, agony. One of the men gazed for a moment at Mike's left leg and how his toes pointed downwards. Then he looked at the bloody bar, with bits of flesh still clinging to it, where it protruded past Mike's right shoulder. He grimaced and cast a quick glance at his partner.

"Jesus Christ!" Mike's voice came from far away.

"Man, am I lucky! I could have got that bar right through my chest. I'd be dead for sure!" he said softly, as the image of the man dying with his guts ripped out, flitted by again.

"Yeah! I can see how lucky you really are," the medic said, exchanging a quick glance with his partner.

When Mike was wheeled into the operating room the first thing he saw was the concern on the nurses faces. He watched through a red haze as someone cut the bloody clothes from his body and an IV needle was inserted into his left arm and from a transfusion bottle, flowed life-giving red blood. Then a young man, in comic relief, held up a dozen cigarettes that had been in Mike's pocket.

"I guess you won't be needing these."

Mike stared wonderingly at the congealed mass of tobacco, paper and blood. He held his bloody hands before his face, examining them minutely for injuries. He was filled with surprise and relief when he realized they were unhurt, and that the blood had come from his main artery, when it had spurted high into the air, landing in the ever spreading pool.

A young nurse bent forward, examining where the bar entered Mike's thigh, just inside the knee but missing the bone and at where it left his leg an inch from his groin and high on the inside thigh. The bar rested under his hip and stuck out past his shoulder with congealed blood on the ridges. Then in slow motion, she succumbed to curiosity, reaching with a tentative finger and gently touching the flesh by the knee.

Mike suddenly sat up, his right fist grazing her nose spinning her around. He fell back onto the blood-drenched stretcher, his chest heaving as he forced air into his lungs. The pain had been so intense it had taken the scream from his throat. A doctor glared at the nurse who regained her balance and retreated.

Mike slipped in and out of delirium, waking once in a white room all by himself yelling for a nurse. A nurse showed him a cord and button to push if he needed her and he slipped back into the dark netherworld. He suddenly woke again with the room nearly full of nurses for he had screamed when he was unconscious. Then, when he felt the soft, warm touch of a young nurse who cradled his head in her arm, the thrashing and swearing slowed.

"Can I," the words were hoarse and the young nurse bent to hear. "Can I have a drink of water? I swallowed an awful lot of blood and I sure the hell am thirsty."

The young nurse looked up and exchanged glances with an older woman.

"Just a swallow?" she asked.

"Well, okay."

Mike felt the cool moisture touch his lips, as the young nurse cradled his head and held the glass for him. He swallowed convulsively, a mouthful of water wetting his parched throat. In less than a minute he spoke again, urgently.

"I gotta go!"

A nurse held a urine bottle while others rolled him partially over. Then someone held his penis so he could urinate into the bottle. Mike wondered idly why he felt no embarrassment as he relieved himself. Then he spoke again.

"I gotta throw up!"

The young nurse held a small basin as he vomited the eggs he had eaten for breakfast. Again, the nurses exchanged glances as he lay back onto the blood soaked pillow. Then an incredulous thought came through the red haze of delirium.

At least I won't have to work on the steel anymore. The image of the blindfolded donkey was driven back into the recesses of his soul and he closed his eyes. The agony in his left leg and the red, hot burning in his right caused the delirium to close in then. He thrashed about, swearing and calling on people who were not in the hospital, while the nurses fussed about, unable to relieve the pain.

Mike was suddenly lucid, as he was wheeled past the reception area en route to the operating room. Then the Gurney stopped and he looked up at a nurse who held the transfusion bottle. People walked by the desk, stopped and stared with Mike glaring back. Finally a nurse covered him with a sheet with only his face showing. Then as the pain came in successive waves and a groan escaped his lips, he glared up at her.

"What the hell's the Goddamn hold up? Why aren't they taking the bar out?"

The nurse stared down at Mike, her face sad.

"It's okay! They're going to start right away."

"When?" Mike growled as another groan came.

The nurse's eyes were moist as she bent to explain.

"A little girl was dying. The doctor had to rush away, but as soon as he's back, he'll start right away."

"I can understand that," Mike said, surprised at his voice and how soft it was. "Just give me something to help the pain."

In a few seconds, a needle was again jammed into his arm and the warm, soft magic of morphine slowly chased away the harsh white heat of pain. He closed his eyes and the nurses exchanged glances once more, while one still held the transfusion bottle with its life-giving red blood.

Mike opened his eyes under a bright glare and the first thing he felt was anger.

"I'll bet the bastards haven't taken that Goddamn bar out yet."

Then he noticed that the sheets were no longer sticky with congealed blood. He turned his head and gazed wonderingly at the crisp white linen and then raised his head slightly to look down at his feet. The bar was gone and his right leg was covered with bandages while his left was in an open cast. Mike lay back and closed his eyes.

"Thank God!" he whispered.

Then he opened his eyes and looked through a large window at gravestones, for a funeral home was next to the hospital. The symbolism wasn't lost on Mike as he wonderingly closed his eyes once more.

While he had been unconscious the bar had been removed and the nurses had washed the congealed blood from his body, replacing the sticky sheets with fresh new ones. They had marveled at his stoicism as they had they rolled him back and forth on the bed.

Mike's reality then became one of sleep, wakefulness, and more sleep for he was receiving one hundred milligrams of Demerol every four hours to keep the pain at bay. At the same time he was injected with three other needles for infection. When he saw the nurses coming with the needles, he prodded his arms and upper thighs to find a spot where he hadn't been injected. If he didn't, the pain from a needle jammed into bruised flesh was intense.

When the bar had rammed through his right thigh, it had dragged his dirt encrusted pants along with it. The impact on his left knee had been so great, tiny bits of gravel and cloth had been imbedded into the bone. The doctor had used a surgical brush to remove it before reassembling the shattered pieces.

The open cast had one drawback. When Mike was sleeping, his left leg suddenly jerked in a spasm. Two nurses were in the room immediately for he had screamed in his sleep. After that he feared sleep but the spasm didn't occur again. He slipped back into the hazy world of drug induced highs and downers when the pain would creep back into his leg and the sheets would be wet from perspiration. Still, his body mended.

All I have to do now is heal he mused wonderingly, gazing out through the window at the gravestones. Then another thought came.

This has got to be the easiest of all hard times.

And it was, for everyone about him was doing their utmost to help. He remembered a different time and a different pain that came from deep within his soul, and how no one had been willing to help. Then he marveled that with the help of drugs, physical pain wasn't nearly as bad as emotional. His family and the years of loneliness had prepared him well.

Within a week he was surprised to see a smiling doctor and nurse enter his room with the bar. The doctor laid it down on a table by the bed.

"Well, here it is! You kept asking for it during the operation."

Mike stared wonderingly up at the doctor for he had no memory of asking. The bar was more than five feet long, and an inch and three-eights in diameter, with ribs running around its exterior. It was indeed a worthy souvenir for it weighed more than thirty pounds.

"Well, some guy's get to keep bullets. I got a bar," Mike said softly and the doctor laughed.

After that, the infection in his left knee fought the drugs and Mike felt the pain grow until he was again awake at night, covered in cold sweat. At times he thought the bandages were too tight. But it was the skin, for the knee had swollen to twice its normal size.

One day, a doctor entered his room with a nurse who carried utensils and a basin. Mike looked up, wondering what was to come.

"I'm going to remove the stitches."

"Do I get something for the pain?"

"No. You're sedated already."

The doctor had never known the white, hot pain of infection and ignored the worried look in Mike's eyes. As he bent, the nurse stood on the other side of the bed with her back to the large window and gravestones. She was an attractive young woman who seemed distant and cold. The doctor held a forceps in his right hand and grasped a stitch, tugging gently to lift it so he could use a scissors.

Mike's body arched suddenly and he lifted off the bed, his forearms smashing into the half table and sending it flying. The doctor jumped while the nurse flew back up against the window and for a mini-second, Mike hung suspended in mid-air. Then he landed back on the bed with a whomp. As his chest heaved and he gulped air desperately, Mike thought a steel knife had been rammed down into his knee for the pain was white hot.

Mike lay on the bed gasping for air, his chest heaving and his head turning from side to side.

"Get a needle!" the doctor yelled and Mike heard the quick slap, slap of the nurses shoes as she left the room on a dead run. In half a minute she was back and he felt a sharp bite in his arm. Then slowly, the gentle warm, lassitude of morphine claimed his mind and a dark peaceful fog closed in.

After that the nurse, was always warm and friendly.

# Forty-six

Mike stared out the window, at the headstones and the fluttering autumn leaves. Then he glanced at the irritating needle stuck into the top of his left hand. The needle was connected to a clear hose which ran up to a plastic intravenous bottle, providing his only sustenance. His body was healing, the broken bones mending back together and the torn flesh becoming one, but there was nothing for his mind to do. He tried reading but could only concentrate for a few minutes, for even holding his head up caused great fatigue. He spent most of his time sleeping.

Then after a week Mike was given his first meal, the same young nurse bringing a bowl of broth and cradling his head in her arm. She was about to feed him with the spoon when Mike stopped her. Her arm was warm and comforting but being spoon-fed made him uncomfortable. He clumsily held the spoon to his mouth but became exhausted quickly and she laid his head back onto the pillow.

The nurse had washed his hair three times to rid it of blood and she had also shaved him. At the same time he fought a never-ending battle against infection and pain. At times he would waken, feel the pain in his left knee begin a faint, throbbing and then grow in intensity until his face was wet with perspiration. When he saw a nurse coming with a needle, he hurriedly poked his thighs or arms to find a spot that wasn't bruised. Then he would slip gratefully into a feathery high, riding a white, fleecy cloud ever upwards. In a couple of hours he would awaken, only to feel the faint throbbing in his knee begin anew.

Then one day, as he gazed pensively out the window, he sensed more than heard the door swing open on well-oiled hinges. He turned his head quickly and stared. There stood Gary and Dennis, looking slightly embarrassed.

"Well," Mike said slowly, as the surprise wore off. "It sure the hell's good to see you."

"Yeah. Likewise," Gary answered. The two men stood, looking at the bed and Mike, his open cast and the bandages on his right leg. As the silence deepened, all three became more and more self-conscious.

"Hey!" Mike suddenly broke the stillness. "I can move my right leg now, see!" He showed them, twisting it back and forth.

"Yeah!" Dennis said, breaking into a sudden grin. "Looks like you'll be up and back on the steel in a couple weeks." He stopped suddenly when Gary glared at him. Then, he stared at the floor. After another painful silence, Gary stepped forward, holding Mike's worn wallet.

"Here! We brought your wallet. There wasn't any money in it."

"I know. I keep it in the bank."

"Well, anyway," Gary cleared his throat, looked at Dennis and then plunged on. "We sorta took up a collection. It ain't much. But it should help."

Mike stared, speechless. Gary laid the wallet down on the table by the bed and stepped back, glancing at Dennis who remained silent.

"Well, I guess we better be going. It's a long flight back to the dam."

Mike was still speechless. Then Gary and Dennis turned to go.

"See ya," Gary said, softly. "Don't drink up that compensation money."

The door swung noiselessly and they were gone. Mike stared after them for a moment and then picked up his wallet. He thought of all the times he had contributed to a man's wife or family after an accident. But the man had always been dead. He tipped the wallet upside down and bills fell onto the sheet covering his lap. He sorted them and began counting, his wonder growing. The crew of twenty had collected five hundred and thirty-seven dollars. In nineteen seventy-two, it was a fair amount. Mike sat dumbfounded as he held the money in his hand and stared out at the gravestones.

They must think I'm smashed up so bad I'll never walk again, he mused. He gazed down at his legs and wondered why they couldn't see the obvious.

Then he thought of his mother describing ironworkers as low people; men who drank and never went to church. Next were more questions, for who can truly say what is the best quality of manhood?


As autumn deepened and the leaves began to shrivel outside the window and beyond the gravestones, Mike pondered his future. And when he was staring pensively out the window, he again sensed the door swing open on well-oiled hinges. He turned quickly, but this time two strange men in business suits stood by the foot of the bed. One held a large book and a couple of brochures. Both smiled warmly.

Mike stared, his eyes narrow, and his body tense.

"Uh, do I know you?" He finally asked.

"I'm Joe!" The first man stuck out a large beefy hand. "And this is Hank."

Mike dubiously shook the proffered hands and stared at the two men. Both seemed out of place in their business suits and he wondered what they were selling.

"Well, you might as well know why we're here," Joe said.

Mike continued staring.

"We're from Alcoholics Anonymous," Joe continued.

"Oh!" Mike's eyes were still narrow. "What'a ya want with me?"

"We were told you were in an alcohol related accident," Joe said hurriedly. "And we thought you might like some help."

He placed a couple of brochures on the table.

"Well, it was nice of you to come," Mike said. "But I'm not an alcoholic." Then he grinned. "I drink my booze in the open, not from a brown paper bag."

Neither of the men laughed and Mike's eyes narrowed again.

"We're not here to convince or convert you," Joe said.

"Good!"

"We're just here to leave you an option. And if you ever change your mind…"

"You'll be the first to know. Believe me!" Mike snapped.

"Well," Joe said sadly and turned to Hank. "We better be going." Then he turned back to Mike. "It's up to you. If you ever need help, our number's on the brochure." Then both men turned and left.

Again Mike stared at the door. Then he glared at the brochures. Jesus H. Christ! He swore contemptuously. That's all I need: Some Bible thumping Sky Jockey telling me how to live my life. He grabbed the brochures and was about to throw them into the garbage pail. But instead, he laid them down on the table and stared pensively out the window. He tried sleeping but sleep wouldn't come and finally he turned back to the table and picked up a brochure. He glanced at the twenty questions, and the statement that If you answered yes to one of these, you may be an alcoholic, and chuckled. Then his eyes fell on a heading, "THE SERENITY PRAYER."

Mike read,
**GOD!** Grant me the **SERENITY**
to Accept the Things,
I Cannot Change.
**COURAGE** to Change the things I can.
And **WISDOM** to know the Difference.

    He pondered the prayer's meaning for a long time. Its simplicity appealed to him and as the leaves shriveled outside the window and the cold wind blew, he returned to it again and again.

    He read the questions asking if he ever had blackouts, if he craved a drink in the morning and if he had ever been hospitalized due to alcohol. He answered yes to the first questions but an emphatic NO to the last. But as the lonely hours crept by he remembered how he had felt the morning of the accident and that if he had not been drunk, it wouldn't have happened. He also wondered what would make him always drink until the bottle was empty.

    One morning two nurses appeared and he was taken to physiotherapy to be fitted for crutches. As he impatiently waited in his wheel chair, his eyes roamed about. A nurse coaxed a pathetic old man, who had broken his hip, to stand and lean on a four-legged walker. When the old man stood shakily, Mike could see the tubes that were inserted into his body, for he had long ago lost control over his bladder.

    Mike watched in wonder, as the nurse placed an arm about the ancient shoulders that once had been strong and broad.

    "Come on, please, just try one step." Her voice was patient. The old man took a hesitant step, followed by another. But at the third he stopped, his head down and his shoulders slumping.

    "Come on, just one more, you can do it," the nurse said softly, tugging gently on the old man's gown. But he stayed where he was, swaying slightly, his head down and his shoulders slumped.

    Mike turned to the nurse, who was adjusting his crutches.

    "Why does she bother?" He asked in wonder.

    The nurse looked at Mike thoughtfully for a moment and then at the old man who had slumped back into his wheel chair, his face damp with exertion.

    "I don't know," she replied, placing a hand on Mike's strong shoulder.

    The old man's rheumy eyes were focused on a vision a long way off, lost in time and memory.

"If we don't keep trying, he'll just give up and die," she finally said.

Mike stared at the old man who was being wheeled out of the ward, his ancient head slumping forward onto his chest.

"I guess I'm pretty lucky, eh!" Mike said suddenly.

The nurse smiled quickly and held out the two crutches.

An instant image of the Serenity Prayer flashed by and Mike thought of the two men from AA and their invitation as he wondered how he couldn't remember one good thing that had ever come from drinking. Then he rose shakily, leaning on the crutches. The nurse grabbed his arm as an instant, vertigo closed in and he swayed.

"I'm okay!" He said grimly, perspiration breaking out on his forehead. He steadied himself and began the long process of learning to walk with crutches.


When Mike was alone in his room, he felt a great, inexplicable loneliness. He stared out at the gravestones for a moment and then pulled the cord by his bed. A nurse appeared and he asked for a portable pay phone. When she had brought it, he dialed carefully and when he heard the operator's voice, inserted the correct amount of change. Then he listened to the familiar ring of the rural party line: *Two, long and one short.*

"Hello!" Someone said gruffly. Mike recognized his father's voice but for a moment he was speechless.

"Hello!" The voice repeated, sounding annoyed.

"Hello! It's Mike."

"Who?" His father demanded.

"Mike!" Mike repeated and then paused, waiting for a reply. When none came, he sighed and added, "It's Metro. Your son."

"Oh!" His father, said and then a silence deepened.

"I'm calling from Thompson, from the hospital," Mike said and then after a pause, "I was in an accident."

"Oh! What happened?" was next and he explained haltingly. When he told of his leg being shattered, his father interrupted.

"Broke it right off, eh?"

"Yeah." Mike sighed again. Then he heard voices in the background and Vincent talking to someone.

"It's Metro!" Vincent said gruffly. Mike heard a voice that was vaguely familiar.

"Hi! It's Allen, your brother. How're you doing?"

Mike paused wonderingly and then began talking slowly.

"I'm okay, I guess. But it's a surprise to hear your voice."

"We're home for a short holiday," Allen explained and then said, "Hear you were in an accident. What happened?"

"I fell," Mike replied. "It was on the job and I landed on a row of rebar. One bar went right through my leg."

"Sounds pretty gruesome!"

"Well," Mike began slowly. "Now I know how those Roman soldiers felt when they were speared," he added, half in jest, feeling vaguely uncomfortable.

"Better still," came from his brother. "Now you know how our brother felt."

"What? What the hell does that mean? Our brother?"

"I was referring to our brother in Jesus Christ," Allen replied for, he had become a born again Christian.

"Oh," Mike said, confused. Then the silence deepened again.

"Well I guess we should send you a card, or something," Allen finally said.

"Don't go to no trouble on my account," Mike answered, his voice harsh in the stillness of his room.

"Okay!" Allen answered quickly and the subject was dropped.

"Well, take care," Mike finally said, after another lengthy pause.

"Yeah. You too," came the answer. Mike heard a click and for the briefest of instants he listened to the hum.

Then he turned and stared blankly out the window at the rows of headstones.